Eric Bishop-Potter has worked as a journalist for the *Daily Mirror*, the *Mail on Sunday*, the Press Association, and the *Sporting Life*. He has also been employed as a public relations executive, a builder's labourer, and a merchant seaman. *A Ruined Boy* is his third book. *Dear Popsy: Collected Postcards of a Private Schoolboy to his Father* was published by Andre Deutsch and Penguin, and his second, *Jimmy, Mrs Fisher and Me*, made its appearance in 2011. Born and educated in London, Eric Bishop-Potter now lives in West Sussex.

A RUINED BOY

Eric Bishop-Potter

Matador
9 Priory Business Park
Kibworth Beauchamp
Leicestershire LE8 0RX, UK
Tel: (+44) 116 279 2299
Fax: (+44) 116 279 2277
Email: books@troubador.co.uk
Web: www.troubador.co.uk/matador

ISBN 978 1780882 659

British Library Cataloguing in Publication Data.
A catalogue record for this book is available from the British Library.

Typeset in 10 pt Palatino by Troubador Publishing Ltd, Leicester, UK

Matador is an imprint of Troubador Publishing Ltd

All the characters in this work are fictional,
as are some of the place names.

For Rene and Jason

You should not have gone murdering people with a hatchet.
That is no occupation for a gentleman.
                          - Fyodor Dostoevsky

PART ONE

CHAPTER 1

Had Honey been given the opportunity of exchanging her mother for one of a more moderate, less slatternly nature, one who paid attention to personal hygiene and did not leave unwashed clothes in a pile on the floor, who swept and scoured and was not excessively fond of bathtub gin, it is doubtful she would have taken it. More likely she would have shied from the idea, dismissed it with a popular expression of the day: Nothing doing.

No – Honey had observed that mothers who were abstemious and odour-free and skilled in the art of household management tended to be harsh disciplinarians, unwilling to allow their children the smallest freedom. Honey was allowed to come and go as she pleased, *do* as she pleased. No restraint was placed on her behaviour. She was, as they say, allowed to run wild.

And that, maybe, is why she ended up as she did – running for her life.

Honey was born Honey Bunn, the illegitimate daughter of Pearl Florence Bunn, a kitchen worker of Stanway, New Drayton (pop 10,000), and Harold Lee Booker, an itinerant truck driver from Springfield, Massachusetts. She was conceived under a late summer sky on a pile of coconut matting in the back of Booker's truck and was born nine months to the day of Booker and Pearl's first meeting – the first of only three meetings, for when Pearl told Booker she was expecting his child he was never seen in New Drayton again.

At birth, Honey weighed 13lbs 7oz, which prompted Janet FitzGerald, the district nurse who delivered her, to remark to her sister: "That Bunn woman has more orifice than Old Toby's collar", Old Toby being the 22-hand shire that pulled their brother's plough.

Although Pearl's hard drinking made her negligent of self and home, it did not, unaccountably, make her negligent of little Honey: she grew to be strong and bright. "That's one lively youngster you've got there, Pearl," Pearl's neighbour Leon Horowitz would say whenever he met mother and daughter on the street or saw them together in the grassless back-yard of their run-down weatherboard, and squatting close to Honey (so close that the inquisitive Honey had, on more than one occasion, reached out and touched the thick purple vein that ran worm-like across his brow), he would add in a lower, more intimate tone: "And a mighty pretty one at that."

At age eight Honey asked who her father was and received the reply that he was "a lying, conniving rat-assed knockaround".

Later, as Pearl mellowed a little, Honey's questions about her father were answered less trenchantly.

"Was he handsome, Momma?"

"All the girls were crazy for him. He could've had his pick."

"And he picked you?"

"I was the one he wanted."

"Why, Momma?" Honey, looking into her mother's face, found it difficult to understand why a man who could have had his pick should have chosen someone with blotched skin and a large fleshy nose.

"It was your momma's build. Your daddy liked his women big up top, and your momma was the biggest." Reading Honey's thoughts, she added: "A girl can have a face like a sack of rocks, but if she's big up top she'll never want for a good-looking man."

The words stayed in Honey's mind, and every night she would stand naked before the cracked mirror in her bedroom and go to work on her young breasts. First she would gently rotate her palms over them, then, cupping them, extend them upwards, stretching them until the skin burned. Stretch, relax; stretch, relax – thirty or forty times, fifty if she were in high spirits. There were nights when she imagined it was Mr Horowitz's hands that were doing the cupping and stretching. Why Mr Horowitz's, she didn't quite understand. Perhaps it had something to do with the thick purple vein that ran across his brow.

At age fourteen Honey's breasts were the size of cantaloupes and, like the Rosenberg trial that was taking place, the focus of much attention. Men of all ages cast lascivious glances in their direction, and women, especially middle-aged women, seeing how firm and shapely they were, experienced a surge of envy. In the school play-yard, boys stared goggle-eyed at them, and the more daring asked: "Hows about a feel?" Occasionally a bribe would be offered: "Let's see 'em in the raw and we'll give you a quarter."

Pearl, noticing the interest being shown in her daughter and fearing a third mouth to feed, warned her of the dangers of allowing a man to get too close. "If a fella starts coming on strong, kick him where he wouldn't wanna show his momma," was her advice.

Honey followed it until the age of sixteen, and then, unable, or not wishing to control her libido any longer, let, as the expression has it, history repeat itself:

She was seated in Tommy's ice-cream parlour on Main Street, a tall glass of chilled sarsaparilla on the counter in front of her, when the door opened and a man of about twenty-eight entered. He wore a navy sweatshirt and trousers and had a face and build that reminded Honey of the fieldworker in the Lucky Strike cigarette advertisement – dark-haired, sloe-eyed and broad-shouldered. He sat two stools away and ordered a vanilla with a nut smother.

Honey, as she sucked her drink through a candy-striped straw, looked sideways at him and absorbed his muscular arms and large rough hands. He was, she thought, better looking than the man in the Lucky Strike advertisement.

The vanilla with a nut smother was brought, and the man, after taking a spoonful of it, turned to Honey and said: "Hi." He smiled a wide contagious smile. "Hot, ain't it?"

Honey wiped away a small dribble of sarsaparilla from her mouth with the back of her hand and said: "It's early yet – it'll get hotter."

"You got a cold?" the man asked.

"No," Honey said.

"Your voice sounds a little husky."

"*Every*one tells me that," Honey said. "It's my natural voice."

"Sounds sexy."

"Everyone tells me that too," Honey said. "Well, the fellas do."

She spoke the truth. Her voice had a surprising richness of tone, an almost baritone timbre, which men found extremely attractive, almost as attractive as her body.

The man smiled again, and Honey noticed that his teeth were

white and glistening, as if he had just bitten into a sharp apple.

"You're a truck driver, I bet," Honey said.

"How'd you figure *that* out?"

Honey said: "Truck drivers and salesmen are the only strangers we get around here, and you don't look dressed for selling ribbons."

"That's for sure," the man said.

"Who d'you drive for?" Honey asked.

The man took another spoonful of ice-cream. "Maxi's Miracle Meatloaf Company," he said. He smiled again. "Crazy name, huh?" After a moment he said: "What's *your* name?"

"Honey. What's yours?"

"Joe. Joe Backhouse." He paused. "An*other* crazy name."

Honey said: "You don't *look* like the average truck driver. Most of them are fat and smell like stewed cabbage."

"*I* don't smell, do I?"

"Not from here you don't."

"That's because I bathe a lot – every day when I can. I like to smell clean."

"You *look* clean," Honey said.

Later, lying on her back on a bed of boxed meatloaf, it would not have mattered to Honey had Joe Backhouse smelled as bad as the drain on the corner of South and Old streets.

CHAPTER 2

"I'm gonna have a kid, Momma."

Pearl looked at Honey coldly for a moment, then slapped her hard across the face. She kept hitting her until her hands were sore, then stopped and said thickly: "How'd it happen?"

"Whaddaya mean, how'd it happen? It happened, that's all," Honey said resentfully. The blows had taken her by surprise: she had expected a deep drawn-out sigh of disappointment, at the most a stare through narrowed lids that said: "You dumb bitch." She felt let down.

"Where'd you meet him? Who is he?" Pearl asked.

Honey said: "I dunno...someone I met at the ice-cream parlour."

"What someone? A local someone?"

Honey hesitated before replying. "No, he's from out of town."

Pearl gave a short contemptuous laugh. "Don't tell me," she said, "he's a truck driver and he's coming back to marry you just as soon as he can." She closed her eyes and said through clenched teeth: "Jesus fuckin' Christ!"

There was a silence between them. Finally Pearl said: "How far gone areyuh?"

"Ten, maybe twelve weeks," Honey said.

"Okay," Pearl said, "tomorrow we get you fixed up."

Honey understood what Pearl meant, but said nevertheless: "Whaddaya mean, fixed up?"

"We get rid of it, that's what I mean," Pearl said.

Honey said evenly: "No. No, we don't get rid of it." She did not know at that moment why she wanted to have the child, but thinking about it later she realised it was for no other reason than to see what it looked like.

CHAPTER 3

"Harry!"

Betty Finn (née Farrell), the subordinate half of the Finn and Farrell comedy act, stood before the bureau mirror in the bedroom of their rented apartment wearing only a pair of blue satin French knickers. She was tall, had dusky red hair and a full, slightly top-heavy figure. Her face was pale and sharply oval and her sea-green eyes were set wide apart on high cheekbones. It was an extremely attractive face. Her husband, Harry Finn, thought it beautiful. "God, you're beautiful, Betty Farrell," he would tell her, drawing her close to him. To which Betty, pleased, would reply: "Cut the corn, Finn", 'Finn' being her pet name for him. They had been married for six years and in that time had appeared together before audiences in perhaps fifty of the hundred or so theatres that comprised America's vaudeville circuit. They had met at the Apollo Theatre in Saint Paul, Minnesota; Finn was compering a variety show there, and Betty was a clerk in the theatre's ticket office. One evening as Betty was leaving the theatre Finn had fallen in step with her and invited her to supper. Two weeks later they were married by special licence. At the time of their marriage Betty was twenty-four and Finn was thirty-six. On Betty's twenty-fifth birthday Finn, to please her, had proposed that she partner him on stage, initially in non-speaking walk-on-walk-off roles and later, when sketches had been written, in roles that were more demanding. They worked extremely well together, and just this summer they had topped the bill at The Grapevine, a small but prestigious theatre in New York's off-Broadway district. They loved each other deeply.

"What is it?" Finn, dressed in a bathrobe, came in from the living room carrying a copy of *Revue*. He was of medium height, stockily built and had dark brown hair parted on the side and brushed back. His face was round and jowled and his nose slightly rubescent from the Old Masters malt whiskey he drank. The most striking of his features were his eyebrows, which were jet black and ran in short, thick dashes above large brown eyes. "What's the problem?"

Betty turned to him, her left breast cupped in her hand. "Harry, look at this," she said.

Finn, with mock solemnity, said: "But mistress, the King awaits me in the Great Hall."

"Harry, this is serious." Her voice was tearful.

Finn tossed the copy of *Revue* onto the bed and went up to her. He kissed her on the forehead. "What is it, baby?"

"I've got a lump on my breast."

Finn looked into her eyes and smiled. "*You* got a lump, *I* got a lump. *All* God's chillun got lumps."

"Don't, Harry."

"Okay, lemme see."

She raised the breast to reveal its underside. She touched a place. "Here."

Finn looked closely and saw a swelling the size of a pea. He brushed it with his fingertip. "Does it hurt?"

"When I squeeze it it does,"

"How long you had it?"

"I just noticed it this morning." After a small pause, she said: "I'm worried, Harry."

Finn ran his finger over the swelling a few times, then gave the breast a curt kiss. Straightening up, he said: "It's nothing – probably a cyst. Forget about it." His tone, because he was anxious, had changed from light-hearted to brusque insouciance. He went to the bed and picked up the copy of *Revue.*

"You know what I'm thinking, don't you?" Betty said. It was more a statement than a question.

Finn quickly, almost angrily, said: "Listen, don't get into a panic over this. You know how these things are: one day they're there and the next they've gone. Give it a couple of weeks and if it hasn't gone by then we'll have a doctor take a look at it."

Betty took hold of a dress that was draped across the back of a wicker chair, made a circle of its opening and stepped into it. As she fastened the buttons she said evenly: "I'm not going into hospital."

"Who said anything about hospitals?"

"I'm not seeing a doctor, either."

There was an awkward silence. Eventually Finn said: "I know what you're thinking and you're wrong."

"Am I?"

"Yes."

"What makes you so sure?"

"It's a feeling I've got."

Betty perfunctorily ran her palms down the sides of her hips, smoothing out the wrinkles in her dress. "I've a feeling about it too; that's why I don't intend seeing any doctors." She looked at Finn in a helpless, pleading way, and Finn, seeing her eyes mist over, went up to her and put his arms around her. "You dope," he said tenderly.

The swelling did not disappear. Each morning, as soon as she awoke, Betty would slide a hand inside the top of her silk pyjamas and tentatively explore the breast with her fingertips. The movements were accompanied by a small prayer which she had learned as a child at school. "Lord, I ask your protection," she would say under her breath. "Protect me from hurt and pain; protect me from those who seek to – " She always located the swelling before the prayer was finished.

After three weeks she decided the prayer wasn't being said quickly enough. If a prayer was to be answered it ought to be completed. She speeded it up and located the swelling just as the last word was said. She kept to the speeded up prayer for a further two weeks, then told herself it was inadequate; it was too short. How could anyone expect results from a scant four-line prayer? It would have to be added to or at least repeated; miracles required effort. She preceded the exploration of the breast with *ten* sayings of the prayer, counting the number of times on her fingers against her thigh. The swelling remained and seemed to her to grow larger. She discarded the prayer and drew into herself. She rejected Finn's advances and turned away from him when he spoke to her. Her work suffered. She forgot her lines and missed her cues. She walked into props unintentionally.

Finn was patient with her, but when during a matinee performance she ran off stage in the middle of a sketch, leaving him to ad lib, he lost his temper. "You want to screw up your life, okay, you go ahead and screw it up, but don't screw up mine," he said in their dressing-room later. "You want to walk around like some goddamn zombie, okay, but not out there on stage."

In bed that night Finn woke to find her in tears. "Hey, hey." He gathered her to him and stroked her hair until she fell asleep.

Next morning over breakfast, he said: "You don't get this thing sorted out you'll wind up in the booby-hatch; you know that, don't you?"

Betty said nothing.

Finn allowed a few moments of silence to pass, then said: "Why don't you have a doctor take a look at you?"

To his surprise, Betty nodded. "Yes, I will," she said quietly.

Finn reached across the table and touched her hand. "That's sensible," he said.

There was a further silence, after which Finn said: "You want me to fix an appointment for you? I know a doctor here who's good. He once fixed *me* up. I ever tell you about the time I got cut in two by a chain saw?"

Betty smiled. "If you would," she said.

"When?"

"I don't know – Friday."

"Okay," Finn said. He sipped his coffee. "Everything'll be fine. Don't worry."

They were appearing in a revue at The Lighthouse, a tiny theatre built in the nineteenth century by the financier Louis Fromanteel for his young wife who enjoyed performing Shakespeare's plays with her friends. With its rococo ceiling and frescoed box fronts, it was one of their favourite entertainment places. Their engagement was for a month and they were in the last week of it.

After the show, on the eve of Betty's appointment with the doctor, they went to a bar a few doors along from the theatre. Finn was in a buoyant mood: Betty hadn't forgotten a line or missed a cue and was smiling and talking again. She seemed confident and was extraordinarily tender towards him. He sensed that for some reason she did not want him out of her sight, and this charmed and delighted him.

It was their first visit to the bar since Betty's discovery of the swelling, and Finn was glad to be back there. He enjoyed a drink after a show and enjoyed listening to what the customers who were there from the theatre had to say about the acts they'd seen. Usually he had three or four whiskies and Betty two gin slings. Tonight he had five whiskies and Betty six gin slings.

"I feel a little cockeyed," Betty said as they left. She took hold of Finn's arm with both hands and pulled him close to her. "Love me?" she asked, looking at him and smiling.

"Hate the sight of you," Finn said, returning the smile.

Inside their apartment, after they'd kissed, Finn said: "I'm down on my feet; I think I'll turn in. How about you?"

Betty ran her fingers down his cheek and over his mouth.

"Mmmm," Finn said.

"I need to freshen up," Betty said.

"Okay, but don't be long."

"I love you," Betty said.

In an upper class English accent, Finn said: "And *I'm* rather fond of you too, don't you know." He smiled and slapped her backside. "Don't be long."

Betty followed him with her eyes as he entered the bedroom and felt tears begin to form. Unbuttoning her dress, she went into the bathroom. She closed the door, eased off her shoes and let her dress fall to the floor. She unhooked her brassiere and tossed it into the linen basket. She followed the brassiere with her dress, then turned to face the mirror that was fixed to the wall above the hand basin. Some of the mirror's backing had come away, causing small blanks to appear in the images reflected in it. After briefly studying her face and running a hand over her hair, she turned on the hot water faucet, unwrapped a tablet of soap and held it under the water. She made a thick lather and smoothed it on to her breast, where the swelling was. She closed her eyes as the warmth penetrated her skin. "Poor baby," she crooned. "Poor baby." Her hand made small rotating movements.

She rinsed off the soap and dabbed dry the breast with a pink towel taken from a stainless steel bar beneath the basin. "Poor baby." She picked up Finn's bone-handled razor that was on the shelf above the basin and opened it out. There was dried soap on the blade, so she dampened the towel and wiped the blade clean. She let the towel fall to the floor. For a moment she looked at herself in the mirror, then, raising the breast, sliced through to the cancer.

CHAPTER 4

Honey experienced her first contraction halfway along Elm Street. The second came on Green Street, and at the corner of Main and South Streets she felt something wet happening between her legs. She had taken a bus into New Drayton to get away from Pearl. Recently they had begun to quarrel. Honey's advanced state of pregnancy had put them both on edge. They saw themselves soon-to-be-encumbered, inconvenienced, their lives spent ministering to a mewling infant. Recently Honey had begun to wish that she had got 'fixed up', but she would not admit that to Pearl.

"Oh!" She clasped her stomach and sank to a squatting position. "Jesus, it's coming," she said aloud. She looked around, but the few people that were about (it was Sunday and eighty in the shade) were too far off to be of help. Across the street she could see Tommy's ice-cream parlour and for a moment she recalled Joe Backhouse, felt a pang of desire for him. She let herself tilt forward and began to crawl the half dozen or so feet to the entrance of the Excelsior Tavern. She had not gone more than a few inches when the Excelsior's door opened and Leon Horowitz, his face screwed up against the light, emerged.

"Honey girl!" He stepped forward, lost and recovered his balance.

"Mr Horowitz, I'm havin' it."

"Havin' it?"

"The baby."

The wool in Mr Horowitz's brain parted fractionally and he said: "Oh. Oh, well now… Well, don't you worry, Honey. We'll get you inside, then we'll call an ambulance."

"We'd better be quick," Honey said brightly. She felt no pain, just minor discomfort.

In jerky, uncertain movements Mr Horowitz took up a position behind Honey, and straddling her, placed his hands under her arms. "Now, don't you try to stand, Honey. Just ease towards the door." He gently lifted her off her knees and back into a squatting position. Honey giggled as she felt Mr Horowitz's hands slide from her armpits to twin points beneath her breasts. Not quite beneath them. "Right, now, here we go," Mr Horowitz said. "Easy does it." Like someone monstrously deformed, Honey gyrated her way to the entrance of the Excelsior Tavern.

"Get the door, Honey."

Honey pushed the door, and as it swung open, Mr Horowitz stuck out a leg to stop it on its return. They worked their way inside.

Carl Lubcek, the Excelsior's owner, wasn't at his usual place behind the long mahogany counter, so Mr Horowitz said to the only customer in the bar, a stranger who sat in the booth nearest the door: "Hey mister, call an ambulance, will you. This girl here's having a baby."

Finn lowered his glass and looked disinterestedly at the crouched couple.

"Hey, mister, this is an emergency," Mr Horowitz said in a hurt voice.

Finn continued looking at them. He didn't know if he wasn't looking at two drunks.

"Mister, please!"

Finn put down his glass and got to his feet. "Where's the telephone?"

Mr Horowitz nodded to the end of the bar. "At the back there – in the corner." To Honey, he said: "Now, Honey, you just lie quiet here while…" He gently eased her into a horizontal position. "Tell them to come quick," he said to Finn.

Finn went off, and Honey said to Mr Horowitz: "Mr Horowitz, the baby's slipping out of me!"

Simulating composure, Mr Horowitz said: "Well, Honey, I guess I'll just have to play at being doctor, won't I?" He smiled weakly and patted Honey's leg. He withdrew a copy of *Racing Scene* from his back trouser pocket, opened it at the centre pages and placed it on the floor. He removed his jacket, unbuttoned his shirt cuffs and rolled up his sleeves. "Now, let me see…" He tentatively raised Honey's dress and peered beneath it.

The child was a third of its way out, its viscous head and shoulders pushing aside Honey's yellow cotton briefs.

"Well now, Honey, I guess I…" Mr Horowitz felt his heartbeat quicken. Often at night, with Mrs Horowitz snoring ferociously beside him, he would picture Honey's young body and the pleasure he would get from undressing it. Now the fantasy was about to become reality. He couldn't believe his luck. "I guess I'll just have to…" Mr Horowitz pulled a red polka-dotted handkerchief from one of his jacket's side pockets, unfolded it and placed it beneath the baby's head. He took a breath, screwed up his face in an expression compounded of distaste and concentration, and gripping the child by its shoulders with the handkerchief, drew it into the world. "Well – " Mr Horowitz grimaced as the placenta emerged. "Well, look what we got here. You got yourself a fine – " He half turned the child, glanced at its genitalia and opened his eyes wide. He cleared his throat. "You got yourself a fine baby boy, Honey. A fine, *big* baby boy." He extended the infant for Honey's inspection.

Honey raised herself on her elbows and scrutinised her son. After a few moments she said: "That's some piece of equipment he's got there – Jesus!" She studied the child's face. "He's cute," she said. Without pausing, she went on: "Mr Horowitz, you think I could have a glass of beer? My throat's so dry I can hardly swallow."

"A beer? Sure you can Honey, but first we got to get you cleaned up. You're a little messy down below here." Mr Horowitz lowered the child onto the pages of *Racing Scene,* thinking, 'There goes my Belmont card, but the kid sure as hell ain't havin' my jacket for a wrapper.' He pulled the pages across the child's body and pressed them to its chest and belly to absorb the mucus.

"Can it breathe?" Honey asked.

Mr Horowitz made a tear in the paper above the baby's face and folded back the two sides. "There," he said. The child let out a small cry, then was silent.

From the end of the bar, Finn called: "The line's tied up."

Mr Horowitz called back: "Keep trying. Don't you leave that phone, mister." He said to Honey: "Now, Honey, you stay put while I get something to clean you up with." He got to his feet and went behind the counter. Next to a chromium basin filled with water he saw a dishtowel. "Be with you in a minute, Mr Horowitz," he heard Carl Lubcek call. He turned and, through the half open door that led to the Excelsior's back yard, saw Lubcek waving to him. "My fuckin' boy don't turn up," Lubcek called again, "so I gotta do the stackin'. Help yourself to a drink. Be with you as soon as I finish here."

Mr Horowitz picked up the dishtowel and plunged it into the water. "You take your time, Carl," he murmured. "I ain't in no hurry."

From the telephone, Finn said: "It's got to be Have-a-Baby week."

"You just hang onto that phone, mister," Mr Horowitz said. He wrung out the dishtowel and hurried back to Honey.

"I sure could do with a beer, Mr Horowitz," Honey said.

"And you're gonna have one just as soon as I get you cleaned up," Mr Horowitz said. He knelt between Honey's legs, hesitated a moment, then got to his feet. "We don't want no-one walking in and seeing you like this, do we, Honey. It wouldn't be – well, it wouldn't be seemly." He went to the door and bolted it. He returned, knelt again, and said: "Now …" For a few seconds he let his eyes take in the spread of Honey's thighs. "First thing we got to do is to get these little old pants of yours off." He laid down the dishtowel, and with clumsy, trembling fingers began to ease off Honey's briefs. "You won't be needing *these* any more."

"There's still plenty of wear in those pants," Honey said emphatically.

"Whatever you say, Honey, whatever you – " Mr Horowitz gazed open-mouthed as Honey's luxuriant pudendum was revealed. "My, you sure have got…" He reached forward, and placing the dishtowel on Honey's thigh, began working it in short downward strokes.

"That feels good, Mr Horowitz," Honey said. She closed her eyes.

"I'm doing my best, Honey," Mr Horowitz said hoarsely. He moved the dishtowel between Honey's legs. "Just think of me as a doctor. That's all I am, a tired old doctor doing his best to clean you up." He raised his other hand, hesitated a moment, then ran it over Honey's belly. "There…Just a tired old doctor who's doing his best to give you the benefit of his – "

"Having fun?" Finn stood over them, his eyebrows half raised in cynicism.

"Huh?" Mr Horowitz started back in surprise and embarrassment. "Well now…" He quickly pulled down the hem of Honey's dress. "Well now, that's got you nice and cleaned up, Honey," he said in an efficient tone. To Finn he said: "You ever seen a prettier kid, mister?" He reached across to the child and patted the paper, which had begun to firm to its body.

Finn said: "You want an ambulance, call one yourself." He went to the counter and eased himself onto a stool.

At this moment Carl Lubcek appeared and said: "Sorry to keep you folks." He was a stockily-built Serbian with a pockmarked face. "My fuckin' boy, he don't turn up today, so I have to do the stackin'." He glanced at Mr Horowitz, who had got to his feet and was standing over Honey. "You havin' trouble there, Mr Horowitz?" Without pausing, he went on: "Leave her, I get the cops. This town's gettin' more like Skid Row every day. Yesterday I had a drunk come in here and 'cos I don't serve him a beer he throws a knife at me. Missed me by this much." He made a half-inch measurement with his thumb and index finger. He smoothed down a few strands of his thinning black hair and wiped massive hands on the half-apron he wore. "What can I do for you people?"

Finn said: "Scotch. A large one."

"Two beers here," Mr Horowitz said.

"I ain't servin' no drunks," Lubcek said, glancing at Honey.

"Carl, this young woman – " Mr Horowitz took hold of Honey's arm and in a caring voice said: "Can you move, Honey? Would it pain you to get to a standing position?" Honey gripped Mr Horowitz's free arm and effortlessly pulled herself to her feet. Mr Horowitz returned to Lubcek. "This young woman, Carl, has just had a baby right here in your bar." There was a note of pride in his voice.

"You kiddin' me?" Lubcek said.

Honey knelt and picked up the child.

"Lemme see that," Lubcek said suspiciously.

Honey held out the baby.

"Hey, wudgyaknow." Lubcek looked at Finn and smiled incredulously. Finn gave a bored shrug. "Whadisit, boy or girl?" Lubcek asked.

"Boy," Honey said.

"Looks like a liddle girl with those lashes."

"You was to see the size of his tube, you wouldn't say that," Honey said.

Lubcek gave a short laugh. "That so? He got a big one, eh?"

"Ain't he, Mr Horowitz?"

Mr Horowitz nodded. "It's a size all right," he said gravely.

In a concerned tone, Lubcek said to Honey: "Shouldn't you be in hospital, you just had a kid?"

Finn said: "You kidding? Trying to get an ambulance in this town is like trying to get a drink."

"Sorry, mister," Lubcek said. He poured Finn his drink and passed it to him.

Finn put his hand in his pocket to pay, but Lubcek said: "On the house. It ain't every day we have a kid dropped here."

"Two beers, Carl," Mr Horowitz said. "This girl's all dried up, ain't you, Honey?"

"Dry as hell," Honey said. She placed the child on the counter and pulled herself on to a stool next to Finn. She looked at him. "Hi," she said. She smiled briefly.

Finn saw a sleepy-eyed, heavily fleshed girl with light brown hair and a wide prehensile mouth, a lewd-looking girl with a prodigious bosom who spoke in a gruff almost masculine voice. "Hello," he said back. His eyes returned to her breasts. 'If they're real,' he thought, 'they'd be worth paying to see.' He guessed her age to be twenty-one or twenty-two. He turned away.

Lubcek passed glasses of beer to Mr Horowitz and Honey. "You drink that," he said, "and I'll try for an ambulance." To Honey he said: "You sure you wouldn't be better off havin' water?"

"Beer's fine," Honey said cheerily.

Lubcek, as he left them, pulled two clean dishtowels from a shelf and slid them along the counter. "Wrap the kid in those," he said. "Get that paper off him."

Finn said: "That paper's stuck hard. You try taking it off, you'll skin the kid alive." He passed the dishtowels to Honey. "They'll give him extra warmth," he said.

Honey spread the dishtowels on the bar and placed the child on them. "Jesus, this stuff's hard as hell," she said, running her hand over the newspaper covering. She flicked it with a fingernail. "Hear that? Hard as hell." She drew the dishtowels around the child and fastened them with a blue butterfly brooch taken from her dress.

"You got a name for him, Honey?" Mr Horowitz asked.

Honey thought for a moment, laughed and said: "How about Dick?"

"We never had a boy," Mr Horowitz said, "but Mrs Horowitz always said, ever we *did*, he'd carry *my* name."

"His daddy's name was Joe," Honey said.

"That's a good solid name," Mr Horowitz said.

Honey looked at the child. "Looks more like a Jo*anne* than a Joe," she said. She unfastened the butterfly brooch and turned back the dishtowels. "This a racing sheet, Mr Horowitz?"

"That's what it is."

"You have a pencil?"

Mr Horowitz took a chewed pencil from his trouser pocket and handed it to Honey.

"He's hung like a horse, we might as well name him after one," Honey said. She raised the pencil over the child, circled it in the air a few times, then lowered it to the paper. She looked at the place where the pencil touched. "Thunder Flash," she said. "Jesus, Thunder Flash!" She laughed briefly. "There's no way I can call the kid Thunder Flash."

"It's a high bred animal," Mr Horowitz said with gravity.

"Maybe so," said Honey, "but it's no name for a kid." She circled and landed the pencil a second time. "Sunnyside Up," she announced. "Sunnyside Up...Sonny..." She smiled. "Hey, that's not bad...Sonny." She turned to Mr Horowitz. "Howd's it sound to you, Mr Horowitz?"

Mr Horowitz asked: "Is that 'Sonny' with a *u* or an *o*, Honey?"

"With an *o*," Honey replied.

Mr Horowitz nodded. "Sounds fine to me," he said.

"Sonny...That's cute," Honey said, smiling and refastening the dishtowels. She looked at Finn. "Howd's it sound to you?"

"Fine," said Finn. "Until he starts drawing a pension."

Lubcek returned and said: "Line's tied up. Give it a coupla minutes, I try again."

Finn said: "I wouldn't want to be shot in the head in this town."

Honey finished her drink and said to Mr Horowitz: "You mind if I have another beer, Mr Horowitz?"

"Sure you can, Honey. A beer here, Carl – " Mr Horowitz looked in Finn's direction " – and a drink for this gentleman. And have one yourself, Carl."

"I'll have a beer with you, Mr Horowitz," Lubcek said. He poured whiskey into Finn's glass. "You havin' one, Mr Horowitz?"

"Not for me, Carl, I got enough here."

Lubcek opened two bottles of beer, passed one to Honey and poured one for himself. "You here long, mister?" he said to Finn.

"Just passing through," Finn said.

"You think we could have some music?" Honey said to Lubcek.

Lubcek reached across to a radio that stood amongst the spirit bottles and turned a knob. A band was playing a foxtrot.

Honey took a swallow of beer and began to sway to the music.

"You sure you're feelin' okay?" Lubcek said. "I don't never heard of a woman soon as havin' a kid is drinkin' beer." There was a slight resentment in his voice.

"Never felt better," Honey said.

Finn studied Honey as she swayed, and an idea that had occurred to him when he had taken his first good look at her seemed suddenly not to be foolish. 'Why not?' he thought. 'It's about *time* I got back to work. She's not Betty, but she has the right credentials – if they're genuine.' He said to her: "Would you mind if I asked you a personal question, Miss?"

Still swaying, Honey turned to Finn and said: "Go ahead."

Finn indicated her breasts with a nod and said: "Are they all yours?"

"Huh?" Honey stopped swaying, glanced down at herself, then stared at Finn. In an even voice, she said: "Well, they sure as hell ain't Captain Marvel's."

Mr Horowitz said in a chagrined tone: "Now look here, mister, that ain't no way to – "

"Okay, okay, don't break out in a rash," Finn interrupted. He took a card from his top pocket and handed it to Honey. "I'm Harry Finn. I work in the theatre."

Honey studied the card.

"I'm an entertainer," Finn said. "A comic."

Honey looked at him with uncertainty.

"I need a partner," Finn went on. "Someone with your kind of build."

"You putting me on?" Honey said.

"My last partner" – Finn hesitated – "walked out on me."

"Why was that?"

"We didn't see eye to eye about certain things."

"And you want a new partner?"

"Right."

"I've never heard of you."

"My credentials can be checked."

Honey looked puzzled.

"You can check out what I say."

"You've got a funny-looking face," Honey said, wanting to believe him.

"How old are you?" Finn asked.

"Twen – " Honey faltered. "Twenty-one."

Mr Horowitz said in a surprised voice: "Why, Honey, you – "

"Twenty-one," Honey said firmly, foreclosing any discussion of the subject.

"Married?"

Honey shook her head. "Uh-uh," she said.

"What do you think of the idea?" Finn asked.

"I'd be on stage?"

"Yes."

"What would I have to do?"

"Just look good; speak a few lines."

"Sounds okay," Honey said, "but I got to think about it." She added, "You sure you're not putting me on?"

Finn raised a hand. "Honour bright," he said.

Lubcek said to Finn: "I sure I seen your face someplace. You ever been in movies?"

"No," Finn said.

Lubcek looked at Mr Horowitz and said in a low voice: "I sure I seen his face someplace."

Finn finished his drink and got off the stool. He said to Honey: "I'm staying at the Drayton Arms. If you're interested, leave a message with the desk clerk there."

Honey nodded and held out his card.

"Keep it," Finn said. From the door, he called: "By the way, the kid doesn't go with the act." He tried the door, unbolted it, and stepped into the sunlight.

As soon as he was gone, Honey went to the telephone and asked the operator for a Boston number.

CHAPTER 5

As Jessica Lansbury waited beside a taxi outside Boston's South Station, her thin, stretched face chilled by a stiff westerly breeze that had suddenly sprung up, the fears that had filled her thoughts the day before; that had kept her awake most of the night, returned. What if there was something *wrong* with the child? What if it was hideously deformed, had an unlovable hump, or a misshapen head? Would she have the strength to say she had changed her mind; that she was mistaken; that she was unable to take the child? She wished she hadn't been so enthusiastic, hadn't cried: "Oh, Honey, yes! Yes, I would!" when Honey in that workman's voice of hers had said: "I've got a baby that needs looking after; you wouldn't be interested, would you, Aunt Jessica?"

The call had come when she was feeling particularly bleak, when she was telling herself that life without someone to care for was no life at all. She had Henry of course, but caring for a husband was not quite the same as caring for an infant: she could not sweep Henry into her arms, bury her face in his flesh and murmur silly baby words. She was thirty-seven, six years younger than Henry, and time was running out. Her chances of becoming a mother were, it seemed to her, vanishing by the minute. She was barren and felt it. She had been thinking of these things when the telephone sounded. At first, because of the depth of the voice and the poor quality of the line, she had imagined she was speaking to a man. "Harvey? Harvey who? Oh, *Honey*. Oh, I'm sorry, Honey, I didn't…It's this line."

Jessica had last seen Honey two years earlier. Henry, to her surprise, had asked her to accompany him on a business trip, and during their car journey she had suggested impulsively that they call on her cousin Pearl. It was a small detour and Henry had agreed.

Neither of them had enjoyed the visit. Henry was put out by Pearl's strong language and criticism of the government ("When's this shit-for-brains administration gonna do something for the low paid of this country?"), and Jessica, for a reason she could not have explained, had felt uncomfortable in the presence of Honey's overdeveloped breasts. Afterwards, continuing their journey, Henry said that Pearl was a disgrace to American womanhood and that it was only too easy to blame one's misfortunes on the government. What was needed, what Pearl needed, was drive, ambition. Look at him, a country boy who'd become the chief buyer for Staley's and the owner of a five-bedroomed house in the best part of Boston.

Yes, life, thanks to what Henry called the doctrine of hard work, had been kind to them. But not as kind as Jessica would have liked: it had not given her what she most wanted – a child.

"Hi, Aunt Jessica!"

Jessica felt her heart thud erratically as Honey, smiling, waved to her from the station's entrance. She hesitated; then, swept momentarily by an unassailable conviction that the bundle Honey was holding contained an infant that was quite perfect, raised a white-gloved hand and waved back.

"Here, wrap him in this," she said when Honey was close to her. She opened the door of the taxi and took from the back seat a blue lambswool blanket – one of a dozen that Henry had had specially delivered from Staley's that morning. "Come, get in. It's cold out here. We don't want the mite catching pneumonia."

They got into the taxi, and, as it pulled away, Jessica turned to Honey, took a deep breath, smiled and said: "Now…let me see him." She held out her arms and received Sonny as carefully as if she were receiving a soap bubble or a fragment of gossamer. She pulled aside the covers that hid his face and felt a butterfly take off in her breast. Sonny was asleep, thick dark lashes curled on apricot skin. "Oh, Honey, he's beautiful," Jessica said. She looked at Honey, her face bright with pleasure. "What do you call him?"

"Sonny," Honey said.

"Sonny," Jessica murmured. "How sweet." Hating herself, she slipped a hand inside the coverings and moved it to Sonny's back and shoulders. Finding no unnatural rise, she sent up a silent Thank You. "Oh, he's beautiful," she said again, and, unable to stop herself, unable to believe that a mother could part with such a treasure without it being flawed in some way, added: "Honey, he's all right, isn't he? There's nothing wrong with him?" She felt her face burn with shame at the question.

"Nothing except his tube," Honey said comfortably.

The butterfly in Jessica's breast turned into a bat. "His tube?"

Honey laughed. "His whip-out."

Jessica remained confused.

"His pisser. It's a monster."

"His piss – Oh…" Jessica felt her face become hot again, this time from embarrassment. She said hurriedly: "It's probably water retention, something of that sort, something not too serious."

"I guess so," Honey said indifferently.

Jessica stroked Sonny's cheek with the backs of her fingers. Without taking her eyes off him, she said: "You shouldn't have made this long journey, Honey. We – Uncle Henry and I – would have come to *you*."

"That's okay," Honey said, "I like train rides."

There was a silence, then Jessica said: "Wouldn't your *mother* have liked to have had Sonny?"

"She don't go much on kids," Honey said.

"But why me?" Jessica asked.

"Momma told me you didn't have a kid of your own, so I figured you'd maybe like to have mine. It was that or putting him in a welfare place."

"Oh, no!" Jessica bent her head protectively over Sonny and quickly drew back as the stench of newly laid faeces rose up. "This young man needs changing," she said.

Honey said: "He's one big stink."

Jessica lowered the window a fraction. "And tell me about this work of yours," she said with genuine interest. "You're going on stage! Oh, Honey it sounds wonderful. How did it happen?"

Honey explained.

"And when do you join Mr Finn?" Jessica asked.

"Soon as I get back," Honey said.

Had Jessica not been holding Sonny, had she not had the luxurious expectation of burying her face in his flesh (washed clean of waste matter) and murmuring silly baby words, she might have felt envious of Honey, might have hardened her mouth. Instead, she smiled contentedly, and when the taxi came to a halt gave the driver an extravagant tip.

"This is some place you've got here," Honey said, stepping from the taxi and looking around. "Just you and Uncle Henry live in all this?"

The house was a white, two-storeyed neo-Georgian structure as broad as it was tall, sheltered by sycamores and cedars and set in half an acre of immaculately tended grounds.

"We have a help who sometimes stays over," Jessica said, and, as if by arrangement, the door opened and a black woman wearing a white apron over a navy dress appeared. "Here she is now," Jessica said. "Millie. She's a treasure." Without taking a breath she called: "Millie come and see what I've brought home!"

Millie came up to them. She was in her mid forties and had wise, chestnut eyes.

Jessica moved the covers from Sonny's face. "Isn't he lovely, Millie?"

Millie studied Sonny for a moment, then said: "He could whip up a storm with those lashes."

Jessica laughed delightedly. "His name is Sonny," she said; then, barely able to control the happiness she felt, added: "This is Sonny's mother, Honey."

Honey and Millie exchanged greetings, and Jessica said warmly: "Let's have some refreshment."

"I've put a tray out," Millie said. "Tea's fresh made."

Inside the house, Jessica said to Millie: "Sonny needs changing. Would you take care of it while I give Honey some tea?"

Millie took Sonny, and Jessica watched with concerned eyes as he was carried up a wide staircase carpeted in cerulean blue. "You know where everything is, don't you, Millie?" Jessica called after her.

"I know," Millie said tiredly, without looking back.

Jessica showed Honey into a large room decorated in green and oatmeal and hung with watercolours of brown and yellow landscapes. An oblong mahogany coffee table set with tea things and a plate of triangular sandwiches stood in front of a white marble fireplace, and there was a long pale green couch with matching chairs.

"Since your call" – Jessica removed her gloves and placed them on the arm of the couch – "I've done nothing but have baby goods delivered. It's been hectic. Tomorrow there's a carriage coming and on Friday blue hangings for the nursery." She laughed and said in a lower tone as if revealing a secret: "It's so useful having Uncle Henry work at Staley's – we get everything discount." In a normal tone, she said: "Before you leave, I'll show you the crib I had delivered. It's beautiful."

They sat at the table on facing chairs, and when Jessica had poured tea and they had taken some, Jessica said: "Honey, there's something I have to ask you." She hesitated a moment, anxious of the answer she might get. Now that she had *seen* Sonny, had held him close, knew that there was nothing wrong with him – nothing visible, that was – it would be unbearable to have to give him up after a few months or years. She would sooner Honey take him back to Stanway that minute than have that happen. "How long will you allow Sonny to stay with us?" she went on.

Honey shrugged and said: "As long as you want, I guess."

Jessica relaxed a little. "But what if your theatre work doesn't come to anything? I don't want to seem a Jonah, Honey, but it's a possibility you have to face. I couldn't bear to take care of Sonny, to get to love him, and then have him taken from me; I couldn't bear that."

Honey said: "It don't *matter* about the work – not coming to anything, I mean; I don't want a kid, *any*way. If the work doesn't come to anything, I'll find something else, something away from Stanway, and if I had a kid with me I wouldn't be able to do that."

"Are you saying that you want Uncle Henry and me to be Sonny's guardians?" Jessica saw a small puzzled look come into Honey's eyes and added: "To bring him up. To be parents to him?"

"Sure," Honey said easily.

For a split second Jessica considered raising the question of adoption but decided against it; it was too early for that; she wasn't a greedy person. She smiled contentedly; she had been given the answer she had hoped for; she had Sonny on a long-term basis. She bit neatly into a fish-paste sandwich, thought it disgusting, and swallowed.

* * *

After she had shown Honey over the house, had, with a feeling of guilt, pressed a hundred-dollar note into her hand, had called and paid for a taxi to take her to the station and waved goodbye, Jessica went into the room where Sonny slept. She looked down at him for a minute, then, bending over him, unfastened his diaper and gently drew it back. From the doorway she heard Millie say: "He's sure gonna give the girls a thrill with *that* thing when he gets older."

CHAPTER 6

Frank Lever's telephone had sounded at 12.30 in the evening.

"Frank, it's Harry. Betty's dead. Can you come over?"

"I'm on my way."

Lever, small, wiry, with flared nostrils and a full head of black-turning-grey hair, had been Finn's agent for a little over twelve years. He had discovered him at The Playhouse, a small back-street theatre in Chicago, during one of his periodic talent-spotting tours. Finn had opened the second half of a variety show there with a convoluted story about a visit to his father-in-law's farm with his wife and two children. Impressed by Finn's zany presentation and immaculate timing, Lever had offered his services as an agent; and Finn, telling himself he would be no worse off with an agent than he would be without one, had accepted. "The first thing we have to do," Lever had said, "is get you some fresh material; some of those gags of yours have hairs on them. Then we have to get your name in print."

At that time, Finn was engaged to appear at The Palace Theatre in New Jersey. On the day that he did, he was equipped with a new set of jokes and his picture under the headline *Comic In Sea Drama* was on the front page of the *Jersey Post*.

According to the report, Finn, while sunning himself on South Beach, had seen a young swimmer in difficulties, and, fully clothed and without any thought for his own safety, gone to his rescue.

The 'rescue' had been engineered by Lever. With Finn's blessing, he had given the swimmer ten dollars to swim fifty yards out and call for help. While the rescue was taking place he had telephoned the *Post* and tipped them off. By the time Finn and the swimmer had reached land an enthusiastic young *Post* reporter/photographer was waiting to get the story.

Finn had played the modest hero ("I'd rather not give my name"), and Lever the inquiring spectator ("Say, mister, aren't you Harry Finn who's playing at the Palace?")

Reporter to Finn: "Is that so, sir?"

Finn: "Well ..."

"Say, Mr Finn, would you mind if I get a picture?"

That night Finn appeared before a capacity audience and received a standing ovation.

Another time, Lever persuaded Finn to go on a hunger strike in protest at the threatened closure of the theatre at which he was appearing in Detroit. After nine days without food (or so Lever and Finn had the Press believe) Finn simulated a collapse on stage. The story appeared in every major Mid West newspaper, and *Variety* devoted a whole page to it.

These and similar ploys had helped keep Finn in work but not got him the attention he and Lever so badly wanted – attention from the radio scouts. Lesser talents were making big names for themselves, but for some reason Finn had remained on the perimeter of his profession. "It doesn't make sense," Lever would say peevishly. "That no-talent cowboy Calloway gets his own radio spot and you're playing Milwaukee. You're worth ten of that prick."

With Betty joining the act, things had improved. There were bigger billings, better theatres to play in. The 'big break' had seemed not too far away. Then the telephone call had come.

After Betty's body had been taken away and Finn had given a statement to the police, they, Finn and Lever, had opened a bottle of whiskey, and when they had drunk that they had gone to an all-night bar for more, Finn finding it difficult to speak for the effort of holding back tears. Lever had stayed with Finn that night and on waking the next morning had found a note pinned to his jacket: *Cancel all engagements. Take care of things. H.*

Three months later Lever received a wire: STAYING DRAYTON ARMS NEW DRAYTON STOP FOUND NEW FEED STOP COME SOONEST STOP HARRY.

Lever had left for New Drayton the next day.

At the bus station they had hugged like brothers, Lever saying: "You cheesehead; you worried me sick running off like that."

Finn had offered the briefest explanation: "I had to get away from the place." He had not told Lever that for two months after Betty's death his eyes had burned from the amount of weeping he had done, that his consumption of malt whiskey had trebled, and that he would sooner have had a tooth pulled than listened to a love song. Instead, he had spoken of the latest theatre news, and now, seated in a booth in the Excelsior Tavern, the talk was of Honey.

"She's not much on looks," Finn said, "but she's got a figure that's perfect for the act. She's got a pair of handles you could stand a drinks' tray on."

"You're sure it's not just the act you're thinking of?" Lever said good-humouredly.

"She's not my type," Finn said. "Too big."

"She's got to be some tough number to give up the kid."

"The kid's okay," Finn said confidently. "It'll do better without her. The old man's a big shot with Staley's. It'll get the best."

Lubcek called from the end of the bar: "You okay for a minute? My fuckin' boy don't turn up, so I gotta clean up out back."

"We're fine," Finn called back and refilled their glasses from a bottle of Old Masters. Lever looked at his watch and said: "Let's hope her timing's better on stage than it is off." He paused, then added: "Or maybe she changed her mind." At that moment the door opened and Honey came in carrying a battered brown suitcase. She was wearing a red dress with padded shoulders, and red high-heeled shoes. Around her throat was a thin band of black satin. She was followed by Pearl, who wore a blue cotton coat over a green printed dress, and faded, purple carpet slippers.

"Here she is now," Finn said.

Lever turned in his seat. "I see what you mean about the handles," he said. Then: "She have a permit for those things?" He raised his eyebrows. "Who's the gorilla with her?"

"Beats me," Finn said.

Honey came up to them. "Hi," she said, smiling.

"Hello," Lever and Finn said together, and got to their feet, Finn moving out of the booth. "Here, let me take that for you," he said to Honey.

Honey handed him the case, and he placed it on the table, against the wall.

"Sorry I'm late," Honey said, "but Momma here decided at the last minute she's got to meet you."

Finn nodded to Pearl who nodded back. Without knowing why,

Finn formed the impression she'd been been drinking.

"Momma, this is Harry – Harry Finn who I'm gonna be working with. Harry, this is Momma."

They shook hands and Finn introduced them to Lever. When Lever had shaken hands, Finn stood to one side to allow Honey into the booth, and Lever moved along on his side of the table to make space for Pearl.

Still standing, Finn said: "Will you have a drink? We've some great Scotch here. Or would you prefer something else?"

"Scotch is fine by me," Honey said, "Scotch okay for you, Momma?"

Pearl loosened her coat from her shoulders and in a cold voice said: "Why not?"

Finn went behind the counter and returned with two glasses. "Here we are, ladies." He sat beside Honey, set down the glasses and filled them with whiskey. He raised his glass and said: "Cheers."

Pearl drained her glass in one gulp and brought it down hard on the table.

Finn slowly refilled it and said: "I guess you're worried about what Honey's getting herself into, Mrs – "

"The name's Pearl," Pearl said in the same cold voice.

"I guess you're worried about Honey, Pearl?" Finn said.

"Could be."

"Oh, Momma, come on!" Honey said. "You couldn't give a *shit* about me."

Pearl shrugged and took a swallow of her drink.

Finn said to Honey: "How was your trip to Boston?"

"Fine," Honey said.

"Your Aunt Jessica like Sonny?"

"Crazy about him."

Finn said to Pearl: "You happy with the arrangement, Pearl?"

"Suits me," Pearl said.

"Momma don't like kids much," Honey said to Lever.

"Who does?" Lever said.

"Frank once got bitten by one," Finn said. "One of the kids in the Robinson troupe, wasn't it, Frank?"

"I got my own back," Lever said. "I fixed it so his rubber duck wouldn't float."

Pearl finished her drink and said: "Men have it easy where kids are concerned."

Finn refilled her glass and, more out of politeness than conviction, said: "Women have it all to do when it comes to raising children."

"Damned *right* they have it all t'do," Pearl said fiercely.

Finn and Lever exchanged a glance, and Honey, seeing this, said: "Momma had a drink before she left home."

"So I had a drink – so why *shouldn't* I have a drink?" Pearl demanded.

Lubcek appeared, and Finn called: "Another bottle, Carl."

Lubcek said: "That fuckin' boy don't turn up tomorrow, he ain't got a job."

Finn collected the new bottle and brought it back to the booth. As he poured, Pearl looked at him and, out of the blue, said: "How do we know you are what you say you are? For all we know you could be a whorehouse keeper."

Honey closed her eyes and said: "Jesus!" In a superior tone she said to Finn: "Pay no attention to her, Harry."

Pearl, as if she hadn't heard, said to Honey: "How do I know he ain't a whorehouse keeper who's gonna dump you in a two-dollar whorehouse in Mexico or some *other* shit-kickin' place?"

"Momma, for chrissake! Mr Finn's business is the theatre not *whore*houses."

"There a difference?" Pearl said sneeringly.

Finn said: "No harm's going to come to your daughter, Pearl." He took from his pocket a duplicate of the card he had shown Honey at their first meeting and passed it to Pearl.

Pearl glanced at it and tossed it on to the table. "That don't mean nothin'," she said.

"Momma why don't you cut it out," Honey said.

"Believe me, Pearl," Finn said with a half smile, "I'm not a whorehouse keeper."

Lever said: "He should be so million-dollar lucky."

Pearl gave Lever a quick, contemptuous glance and helped herself to another drink.

There was an awkward silence before Honey said to Finn: "I was so excited last night I didn't get to sleep."

Pearl, rolling her head from side to side, said in a mealy, baby voice: "I was so excited last night I didn't get to sleep." She took a drink, coughed on it and allowed a dribble of saliva to reach the turn of her chin before wiping it away with the back of her hand. "A whorehouse, that's where you'll finish up," she muttered.

Honey, looking at her, said: "You know something? You're one big stinking mess."

The words and the way in which they were spoken made Finn feel vaguely depressed. "Hey, hey," he said uneasily, "let's be friends."

They drank steadily on, Pearl staring sullenly into her glass, while Lever and Finn reminisced and Honey listened.

When they had drunk four fifths of the second bottle, Lever looked at his watch and said: "I have to go."

Finn looked at his watch and said: "You've time for one more," and topped up Lever's glass.

Lever said: "Okay, one more, then I got to go."

Honey said: "Can't you stay a while longer, Frank?" Her voice was pleading, but there was a note of insincerity to it. She wanted Finn to herself.

"There's an act I want to catch in Baltimore," Lever said.

Finn said: "Frank's always on the look-out for the next ten per cent."

"From *you* in the past three months I got ten per cent of nothing," Lever said.

"Touché," Finn said.

Pearl, who seemingly hadn't been listening, suddenly turned to Lever, jerked her head in Honey's direction, screwed up her eyes and said: "You think she's got big tiss?" Her voice now was blurred and rough.

"Oh, Jesus!" Honey said.

Without waiting for a reply, Pearl swung back and faced Finn. "You think she's got big tiss?" It was more a challenge than a question.

"Well – " Finn began.

"You shoulda seen *mine* when I was her age," Pearl said. Her face broke into a dazed smile. "I had the best tiss in Stanway – in the whole goddamn State. My tiss were *twice* the size of hers. I had fellas breakin' their balls to get a look at 'em."

Lever finished his drink in one swallow and said: "I got to go." He started to rise.

Pearl spread her palms, gathered up as much of her breasts as she could and turned to him. "I could out-tit anybody in those days," she said. "Nobody had bigger tiss n'mine."

"Sure, Pearl," Lever said tiredly. "The best. Now let me out."

"You bet your ass the best," Pearl said. She looked wistfully at her massed flesh for a moment, then let it fall.

"Come on, Pearl, I've got a tight schedule," Lever said impatiently.

Pearl, without looking at him, grabbed his arm and pulled him down. "If you'da seen *my* tiss when I was her age, you'da wanted *me* for your whorehouse," she said to Finn.

Honey said: "Okay, Momma, now let Frank out."

"Yes, Momma, let Frank out," Lever said sourly.

Pearl looked at Honey and said sneeringly: "You think your tiss are big? Mine would've made yours look like a couple of two cents kids' marbles."

A faint flush of anger came into Honey's cheeks and, forgetting for a moment that she wanted to impress Finn, she said: "You make yourself sound like you were some kind of fucking freak."

Lever got to his feet again and said to Pearl: "Move your ass, Pearl." Without waiting for a response, he bulldozed into her legs and forced his way past her.

Finn rose and said to Honey: "Take care of your mother while I have a word with Frank." He walked to the door with Lever.

Lever opened the door, and Finn said to him: "I'll see you in three weeks. If you can't make it, leave a message. We should be ready by then. It's not as if she'll be playing Lady Macbeth."

Lever glanced across at Honey and said: "You sure you know what you're taking on? She's got the build all right, but she's not exactly Miss Society Page."

Finn said: "She'll be okay. It's just she's lost a little of her charm school gloss."

Lever smiled laconically and shook his head.

Finn said: "Take care of yourself."

"You too," Lever said. "And behave yourself with Momma." He shook his head again. "Jesus, what a gorilla!"

Finn watched him until he was out of sight, then returned to the booth. Pearl was asleep in a corner of the booth, her mouth open and her head resting against the wall. A piece of her hair had come loose and stuck out awkwardly from her temple. Looking at her, Finn felt a vague sympathy for her. He sat down and said to Honey: "How much did your mother have to drink before she left home?"

"I dunno," Honey said. Then, emphatically: "Enough."

Finn glanced at his watch. "We've an hour to kill before the train leaves. We'll let her sleep awhile, then put her in a taxi."

Later, on their way to the station in the same taxi that had dropped off Pearl, Finn said to Honey: "Your mother has a lot of spirit."

"*She's* okay, I guess," Honey said, shrugging.

"Will she be all right in the house on her own?" Finn asked.

Honey gave a small laugh. "As long as she has a drink in her hand she'll be as happy as a hog in horseshit."

Finn winced inwardly and after a moment let his thoughts go to Betty.

* * *

And Pearl, resting now on a broken couch in the living-room of her delapidated weatherboard, her mind still dazed with drink, her eyes closed against the bare ceiling light, let her thoughts go to Honey. 'You lucky bitch,' she thought. 'You've got it all and I've got nothing.' In her mind's eye she saw Honey's face, then saw it recede and blur and become clear again. It blurred a second time and suddenly she saw Honey in a bawdy house in a flame-red dress, drinking from a tall misted glass in the heat of a high plains afternoon. She saw a door open and a lean dark-haired man enter. She saw Honey rise from a chaise longue and go to him. She saw Honey's face dissolve and re-form into a face that she recognised as her own, and she saw herself lead the man by a hand to a perfumed turned-down bed, slip from the flame-red dress and stand naked before him. She saw the man caress her body, saw her body as it once had been; then she saw the man begin to unbuckle his belt. "Oh, Jesus," she moaned as the picture faded, "why ain't I a whore in a whorehouse?"

CHAPTER 7

They went to the boarding house where Finn and Betty had always stayed whenever they were appearing at one of New York's fringe theatres. Its proprietress, Ida Petchnikopf, described it in the advertising columns of *Variety* as a *Theatrical Rooming House*, and theatrical it was – a large grey-bricked edifice with soaring chimneys, tall, narrow windows, and spiky wooden trimmings that hung from its eaves like so many ugly stalactites. The children of the neighbourhood called it The Crazy House, not so much for its grim appearance than for the odd-looking people that came and went through its arched portico – men wearing ancient astrakhan coats and spats, and over-cosmeticised women who gestured extravagantly and clacked along on run-down high-heeled shoes. Ida Petchnikopf had inherited the house from her husband Boris, an animal trainer for circuses, who had met his death in Nebraska when a bear he was breaking in turned on him and disembowelled him. Ida had had the beast shot and its head fixed to a shiny black plaque, which she had hung in the entrance hall. Over the years the head had suffered a number of embellishments: a young actress had painted its nose with scarlet nail polish and blacked out two of its middle teeth, and when one of its eyes had gone missing someone replaced it with a ball of silver paper. A cigarette stub was glued to its lower lip, and two cherry stones dangled by joined stalks from a bottom incisor. It was affectionately known as Cedric and had become something of a good luck piece (the story ran that those who kissed its brow would be rewarded with fame and riches). Looking at it, Honey thought it cute.

Ida Petchnikopf looked up from her directory of rooms and said to Finn: "Sorry to hear about Betty." She was thin and sallow-skinned and spoke the words flatly, without a trace of sincerity.

"Sure," said Finn equally flatly. Finn did not like Ida – she was cold and humourless – but she kept a clean house and her food was first rate. "How's business?" he asked.

"They come and they go," Ida answered.

Finn presented Honey, who gave a small nod and received a smaller one in return.

"Double or singles?" Ida asked.

"Singles," answered Finn, aware that Honey was looking at him expectantly.

"Four, and nine," Ida said.

They signed the register and Finn paid three weeks' board in advance.

When they got to their floor, Finn said: "I'm going to clean up and rest awhile. I'll meet you downstairs in forty minutes and we'll take in some of the sights. How does that sound to you?"

"Swell," Honey said brightly.

In his room Finn removed his shoes and jacket, drew the curtains and lay on the bed. Almost immediately he smelled the lavender water that Ida Petchnikopf scented the pillows with, and a split second later recalled something Betty had said to him after they had made love on their first night there – "If you ever stopped loving me, Harry Finn, my heart would break." He tried to picture her as she was then, but saw her as he had last seen her. He closed his eyes against the tears that had begun to form and drifted unhappily into sleep.

He awoke after thirty minutes, depressed and nauseous. He tried to remember the dream he'd had but was unable to. He knew it was something unpleasant, but that was all. He washed, put on his shoes and jacket and went downstairs.

Honey was waiting for him in the entrance hall. She had changed into an electric blue silk dress and a short spiky fur coat, which made Finn think that the first thing he had to do was to get her some new clothes. He smiled briefly and said: "Let's go, shall we?" He walked ahead of her to open the door, and opening it, came face to face with a slim, swarthy man wearing a reefer jacket and tight, navy trousers that flared at the bottoms. He had jet hair flattened to his skull and a pencil-thin moustache.

"Harry!" The man's mouth parted to reveal perfectly matched teeth.

"Hello, Bobby,"

Finn and the man shook hands.

"Long time no see," the man said. "Where you been hiding?"

"Here and there," Finn said, and added quickly: "How are things?"

"Terrific, just terrific. I'm playing the Starlight."

"The big time, eh?" Finn said.

"It beats Barney's Beer Hall," the man said.

"This is Honey," Finn said. "Honey Bunn. She's joining the act."

"Yeah, I heard about – "

"Sure," Finn said, cutting him short, but pleasantly so.

"This is Bobby Malt," Finn said to Honey. "Stage name Pierre Lavelle. The best dancer in the business."

Bobby Malt revealed his teeth again and by way of confirming Finn's words wriggled his hips wildly, raised his arms high above his head and rattled his heels with extraordinary celerity on the stone step. "Ole!" He clapped his hands rhythmically and slowly circled on the spot, his back arched and his eyes half closed.

Honey laughed with pleasure.

He came to a halt and said to her: "Pleased to meet you." He smiled. "Honey Bunn – that your real name?"

Honey nodded.

"Why don't you catch the show tonight?" Malt said to Finn, but concentrating on Honey. He slipped a hand inside his jacket and produced two tickets.

"Can we?" Honey asked Finn.

"Why not?" Finn said.

They said their goodbyes, and as they walked away, Honey said: "He's something else."

"Beware of men with thin moustaches," Finn said.

They went first to the Empire State Building, where they took an elevator to the observatory balcony and, it being a clear day, saw fifty miles over Manhattan and the harbour, New Jersey, the Hudson River, Queens and the East River.

Next they rode on an open tramcar and from its top sighted the New York Public Library and Scribners Bookstore and Radio City Music Hall. They saw the Rockefeller Centre and Cartiers and Tiffanys and St Patrick's Cathedral and on 58th and 59th Streets the Plaza Hotel.

From Midtown Manhattan they went to Times and Herald Squares and after they had window-shopped at Gimbel's and Macy's and eaten a hamburger, took a taxi to Broadway to gaze at the theatres.

But it was the *people* of New York that most interested Honey. While Finn pointed out a building or landmark, she cast surreptitious glances at them and saw in their eyes, or fancied she saw, a steady light of expectation, as if they knew with absolute certainty that something wonderful was going to happen in their lives and that whatever that wonderful thing was it wasn't too far off – around the next corner or on the next block, moving towards them, diamond bright and unstoppable. They returned to Times Square, and here they heard a man greet another – "Hiya, George! Boy, you look terrific! How d'you do it, you old son of a gun? Boy, seeing you is just about the best thing that's happened to me today." Ping, ping, ping. Music being played on a stretched rubber band, Honey thought.

"Come on," Finn said. He took Honey's arm and steered her to a narrow side street that smelled faintly of disinfectant.

"Where're we going?" Honey asked.

"To get you something to wear."

They came to a small shop that stood between a furrier's and a florist's. The shop had fresh blue and white paintwork and a sign that hung from a wrought iron fixture which said *Harriet's Fashions*. Displayed in its one window was a single black dress draped over a white wicker chair. Finn knew the shop through Betty, who had discovered it on her first visit to New York and been impressed by the stylishness of its clothes and the reasonableness of its prices.

They went in, and an assistant came up to them.

Finn said to Honey: "Have a look round and choose yourself a couple of outfits. I'll collect you in an hour. There's something I have to do." He took the assistant to one side and said: "Don't show her anything you wouldn't want your favourite aunt to wear. And I'd like to see change from two hundred."

He left the shop, found a telephone booth, and after consulting the address book he carried, dialled. A few seconds later he heard a tinny female voice say: "Broadway Rehearsal Rooms. Can I help you?"

"I'd like to hire a room for tomorrow and Wednesday," Finn said. The voice replied: "I'm sorry, Sir, we're fully booked."

"How about Thursday?"

"We've nothing available until Friday of next week."

Finn thought for a moment, then said: "Okay, thanks," and replaced the receiver. He consulted his address book again and dialled a second number. After a short wait, he said: "Reverend Coates, it's Harry Finn. Yes...Yes...You too, Reverend. Reverend, I have a favour to ask."

Finn had made it a rule never to ask favours of anyone unless they were owed, and this one was. While appearing at The Royale in Brooklyn, a small red-faced man had approached him backstage and introduced himself as the Reverend James Coates, vicar of St Edward the Confessor's in South Bronx. In a tired voice Coates had told him he was organising a Christmas party for a group of underprivileged children and wondered if Finn would be generous enough to provide the entertainment. He'd petitioned entertainers at other theatres but they'd turned him down. Of course, there would be a payment, but it wouldn't be large, there was very little in the coffers – just fifteen dollars. Finn, smiling, shaking his head no, had said: "Sorry, Reverend, but I got a wife and ten kids to support." At that moment Lever had come up, and Coates, perhaps sensing that Lever held sway over Finn, had said: "They are children who have suffered greatly. You have no idea what your presence would mean to them." He had looked at Lever, who, looking at Finn, had asked: "What's going on?" and Coates had repeated his story. At the end of it, Lever had said: "We'll be glad to help out, Reverend." At that, Finn had taken Lever to one side. "What's the big idea?" he'd demanded; and Lever, grinning, patting Finn's cheek, had answered: "Publicity, pal, publicity."

The party was held in St Edward's church hall, a low, brick building which stood a few feet from the church and next to a hoarding that advertised Chesterfield cigarettes. St Edward's itself was a flinty building with broken windows and black, blistered paintwork. Spindly rose bushes grew against its sides, and caught on their thorns was the windblown refuse of the city: an ancient Hershey bar wrapper, a cellophane envelope that once had held nylon stockings, a nylon stocking, wisps of tissue paper, a particularly spent prophylactic. Passing it, Finn had thought it devilishly ugly, doubted that it attracted many worshippers. Finn tended to look upon churches as theatres, and in his experience the more warmth a theatre radiated the greater were its chances of being filled. St Edward's, he'd decided, would never have a *House Full* sign outside.

The party was a success, and afterwards, after photographs had been taken (Lever, as usual, had alerted the Press), Coates had given Finn his telephone number, saying: "If ever I can be of help to you, don't hesitate to call me."

Now Finn said to him: "I'd like the use of your hall."

"It's yours whenever you want it," he heard Coates say.

"Just for a few days."

"It's hardly ever used. There's no call on it. You can have it for as long as you wish."

They spoke for four or five minutes – Finn explaining why he wanted the use of the hall, and Coates reminiscing about the party. Eventually Finn said: "I've got to go now." He wanted a drink badly. He looked across the street to where the Tower Hotel stood. People were entering and leaving through its revolving doors, their faces momentarily greening as the foyer's emerald spotlight caught them. "Goodbye, Reverend – and thanks." He left the booth, crossed the square and went into the hotel's Night Owls bar.

He ordered a whiskey sour and carried it to a deep leather chair that stood away from the glare of the bar's single chandelier, close to the door.

There were three other customers – a woman away to his left seated at a glass-top table, and two men who stood together at the counter, both smartly dressed in dark suits. One was heavily built, with thick red hair, and the other slightly built and balding. They spoke in loud voices, their conversation interspersed with raucous laughter, which made Finn think they were there to get drunk and had reached that stage in their drinking when everything the other said was excruciatingly funny. The woman was middle-aged and had a sharp but not angular face and copper-coloured hair tied in a knot at the nape of her neck. She wore a plain red-rust cardigan over a white shirt, and a simply-tailored red-rust skirt. Finn thought her extremely elegant – not a woman's woman. Taking stock of her,

Honey came into his mind. Honey, he decided, could *never* look elegant. He could take her to a top Parisienne couturier, spend ten thousand dollars on her and she would still look like a gang-moll in a B-class movie. He wondered cynically if Harriet's Fashions were having difficulty in finding something in her size, if they had a tape measure long enough to go round her chest. He had two more drinks and returned to the shop.

Honey was wearing a loose-fitting navy and white suit and a cream shirt that had a blue paper orchid pinned to its front. Her shoes were the same colour as her shirt. The suit was smartly cut but had a look about it that said to Finn that it had come from the rail reserved for Harriet's older, heavier customers. "How do I look?" Honey said, smiling.

"Fine," Finn said.

"I had them fix a paper orchid to the shirt to jazz it a little."

Finn nodded.

"I got the same outfit in cucumber – they're not exactly hot on colours here – and a second pair of shoes and a coat. The coat's a little last century, but that's okay, I'll fix it with some trim."

Finn went to the assistant, who was standing at a small desk at the rear of the shop. He said to her: "The clothes are fine. What is there to pay?" He wondered if she was thinking that Honey was his floozy, and supposed that she was.

"A hundred and twenty dollars, sir."

Honey came up to them and in a hard, superior voice said to the assistant: "I'll keep these on. Have the stuff I came in with delivered with the other stuff."

Finn looked at her coldly, and for a moment hated her. He paid, and wrote down their address.

In the street he wanted to say something to Honey about the way she had spoken to the assistant, but found himself unable to. He was dismayed to discover that he felt intimidated by her. "How about something to eat?" he said brusquely.

"I'm starved," Honey said. She did not thank him for the clothes.

"Ever eaten Chinese?"

"No, but I'll try anything once." She spoke the words suggestively, and to Finn's embarrassment took hold of his arm.

They went by taxi to Chung's, which was close to the Starlight Room on Shelbourne Street and which, despite its dinginess, had the reputation for serving the best Chinese food in New York. Rodgers of Rodgers and Hammerstein ate there, as did Alice Faye.

They sat at a zinc-topped table next to a window hung with threadbare red and white check curtains. Honey, as she settled herself, looked disapprovingly at them and said: "*All* Chinese places like this?"

"The food's good," Finn said bluntly. He ordered a duck dish and side dishes of noodles, rice, and fried pork in sweet and sour sauce.

As they ate, Honey said: "We don't have no Chinese places in Drayton, just regular eating places. We got a place run by an Italian but he don't sell nothing but hash and ham." A noodle fell from her fork and draped itself over the orchid on her shirt. "Shit!" She carefully removed the noodle and dabbed at the grease mark it had left with a napkin. "Frank Ferranti," she went on. "Every waitress ever worked for him he screwed. Once, I looked through the serving hatch and caught him screwing a waitress up against the ice-box. He looked at me while he was doing it and said, 'Give me a coupla minutes, willya, Honey?' just like he was fixing a ham on rye."

From Chung's they went to the Starlight Room and got there as it was filling. A ten-piece band was playing a quickstep and four couples were dancing with conscious precision on a raised marble platform in front of the dining area.

Honey went to the powder room and returned ten minutes later with her face freshly painted and her hair wetted at one side and fashioned into a wave.

"Let's have a drink, shall we?" Finn suggested.

They made their way to a long S-shaped bar at the back of the floor, where thirty or forty people had gathered to pass time before eating.

Finn bought drinks and they stood with them at the counter, Honey studying the dancers, and Finn the faces of the people around him. After a while, Finn said: "See that tall man over there with the silver hair? He's a big Broadway producer – Joseph Kirschell. The man with him is David Lord the songwriter. He wrote *Goodbye Sad Eyes* and – " He broke off, angry with himself for having tried to impress her. He asked himself what he was doing in the Starlight Room – or any other place for that matter – with a woman who swore like a waterfront worker and was rude to shop assistants. He wished he was back in the Tower Hotel.

A man with a large wen on his temple came up to them, squeezed Finn's arm, and said: "Awfully sorry to hear about Betty, Harry. You know how we all felt about her. In my book she was the best." He added in a low, intense tone: "Christ, what a rotten thing to have happened."

Finn said awkwardly: "Yes, thanks, Tommy." He felt suddenly exhausted.

"We'll have a drink sometime," the man said.

"I'll look forward to that," Finn said.

The man smiled kindly at Honey and moved away.

Honey swallowed some gin and said: "Who was that?"

"Tommy Deacon. He's a comic on radio."

"Never heard of him," Honey said.

"He's a very funny man," Finn said tiredly.

"Betty was the partner you told me about, wasn't she?" Honey said.

"Yes," Finn said.

"I guessed she was."

A few moments of silence went by, then Honey said: "It's none of my business, but what happened to her?"

"She died," Finn said.

"How'd she die?" Honey said matter-of-factly, as if she were asking the time.

Finn thought: 'She'll find out, anyway', and said: "She killed herself."

"Killed herself?" Honey said, still in a matter-of-fact voice. "What she wanna do a dumb thing like that for?"

Finn felt his face grow hot and the muscle at the back of his neck contract and become solid. He wanted to reach out and take hold of her throat and say: "Damn you, why don't you keep that big mouth of yours shut." Instead, he said softly: "She had cancer."

"Jesus," Honey said, her voice taking on an anxious note. "Where?"

Finn looked into her eyes for a long time, then let his gaze go to her breasts. "In the breast," he said deliberately.

"Jesus," Honey said again. "What a place to get it."

Finn decided that if she were less than very good at tomorrow's rehearsals he would give her a hundred dollars and send her back to New Drayton.

CHAPTER 8

He had told her to be ready to leave at nine, but expected her to be late: they had done a great deal of walking and drunk a debilitating amount of gin. Also, he suspected she had spent the night with Bobby Malt. Malt had joined them at the bar after his performance (an extraordinarily athletic one that had had the diners neglecting their food to watch it) and paid Honey extravagant compliments. Dancing with her, he had held her tightly, his mouth against her cheek. Later in a taxi taking them to Ida Petchnikopf's Finn had heard them sighing words to each other and the sound of clothing being disturbed. He had said goodnight to them and left them talking outside Malt's room, which was two doors down, across the corridor from his. Undressing, he had heard their voices, then a door close and cut them off. If Honey had spent the night with Malt and Malt had lived up to the reputation of being an indefatigable lover, she would, Finn speculated, have managed only a few hours sleep. She would be tired and hung over and late.

But he was wrong. She was waiting for him downstairs and looking as only very young women are capable of looking after a night of unrelieved love-making – refreshed.

She had had her breakfast, she told him, so he left her with a magazine in a room near the reception desk that served as a card and reading room, and ate alone.

On Tuesdays it was scrambled eggs on toast followed by more toast, and blueberry jam. Tomorrow it would be grilled herrings, and on Thursday fried chicken livers and tomatoes; the menus at Ida Petchnikopf's never changed, which suited Finn and was another reason why he chose her house as his base when in New York. It made life easier; he found it comforting to know what the next day's meal would be; he did not enjoy surprises, especially culinary ones. As far as he was concerned, food, like the colour of one's mother's hair, was something a man shouldn't have to spend time worrying about.

Over coffee he scanned the front page of the *New York Times* (there was a copy placed on every table) and read that there had been another gangland killing. It was the third that month, the report said, and police expected reprisals. The dead man, as in the previous killing, had been an associate of Sylvano Mastrioni, the Mafiosa's controller of New York's east side. Finn had once seen Mastrioni in the lounge of the Plaza Hotel. He was accompanied by two very rouged young men who spoke in sibilant, falsetto voices and who, whenever they addressed him, moved close to him and fussed with his jacket. Mastrioni, for his part, had neither spoken nor changed his bored expression; he'd moved only to raise a drink to his lips and once to slap away fingers – nails brightly lacquered – that fluttered over his tie like so many tiny red butterflies. Finn had been reminded of a photograph he'd once seen of a Mandarin, aloof and inscrutable, seated between two concubines who giggled into their palms.

Finn finished his coffee, wiped his mouth on one of Ida Petchnikopf's hand-embroidered napkins and collected Honey. In a taxi, he said to her: "We'll most likely run into a priest, so I'd like you to watch your language."

Honey started to say something but was interrupted by the driver. "How about that Mastrioni hood gettin' it? Third one this month. You read about it?" He was bull-necked and wore a dark green tartan muffler that was speckled with dandruff. "Pretty soon Mastrioni's gonna get worked up. Guys like him don't take that kinda stuff lyin' down."

Finn, by way of reply, said: "He's a mean man."

"You ain't gonna believe this," the driver said, "but I once had Mastrioni in this cab." He glanced over his shoulder at Honey. "Right where you're sittin', lady." He paused to change gear and pull in front of a dark blue limousine. He decelerated and said: "The guy's a faggot, you know that? Had two kids with him."

The air in the cab was hot, so Finn wound down a window.

"You wouldn't believe what they was doin' back there," the driver went on. "If it wasn't for the fact it was Mastrioni, I'da kicked him out. Real crude stuff – y'know what I mean?" He paused. "Don't get me wrong, I ain't no Holy Joe; I like havin' fun like anybody else – and when I say fun, I mean sex fun, if you'll excuse the expression. But there's sex fun and there's sex fun." He ran a hand over his hair, dislodging a single flake of dandruff. "I seen some real heavy stuff back there, but nothin' like what I seen Mastrioni and his little pals doin'." He shook his head. "Like I said, if it wasn't for the fact it was Mastrioni, I'da kicked him out, but I got a wife and kids and I ain't gonna be much use to them if I got a coupla slugs in the head." He slowed, looked out of his side window and said: "Jesus, this traffic gets worse." He picked up speed again and continued: "Mastrioni ain't the *only* hood I had in this cab. Another time I'm flagged down on 102nd and this guy asks me to take him to Belvedere. I tell him that's a fifty mile trip, and he says: 'So who's askin' for a geography lesson' – real Jimmy Cagney stuff." He cleared his throat. "Anyway, the guy gets in and I notice he's scratchin' hisself...*all over*. Christ, I never seen anyone scratch hisself so much. 'You okay there, pal?' I say; I'm scared he's got somethin' catchin' – like somethin' he could give the seats. It don't register that I got Scratch Jackson in the back. Scratch Jackson! That guy wiped out more people than the plague.

"Anyway, I drop him at a joint in Belvedere – you shoulda seen this place, a real million dollar pile; like somethin' outa the movies – and the next day I read he's been found with his throat cut and his anal passage – that's the name the cops give it – his anal passage givin' house room to a broom handle. I figured he'd arranged a meet at the place I dropped him at, only the guy who opens the door and says, 'Come on in, Scratch' ain't the person he's *suppo*sed t'be. You get the picture? Like he was set up. That's how I figured it.

"Anyway, gettin' back to Mastrioni: my old lady once had a run-in with one of his hoods." He glanced over his shoulder again. "You ain't gonna believe this. This story is so horrific you ain't gonna believe it." He cleared his throat. "My old lady's out buyin' onions for the stew she's makin', when this guy comes up and pushes in front of her. When I say pushes, I mean *pushes*; and she's comin' up seventy at the time." Glancing at his rearview mirror, he went on: "Now, my old lady don't take that kinda crap from nobody. I seen her, when I was a kid, kick shit out of a guy who tried to jump a bus queue; they don't come any tougher.

"Anyway, this guy pushes her, and she gets hold of him by the coat and starts hollerin' and screamin'. She won't let go of him. And you know what the guy does?" He paused for effect. "He smacks her in the mouth – in the mouth! – an old lady of seventy. When I say smacks, I don't mean a back-of-the-hand smack like you give a kid, I mean with the fist. Bam! He laid her out. That's the kinda shit Mastrioni's got pitchin' for him."

A car horn sounded and Finn closed his eyes against it, kept them closed.

"How can a person hit an old lady in the mouth just 'cos she's demandin' her rights as a human citizen? You tell *me*, pal. That guy's gotta be some kinda animal."

After a little silence, he said:

"My old lady, she was never the same after that. Had to have everythin' mashed up 'cos her jaw was hurt so bad. Couldn't chew anythin'. She looked a real fuckin' mess, too – 'scuse my French, lady – 'cos her face was all twisted up. I wanted go look for the sonofabitch, but the old lady says, 'No, they'll blow you away, Alex.' And I guess she was right – they woulda done. But like I said, Mastrioni hisself is a faggot. Jesus, what he had those kids doin' with him! And when I say kids, I *mean* kids. They couldna been more than seventeen. Ever I caught a kid of mine doin' what they was doin', I'd take his fuck- I'd take his head off. Disgustin' ain't the word."

"What were they doing?" Honey asked.

The driver half turned. "If I was to tell you, lady, it'd mean my licence." He laughed and slowed down as a traffic light changed to red.

* * *

Pinned to the door of the church hall was a message from Coates saying he wasn't able to greet them; he'd been called away on business; they should help themselves to refreshments, which they would find in the back room.

They went inside and when they had drunk coffee poured from a flask, Finn moved aside chairs and tables to make a space. "Okay," he said, "let's get started." He took from his jacket pocket a piece of chalk which Ida Petchnikopf had given him from her work basket, and drew a large oblong on the floor. "This," he said, "is a bed, and this" – he drew a three-foot square next to the oblong – "is a table that has a call button on it. This" – he drew a long straight line – "is the edge of the stage, and this a door, back of the stage." He stood upright and looked at Honey. "Okay? Any questions?"

Honey shook her head no.

Finn removed his jacket and placed it on a table. "This particular sketch," he said, "takes place in a hospital room. I play the patient; and you the nurse.

"When the curtain rises, I'm in bed, smoking a cigarette and reading the racing sheet.

"I put the cigarette into my mouth to turn a page, and when I take the cigarette back into my hand, I drop it. I search for it, but can't find it. I get into a sweat and call for the nurse – *you*." He paused. "It doesn't sound much, but it works. Let me show you…"

Finn lay on the floor and raised his back, suggesting it was supported by pillows: Finn a malingering patient studying a racing paper and smoking a cigarette, then dropping the cigarette and searching for it: tentatively feeling beneath the bedsheets, beneath himself, peering under the bedsheets, running a hand under the pillows, becoming more and more agitated, throwing off the bedsheets, and finally, in panic, pressing the call button and calling: "Nurse! Nurse!"

It was comedy of a very high standard – a composite of W.C. Fields, Eddie Cantor, and Groucho Marx, perhaps too reminiscent of Groucho Marx for Finn's own good.

He sat up and said: "Now, when I call 'Nurse! Nurse!', you come on stage through that door." He got to his feet and crossed to the chalked door. "Through here. Imagine this is a door and you've just heard me call, 'Nurse! Nurse!' This is what you do. Watch carefully."

"You've got chalk on your pants," Honey said matter-of-factly.

Finn stared at her, stunned, as if he couldn't believe what he'd heard. He let several seconds pass, then in a hard, deliberate tone said: "Never mind about the chalk. It doesn't *matter* that I've chalk on my pants. Just pay attention." He was perspiring heavily and his left knee hurt from his exertions. "Just pay attention or we'll call it a day right now and you can go back home to your mother." He brushed angrily at the back of his trousers.

When he'd composed himself, he said: "Okay, this is the door."

Finn went through the motions of opening and closing a door. Now he was a nurse – bustling and efficient – a nurse smoothing down her uniform, conscious of her figure, walking with quick, small steps to the bed, smiling a wide smile and throwing fluttering glances at a make-believe audience. "Mr Finkelstein! What on earth are you doing? (this spoken in falsetto). Heavens! If Doctor Wilberforce knew you'd been smoking again…Well, I don't know…"

Finn, still the nurse, mimed searching the bed for the cigarette. Then he lay on the chalked bed again and in the patient's voice and with much rolling of the eyes said: "That ain't no *cigarette* you've got hold of, nurse!" He grinned lasciviously.

"Okay – now let me see you give it a try. There's more to it than that, but we'll get to that later." Finn got to his feet, went to a chair, and sat down. His knee still hurt, and he was experiencing a vague feeling of despair. He half hoped that Honey would fail the 'test', that she would be so impossibly bad that at the end of the day he could say to her: 'I'm sorry but I don't think it's going to work out the way I'd hoped it would', and put her on the next train to New Drayton.

"Okay," he called. "Now, don't worry. Just do the best you can."

PART TWO

CHAPTER 1

Honey, her head beneath a bedsheet, slowly rotated her hips. She waited until the whistles were sustained and shrill, then surfaced and faced the audience. "Mr Finkelstein!" she cried, her eyes open wide in mock astonishment. "You're sure it's not a *cigar* we're looking for?"

The audience laughed and a rough voice called: "Corona or Tom Thumb?"

"Felt more like a Panama Special to me," Honey called back.

The audience laughed again, and a stout woman seated in the stalls choked on the popcorn she was eating.

It was the height of summer and the temperature on stage in Cincinnati's Phoenix Theatre was 105 degrees, which made Finn glad he'd decided to work with a single sheet instead of the usual sheet and blanket.

Honey bent over him and he held his breath against the effluvium of perspiration that hovered around her. In the five years they had worked together – five years in which they had grown to hate each other with an almost animal-like ferocity (Finn hating Honey for her vulgarity and insensitivity, she hating him for his contempt-filled eyes and self-pity) – he had never known her to bathe more than once a week.

"Mr Finkelstein, this is too much!"

"You bet your life it's too much! Why d'you think I got five women wantin' to marry me! *C'mere!*"

"Mr *Finkel*stein!"

The curtain came down to applause.

Finn threw back the sheet and swung his legs over the side of the bed. He unbuttoned the pyjama jacket he wore and saw that the hairs on his chest were drenched and flattened to the skin. He got to his feet and said to Honey: "You *smell* bad, you know that?"

Honey unpinned her nurse's hat and shook loose peroxided hair. "Not as bad as this fucking act," she said.

"If this act smells, then go find another," Finn said.

"If I did, you'd be writing gags for match books," Honey said. "Without me you wouldn't have a pot to piss in – or a bed to put it under."

"Go to hell," Finn said. He removed the pyjama jacket, wiped his chest with it, and strode off stage.

"What's the matter," Honey shouted after him, "THE TRUTH HURT!"

In their dressing room a small fan was working, and Finn sat on a chair in front of it and let the air play on his face and throat.

Honey came in and kicked the door shut with her heel. She threw her nurse's cap into a wicker props basket that stood in a corner of the room and unbuttoned her uniform. She wore nothing under it.

Finn glanced at her reflection in the mirror that ran the length of the wall, and seeing her breasts, was overcome with a feeling of revulsion. He didn't quite understand why he found her breasts so offensive; most men ached to get their hands on them. Perhaps it was something to do with Betty's death. Perhaps he saw them as a cruel, caricatured reminder of it.

Honey sat at the make-up bench and quickly, expertly made repairs to her lipstick and mascara. She vigorously brushed her hair, then went behind a black rice-paper screen and changed into a low-cut, tight-fitting silver dress made of aircraft fabric. She returned to the bench and from a score or more of glass and china containers selected a blue scent bottle that trailed a pink ball on a tube. She pointed the nozzle at her throat and squeezed the ball.

Finn grimaced and turned his head away as a cloying, hyacinthine smell filled the room.

There was a knock at the door and a young voice said: "You're on, Miss Bunn."

Honey, with the merest contemptuous glance at Finn, left the dressing room and made her way back to the stage.

Waiting for her in the centre of the stage, a microphone in his hand, was the theatre manager, Bob Masters.

Masters was tall, heavily built, with closely set eyes and a nose broken in two places.

"Swell show," he said as Honey took a position alongside him. "Full house again."

"Huh-huh," Honey said.

Both knew why the theatre was full.

Masters gave a signal to a man in the wings and almost immediately the curtain began to rise. Simultaneous with the curtain rising, a drum roll sounded and a few moments later a chorus of whistles broke out as Honey was sighted.

Honey widened the smile she'd assumed and waved to the audience.

When the curtain was fully risen, Masters waited for the whistles to die down, then raised the microphone. "Okay fellas, this is it," he said. "This is what you've been waiting for all evening." He placed a paternal arm about Honey's shoulders. "Here she is, you guys – the gal with the biggest pair of" – he corrected himself with a cough – "with the biggest personality since Annie Oakley." He let a fresh fusillade of whistles subside, then looked around the theatre. In a concerned tone, he said: "Pretty hot out there, isn't it?" He waited for a response. "Well, isn't it?"

"YEAH!"

"I know it's hot out there, because I've been standing at back, watching the show." He turned to Honey and looked her up and down, letting his eyes rest on her breasts. In a low, throaty voice, he said: "Pretty hot up here, too!"

Now there were cries of "Whoo-ee!" and somebody barked like a dog.

"Well, let me tell you fellas something – IT'S GONNA GET A WHOLE LOT HOTTER!"

The person with an aptitude for dog mimicry made a high-pitched howling sound and there was stamping of feet and pounding of arm rests.

Masters raised a hand for silence. He was about to say something, when a voice called: "Come on, get on with it."

"Yeah, get on with it," another voice called.

"Okay, okay," Masters said good-humouredly, "but before we do, let me for the benefit of those of you out there who've been living on the moon for the past couple of weeks, explain what's about to happen."

There was a slight murmur of discontent.

"This won't take a second," Masters said. Then: "What's about to happen is, Honey here is going to come down among you and find herself a fella; it could be *any one of you out there* – and the fella she finds could be in for one helluva treat...one H-E-L-L-U-V-A treat, because that fella's name will be put into a hat along with the names of all the *other* fella's Honey's taken a shine to in past shows, and at the end of her run here in two weeks she's going to draw one of those names out of the hat – and the name she draws – WOW!" – Masters paused and rolled his eyes – "is going to have a night on the town, all expenses paid – dinner and dancing, chauffeured limousine – with none other than little" – he glanced at Honey, who throughout the spiel had smiled and shaken her backside – "Did I say little!" He leered and went on: "With none other than Miss Honey Bunn Dynamite herself!"

There was a furious roll of drums followed by a crash of cymbals.

"I'm waiting, Honey," a wag called.

"Let me be your honey bee," another cried.

Masters, smiling, raised his hand again. "You like the idea, huh?"

"YEAH!"

"Okay, let's get on with it. Let's have some fun here tonight." He turned to Honey. "Are you ready, Honey?"

Honey nodded and fluttered her lashes in coy fashion.

"That don't look ready to me, does it to you, fellas?"

"NO!"

"She can do better than that, can't she, fellas?"

"YEAH!"

Masters ran a hand over Honey's backside and in his throaty voice said: "Come on, baby, let's *show* these guys!"

Honey looked at him and flicked out her tongue.

Masters put his face close to hers. "Y-e-a-h..." he said lasciviously.

Honey closed her eyes and swivelled her hips. Suddenly she spread her legs, threw up her arms and thrust forward her pelvis. It was a movement of animal-like sensuality which brought whoops of delight and encouragement from the audience.

She repeated the movement; repeated it again. A drumbeat took it up. Bap. Bap. Bap. The movements became faster. Bap-bap-bap-bap-bap.

Masters turned to Honey, stooped down low, and began rotating his arm as if he were cranking a car.

Bap-bap-bap. The thrusts and the drumbeat became urgent. A man got to his feet and was joined by others. Masters, still cranking, shouted: "Go, go go!" The audience took up the call. "GO, GO, GO!" Bap-bap-bap-bap-bap-bap-bap-bap. "Go, go, go!" Masters screamed. The woman with the popcorn got to her feet and began emulating Honey's movements, her eyes closed and her mouth working orgasmically.

"GO, GO, GO!"

Honey rolled her head.

The woman with the popcorn moaned.

Honey moaned. "Ooooooooooo!"

"Oh y-e-e-e-e-e-s!" the popcorn woman called.

Honey's movements slowed, became laboured, ecstatic.

Bap. Bap. Bap.

"Aaaaaaaaaaaaah!" Honey gave a violent thrust. Gave another.

"Oh, yes, yes!" The popcorn woman cried out as if in pain.

"Ooooooooooooh!" Honey went again.

The audience grew quiet, conscious that something climactic was about to happen.

"Aaaaaaaaaaaah!" Honey gave a final thrust and let her head fall to her chest. She hung limp, her arms at her sides. Now there was complete silence. Those of the audience who were standing looked around at the people who had remained seated, and appeared disorientated, the way dancers on a dancefloor do when the music stops without warning and the lights go on. They returned awkwardly to their seats.

Honey, as if drained, remained motionless for a few moments, then suddenly straightened up and smiled a wide smile. She waved two-handed, and after a second's hesitation the audience, their self-confidence restored, cheered and waved back.

"I guess she's ready!" Masters cried.

"YEAH!"

There were five or six clashings of cymbals and Honey, a spotlight focussed on her, walked quickly across the stage and down the half dozen steps that led to the stalls. She stopped on the bottom step and called: "Hi, fellas!"

"Hi!"

"Lemme hear you!" She cupped an ear and leaned forward.

"HI!"

Honey moved, or rather she bounced, to the centre aisle, and as she did so, the drum started up again, this time with a dum-de-dum dum-de-dum beat that circuses play when the clown walks. From all parts of the theatre came calls and whistles.

"Here, Honey, here!"

"Aw c'mon, Honey-baby, daddy needs you. Come to daddy."

Honey, smiling, bounced along the aisle, studying the faces that were turned towards her. Once, she stopped to say to a cadaverous seventy-year-old with broken, yellow teeth: "You're cute." She bounced on until she got to the top of the aisle, then turned, blew half a dozen kisses and bounced back down again.

"Pick *me*, Honey. Here!"

"I got what it takes, Honey!"

"Hubba, hubba!"

Honey with little sideway steps avoided hands that tried to touch her.

When she reached the well of the theatre, she stopped and looked up at Masters, who had remained on stage.

"You found one?" Masters said into the microphone.

Honey nodded.

"Honey's found herself a fella, folks!"

"Whoo-ee!"

"How old's this fella you've found, Honey?"

Honey shrugged.

"Fifty?"

Honey frowned and shook her head, showed the frown to the audience.

"Younger?"

Honey nodded vigorously.

"Much younger?"

Three deliberate nods.

"Twenty?"

More deliberate nods.

"Twenty!" Masters cried. "Honey's found herself a college kid!"

"WHOO-EE!"

Honey turned to the audience and grinned, rolled her eyes.

"Okay, let's see who the lucky fella is. Go show him to us, Honey."

Honey, to the accompaniment of the drum, walked briskly up the aisle.

"Here I am, Honey!"

"I'm waiting, baby!"

"Honey!" a female voice called.

Honey stopped at a row of seats in the middle of the theatre and almost immediately a second spotlight came on and began sweeping the people seated there.

Honey squeezed her way past a dozen or more legs until she came to a slim youth with unruly light brown hair. She looked down at him for a while, then took hold of his hands and pulled him to his feet.

Whistling and cheering broke out, and the youth, evidently embarrassed and not knowing what was expected of him, looked nervously around.

Honey put her arms around his neck and somebody called: "Go to it, fella!"

In a stage whisper, Honey said to the youth: "Hello, handsome – what's your name?"

"George," the youth said softly.

"George who?"

"George Bellamy."

"George Bellamy, ladies and gentlemen," Honey called.

"Wanna trade, George?" somebody shouted. "My old lady for the doll you got there?"

"You're a good-looking fella, George," Honey said.

The youth blushed.

"You like me, George?"

"Sure."

"They can't hear you, George."

The youth cleared his throat. "Sure," he said in a louder voice.

"Louder, George."

"SURE!" he shouted, his courage growing.

"You like the way I look, George?"

The youth glanced at Honey's breasts, which were touching his chest. "Huh-huh."

"A lot?"

"You bet."

Honey put her face close to his and whispered: "Give 'em a squeeze."

The youth, flustered, looked down at the people seated either side of him.

"Give 'em a squeeze, you jerk," Honey hissed.

The youth raised a hand and before he could change his mind, Honey took hold of it and pulled it hard against her breast. She closed her eyes in mock ecstasy. "Oh, George!" she cried. "Mmmmm...Oh, lover! Mmmmm... Oh, you're driving me crazy, George."

People were getting to their feet again.

"Give 'em a squeeze for *me*, George!" someone called.

"I got bigger hands'n he has, Honey!"

Honey pulled the youth tightly to her and kissed him on the mouth, forcing her tongue between his teeth. It was a lingering kiss that brought a further burst of whistling. Eventually she broke away and said: "Oh boy, you sure are a kisser, George Bellamy. Wow!" Then: "George Bellamy, ladies and gentlemen. Let's have a hand for George Bellamy."

There was loud applause as the youth waved to the audience.

Honey moved in close to him again and ran a hand over his crotch. "Meet me at the stage door in half an hour," she whispered. She moved out of the row of seats and into the aisle. The drum started again, and Honey, smiling and brushing with her fingers the hands that were held out to her, returned to the stage and Masters.

"George Bellamy," Masters said with deliberation. "Okay, George your name goes into the hat." He took a pen and paper from his pocket and made a show of writing down the youth's name. "Okay, folks, that's it for tonight. Come back tomorrow – and bring grandpa

with you. You never know…" The curtain slowly descended.
"Goodnight, everyone."

* * *

Finn's intention had been to leave the theatre and go to the nearest
bar as soon as Honey had left the dressing room, but the cool air of
the fan had delayed him and he was still there when she returned.
He glanced at her and noticed that her lipstick was smudged and her
face flushed.

"When they gonna do something about the heat in this dump?"
she said angrily. "It's as hot as hell out there. If it's like it tomorrow,
I'm not going on." She sat at the make-up bench and began
redecorating her eyes.

"You'll go on," Finn said in a bored tone.

"Oh yeah? We'll see if I go on or not."

"You'll go on if only to find yourself a bed partner for the night."

Honey stopped applying mascara and said to Finn in the mirror:
"Don't count on it."

Finn shifted in his chair to let the air from the fan reach his side.
After a minute's silence he said: "Who's the lucky fellow got the
come-on tonight?"

"What's it to you?" Honey said.

"Oh, you know me," Finn said easily, "I like to keep abreast of
things." The pun was intentional and he chuckled inwardly over it.

Honey elongated her upper lip to apply powder to the sides of
her nose. "You know something, Finn?" she said when she was
satisfied with the result, You're not funny any more." She turned to
face him. "In fact, you're just about the unfunniest person I ever came
across. You're so unfunny, you're pathetic."

Finn turned his other side to the fan. The words, although he
didn't show it, wounded him. In retaliation he said: "Well, make sure
you wash the stink from yourself before you meet him. You don't
want the poor guy passing out while he's making it with you."

Honey turned back to the mirror. "You don't want the poor guy
passing out while he's making it with you."

It was an astonishingly accurate impersonation of Finn's voice, and hearing it, Finn felt his stomach tighten. For a moment it was as if he had ceased to exist, lost his identity – an eerie, baffling experience made the more baffling by the words having come from a woman – a woman with shoulder-length bleached-blonde hair and scarlet lips. There was an additional reason why Finn's stomach had tightened: the impersonation had reminded him of his vulnerability as an entertainer. He thought about the day he and Lever had heard Honey's voice mimicry for the first time. The three of them were travelling by car to Atlantic City, he and Honey for a theatre engagement and Lever to sign up a violin and patter act. Lever was recounting a movie he'd seen two days before, when, out of the blue, Honey had given wonderful voice impersonations of the movie's two main actors – James Cagney and Humphrey Bogart. He and Lever, their eyebrows raised in astonishment, had exchanged a glance, but had said nothing. Later that same day, over a drink, Lever said to him:

"You know, Harry, with the talent Honey's got she could be out on her own. Don't ever let a smartass agent like me get his hands on her, or you'll be in trouble."

"Trouble? What d'you mean, I'll be in trouble?" Finn had responded angrily. "You think I couldn't get by without her? You think I couldn't get by without that tit freak?"

"Come on, Harry," Lever had said in a pleading tone, "you know I think you're number one, but you've got to realise: things aren't the same any more; you know they're not." Then, lowering his voice, as if revealing a secret: "I'll level with you, Harry: you've got to stick it out with Honey. You need her more than you think you do. You get rid of her and you'll have to find yourself a feed who's prepared to give the customers free pussy every night; and believe me, feeds like that are hard to come by." He'd paused. "Why d'you think we get the kind of houses we get? Ever wonder why the customers are mostly males? You think they're there to hear a few gags or see some bozo juggle bananas? You think they're all in love with Harry Finn? I wish it were like that, but it's not. They're there because they're hoping that maybe they'll be the guy who gets to screw the dame on stage." He'd paused again. "Word gets around. Why d'you think you're booked solid for the next ten months?" He'd smiled grimly. "I'll tell you why: because yours is the only act whose feed sleeps with the customers.

Okay, the places you play in may not be Carnegie Hall, but you're making more dough now than you've *ever* made. If you wanted, you could work eight days a week, twenty-five hours a day, so go easy on the I-don't-need-that-tit-freak routine. *You* need her; *I* need her. Not counting Harry Finn, the acts I've got in regular work wouldn't pay the milk bill." Sighing heavily, he'd continued: "You know how many theatres closed last year? Fifteen. Music Hall's dying on its feet. It's all movies now. Okay, so one day Honey's handles will go. When she hits thirty, thirty-five, they'll be like her old lady's – hanging round her waist. What's she got – another seven, eight years? So stick with it. Make a pile while you can."

And so they had not, *did* not, encourage Honey to develop her talent. Whenever she surprised them with an impersonation (always of a male – usually of a movie star, or of someone they knew) they passed it off with a simple: "That's not bad. Needs a little work, but not bad", as if there was nothing at all remarkable about a woman speaking in a man's voice.

Finn said to Honey now: "I've heard better at Amateur Nite at the Roxy."

Honey gave him a look full of hatred, then went behind the rice-paper screen. After a short while she reappeared wearing a white dress with vertical blue stripes and a heart-shaped neckline. She looked at her reflection in the mirror, wiped away a speck of something from the corner of her mouth with a finger, and picked up her purse. "Goodnight, funnyman," she said sneeringly. She gestured with her head towards the fan and said: "Stay in front of *that* long enough and it'll maybe blow away the cobwebs from those gags of yours." She started out of the room.

"If you see a bridge, jump off it, will you?" Finn called after her.

He heard her heels clack down the stone corridor and when their sound had died he reached behind him and pushed the door shut. The air from the fan pelted his chest and he slid lower in the chair to let it get to his neck. He watched the blur of the fan's blades for a while, and then dressed and left the theatre. As he made his way to a bar across the street, he hoped he wouldn't run into Honey and her partner for the night. In a tired, dispassionate way he wished Honey was dead.

They returned to New York in February; Honey had told Finn she needed a rest, and Finn, although he hadn't said so, needed one too.

Finn took a room at Ida Petchnikopf's house, and Honey booked into a small hotel just off Herald Square.

On her second night in the city, Honey went to the Starlight Room. Since her visit there with Finn, she had gone there again and again – not because she enjoyed the Starlight Room's atmosphere especially – it was too formal for her taste – but because she enjoyed the entertainment it provided.

Towards the end of the evening she noticed a man wearing a black overcoat approach two men standing at the bar and speak briefly and clandestinely with them. She saw the man turn to leave, then turn back and stare at her. She returned the man's stare, and after a moment's hesitation he came up to her. He was in his early thirties and had high cheekbones, a small blunt nose, and widely-spaced chestnut eyes. With his ivory skin and dark, slicked-back hair, Honey thought him the most attractive man she had ever seen. "Meet me here tomorrow at seven," the man said to her, then turned and walked briskly away.

The man was Thomas Calvino, procurer of boys for Sylvano Mastrioni.

INTERLUDE

Thomas Calvino arrived in New York from Naples with his parents at the age of eleven. His mother found work as a button-hole maker in a garment factory, and his father, after months of being unemployed, was taken on as a waiter at Rimbeau's restaurant on East 52nd Street, a short tramcar ride away from the two-roomed cockroach-infested apartment he rented in the Bronx district. Calvino, meanwhile, had joined a street gang and quickly gained the reputation of being a psychopathic bully and vicious degenerate. Parents told their children to avoid him. Parents avoided him.

On his fifteenth birthday Calvino was taken by his father to Rimbeau's and given a job as a kitchen hand. Three years later and to Calvino's great delight his father dropped dead from a heart attack (Calvino had disliked his father almost as much as he disliked his mother – his father for his heavy handedness and his mother for her meanness) and Calvino was offered his job. Suddenly he'd become the youngest waiter on East 52nd Street.

Although he found waiting on tables demeaning, Calvino was proud to wear the black Rimbeau costume: it fitted him well, complemented his ivory complexion, drew attention to his slim figure. Never had he had trousers cling quite so tightly to his hips. Women and not a few men gave him admiring glances. He received good tips.

One Friday evening, four months after his promotion, he was taken to one side by Rimbeau's Maitre D'hotel, Mario Marinelli, and told: "You're working Table Six."

"But I'm on Four," Calvino protested. "I got a nice piece of change coming from that party – they ain't no ham 'n' eggs number."

"*Mastrioni* wants you," Marinelli said.

"Mastrioni? He here?" Calvino looked across at Table Six and saw two men – one squat and fat, and the other solidly built with large almond-shaped eyes that slanted downwards.

Mastrioni dined at Rimbeau's once or twice a month, but Calvino had never seen him; on the nights Mastrioni had eaten there he'd been absent. This had irritated him: Mastrioni was a big tipper.

"Wha'dya mean, he wants *me*?"

"He's asked that you wait on his table." Marinelli smiled and added: "Maybe he's hot over you."

Calvino coloured: he knew of Mastrioni's reputation. There was a story that he had once taken a waiter on a trip to Acapulco and bought him a dozen suits. (When Calvino was told the story, his face had burned with envy.)

"Don't let's keep the man waiting," Marinelli said.

Calvino went across to Table Six. "Good evening, gentlemen," he said.

The man with the almond eyes looked up at him and studied his face. "What they call you, kid?" His voice was soft. Calvino noticed that his forehead was heavily pockmarked.

"Tommy. Tommy Calvino." Calvino offered a menu and had it brushed aside.

"You new here, Tommy?"

"New on tables, sir."

"How old you, Tommy?"

"Nineteen."

"You're a good lookin' kid."

"Thank you, sir."

"You know who I am?"

"Sylvano Mastrioni," Calvino guessed.

Mastrioni smiled. "Those pants sure look neat on you, Tommy. A great fit." He turned to the man with him. "Don't they fit Tommy great, Benjie?"

"Like a rubber," the man said. Both men laughed.

"You got a girl, Tommy?"

"No sir."

"You ain't interested in girls, that it?"

"Yes sir."

"Yes you are, or yes you ain't?"

Calvino thought quickly. He saw himself in Acupulco with a dozen suits. "I can take 'em or leave 'em," he said.

"Good," Mastrioni said. "Girls can be trouble. Benjie here took a slug from one just last year. Ain't that so, Benjie?"

"I got the mark that says I did," Benjie said and tapped a spot on his shoulder.

"Would you care to order, Mr Mastrioni?" Calvino asked.

Mastrioni looked steadily at him for a few moments. "Rib-eye. Rare. All the trimmings. Twice."

In the kitchen, Marinelli said to Calvino: "What the big man have to say?"

"He said I looked cute, which I do." Calvino fluttered his lashes and waved his backside.

Marinelli laughed. "You keep your hand on it, or he'll have it for dessert," he said.

Mastrioni and his companion ate their meal and Mastrioni paid for it with a fifty-dollar bill. "Keep it," he said when Calvino brought him his change. It was the biggest tip Calvino had ever received. He thanked Mastrioni, who smiled and said: "How'd you like to work for *me*, Tommy?"

"What kind of work would that be, Mr Mastrioni?" Calvino asked.

"I can always use a good collector."

"I got a good job here. It pays well." Calvino said. He paused. "What'd be my take with *you*?"

"What you get here: fifteen a week – with another ten in tips? How does two hundred a week sound, and no rent to find?"

Calvino stifled a gasp. "It sounds good."

"There'd be other work," Mastrioni said. "Nothing too heavy. Just a little entertaining work." He reached out and brushed the inside of Calvino's leg with the backs of his fingers. "You get the picture?"

Calvino didn't answer immediately. He considered the proposition. The only 'entertaining work' he'd done had been done with girls, and he'd enjoyed it. He wasn't sure if he would enjoy entertaining or being entertained by Mastrioni. Then he thought of the two hundred dollars a week he would get and what they would buy. He also thought of his mother: he would no longer have to live with her.

"Sure. I get the picture," he said. He moved his legs a little farther apart.

Calvino moved in with Mastrioni a few days later. He did not tell Marinelli of the move because he knew that Marinelli would despise him for it, but he told his mother, who, after closing her eyes and murmuring rapturously: "At last we got somebody in the Mafia", asked him: "So how much you planning on giving me from your forty-dollars-a-week salary?"

Calvino shared Mastrioni's bed for six months (an experience he found not wholly unpleasant) and then was replaced a young light-haired mechanic who had changed a wheel on Mastrioni's car.

Calvino was not put out at being replaced: He could now pursue girls without upsetting Mastrioni, and Mastrioni had been generous: he had doubled his salary and given him a small apartment in one of the blocks he owned – rewards for his personal services and for his performance as a collector. As a collector, Calvino had come to be highly regarded – this by reason of his meticulousness in the carrying out of his duties: his takings were always accurate to the dime, and he never handed them in without they had first been checked and sorted. He also saw to it that damaged or stained bills were exchanged at a bank for fresh ones. ("If only *all* my collectors were like you, Tommy," Mastrioni would tell him, sighing.)

After ten years as a collector Calvino decided he wanted something better; he went to Mastrioni and asked to be promoted to executioner. Mastrioni agreed and put him to work at once, naming as his 'target' Frank Pittelli, third in command to Joe Rizzocco who controlled New York's West Side and was seeking to extend his territory. (Pittelli, Mastrioni had learned, had visited a restaurant on New York's East Side (Mastrioni's ground) and demanded a two-hundred-dollars-a-week protection fee. Mastrioni had felt drawn to act.) "I want Pittelli made an example of," he told Calvino. "Rizzocco and his shitlickers got to learn to stay on their own side of the fence. You do a good job on Pittelli, Tommy. Make him bleed a little before you stiffen him. Make me proud of you, Tommy."

Two days later Pittelli's body was found in the back of his car. His nose and lips had been removed and there was a gaping hole in the side of his head. Embedded in his neck, below the right ear, was a large wooden-handled hook, the type of hook used by stevedores to move heavy objects. The young policeman who discovered the body was hospitalised for trauma.

Calvino was given other such assignments: Alfredo Terzic (ears removed, ice-pick in skull); Leo Sempravinci (arms amputated at elbows, throat cut); Ricardo Carbolini (face blown away with a shotgun); Bruno Beldonni (legs broken, decapitated); Giorgio da Silva (flayed with a heavy chain, buried alive); Valentine Rimi (eyes torn out, bullet in temple).

And there was Lady Millicent Palfrey, Joe Rizzocco's English girlfriend, who, in the Stork Club one night, had swaggered up to Mastrioni and in a slurred, cut glass voice called him "a frightful old faggot". Incensed, Mastrioni ordered that Palfrey "die screaming".

Calvino burned her to death with a blowtorch.

Calvino's work as an executioner gave him much pleasure. He relished the stalking and snaring of the victim, enjoyed the killing itself. But his real pleasure came from the devising of the punishment; for it was Calvino's policy that no two victims suffer the same fate – this to add interest to the job and to maintain and promote the reputation he had for innovation (nobody in the Mastrioni organisation had performed amputations or forced a victim to swallow his own eyes, as in the case of Valentine Rimi).

Sometimes Calvino would spend a whole day contemplating a new punishment. He did so when, not long after his despatch of Millicent Palfrey, he was ordered to eliminate Vito Fellini, a new recruit to the Rizzocco organisation, whose crime had been to spit on the grave of Mastrioni's mother.

Armed with a razor-sharp hunting knife, Calvino went to Fellini's apartment, forced an entrance, and dragged Fellini naked from his bed. He was about to disembowel him (after much mind-changing he had settled on disembowelment), when the door opened and the cleaning woman came in; he'd forgotten to slide the safety catch. He ordered the woman out, but she came at him screaming and swinging the bucket she was carrying.

Calvino fled, a deep cut in his head from the swung bucket.

Next morning Mastrioni tossed him that day's newspaper, featured on the front page of which was the headline: *Hit Man Hollers Murder!* A sub-headline declared: *Cleaning Woman, 70, Routs Intruder.*

"It ain't good enough, Tommy," Mastrioni said. "People, they laughin' at us. One of my team gets taken out by some old broad with a tin bucket."

Calvino asked, pleaded, to be given another chance; but Mastrioni shook his head no. "You need a rest, Tommy," he said. "You bin doin' too much. Anyway, I got *other* work for you – more important work, personal stuff. You're the right person to handle it. I don' want no one else. You got the right face. You got the kinda face kids go for."

And so it was that he became Mastrioni's procurer.

CHAPTER 2

Jessica, standing at the tall French windows, sighed. The large cloud that had positioned itself above the trestle table looked decidedly ominous. She had instructed Millie and two hired helpers to station themselves at the table and at the first spot of rain to pack the food in wicker baskets and carry it into the house. Henry was standing by too. He waved to her now. Jessica smiled and waved back, then turned from the window and went into the hall. At the foot of the stairs she called: "Come along, Sonny dear, your guests will be here at any moment." She strained to hear a reply, and not hearing one started up the stairs. Her head ached slightly. She hoped Sonny was not in one of his moods; that he would not make one of his scenes.

He was sprawled on a couch in his playroom, abstractedly fingering a dark brown curl that had fallen across his forehead. He was dressed in plum-velvet breeches, a lilac silk blouse, patent leather shoes that buttoned at the sides, and white socks. He was an extremely beautiful child.

"Sonny dear, do come along," said Jessica, a little breathless from her climb of the stairs. "Your guests will be arriving at any moment. What will they think if you're not there to greet them?" She went to him. "Come along, darling." She knelt beside him and lightly touched his hair. She worried that the curls at the back, where his head rested on the couch's arm, would be flattened.

"I hate parties," Sonny said.

"We *all* do, dear, but we have to have them," Jessica said soothingly. "It's expected." She took hold of Sonny's hand and gently brushed it with her thumb. She marvelled for perhaps the ten thousandth time at the exquisitely formed fingers. After a while she took the tips of them into her mouth.

"It looks about to rain," Sonny said. He paused. "I *like* the sound of rain." He slowly moved his fingers so that their nails tapped rhythmically against Jessica's upper dentures. "Rain is sweet," he added.

Jessica caught a finger between her teeth and gently bit upon it.

They stayed close like this for several minutes, Jessica thinking she would like to stay biting on his finger for ever.

"Oh well, if I *must* go down, I suppose I *must*." Sonny pulled his fingers roughly from Jessica's mouth and swung his legs over the side of the couch. "But I know I shall hate every minute of it."

"I know, dear," Jessica said, "but we must try to put on a brave face. No, keep still a moment while I fix your hair. We don't want it looking crushed." She sat alongside Sonny and fluffed and flicked at his hair, wetting her fingers with saliva and fashioning back into shape those curls that had been flattened. "Now, stand up and let me look at you."

Sonny got to his feet on the couch and began to bounce on his toes.

"Keep still, darling." Jessica adjusted his socks.

"I should so love to know what it is that you and Uncle Henry have bought me for my birthday," Sonny said. He spoke the words softly, dreamily.

"Sonny, I can't *possibly* tell you – it's to be a surprise."

"Please, Mumsie."

The word made Jessica tremble. As soon as he had been old enough to have a little sense, they had made a point of telling him they were not his true parents (they did not want him being made upset by hearing it second hand), but they lived in the hope that he would one day come to accept them as such. His calling her Mumsie, even though she knew he used the name only when he wanted something, strengthened that hope.

"Oh, Sonny, Uncle Henry would be so angry."

"Please, Mumsie." He took her face in his hands, and, looking into her eyes, smiled a radiantly sweet smile.

Jessica sighed. She found the smile almost irresistible. "Oh, Sonny, what am I – "

"Please, Mumsie." He drew a breath, held it, and kissed her on the mouth.

"Sonny…"

"*Please.*"

"Oh…"

"Please, darling Mumsie." He covered her face with small kisses.

Jessica's head became light. She heard herself say: "It's what you wanted, darling." Her words came in little gasps.

"A rat maze!" Sonny bounced wildly on the couch, his hands clamped to the sides of Jessica's face so that her head was forced to rise and fall with each bounce. "Rats, too?"

"Two…darling," Jessica said breathlessly.

"Black?"

"Yes – but – you – must – promise – me – that – you – will – never – let – them – loose – in – the – house."

* * *

In the garden, Henry looked again at the cloud and thought he detected movement. When he was sure that he had, he said to Millie: "Well, Millie, I think we can uncross our fingers." As he spoke, the sun slowly broke through and scythed back the shadow on the lawn. "Now we must hope the cakes don't melt."

Millie raised her face to the sun, as if testing its strength. "*They'll* be okay," she said after a moment.

Henry addressed the helpers. "All right, I don't think we'll be requiring those," he said, indicating the wicker baskets. "Perhaps you'll take them into the house. We don't want the guests falling over them and breaking something."

"And here they come," Millie said.

Henry turned and saw half a dozen children racing across the lawn. They were followed at a snail's pace by Sonny, who was looking disconsolately at the ground.

"Get a move on thar, young Sonny," Henry called. "Let's git this har show on the road. We got a heap of entertainin' t'do today and we cain't have no feet-draggin'. Not today we cain't, no sirree."

There wasn't a day that went by that Henry didn't lapse into cowboy talk. Every evening on his return home from work he would greet Sonny with: "Howdy, mister. How ya'l doin' thar?" and come the boy's bedtime he would look up from *The Wall Street Journal* and say: "Reckon it's time to hit the hay, old timer." When dinner was about to be served, he would call: "Chow's up!" His father had used similar speech to *him* as a child and he'd enjoyed it. He assumed that Sonny enjoyed it too, though there was never any indication that he did. There was never a 'Be right there, Hank', or 'Okay, pardner' – not even a 'Yep' or 'Nope'. Had Henry known that Sonny hated cowboy talk and winced every time he heard it, he would not have held it against the boy: like Jessica, he was besotted with him, bedazzled by his beauty. On his desk at Staley's were two silver-framed photographs of Sonny at age four that were forever being picked up and admired by staff and visitors. "Oh, how cute!" they would say, or, "Oh, what gorgeous eyes!" Once, Staley's chairman Harold Dobbs and his wife Olga had called on him during a tour of the building, and Olga Dobbs, on seeing Sonny's picture, had said: "Is that your daughter, Mr Lansbury? She's perfectly lovely." Henry, for some reason, had not corrected her. In times of stress (when, say, an order had gone astray, or his secretary had forgotten to change the date on his desk calander) Henry would look at the photographs and be calmed by the sweetness of Sonny's smile. Sometimes when the stress was almost impossible to bear (the receiving of a critical memo from the director of sales, say) he would look at the child's face and feel tears of love and self-pity well up.

More children arrived. At first they hung back close to the house, then, catching sight of the other children, spurted across the lawn to join them. "Hi, Sonny!" they called as they passed him, and for the most part were ignored.

When the last of the guests had arrived, Jessica came out with the parents. She had hold of Verna Lugmann's arm and was laughing and gesticulating. Verna was Jessica's best friend. They had met at the hairdresser's and discovered they had a mutual interest in kitchen recipes and astrology. Like Jessica, Verna was thin-faced and of similar height and colouring. On several occasions they had been taken for sisters, which irritated Jessica: Jessica thought Verna plain.

Jessica and Verna caught up with Sonny, and the three of them made their way towards Henry. When they reached him, Verna said: "I was just saying to Jessica, Henry: every time I see Sonny I want to get hold of him and hug him to my face."

"I guess he is a hug-able son of a gun," Henry said proudly. He felt an urge to reach down and touch Sonny's hair, perhaps ruffle it a little, but he knew that Sonny would object, say, 'Stop it!' and he did not want the hurt of rejection. In bed at night with Sonny asleep between them, he and Jessica would turn on their sides and brush away the curls that had fallen across his brow, every so often looking at one another and smiling their adoration of him.

"My, that spread looks utterly delicious, Jessica," Verna Lugmann said. "And how the turquoise matches with the black. Turquoise and black cakes and black china.... How decadent!"

"They're Sonny's favourite colours," Jessica said. "*Everything* would be turquoise and black, if Sonny had his way." She looked at Sonny, who had seated himself at the table and was gazing across at the children, who were playing tag. "Isn't that so, Sonny?"

Sonny, without looking at her, nodded.

"Aren't you in a play mood today, Sonny?" Verna Lugmann asked soothingly.

"No," Sonny said.

"He's a bit of a lone ranger is our Sonny," said Henry. "A regular lonesome cowboy. Ain't that so, pardner?"

Sonny bit on the inside of his cheek.

The other parents gathered at the table and, like Verna Lugmann, admired the cakes and Sonny – mostly they admired Sonny.

"Sonny, you've got lashes a woman would kill her canary for," Mrs Lewis Brankelfort of Brankelfort's Eradication Services said.

Sonny loathed Mrs Brankelfort, but enjoyed receiving compliments from her – from anyone. He turned and gave her a wide smile. "Thank you, Mrs Brankelfort," he said, and, still smiling, lowered his eyelashes twice.

"Oh, what a darling!" cried Mrs Brankelfort.

"The glorious thing about children," said Mrs Herbert van Lodz of Lodz Disposables, "is that they don't know how beautiful they are. If they knew how beautiful they were they could rule the world. With *that* face Sonny could have anything, anyone he wanted. With *that* face he could have Einstein."

Verna Lugmann looked puzzled. "Einstein?" she queried.

"Einstein," said Mrs van Lodz confidently.

Henry cast a glance at the sky and saw a mass of cloud rolling in from the east. "I think it might be wise to start," he said to Jessica.

"If you think so, dear," Jessica said. "Shall I have Millie get the children?"

"No, it's all right, I'll call them." Henry climbed on to a chair and cupped his hands to his mouth. "COME AND GET IT! COME AND GET IT!" he called.

The children stopped playing and stared across at him. For a moment it looked as if they weren't going to respond, but Henry beckoned and called again, and they moved towards him.

When they were gathered at the table, Millie and Jessica and one of the hired helpers began removing the glass covers and linen napkins that protected the plates of food and jugs of lemonade. One huge glass cover protected a cake with six candles.

"Sit down now, children; any place will do," Henry said.

The van Lodz boy bounced on to the nearest chair and immediately reached for a cake.

"No, not yet, Carly," Henry said sternly. "First, Sonny has a few words to say to us."

"Wipe that filth from your nose, baby," Mrs van Lodz called to her son. She turned to Mrs Brankelfort. "Pick, pick, that's all the boy does. See how big his nose is – how spread out it is? That's what picking has done." She lowered her voice to a whisper. "Talking of size, did you know that Sonny has a sprinkler the size of a man's?"

"A …You mean …"

"His penis." Mrs van Lodz spoke the word sibilantly. "Mr van Lodz was shopping for a few things with Carly last week and needed to go to the men's room. While they were…re*lieving* themselves, Carly looked across at Mr van Lodz and said, '*Sonny's* got one as big as yours, Pop.'

"Can you imagine: a child of Sonny's age with a full size…Unless of course Carly was exaggerating – you know how children exaggerate – but I got to thinking, and it occurred to me that I'd never seen Sonny in a bathing suit. Whenever we have bathing parties, Sonny always wears his everyday clothes. Haven't you noticed that Sonny never wears a bathing suit?"

"Why, yes…Now that you…"

"Jessica says she doesn't want Sonny bathing outdoors because he chills easily, but maybe there's more to it than that; maybe it's because she doesn't want anyone to see his bulge. You know how men *bulge* in bathing suits; you just can't help noticing it. Boys too. Have you seen the eldest Harrison boy?"

"Why, I can't say that I…"

"I've asked Mr van Lodz to check again with Carly – just casually, you understand, over a game of checkers or something; I don't want Mr van Lodz to make a meal of it; I don't want Carly developing anything Freudian."

Mrs Brankelfort looked across at Sonny, who was standing on a chair delivering a thank-you-for-being-here speech to his guests.

"Furthermore, it…"

"*Furthermore!*" echoed Mrs van Lodz. "Such a big word for a small boy. Where does he *get* such words from, will someone tell me?"

"Jessica reads Henry James to him," said Alice Cantrail of Cantrail Mattresses.

"Henry James?" Mrs Brankelfort said vaguely. Her eyes travelled to a point on Sonny's breeches. She fancied she saw…But no, Mrs van Lodz's words, she told herself, had played tricks with her imagination.

For he's a jolly good fellow
For he's a jolly good fellow
For he's a jolly good fe-el-low
And so say all of us

Henry clapped his hands as he sang, and, looking around, nodded to the others, tacitly demanding that they join in.

And so say all of us
And so say all of us

Throughout the singing, Sonny gazed at the faces turned brightly towards him and thought them hideous – the Brankelforts and the Cantrails and the van Lodzs, especially the van Lodzs. He wished everyone would go home and leave him alone with his turquoise and black cakes. Not that he would eat them. No, he would simply sit and admire them. Well, he might sample a fragment of one – a black one; run his tongue over one of its rounded corners, taste the sweetness of the icing, bite into it. He saw in his mind's eye the black icing against the coral pink of his tongue and felt strangely excited.

For he's a jolly good fe-el-low
And so say all of us

When the singing and the applause had stopped, Jessica, for no particular reason, looked back at the house and saw two figures – a woman and a man – striding across the lawn towards her. She wasn't certain, but the knotting of her stomach told her she recognised the woman.

"Henry!" she called anxiously. Then, as the figures drew nearer: "HENRY!"

* * *

There were nights when Jessica would wake with a scream in her throat.

The dream, or rather the nightmare, was always the same: the bedroom door would burst open, and Honey, naked from the waist up, would swoop on them as they slept and tear Sonny from her arms. Jessica's cries would rouse Henry, who would leap from the bed and start to fondle Honey's breasts. In a corner of the room a hairless cat grinned insanely and scratched at its throat until blood gushed.

"Henry, save him! Save Sonny! Don't let Honey harm him!" Jessica would strain forward, tears burning her eyes. "Please Honey, don't harm him; don't harm the boy." And she would add words which when she recalled them the next day would seem foreign and horrible to her: "Take *my* glisten spult, Honey. Have *my* glisten spult. Look – my spult is better, stronger. Here, see how strong it is." She would plead with Henry again:

"Please, Henry, save Sonny! Save the boy!"

Henry would take Sonny from Honey, but instead of returning him to the bed would set him astride one of Honey's breasts. Then the three of them – Honey, Henry and Sonny – Sonny naked and riding the breast for all he was worth, his feet locked tightly beneath it – would look down at her and grin the mad cat's grin.

The dream would change: Now Henry crouched in the corner, the cat hanging by its claws from his chest. Sonny was no longer riding the breast but was being held aloft by Honey, who, looking up at him, half rotated him so that his member, engorged and purple-headed (Jessica's dreams always were in colour), swung this way and that.

"Oh, God, no!" But as Jessica cried out, Honey would lower the child's sex into her mouth and begin to chew on it.

Jessica had experienced the dream for the first time on the eve of Sonny's third birthday. She told Henry of it, and he had sympathized; placed an arm round her and drawn her to him, something he hadn't done in a very long time. He told her to put the dream from her mind and think of something pleasant – gardening. Had she not said she had a clump of agapanthus to plant? A month later the dream returned; and Jessica, unable to stop herself, once again told Henry of it; or, more exactly, told him ninety per cent of it: Henry hadn't allowed her to finish (a caustic memo from Staley's director of sales the previous day had put him in no mood for dreams). "For God's sake shut up!" he shouted when the penis-chewing scene was reached. "I don't want to *hear* about cocks – Sonny's or anyone else's. Is that all you think about – Sonny's cock!" And throwing down the *Wall Street Journal* he was reading: "You're sick, Jessica. You need help. Go see your doctor."

Whenever they had spoken of Sonny's penis they had referred to it as 'his person'. To hear it referred to in the vernacular had shocked and upset Jessica. But Henry had been right: she *was* obsessed with Sonny's penis – or, rather, its size. She saw it as a ghastly joke played on the boy by nature; a grotesque disfigurement of something inexpressibly beautiful. She felt as an artist might feel at the sight of the Venus de Milo with simian arms. In addition to being obsessed by the size of Sonny's penis, she was also obsessed with the idea that Honey would one day turn up and take Sonny from her, tear him from her arms, as in the dream, and she would never see him again.

On the day after Henry's outburst she had taken his advice and called on Doctor Wolfgang Schneider – ostensibly to renew a prescription for the vitamin tablets she was taking (vitamins B12 and E (she was anaemic and lacked vitality)).

"And how is dat boy ob yours?" Doctor Schneider asked, writing the prescription. "Still brimmin' mit helt?" A German by birth, Doctor Schneider had spent the best part of twenty years in the West Indies as a missionary worker, a tour of duty that had given his English a curious tropical flavour. "Still full ob de joys ob spring?" He was small and round and bald and wore pince-nez.

"Sonny? Oh, he's fine, thank you, doctor. I sometimes think he's *too* healthy."

"You nebber can be *too* helty, dear lady. Nebber *too* helty." Still smiling, Doctor Schneider handed her the slip of paper.

"Thank you, doctor." Jessica made a pretence of leaving: she stood up, pulled on her gloves. "However, there is *one* thing…"

"Ya?" Doctor Schneider remained smiling.

"Sonny…I'm rather worried…It's his…I don't know what to…I keep having these terrible dreams…I can't…" The tears that had suddenly built up, spilled over.

"My dear Missie Lansbury, what on ert is de madder?" Doctor Schneider pressed the not-to-be-disturbed button on his desk. "Now, now, enuff ob dis." He hurried over to her, laid a hand on her shoulder. "Kom, zit down."

"I'm so dreadfully…" Jessica sobbed uncontrollably. "The dreams…"

Doctor Schneider went to a water dispenser and thrust a paper cup beneath its nozzle. "Now, now…Drink dis. Here, drink."

Jessica took the cup and sipped.

"Dat's bedder. Now, dry yo eyes and tell me vot it is dat's trublin' you. Ib you haff a problem you must tell me. I inzist on dat. Dat is vot I am here fo. Do you understandt? Dat is vot I am here fo." He patted her arm reassuringly and returned to his desk.

"I don't know how to be begin, doctor. It's all so…" Jessica dabbed at her eyes with a tiny blue handkerchief, one of a treasured half dozen that Sonny, with Henry's help, had bought for her as a Thanksgiving Day gift.

"Take your time. Dare is no hurry. I haff all de time in de vurldt; all de time in de vurldt."

"It's Sonny's…" Jessica felt as though she were alone in an ocean and about to sink. She drew a deep breath. "It's Sonny's person, doctor."

Doctor Schneider smiled, nodded. "Ya, ya, hiss person. Vod abowd hiss person? Vot person?"

"His…penis, doctor."

"Oh, de penis. Ya, vod abowd de penis?" He spoke the words so matter-of-factly, jocularly almost, that Jessica wondered if he had understood her; she had expected a more reverential tone.

"His penis, doctor," she repeated.

"Ya, ya. I hear; vod abowd it?"

"It's…it's its size, doctor. It appears to be…"

"Too small, eh? You tink it iss too small?" Doctor Schneider interrupted. "My dear Missie Lansbury, ib I were to tell you how many mudders kom to me mit de same vorry, you wooden belieb me. Ebery mudder seems to tink dat dare childt's penis iss too small. I tell dem, 'Wait; wait; it will grow.' But still day vorry."

"No, doctor, it appears to be…overly large."

"Oberly larch? Svollen, you mean?"

Jessica straightened out the blue handkerchief she had screwed into a ball. "Overdeveloped…in size, doctor. It appears to be too *big* for a child of Sonny's age."

There was a silence. Doctor Schneider picked up the paper cup that Jessica had placed on his desk and jiggled its contents. Eventually he said: "My dear lady, you understandt dat often de berry young hab de erection. De erection is not uncommon in chiltren ob two or tree munts. Dare hab been instances…"

Jessica interrupted. "I'm talking of it in its relaxed state, doctor."

"Aah, I zee – it's relaxed state. Ya, dat is different. Oberly larch, eh?"

"Yes, doctor."

"Vell, vot you must do is bring de boy to me so dat I can hab a look at him. Vill you do dat?"

Jessica nodded.

"In de meantime, I vill gib you sumtin' for de nerbs. You say you bin habin' bad dreams?"

"Yes."

"Abowd de boy's penis?"

Jessica felt her face grow hot with embarrassment. "It has more to do with the boy being taken away from me."

"Ah, dat is de fear dat koms mit lub. Zomtimes lub can be a terrible ting. It tears at de heart and de mind. Now – " He stood up, a second prescription in his hand. "Next time, you bring de boy."

Jessica had waited a week before returning with Sonny. (It had taken her that long to recover from the ordeal of her previous visit.)

"Ah, dare is de boy," Doctor Schneider said as they entered his office. "Do zit down, Missie Lansbury." And when she was seated,

Sonny on her knees: "And how hab you bin feelin'? Hab you bin takin' de tablets I prescribed?"

"Well…"

"Goot." Doctor Schneider turned his attention to Sonny. "Dat face! Dare has nebber bin a priddier child in dis obiss. Nebber hab I seen a priddier child. He has de eyes ob a boet."

Sonny played with a button on Jessica's coat.

"Zonny." Doctor Schneider waggled his fingers. "Zonny… Look, Zonny."

Sonny looked at Doctor Schneider and smiled.

"Zonny, vill you let me take a liddle look at you?"

Sonny continued smiling.

"Ya? Ya! Goot. Kom den. Kom." He got up from his desk and walked round to where they were sitting. "Now…" He lifted Sonny from Jessica's lap and stood him on the desk. "Vod a bik boy you geddin', Zonny. You nearly as bik as me."

To her shame, Jessica couldn't help thinking that in one respect Sonny was perhaps bigger than Doctor Schneider.

Doctor Schneider removed the boy's coat and handed it to Jessica. "Dare we are." He eased down Sonny's perfectly tailored tweed breeches. "Now…" He lowered Sonny's underpants.

Jessica had been determined not to be present during the examination. For a reason she was unable to fathom, the sight of Sonny's 'person' made her nervous and disoriented. She would, she had decided, make an excuse to leave while the examination was taking place. If that were not possible – if, say, Sonny were to cry out at her leaving – she would look out of the window, or read the gardening magazine she had brought with her.

She did none of these things. To her amazement she found herself watching Doctor Schneider as he felt with finger and thumb along the young flesh, watched him raise it, study its underside, raise the tight purple sac (Doctor Schneider's office was not the warmest of places), press the leg-flesh on either side of it, raise the organ again (as gently as her gardener would raise the cup of a fuschia, Jessica thought dully), turn it this way and that, and – Oh! – weigh it in his palm. Jessica felt her stomach stir, felt it fold over; heard a drumming in her head. She tried to fix her eyes on the photograph of Doctor

Schneider standing with a group of half naked natives that hung on the wall behind his desk, on the curious pear-shaped stain on one corner of it, but they returned to Sonny's genitalia.

Doctor Schneider pulled up Sonny's underpants and breeches, tucked in his shirt, and set him in Jessica's lap. "Vell, Missie Lansbury," he said as he returned to his chair. "I tink you vorry ober nuttin'." He smiled at her. "Sho, Zonny's peniss is larch for a child ob hiss aitch; and I must be honest mit yo, it is un*yooshally* larch – how old is he, tree?"

Jessica nodded.

"But zo vot! It is a goot regular shape and it ain't gibbin' him no trubble. It vurks okay, doan it?"

Jessica nodded again.

"Ya, ob course it duss, and we should tank de Lord dat it duss. Ib it didden, den ve *vood* hab sumtin' to vorry abowd."

"But if it were to…"

"Ged bigger?"

Jessica felt her face become hot again. She fiddled with Sonny's shirt collar. "Yes," she said.

"Vell, it *vill* ged bigger. Ob course it vill ged bigger, but zo vill Zonny, zo vill de boy." He spoke the words as though they were a revelation. "Who knows," he continued, "maybe Zonny's gonna be a zigs fooder and as vide as a parn door. He'll need de pards to match."

Jessica remained troubled. She shook her head sadly.

Doctor Schneider tried a new tack: "My dear Missie Lansbury" – he spoke softly, confidentially – "dare are plenny ob men who would gib dare ride arm for a big – "

"Please, doctor, please…" Jessica lowered Sonny to the floor and began working his arms into his coat. "Please…"

"Berry well, but you must stop dis wurryin'. Id voan do you no goot and id voan make de penis smaller. You hab to adjust yo mind to dat fact." He opened a drawer in his desk. "Here, take dis home mit you. I tink you vill find it most helpful. Your problems ven you read it will seem like nuttin', ob dat ah'm sho."

Jessica buttoned Sonny's coat and slipped his hands into the mittens that hung from the sleeves on silk tapes. "Thank you, doctor."

She took the slim volume that Doctor Schneider held out to her and without a glance at its title (*Medical Phenomena: The Male Reproductive Organ*) thrust it into her purse. "Thank you. Good day, doctor. Come along, Sonny."

That night, while Henry and Sonny slept, Jessica had settled herself in an easy chair in front of a log fire and, with hands that trembled slightly, turned to the page in *Medical Phenomena* which showed a naked fourteen-year-old Tibetan goatherd.

* * *

"HENRY!"

Yes, she was certain now: the woman striding towards her, her body encased in pink, her arm linked to that of the man matching her stride, was Honey. "Hi," she heard her say, and a few moments later felt arms around her and a stab of breasts, the prick of an earring on her cheek.

"It's swell to see you again," Honey said, when the embrace was over.

Jessica wanted to moan, but instead said: "Why, Honey, what a surprise!" She reached out blindly for Henry, who now was at her side.

"Hello, Uncle Henry." Honey smiled at Henry and they shook hands. "I didn't think I'd recognise you after all this time, but you haven't changed a bit. A little less hair, maybe." Before Henry could say anything, Honey darted a look at the children seated at the table and said to Jessica: "Don't tell me – it's a party for Sonny. It's Sonny's birthday."

"Yes, it is," replied Jessica.

"What I tell you?" Honey looked at her companion. He was tall and gangling and had the colouring and features of a Red Indian, features that had attracted Honey when a spotlight had picked them out. He carried under his arm an oblong package wrapped in gift paper. Henry had the feeling he knew him from somewhere. "This is a friend of mine," Honey said. "Joe – " She looked at the man and wrinkled her brow. "*How* d'you say your name again?"

"Chippupquick," the man said awkwardly. He shuffled large feet.

"Joe Chippup –" Honey gave up, dispensed with the introductions, and said to Henry: "I guess I should of let you know I was coming, but it was a spur of the moment thing. I suddenly saw what day it was and straightaway grabbed a cab. I'm playing at The Music Hall on Tremont Street."

Jessica raised her eyebrows in surprise.

Honey said to her: "Yeah – right here in Boston." In the same breath, she added: "I bet you thought I'd forgotten it was Sonny's birthday?"

Jessica smiled and shook her head in a vague manner. She felt faint.

"I guess I should of come before this," Honey went on, "but I've never played in Boston before. If I'da played here before, I would of." She scrutinised the children and said to Jessica: "Where is he? Which one is Sonny? He's not the fat kid in the middle is he?"

Jessica looked across at the table and saw the "fat kid", Carly van Lodz, his mouth swollen with food, reach for a ham sandwich. Next to him sat Sonny, an arm thrown over the back of his chair in a bored fashion.

Jessica took hold of Honey's arm. "Honey could we go into the house? There's something I want to discuss with you."

"Sure," Honey said. "But first show me Sonny. Point him out. I'm crazy to see him."

Jessica sighed. "He's the one next to the fat – to the plump child," she said. "The one with the curls."

"The kid in lilac?" Honey screwed up her face. "The one who looks like something out of the *Junior Miss* catalogue?"

"Please, Honey." A rat gnawing at her stomach, Jessica propelled Honey towards the house, Henry and Chippupquick following behind.

Inside, Henry poured drinks, and when they each had a glass in their hand and were seated, Jessica said to Honey:

"As you know, Uncle Henry and I have had Sonny for six years and in all that time, Honey, you haven't once visited him. It would be terribly unfair both to Sonny and to us if you now were to take him away, to uproot him from what he regards as his home." She took a breath. "I know that as his mother you have every right to ask for his return, but you must consider the anguish it will cause, the terrible anguish, Honey. Sonny is our life." Jessica swallowed the lump that had come into her throat and continued: "Although we have made it perfectly clear to Sonny – out of respect to you – that we are not his parents, we hope that in the not too distant future he will come to regard us as such. Indeed, there are times when" – the lump in her throat rose again – "when he calls me 'Mumsie'." Jessica's eyes filled with tears and she lowered her head.

"Now, now." Henry reached across and touched her arm. "Don't upset yourself," he said.

"But I'm not here to take Sonny," Honey said. "I'm just here to *see* the kid. I couldn't take him away even if I wanted to. He wouldn't fit with my work."

"Oh, but I thought…" Jessica's relief was palpable. "You see, I've been so worried that you might…I've been having the most awful… Oh, you don't know how relieved I am." She glanced at Henry. "How relieved we *both* are."

"As far as I'm concerned," said Honey, "he's yours." She glanced at her glass, which was almost empty.

"But Honey, why have you waited so long to visit him? Six years!"

"I suppose I should of come before, but I haven't had the time. When I'm not working, I'm travelling." Honey held out her glass to Henry. "Would you mind if I have a refill, Uncle Henry?"

"Of course not!" Henry slapped his legs and got to his feet. "Let's *all* have a refill. After all, it's Sonny's birthday. It's a day to celebrate."

"I'm dying to see him," Honey said to Jessica. "Close up, I mean. Jesus, I never would of known he was my kid if you hadn't pointed him out to me. I guess I expected him to look a little more…I dunno …rugged."

Henry refilled the glasses and said to Honey: "You have to understand that Sonny knows very little about you. We have told him that you are in the theatrical profession and that your home is in New Drayton, and that is all. As far as Sonny is concerned, you are his mother in name only. You should not expect any display of affection. It is likely he will regard you as a total stranger. That is something you must expect. No one can be expected to show affection to someone they don't know – certainly not a child. You understand that?"

"I can take it," Honey said cheerfully. She turned to Chippupquick and said: "You got the kid's present, honey?"

Chippupquick reached down by the side of his chair and handed Honey the package he had been been carrying.

"This is for Sonny," Honey said, extending the package to Jessica, "though after seeing him I doubt he'll be much interested in it. It's a baseball bat."

Jessica took the package with a smile. "I'm sure he'll love it," she lied. "Thank you."

"One further point, Honey," Henry said slowly. "We have told Sonny that his father is dead. We thought it a kindness to do so. We have told him he was killed in a yachting accident, so I would ask you when you meet him – "

"Honey," Jessica interrupted, "do you think it *wise* to meet Sonny?" Her voice had a hysterical edge to it. Henry's words had made her stomach tighten in panic. She saw herself introducing Sonny to his mother ('Sonny, I have a surprise for you'), saw the look of distaste on the child's face as Honey in her gruff voice greeted him. That would be horrible. But more horrible would be her having to introduce Honey to her friends. From the start she had made them aware that Sonny was not her child, that she was unable to have children. What she had *failed* to do was to correct the impression they had formed of Sonny's mother. Whenever they had asked about her she had told them what she had told Sonny – that she was in the theatrical profession. Without exception they had assumed that Honey was in the legitimate theatre. "How wonderful it must be to play Ophelia," Connie van Lodz had said, and Jessica had given a slight smile and changed the subject. Now, or very soon, the van Lodzs and everyone else would know the truth of the matter.

"A meeting with his mother after all these years," Jessica went on, "could have the most devastating effect on a child of Sonny's age. Wouldn't it be wiser to leave a note for him – write him a note and leave without seeing him?" She felt on the verge of collapse. "Don't you think that that would be wisest thing to do, Honey?"

"I'd like to *meet* the kid," Honey said. She hardened her voice. "As his mother, I have that right."

"Yes, of course you do," Henry said, and reading Jessica's thoughts, added: "but perhaps it would be better to meet in private. Privacy in matters of this nature is – " His words were cut short by a crash of thunder followed almost immediately by the sound of battering rain.

"Oh dear." Jessica hurried to the French windows. "Oh, they'll get drenched." She saw the children and grown-ups running, heads down, towards the house. She saw Connie van Lodz in her flight push Carly van Lodz roughly to one side as he tried to cross in front of her, and she saw Millie holding a linen napkin above Sonny's head. His curls would be saved

Henry joined her and said: "Some party."

"I feel a little headachey," Jessica said.

Honey called: "Would you mind if I help myself to a drink?"

"Of course not, Honey; please do," Henry called back. "Perhaps Mr Chippup – Perhaps your friend would like one, too."

The children and their parents crowded into the room, and Jessica, as if in a stupor, sent Millie for towels to dry themselves on. She noticed that Carly van Lodz was licking ferociously at an iced cake. She looked for Sonny and saw him standing, arms folded, by the door. She went across to him and gently felt his hair for damp.

"Who are those people?" he asked, sullenly.

Jessica looked to where Sonny was looking and saw Honey turn from Chippupquick and look in their direction.

"Sonny dear, I have a surprise for you." As Jessica spoke, she saw Honey rise from her chair and walk towards them. "You'll never guess who's here to see you today. You simply won't believe who has – "

"Hi, baby." Honey was upon them, squatting in front of Sonny, an overly large whiskey in her hand. "Do you know who I am, baby?"

Sonny pulled back as Honey took hold of his arm.

"Honey, I think we should go somewhere a little more private. This is not the place for – " Jessica looked nervously round the room. "Perhaps the study…"

"Aren't you gonna give your momma a hug, baby?" Honey gave a tug at Sonny's arm.

"You're *not* my mother," Sonny said contemptuously. "My

mother is an actress." He gave Honey the merest look of irritation, then looked away.

"I got you a baseball bat for your birthday. Ain't that worth a hug?"

Still looking away, Sonny said: "I loathe baseball." He tried to free his arm, but Honey held on to it. "Let go of me!" he ordered.

Honey looked up at Jessica and said: "Tell the kid who I am."

Jessica felt perspiration break out on her neck. She desperately wanted Henry on hand to take charge of the situation. She looked for him and was relieved to see him coming towards them. "Honey," she said, "not here. Let's step outside where we – "

"Tell the kid who I am." Honey's voice had taken on a hardness again.

"Oh, Henry!" Jessica sent up a prayer of thanks as Henry arrived.

"Honey, this is not the time. Come." Henry hauled Honey to her feet.

"Hey, what the hell d'you – " Before she could finish, Henry called out: "Ladies and gentlemen, boys and girls, I have a treat for you. Our birthday boy here" – he looked adoringly at Sonny and placed a hand on his shoulder – "is going to entertain us with a song."

Above the murmur of approval, Henry thought he heard a groan. He sensed that it came from Gretchen Pakerman of Pakerman's Haulage and made a mental note to cancel her credit facilities at Staley's.

"Come, Sonny. Jessica." Henry released his grip on Honey and led the way to a piano which stood to one side of the room. When he reached it he pulled up a chair and stood Sonny on it. "Quiet everyone," he called. "Come on now, give our boy a chance", and when he had their attention: "Sonny has chosen to sing for us a song made popular by Mr Al Jolsen, a song which just happens to be my" – he looked at Jessica, who had seated herself at the piano, and corrected himself – "our favourite number. It is called, appropriately enough, *Sonny Boy*."

There were more murmurs of approval, and Connie van Lodz was heard to say: "I love that number. Every time I hear it, I weep. Jolsen: he's so adorably Yiddish."

Jessica looked up at Sonny, smiled encouragement, and began to play.

They had rehearsed twice a week for the past three weeks. Sonny had wanted to sing *Greensleeves*, but Henry, with Jessicas's support, had argued that *Greensleeves* would not be suited to the occasion. "It's more like a hymn, pardner," he told Sonny. "The folks won't take kindly to it. We gotta give 'em sump'n a mite more powerful than *Greensleeves*." Sonny had stamped and sulked and given in only when Henry had promised him a pair of shoes with buckles on them.

> *Climb upon my knee, Sonny Boy*
> *Though you're only three, Sonny Boy*
> *There's no way of knowing*
> *There's no way of showing*
> *What you mean to me, Sonny Boy*

Sonny's voice rose clear and sparkling into the air.

> *When there are grey skies*
> *I don't mind those grey skies*
> *You make them blue, Sonny Boy*

Henry felt his eyes fill with tears, as they always did when Sonny sang (*Danny Boy* was a sobbing affair), and Connie van Lodz sniffed into a towel.

Suddenly from the back of the room came the sound of Jolsen himself.

> *Friends may forsake me*
> *Let them all forsake me*
> *I still have you, Sonny Boy*

The rich, sonorous tones of the famous Jewish entertainer took over from Sonny's sweet soprano sound, swept it away, swamped it. Faces that were fixed on Sonny turned and focussed on Honey.

"My God," Connie van Lodz exclaimed, "it's a woman!"

Sonny stopped singing and glared at Jessica to stop playing; but Jessica, mesmerised by what she was hearing, played on. She continued to play even when Sonny turned on his chair and kicked in two of its wooden spokes.

> *I still have y-o-o-o-o-o-u, S-o-n-n-n-n-y B-o-o-o-o-y*

Honey finished the song, and a dozen applauding guests gathered round her.

"My dear, that was amazing," Connie van Lodz said. "If I hadn't heard it with my own ears, I should never have believed it." In the same breath she added: "May I introduce myself? – Mrs Herbert van Lodz."

She glanced at Honey's breasts and experienced a pang of excitement.

Honey said: "I'm Honey Bunn, Sonny's mother."

"Sonny's *mother*? *Jessica's* Sonny?"

Honey took a mouthful of whiskey and nodded. "Huh-huh," she said when she had swallowed.

Connie van Lodz opened her eyes wide and looked at Verna Lugmann, who raised her brows. Still looking at Verna Lugmann, Connie van Lodz called: "Jessica! Jessica dear, where are you?"

Jessica, still seated at the piano, felt the pierce of Connie van Lodz's 'dear' (Connie van Lodz addressed her friends as 'dear' only when she had something poisonous to say to them) and smiled bleakly at Henry. "We have to get this over with," she said.

Henry glared at her. Her accompaniment of Honey had been a betrayal of Sonny: she had allowed Honey to steal his limelight. He wanted to slap her face. He lifted Sonny from the chair and in an abrupt voice said to Jessica: "Go with Sonny to the study. I'll join you later."

Jessica got to her feet and took hold of Sonny's hand. "I'm scared," she said to Henry.

"We knew this would happen *one* day," Henry replied.

"Knew *what* would happen?" Sonny asked sulkily. "Who is that awful woman?"

"Come along, darling," Jessica said.

Henry followed them with his eyes as they moved into the group that circled Honey. He took stock of Jessica's thin hips and legs and thought them ugly. He noticed Sonny's hips and worried that he thought them beautiful. He saw a hand reach out to detain Jessica, and saw Jessica avoid it. He looked down at the chair on which Sonny had been standing and lovingly touched the kicked-in spokes. As he looked up he saw Chippupquick and knew where he had seen him before. He was Staley's odd-job man.

CHAPTER 3

Finn had arranged to meet Lever in the Tahiti Bar on Lower Manhattan's 42nd Street at seven thirty, but because he wanted some time to himself he got there an hour early.

He ordered a large Old Masters, drank it quickly, and called for another.

Over the second drink he studied the life-sized paintings of Tahitian girls in grass skirts that adorned the bar's walls. He noticed that one, incongruously, had green eyes and a Cupid's bow mouth.

After a while he turned away from the paintings and concentrated instead on what had taken place late that morning:

He had been called to the telephone and heard Lever ask: "How does a part in a movie grab you?"

There was a time when his response would have been: "Screw the movies." He was a professional entertainer, and, so far as he was concerned, professional entertainers appeared on stage, not on celluloid. Celluloid was for amateurs. But things were different now, and his reply had been: "What's the deal?"

Lever had been slow in answering. Finn had heard talk at the end of the line, and Lever, on getting back to him, had said: "Look, I have to go. There's a guy here who owes me. Meet me at the Tahiti at seven thirty. I'll fill you in there."

All afternoon Finn had pondered Lever's words and the questions they raised. How big a part? How much would it pay? More importantly, would it rid him of Honey?

He was playing with these questions again when a man and woman entered and sat at the bar two stools along from where he was sitting.

Finn looked at them in the mirror that covered the wall behind the counter and saw that the woman was in her late twenties and had auburn hair that reached her shoulders. She wore a tailored oatmeal coat and carried a crocodile-skin handbag. Her face was puffed and blotched, and Finn formed the impression that she had been crying.

The man was in his forties, heavily built, and wore a light brown suit.

The man ordered two dry martinis and paid for them from a wad of notes taken from his back trouser pocket.

It was a good two minutes before the couple spoke.

"C'mon, baby, don't be like this." The man's voice was pleading. He placed a hand on the woman's neck and had it shrugged off. "Baby." The word was drawn out.

"You tried to degrade me," the woman said. "I thought we had something special, but you tried to degrade me."

Finn tried his best not to listen.

"It's only a doggie, baby."

"It's disgusting. How could you have asked me to do something like that?" She sipped her drink. "When I first met you I thought you were the kindest, most loving man in the world, but all the time you wanted to degrade me – and with Spud. I love that dog. I buy him" – she broke off and sipped her drink again – "the best cuts."

"I know, baby. *You* love old Spud, and old Spud loves *you*. That's why I thought – "

"Oh God, stop it! I feel sick just thinking about it."

They were silent for another minute or so, then the man said: "I love you, baby – you know that."

Without looking at him, the woman said coldly: "If you love someone, you don't ask them to do what you asked *me* to do." She touched her hair. "They put people like you in prison; you know that, don't you? If I were to go to the police and tell them what you wanted to have me do with Spud, they'd arrest you."

"I love you." The man's voice was sensuous. "I love you so much." He paused. "I love you." His hand went to the woman's neck again and this time she let him keep it there. "It's only a doggie, baby."

"Don't, Greg, please."

"Won't you do it for me? You would if you loved me. If you loved me, you'd do it. Oh, baby, I love you so." He leaned across and kissed her cheek.

The woman turned and faced him and said: "Greg, it isn't right. Don't you see that it isn't right? My God, if you don't see that it isn't right, then there's something terribly wrong with you."

"Anything is right if you love someone, baby. If I didn't love you and asked you to do something like that, then, sure, it wouldn't be right, but I love you. Oh God, I love you." He kissed her cheek again. "You love me too, don't you? Say you love me. Say it. Say it."

"No."

"Yes. Say you love me. Say it. You love me. Say it."

"Oh, yes. Yes, I love you, only – "

"Say you'll do it. Say you'll do it for Greggie. Say it. Say it."

"No – I couldn't. I couldn't, Greg."

"You could. You could if you loved me. Say you love me. Say it."

"I love you."

"Say you'll do it."

"No. Oh, I don't know… "

"Say you'll do it."

The woman in a serious voice said: "If I do, Greg, it will only be this one time. You must promise me you will never ask me again."

"I promise, sweetheart. Just this one time." The man got up off the stool. "C'mon, let's go back now. Leave the drinks." He kissed the woman on the cheek and took hold of her arm. "Come on, baby."

As they left, Finn heard the woman say: "I'm glad I wore my light coat tonight – I'd've baked in fur."

Finn lighted a cigarette and let his thoughts return to Lever's words and their suggestion of Hollywood. He pictured himself making a screen test. He was wearing a loud, check suit with tyre marks down the front and back. He heard himself deliver the line – "I'm just off to the doc's for a check up: I'm feeling a little run down." He smiled. It was a joke he had written himself and he was proud of it. He would follow it, he decided, with a dozen or more doctor/patient stories and finish with his bar-room-drunk act. He had just got to the part where he was stumbling over a chair when Lever came in.

Finn glanced at his watch and felt faintly annoyed that Lever was early. "What'll you have?" he asked.

Lever asked for a beer.

Finn ordered a small beer and a large Old Masters.

Both men sat in silence for a while, then Finn said: "You should've been here ten minutes ago, you'd've heard some great dialogue." He described the couple that had left – making the woman to be more attractive than she was – and gave an almost word for word account of their conversation. When he had finished, Lever said: "Let's hope old Spud knows how to treat a lady."

"I wouldn't mind being Spud myself, right now," Finn said.

"Some dogs have all the luck," Lever said.

They finished their drinks and Finn called for two more.

Finn finished his drink quickly and signalled to the barman for a refill.

"Aren't you hitting that stuff a little hard?" Lever said.

"I can handle it," Finn said.

"It doesn't make hair grow, you know."

Finn raised his eyebrows and in a slurred English accent said: "It has other reshtorative powersh, old boy."

Lever laughed.

"So what's this about me becoming a movie star?" Finn asked.

Lever put down his glass. "Nothing's fixed yet. There may be a part in a Tiny Templar movie, but there are still a couple of things to be worked out."

"Like what?"

Lever rotated his glass on the bar top before replying. "Like whether or not Honey passes the screen test."

"Honey? What's *she* got to do with this?"

"Templar wants a dame with big handles for the new movie he's making. So far, the studio hasn't come up with one."

"There must be a million dames in Hollywood with big handles."

"Not as big as Honey's. Templar wants 'em *real* big. He's seen maybe two hundred pairs of tits and turned them all down."

"So where do *I* come in?"

"I put the word around that *I've* got the dame if *they've* got a part for *you*. Templar's okay'd this. Provided Honey's handles are big enough – and they will be – and she looks okay on celluloid, you're in."

"So I'm getting in on Honey's ticket, is that it, Frank?" Finn swallowed some whiskey. "No fucking deal. If I make it to Hollywood, I make it under my own steam. I don't want a goddamn thing from that bag of pus."

"For chrissake, Harry, don't be dumb," Lever said. "Don't be fucking dumb. This is the break we've been waiting for."

"What *you've* been waiting for, not *me*."

"What's *that* supposed to mean?"

"Nothing."

"If you're trying to tell me something…"

"Forget it." Finn looked at the bar counter. He felt a momentary shame for having doubted Lever's integrity; Lever had always been honest with him. "Anyway, what part do I get to play – Tiny's kid brother? I'm a little on the tall side for that, wouldn't you say, Frank?"

Lever's voice when he answered had a coldness to it. "Your part hasn't been fixed yet, but I've let Paragon know you play a great drunk. There's always a hotel bar scene in a Templar movie and you'd be perfect for it."

"Christ, an extra! Is *that* what you're saying? A fucking extra!"

"No, that's *not* what I'm fucking saying," Lever said angrily. "You get a part. Okay, it maybe won't be too big a part, but it'll get you noticed, and that's the name of the game – getting noticed. How d'you think Templar and the rest of the big deals got started? You think they just walked into a studio and said, 'Hey, look everyone, I'm here', and straightaway fell into a lead part? You start from the bottom and work your way up – that's the way it works in Hollywood." Lever scratched his neck angrily. "Look, if you're not interested, it's okay with me."

Lever ordered more drinks and the two men sat in a difficult silence over them. After a while Finn said: "What kind of money we talking about?"

"Three, maybe four hundred for a couple days' work, plus expenses." He added quickly: "The money's not important. What's important is that you get a start in movies."

"Does Honey know about this?"

"I'm seeing her tomorrow."

"Maybe she won't want to know. Maybe she won't want to leave that hood of hers. You know she's talking about *marrying* the creep?"

"Honey'll want to know. What dame doesn't want to know about Hollywood?"

Lever lighted a cigarette, blew out smoke and said: "So what d'you say? You want in or out?"

"Why not?" Finn said. "It can't be any worse than the deal I've got going for me at the moment."

"You shouldn't let Honey get to you," Lever said.

"You don't know her like I do. She's poison."

"She's no Mary Poppins," Lever said philosophically.

"I'd like to beat hell out of her," Finn said.

"That wouldn't solve anything."

"You know what she did to the kid in the high wire act yesterday? Knocked two of her teeth out. The kid borrowed a lipstick without asking her permission. A *lipstick*, for chrissake!"

"She's a real sweetheart," Lever said.

"I hate her damn guts."

"What's this about her marrying Calvino?"

"That's what the word is."

"He's a heavy hitter."

"They'll make a perfect match – like stink on stink." Finn's hatred of Honey welled up. Her attack on the girl had sickened him. He had seen many fights back stage but there was usually nothing more to them than a lot of loud, angry words. Honey had thrown herself on the girl and pounded her with her fists. Afterwards, when he had remonstrated with her, asked her just what in hell did she think she was doing beating up on a kid like that, she had looked at him with narrowed eyes and said: "No two-bit wire walker is gonna fuck with *my* property. She does it again and I'll break her feet."

Finn saw himself beating Honey's head with a length of lead piping and said: "When do we leave?"

"Sunday," Lever said. "Paragon need the handles quick. They're way behind with their shooting schedule."

"What about the Tivoli booking?"

"I can fix that. I've a singing cat act they can have."

Finn smiled and shook his head. "Where d'you find 'em?" he said.

"This cat's real cute," Lever said. "Last place it played, it jumped on a dame in the audience and crapped in her lap." He paused. "Talking of pussies, I hear Honey was found having hers eaten by a stagehand at the Metropole."

"Two."

"Two? At the same time?"

"They took turns."

"Who says there's no romance left in the world?" Lever said. There was a silence, then Lever said: "Anyway, I've got to move." He drained his glass and swung off the bar stool. "Be ready to leave at seven, seven thirty Sunday morning. I'll pick you up."

"What about tickets?"

Lever smiled and patted his breast pocket.

Finn looked ruefully at him without speaking.

From the door, Lever called: "Go easy on the sauce."

"Go to hell," Finn called back good-humouredly.

Finn had four more Old Masters, then left.

It was a clear night with few people about. As he walked, Finn's thoughts wandered from Lever to Hollywood and from Hollywood to the woman in the bar. He wondered what breed of dog Spud was. He thought: I don't even have a dog to make it with.

CHAPTER 4

Honey rang the bell of Calvino's apartment, waited ten seconds, then rang it again. She was about to ring a third time when the door opened.

"The hell you been? I've been calling you all morning." She walked briskly past Calvino, slipped off her coat and threw it onto a chair.

"I been sleepin'," said Calvino thickly. He wore a crumpled singlet and pyjama trousers. "Where you *think* I fuckin' been, out pickin' bluebells with the fuckin' brownies?" He scratched angrily at his groin.

Honey briefly admired his solid shoulders and said: "Baby, you're not gonna believe this." She went up to him and placed her hands on his biceps. "Baby, guess what? I got a part in a movie. Lever's fixed me a part in a Templar movie. I leave for California on Sunday." She pulled down his head and kissed him. "Jesus," she said when they'd parted, "I'm so excited!"

Calvino wiped lipstick from his mouth with the back of his hand and said: "A movie? You kiddin' me? Gimme a cigarette."

Honey took a cigarette from a silver-plated box that stood on a coffee table, lighted it quickly with a lighter that matched the box, and handed it to him. "It's not a big part but it's a start. It's what I always wanted." She gave a little laugh. "Lever says they can't do the movie without me. I got the *figure* they want. I get to play a scene with Templar." She laughed again. "Baby, I'm so excited I could yell."

Calvino held out the cigarette so that Honey could see the lipstick mark she'd left and said: "Look at this. For chrissake, why d'you have to wear so much shit on your face?"

Honey stared incredulously at him for a moment, then sat down suddenly on a couch. "Oh, boy, I don't believe it, I just don't believe it," she said. "I tell the jerk I've got a part in a Templar movie and all he can say is, 'Why d'you have to wear so much shit on your face?' Christ, you're really something."

Calvino flung the cigarette into the fireplace, turned on her and said: "Who the hell you think you're talkin' to? You better watch that fat mouth of yours or you may get it hurt. You ain't no fuckin' movie star yet. Not yet you fuckin' ain't."

Honey smiled. Calvino's words had warmed her. *You ain't no movie star yet.* The 'yet' said to her that one day she might be. She saw herself at a film premiere trailing a white ermine cape and signing autographs. She stood up and went to him. "Baby," she sighed, "don't let's fight, I feel good today." She put her arms round his neck and pushed herself against him. "Don't let's fight, lover." Her voice was throaty.

"Sure. Sure." Calvino ran his hand over her back.

"Come on, baby." Honey searched for his penis, found it without difficulty, and led him by it to the bedroom and the bed.

When they had finished, Calvino said: "I hear this Templar guy has his dames do some strange shit. And when I say shit, I mean shit."

"Where'd you hear that?"

"Mastrioni. Mastrioni's got some heavy deals goin' with movie stars."

"Mastrioni's into some strange shit hisself," Honey said.

Calvino was silent for a moment. Then he said: "He wants 'em younger. He wants real *young* meat now."

"How young?"

"Fourteen."

"Jesus."

"It ain't easy – findin' 'em, I mean. Last night he kicks out this sixteen-year-old kid – a real nice, beautiful-lookin' kid, well brought up – his old man's a judge – and says to me, 'Find me something a little younger, Tommy.'

"'Like, *how* young?' I say, and he says, 'I dunno – younger. Fourteen.'

"'Fourteen's trouble,' I say, and he says, 'Yeah, trouble for you, you don't find me one.'" He cleared his throat. "I got to go out today and find fourteen-year-old meat. Where the fuck do I find fourteen-year-old meat? I gotta go hang around a school gate wavin' a bunch of fuckin' lollipops."

Honey turned on her side and brushed Calvino's cheek with the backs of her fingers. "Let's get married, baby," she said. She ran a finger over his mouth. "We're good for each other." She spoke dreamily. "We could get married in California – in Hollywood. A Hollywood wedding. Wouldn't that be swell?" She saw herself in a pink and white suit and a picture hat with ribbons flying from it. "What d'you say, baby?"

"Huh?" Calvino said. His thoughts were on fourteen-year-olds.

"Let's get married, baby."

"You outta your roof!" Calvino swung his legs over the side of the bed. "You know I can't walk out on Mastrioni. I walk out on Mastrioni, I'm fish feed."

"I'm not asking you to walk out on Mastrioni," Honey said hotly. "For chrissake! Take some time off. Tell him you wanna get married."

That's not possible – not yet it ain't."

"Yeah," Honey said sneeringly, "Mastrioni first and me second. Well, while you're finding Mastrioni *his* meat, maybe somebody'll be finding *mine*."

* * *

After Honey had gone, Calvino drove to Belvoir Drive and parked outside Brookmayer's Music Academy. The students were beginning to drift out in ones and twos. He saw a boy with blond hair carrying a violin case and pondered what his approach should be. It had been easy with the sixteen and seventeen-year-olds – a straightforward proposition: "How'd you like to make a lot of dough? All you got to do is be nice to a friend of mine – a real rich guy. You be nice to him and he'll give you anythin' you want." But fourteen-year-olds…

As the boy drew near, Calvino opened the door of his car and leaned out. "Hey, kid," he called. "C'mere."

The boy glanced at Calvino and continued walking.

"Hey, kid, c'mere."

The boy turned and walked back.

"Hi, kid." Calvino smiled. "How old you, kid?"

"Fourteen."

"Fourteen, huh." Calvino paused, not knowing if he should produce money. "Kid," he said finally, "how'd you like to play your violin for the queen of New York City?"

CHAPTER 5

The showing of the screen test had been scheduled for ten o'clock in Studio Four and Templar was late. He pushed open the swing doors and walked with small rapid steps to a row of seats reserved for Paragon executives and leading actors. He wore a light grey suit (loosely cut to conceal his ungainly hips), a silver and red bow tie, and heavy brown shoes. He was smoking a Countryman pipe.

"Good morning." His voice was low and harsh and anyone hearing it for the first time might have thought it more suited a man twice his height: Templar stood three feet ten inches.

Dick Caswell, one of Paragon's more competent assistant directors, pulled down the seat next to him, and Templar clambered onto it. Behind them sat Caswell's secretary, Doris Capper, and Gerry Kramer from Paragon's publicity office.

"Okay, we're all here," Caswell called.

The lights dimmed and there was a hum of machinery from the projection room, followed by the clack of loose celluloid being caught up and spooled.

In a low voice Caswell said to Templar: "A swell party, Tiny. Really swell. Boy, did I have a skinful." Looking at Templar, Caswell saw him as he had seen him the previous evening – naked on a yellow oilskin, his wrists tied together above his head and his body smeared with the entrails of a freshly slaughtered lamb. Caswell had known the mess was from a freshly slaughtered lamb, because a lamb with its stomach and neck cut through was lying steaming on a second oilskin, a little blonde, naked like Templar, kneeling beside it reading from a bible. Embarrassed, Caswell had said: "Gee, I'm sorry, Tiny, I was looking for the bathroom", and had closed the door on them.

The clack of celluloid stopped and a yellow stream of light illuminated the screen, upon which appeared: LITTLE BIG SHOT CASTING TEST. PARAGON PRODUCTIONS. TAKE ONE. HONEY BUNN.

The words were followed by a few moments of blank screen, then

Honey appeared. She wore a plain white shirt, a tightly-belted black skirt, and black high-heeled shoes.

A voice from the screen said: "Okay Miss Bunn, will you profile for us, please."

Honey turned sideways and perceptibly pulled back her shoulders.

"Wow!" Caswell said, and Kramer whistled appreciatively.

"Fine, Miss Bunn," said the voice. "Now let's see you walk a little. Turn and walk to the backcloth."

Honey did as instructed.

"That's beautiful," the voice said. "Thank you."

Honey did an about face and broadened the smile she wore.

"Would you like to tell us something about yourself, Miss Bunn?"

Honey said: "My name is Honey Bunn and I come from Stanway, New Drayton, where I live with my mother, who is a church worker.

"Both of us are great fans of Mr Templar and think his last picture, A Titch In Time, just about the funniest picture ever made." Her voice had an appealing breathlessness to it. She paused briefly before adding: "I guess that's all." She smiled, then took a deep breath, which made her chest seem bigger than it already was.

"Thank you, Miss Bunn. That was very nice, *very* nice. We'll be getting in touch with you."

"Thank you," Honey said.

The screen went blank and the voice was heard to say: "If you had tits like that, Harry, I'd marry you tomorrow."

A second voice said: "If I had tits like that – " Then: "Shit!" and there was the hollow sound of a microphone being switched off.

The lights came back on and Templar said to Caswell: "She's no Hedy Lamarr, but she'll do." He turned to Doris Capper and said: "Have Miss Bunn call on me at my bungalow first thing tomorrow." He wriggled to the edge of his seat and dropped lightly to the floor. "I'd like an early start tomorrow," he said to Caswell.

"Sure, Tiny," Caswell replied. "She'll be great. A swell figure."

Templar nodded, nodded at Doris Capper and Kramer, and hurried away.

Waiting for Templar outside was a cream limousine with smoked glass windows and white-rimmed tyres. A chauffeur in a pale blue uniform leaned leisurely against it chewing a matchstick. Seeing

Templar, he came to attention and pulled open the rear door. Without looking at him, Templar said: "Straight home, Max", and clambered inside.

The car moved off and Templar rested his head against the back of the seat and closed his eyes. He felt exhausted. He hadn't slept well. The thought of Caswell having seen him on the oilskin had kept him awake most of the night. By now, he told himself, if Caswell had lived up to the reputation of being a gossip, the story would be all over the lot.

At the main gate the car stopped, and Sam the gatekeeper came out of his box and hurried over to it.

Templar wound down the window, and Sam leaned through and said: "Excuse me, Mr Templar, but I got a message for you."

"What is it, Sam?" Templar made an effort to sound pleasant. Sam was one of his greatest fans: he had sat through eight performances of *A Titch In Time*.

"I got to ask you to see Mr Blickerman straight away. At his home."

Templar smiled weakly and said: "Thank you, Sam."

"You're welcome, Mr Templar."

Templar wound up the window and said: "You heard that, Max? Blickerman's." To himself he said: "You bastard, Caswell." He closed his eyes again and rehearsed what he would say to the head of Paragon Productions:

It was just a gag, JB. There's this cute little extra who can't stand the sight of blood. Every time she sees – '

In imagination he heard Jake Blickerman's thick Jewish voice break in:

So you get yourself a sheep (the story would have grown) *and you cut it open in front of her, is that what you're telling me?*

The car turned into Paragon Avenue, where most of the screenwriters lived, and headed north towards Paradise Hill.

Templar recalled the *last* time he'd been summoned to Blickerman's house. Then it had been over an incident involving a Paragon Princess (the name given to the studio's starlets) who had run sobbing from his lot bungalow straight into the arms of a patrolling security guard.

Blickerman had sent for him the next day.

"You want to do that kind of stuff – and I have to say that both myself and Mrs Blickerman find it puzzling that a man of your talent should go in for that kind of perverted filth – then do it with someone outside Paragon. You do not do filth with a Paragon Princess." Blickerman had wiped sweat from his brow with a large white handkerchief. "You know the picture that girl starts work on next week?" His face had grown red, his voice louder. "*Sweet Sixteen. Sweet Sixteen*! And you're trying to stick salamis into her. You want to corrupt her? You want to ruin her performance? You know how much we *budgeted* for that picture?"

* * *

The Blickermans' white marble house with its four dorric turrets stood in two acres of wooded land half way up Paradise Hill, a position which distressed Mrs Blickerman to the point of paranoia. She wanted, ached for, the pink house that stood on the crest of the hill. She felt she was entitled to it; after all, she was the wife of one of Hollywood's most powerful figures. Such eminence, she reasoned, demanded the loftiest location. Her husband had made repeated offers to buy the property, but its owner, the tango-loving widow of a tin baron, had turned them all down – even one which included a dancing part in *Carnival Capers*, Paragon's multi-million-dollar musical extravaganza. Mrs Blickerman had done her very best to overcome her disappointment, but there still were days when she would climb to a turret, focus her mother-of pearl opera glasses on the pink house, and sigh operatically.

* * *

The car drew to a halt, and Templar, his heart thudding against his chest, got out.

Waiting for him at the top of broad, white steps was Blickerman's portly butler, Williams.

"Good morning, sir. Mr Blickerman will see you in the Great Room. If you will follow me, please."

At a stately pace, Williams led Templar to a large metal-studded door and turned a brass handle.

Blickerman, tall and bald with a long pink face, was standing by the fireplace, one hand resting on the mantel, the other gripping the revere of his jacket – a pose suggested by Mrs Blickerman for moments of seriousness with employees. It was the pose he had struck when issuing the salami reprimand.

"Hello, JB." Templar attempted to sound cheerful.

Blickerman held the pose. "Come in, Tiny. Come in, please." His voice was light, almost friendly.

"I got your message, JB." Templar trotted across a floor of ivory-coloured marble.

"Of course you did. You wouldn't be here if you hadn't – unless you happened to be passing and decided to drop in. But why would you want to do that? You've got more important things to do, a big movie star like you." The voice was still light but the friendliness had gone.

Templar felt a lurch of panic. His thoughts went involuntarily to Carlos Ramirez, Paragon's great screen lover, who, in a fit of over confidence, had suggested to Mrs Blickerman that she wanted him to make love to her ('Admit it, bebby, admit you'd like to have me screw the ass off you'). Blickerman had ruined Ramirez's career by giving him second billing to Rusty The Wonder Dog.

"Sit down," Blickerman said. He nodded at a chair, and, flea-like, Templar catapulted himself into it.

"Well, Tiny – " Blickerman scratched his neck ruminatively, "I hear you had quite a party last night."

"Just a little get-together with a few of the crew, JB."

"Quite a party," Blickerman went on. "I hear you were the star attraction, or should I say the star exhibition?"

"I don't – "

"Don't interrupt me, Tiny, please." He seemed to be in pain. "I also hear you've gone into the slaughtering business…set up a slaughtering business in your bedroom, I hear." He shifted his feet. "Isn't that a little messy? What about your beautiful furnishings? Won't they get spoiled with all that blood? You paid a lot of money for those furnishings. I know, because Mrs Blickerman helped you choose them. Mrs Blickerman tells me you got a carpet in your bedroom cost you two thousand dollars." He shifted his feet again and said: "So how come you're committing animal slaughter on it – cutting up sheep on it. Isn't it – "

"Look here, JB," Templar broke in, "I don't know who's been dishing you this stuff, but you've got it all wrong." His voice came from a constricted throat.

Blickerman went over to him, placed his hands on the arms of the chair and thrust his head forward. "You interrupt me again," he said, "and as sure as there's shit in a camel I'll bounce you all round this room." He stood up straight. "You sit there and listen." He made to walk away, then turned suddenly and screamed: "YOU LISTEN!"

Templar swallowed. "Okay, JB. Sure."

"Sure." Blickerman returned to the fireplace. "Now then – " He brushed something from his sleeve before continuing. "I been told you carved up a living sheep and covered yourself with its guts while a girl, also covered with guts, read from the bible. What's more, I heard not only is the girl a *Paragon* person but is playing in one of our *religious* pictures." His face began to look swollen and red. "If this is true what I've heard, then a lot of that picture is going to have to be re-shot, because there's no way that a girl who covers herself with animal guts and reads the bible to some crazy pervert is going to appear in a Paragon *religious* production." He shook his head twice. "No way is that going to happen." In a rising voice, he said: "Have you any idea what the *Christian Monitor* would do if they got hold of the story? *Have you any idea, you midget bastard!*" Blickerman clenched his fists, half crouched and took a long loping step towards Templar. "Never mind about the *Christian Monitor*, you filthy piece of shit," he roared, "do you know what this will mean in terms of extra production costs!" He stayed crouched for a long time, then straightened up and took a deep shuddering breath. In a calmer voice, he said: "Okay; okay. Now let's hear what *you've* got to say. Let's hear *your* side of things. And it better be good. It had better be the best, or you'll be out." He smiled grimly. "Now.... *Now* we'll hear."

Fear fired Templar's imagination. He swallowed again and began:

"First, JB, the sheep you're talking about wasn't a sheep, it was a lamb, and second, it wasn't a real lamb, it was papiér maché – you know, cardboard. I had one of the prop boys make it up to throw a scare into Dick Caswell. I don't know if you know it, but Caswell can't stand the sight of blood. Every time he sees blood he faints clean away." He paused. "Me and a couple of the gang thought we'd have a few laughs, take him down a peg or two – he's been getting awfully swollen headed recently – so, like I said, I got one of the prop boys to make up this lamb and paint it so it looked like the real thing. He did a swell job. Then we fixed things so that Caswell would find me in the bedroom with it." He gave a small, fake laugh. "All this stuff about it being a real sheep is just baloney."

Blickerman looked at him coldly. Presently he said: "Let me get this straight. The sheep wasn't a sheep, it was a lamb, and the lamb wasn't a real lamb, it was made of cardboard."

"That's the way it was, JB."

"So what about the guts and blood? *They* were made of cardboard, you're telling me? You're telling me you had cardboard guts over you?"

Templar felt inspired. "Not cardboard, JB, rubber – strips of rubber dipped in ketchup."

Blickerman looked down at his shoes. The story sounded plausible. It was the kind of thing that went on in Hollywood, and, after all, no one had produced any evidence, not even an ovary or a scrap of intestine. He thought of the additional production costs. He wanted desperately to believe Templar. Still looking at his shoes, he said: "And what about the bible? You're going to tell me the bible was made of *marzi*pan?"

"No, JB," Templar said, "I'm *not* going to tell you that. It *was* a book, but it wasn't the bible. I love the bible. It means a great deal to me. I get a great deal of comfort from it. I always have." He sensed that Blickerman threequarters believed him. One more push and he'd be home free. He decided that a display of pique was called for. "And I'm not going to sit here and have it suggested that I would abuse it in any way. I won't take that, JB. Not even from you." His effrontery astonished him.

He went on: "If you really want to know, if it's *that* important to you, the book the girl was reading from was *Gulliver's Travels*. It happens to be her favourite novel, and it also happens to be mine. In fact, it would make a great picture, but that's beside the point. We were passing the time with it while waiting for Caswell to walk in."

Blickerman studied Templar's face. He didn't trust him. Eventually he said: "If ever I find you lied to me, you'll never work again." He turned his head away. "Now get out."

In the car on his way home, Templar said to Max: "You got rid of that sack of stuff I left out last night, didn't you, Max?"

"Yes, sir," Max said. "Incinerated it. Smelled real bad."

CHAPTER 6

Honey had been told that Templar liked his women big, blonde, and brash.

"Brash? Whaddaya mean, *brash*?" she had asked her informant, a young waitress in the Paragon studio canteen.

"Well, he likes them enjoy a joke. *You* know, crude stuff; like, really *crude* stuff. Personally, that kinda stuff don't appeal to me."

"It doesn't?" Honey had been genuinely surprised.

"Another thing about Templar: he likes his women take the initiative. You know...with sex and stuff."

"How d'you know all this? You dated him?"

"No, but my sister has. He was dating my sister for a while...until she couldn't take him no more."

"I heard he was freaky."

"Most of 'em *are* out here. But Templar's *really* mixed up."

"What'd he have your sister do?"

"Breast feed him. Stuff like that – him naked and everything. Real crazy stuff."

* * *

Honey ran a hand over her hair and knocked on the door of Templar's white-walled bungalow on the Paragon lot.

"Yes? Come in."

Honey went in.

Templar was standing before a mirror. He was naked except for a towel round his waist.

"You wanted to see me, Mr Templar." Honey gave a wide smile. "I'm Honey Bunn."

She closed the door and took off her blouse and skirt. She wore nothing beneath them. Going up close to Templar, she said: "You heard the one about the cop who finds his wife screwing with the delivery boy?" She unfastened Templar's towel, took him into her arms and fed a rosy nipple into his astonished mouth. "One day this cop comes home unexpected…"

CHAPTER 7

It was the fourth Take, and Finn was becoming bored. It seemed to him that Caswell was unsure of what he wanted (in Take Two he had called for noise; then, in Take Three, he had wanted silence. Now he wanted noise again – but at a lower level). 'Christalmighty,' Finn thought, 'why can't he just get on with it!' He closed his eyes in exasperation.

"That's fine," Caswell called. "Let's keep it like that." In a louder voice, he said: "But will the man in the white coat at the bar not *slump* quite so much? Place your elbows on the counter, but don't get too low down. And the man next to him: don't look at the drunk when he *enters*, look at him when he brushes past you." He sighed audibly. "Okay, let's try it once more."

The setting was the crowded bar of a large run-down hotel somewhere in the mid West. The action was a variation on the old cowboy theme: a door opens, the bad men (in this case a gang of bungling bank robbers) swagger in, the customers, with the exception of the town drunk, scatter. Finn as the drunk had thirty seconds of screen time – a minor part. Templar wasn't in the scene. He would make his entrance when the drunk had been thrown out.

"Okay, take your places."

Finn left the set to wait for his cue. He would have liked to leave the lot – to walk out of the studio into a *real* bar. He wasn't enjoying picture-making. He preferred the real theatre with a real audience. Here it was too impersonal. Here the *make-believe* was real.

His cue came and he lurched through swing doors. He wore a suit that was a size too small and a battered top hat. As if blinded by lights, he screwed up his eyes and took a step backwards; then, focussing on a point in the distance, he gathered himself and made his way slowly, jerkily towards it.

In the bar were small round tables, at which sat costume extras drinking coloured water.

Coming to two tables set close together, Finn hunched his

shoulders, clamped his arms to his sides and, with all the care that a man on a thousand-foot-high ledge might take, edged his way between them.

For the third or fourth time that morning, Caswell said to the continuity girl: "This guy is great."

Finn negotiated a waiter, took a few tottering steps to his left, and collapsed onto a chair.

"Cut!" Caswell rose from his director's chair. "Okay, that was fine, everyone. Thank you."

They broke for lunch, and as Finn walked off the set Caswell caught up with him and fell in with his step. "You were fine, Mr Finn. The best drunk I've ever seen."

"And you've seen a few drunks in your time," Finn said tiredly.

Caswell laughed. "I mean it. You were terrific."

"It took a lot of bar-hopping to get it right," Finn said.

"I'll bet," Caswell said.

"I take it you won't be wanting me any more," Finn said matter-of-factly.

"Your work's finished here, I'm afraid, but don't leave town for a couple of days – Tiny may want to reshoot. Tiny has the final say around here, you know."

Finn detected a trace of bitterness in Caswell's voice.

"Make sure you leave a forwarding address or a number where we can contact you. It's possible we may be able to put something your way at a later date. In fact, I'm sure we can."

They parted and Finn went to the dressing tent, changed his clothes and took a Paragon bus off the lot. He had planned to go straight to his apartment and rest, but the spring weather was warm and he decided to make the most of it. Lever had told him of the houses on Paradise Hill. He would take his advice and see them for himself.

He left the bus at Paragon Boulevard and made his way to a row of mock Tudor shops that were across the road from the bus stop and half hidden by a line of laburnum trees. Although it was midday there were no people about. He saw only a blue Siamese cat that arched its back as he passed and looked at him with malevolent eyes.

He wanted cigarettes, so he went into a shop that displayed

expensive pipes and smokers' accoutrements in satin-lined cases and ordered a pack of Chesterfield from a tall silver-haired man with soft blue eyes and a John Barrymore profile.

"How do I get to Paradise Hill?" Finn asked, pocketing his change.

"Turn right out the door, then take the fourth right into Venus Avenue. You'll find Paradise at the end of Venus." The voice was slightly falsetto and the idea occurred to Finn that he had been given directions by a former Paragon star who had failed his 'talkies' test.

Outside, Finn raised his face to the sun for a few moments, then, after admiring a hand-made pair of shoes in the window of a shop a few yards along from the one he had just left, headed in the direction of Paradise Hill.

As he walked, he thought of Caswell and decided he liked him. He was a little too self-satisfied, perhaps, a little too self-important, but he seemed genuine enough; his praise of his work on the set hadn't been spoken mechanically.

He came to Paradise Hill and saw a steep rise of land divided by a white brick road that ran in a straight line to the top. On either side of the road, built on steppes cut into the land, was a collection of oddly designed houses. Each was pastel-coloured and each more elaborate than the other. Where one featured towers shaped like giant tulips, the towers of the house above it twisted and turned in corkscrew fashion. Where one had a giant oyster shell for a roof, the roof of the house that overlooked it soared and dipped like a funfair ride. Lever had told him to look for the home of Constance Maybury, Paragon's sex goddess, and now he saw it – a huge heart-shaped structure made of lavender glass.

A heat haze hung over the rise, creating momentary illusions of movement, and looking at the heart house, Finn saw it shudder convulsively, as if life had been breathed into it.

He suddenly felt very tired, but a compulsion to see the pink house that topped the rise like the last piece of confection on an extravagant wedding cake made him move on.

* * *

"Yoohoo!"

He had stopped outside a high wrought iron gate, and a woman with white hair was waving to him from a balcony.

He took out his handkerchief and wiped sweat from his eyes. His legs trembled from the effort of the climb and he had difficulty in breathing.

"Yoohoo! Please come. Come!"

There was a note of urgency in the woman's voice, which made Finn think she might need help.

"Yes, come!" The woman beckoned to him.

Finn wiped his neck. He was thirsty. He would find out what she wanted and perhaps be given a cold drink for his trouble. He slid back the bolt of the gate and made his way through oleander bushes that had been allowed to grow unchecked.

When he was at the walls of the house, the woman called down: "Do come up, Mr Blickerman."

Finn had seen pictures of Jake Blickerman and thought it odd that he should be mistaken for him. He climbed pink marble steps and passed through a small archway.

She was standing facing him, smiling. "Mr Blickerman – " She came forward to greet him. "How nice to see you again."

She was wearing a yellow silk dress tied at the waist with a piece of green chiffon, and green satin ballet pumps. Finn took her to be in her early sixties.

"When I saw you outside, I thought for a moment you were going to ignore my call. That would have been too naughty of you, I get so few visitors." She giggled, then gave a small nervous cough as though to check herself. "Do sit down and rest. You look so hideously hot, poor man. That hill… So killing."

Finn pulled a curlicued wrought iron chair from beneath a white wooden table and sat down. On the table was a phonograph with a record on its deck.

"I'm afraid you've made a mistake," Finn said. "My name isn't Blickerman, it's Finn. I was walking by when I heard you call. I thought you were in trouble. That's why I came up."

"Trouble?" The woman opened her eyes wide in surprise. "Why, Mr Blickerman, what an idea!" She fluttered her lashes. "Trouble –

trouble from whom? Why, it's as quiet as a grave up here." She giggled again and gave the nervous cough. "Come, be honest, Mr Blickerman, you are here to negotiate." She put a hand to her throat. "What persistence! How keen you must be to possess my little house. How Mrs Blickerman must love it! I sometimes see the glint of her binoculars, you know. I sometimes wave to her as she glimpses me through them." She flicked up the tails of the chiffon that hung from her waist and executed a child's skip.

Finn wiped round his mouth and throat. "Would you have a glass of water?" he asked.

"My dear man, of course." She came towards him. "But first" – she turned the handle of the phonograph, moved a lever to set it in motion, and placed the needle-head on the record. "But first we must dance."

An accordion began to play a tango tune and she took hold of Finn's wrists and pulled him to his feet.

Finn resisted, but she locked an arm round his waist.

"Look here, lady – "

She moved him into a tango. "Don't you just *love* the tango, Mr Blickerman?" She closed her eyes as if in ecstasy. "I usually tango alone, but there are days when I ache for a partner."

"Lady – " Finn felt sick and his head swam. He tried to twist himself free, but she tightened her grip on him.

"I'm afraid I must disappoint you once again, Mr Blickerman: my house is not for sale. I could never give it up." She propelled him forward with long raking strides. "Not even for a dancing part in one of your clever talking pictures."

With a suddenness that took Finn by surprise, she reversed her hold on him. Now they were facing in the opposite direction, hip to hip, taking short, jerky steps. "My husband had it specially built for me, you know. " She stopped abruptly, spun in to face him and reversed her hold on him again. Their faces were very close. "It was his wedding present to me." She fluttered her eyelids coquettishly, then suddenly leaned backwards, pulling Finn over her so that he had to balance on one leg. "We spent our wedding night here."

They regained an upright position and moved forward. "It was my husband who taught me to tango. Mr Carlsen was besotted with the tango. Besotted!" She giggled again but there was no cough this time. "We tangoed on this very balcony on the night of our wedding." She jerked Finn to the left and right. "No, I could never give it up." She swung Finn round, released her grip and gave him a violent push.

Finn staggered backwards and felt the small of his back connect with the balcony wall.

"Oh, God!" He stretched out his arms.

As he fell, he heard hysterical laughter.

INTERLUDE

The studios and offices of Paragon Productions occupied sixty acres of prime land two miles south west of downtown Los Angeles. They had been built on the instruction of Eugene Blickerman, the eldest son of Frederick Blickerman whose fortune – made in the Chicago stockyards - Eugene had inherited at the age of 30.

Now deceased, Eugene had been both loved and respected – loved by his employees for his generous treatment of them (he had paid the highest wages in Hollywood), and respected by the Hollywood intelligentsia for his, in their opinion, enlightened approach to picture-making; enlightened because, unlike his opposites, Eugene had made pictures not to increase his wealth but to educate the masses. While all other studios thrilled audiences with the likes of *Rooty Rides Again* and *The Exploits of Emily*, Paragon, under Eugene's leadership, had bored them to the point of coma with the likes of *A Pilgrim's Progress* and *Hamlet*. Paragon's pictures had been what the movie industry terms 'sleepies'. There are 'weepies', creepies', and 'sleepies'. Paragon, with Eugene at its helm, had made 'sleepies'. That is why Paragon had lost of ten million dollars a year and why, when Eugene announced he was to film Proust's *Remembrance of Things Past*, Jake Blickerman, Eugene's younger brother, had had him knocked down by a truck.

Two days after Eugene's death (his skull crushed, Eugene had died instantly) Jake had called a meeting of executives and actors and informed them that his brother, because of his dedication to Paragon and his love of the motion picture industry, would be buried in a dip of unused land at the back of Stage Fifteen. Furthermore, as a parting gift from Eugene and to perpetuate his name, the land would be turned into a burial ground, where Paragon staff could, if they wished, be interred free of charge. It would be known, Jake had announced – and there were some who thought they saw the suggestion of a smile in his eyes when he made the announcement –

as *Eugene's Valley of Sleep.*

That was sixteen years ago. Since then, *Eugene's Valley of Sleep* had, not counting Eugene, become home to six people: three costume extras, killed when scaffolding collapsed on them; a stuntman who broke his neck jumping from a window; and two English screenwriters who gassed themselves in a suicide pact.

CHAPTER 8

"I'd be breaking the rules," Paragon's personnel girl, a Deanna Durbin lookalike, said when Lever made application for Finn's burial. "The Vale is reserved for those who were in Paragon's employ at the time of death. Mr Finn had *left* our employ."

"For chrissake," Lever protested, "he just finished work that day. He hadn't even picked up his pay cheque."

"He hadn't?" The girl's manner relaxed. "Well, I guess that *does* alter things. If he hadn't collected his pay cheque, I guess that makes him Paragon – if we stretch the rules a little." She smiled conspiratorially and handed Lever a brochure. "I'm afraid Mr Finn is eligible for Section C tablets only. There's a tear-out Last Message form in back, if you'd care to complete it. Fifty characters maximum."

* * *

The funeral was held two days after a coroner decided that Finn, as an intruder in the Carlsen residence, had met his death accidentally. It was attended by Lever, Honey, Tiny Templar, and Caswell.

Templar hadn't wanted to go. "The guy was a nobody," he said to Honey. "I didn't know the guy. Why should I go to the funeral of someone I didn't know?"

"For *me*, daddy-baby. For mommy. For daddy's big mommy."

Since her suckling of him, they had met frequently, though always secretly, at his home at night. Templar's chauffeur Max would collect her in the limousine and take her to him. This secrecy irritated Honey. She wanted to be seen with Templar in public; wanted the glamour and attention that went with being seen with someone of his fame. But Templar, because it was a rule of his that he be seen only with women of star or starlet status, kept her out of sight. In retaliation, Honey teasingly repulsed the more depraved of his advances – "Baby, you're too much!" or, simply, "Baby!" Frustrated, Templar sulked and considered ending the relationship; but the thought of one day seeing Honey's body smeared with viscera, of seeing (through a pane of glass) her buttocks in the throes of intestinal evacuation – made him continue with it. Also, he knew that if he were to discard her, he would have difficulty in finding a suitable replacement: women of Honey's disposition were hard to come by: nothing he said or suggested disgusted her. There was a further problem: lately he had begun to fall in love with her.

"What's in it for *me*?"

"What would daddy like?"

"You know what I'd like."

"You be good to mommy and mommy'll be good to daddy. You take mommy to the funeral and afterward to the studio canteen, and when we get back home mommy'll get out the glass and do poopies like daddy wants."

"You mean that?"

"Yes, baby."

"You *really* mean that?"

"Yes, baby."

"You'd better."

"Daddy'll take mommy to the funeral, then?"

"Yes, goddamn it, daddy'll take mommy to the funeral."

He had kept his word. The next day Max drove them to Stage Fifteen and parked in one of the bays reserved for executives. As they left the car, a call-boy passed them holding a suit on a hanger. He looked back at Honey several times as if trying to place her face. Honey laughed and waved to him, envisioned him talking with other call-boys during their lunch break: *You should of seen the dame Templar had with him today. Boy, what a build!*

At the end of the lane that ran between Stages Fifteen and Sixteen they came to a dip of grassland planted with willows and mountain ash and enclosed by a white picket fence. Above a gate was a sign in gold script that said, EUGENE'S VALLEY OF SLEEP. THIS GARDEN OF REMEMBRANCE IS DEDICATED TO THE MEMORY OF EUGENE BLICKERMAN, A TIRELESS PIONEER OF THE MOTION PICTURE INDUSTRY AND FORMER HEAD OF PARAGON PRODUCTIONS.

They went through the gate and saw Caswell, Lever, and a priest standing by an open grave.

"Hello, Tiny. Hello, Miss Bunn." Caswell greeted them.

"Hi." Honey gave him a bright smile. "Hi, Frank." She glanced at Lever, then into the grave where Finn's coffin lay.

Lever was surprised to see her: when he told her of Finn's death she had reacted absently, shrugged her shoulders.

"This is Frank Lever, Finn's agent," Caswell said to Templar, "and this – " he indicated the priest " – is Father Henderson."

The priest was small and pale and had sparse beige hair. His clerical collar was yellow like an old photograph and had a smear of dried blood on it. He leaned forward, took Templar's hand and shook it vigorously. "I recognised you immediately," he said. He gave a long, viperish grin. "I'm a great follower of yours, Mr Templar, a disciple you might say. Perhaps when the service is over you'll be kind enough to sign my prayer book." He drew a slim leather-bound volume from his pocket.

"Shall we start, Father?" Caswell said coldly.

After the ministrations and after Templar had signed the priest's prayer book (*Best wishes – T. Templar*), Honey and Templar walked to the studio canteen and got there as food was being served. The seats on the Big Table (for VIP's and their guests) were taken, so they chose a window table. As they made their way to it Honey stooped and took hold of Templar's hand. Embarrassed, hoping he hadn't been seen, Templar glanced across to the Big Table and saw Roland Burgess, Paragon's top producer, wave to him, then turn to Coleman Hennessy, his director, and whisper something (*Look who's just walked in, Tarzan and Cheeta*). He heard Hennessy laugh and felt a rush of anger towards Honey. She had made a fool of him to get herself noticed.

When they were seated, a waitress came up and handed Templar a menu. "What'll you have, Mr Templar?"

Templar passed the menu to Honey, who, without looking at it, handed it back. "You order, sugar," she said.

Templar studied the list of food. "A plain salad for me," he said to the waitresss, "and" – he would get his money's worth – "and the lady will have a chicken-liver curry."

CHAPTER 9

They were into the second days' shooting of *Tom Thumb Meets Count Dracula* and Honey was late on set. It was Honey's and Templar's fifth picture together. After *Little Big Shot* had come *Wee Won The War*, and after *Wee Won The War*, *Size Right!* and *Small Fry*. In *Little Big Shot*, Honey had played Templar's mistress, in *Wee Won The War*, his nurse, in *Size Right!*, his wife, and in *Small Fry*, his secretary. The pictures had been well received: *Movieworld* had hailed *Small Fry* a comic masterpiece, and *Take One*'s reviewer, Julius Reed, had reported that Templar was as funny as Chaplin at his best. Honey had been named too. "By the way, fellas," Vic Swainland of *Peek!* had written, "catch Honey Bunn who plays Templar's little woman. Did I say little? Wow!" And Eddie Pinkerton of *Flickthroo!* recorded: "Miss Bunn has a figure like a rigger only bigger." During the making of the pictures, Honey had taken as lovers an electrician, a scene-shifter, a carpenter, a call-boy, an extra, a floor sweeper, a camera loader, and a props man.

"Christ! Where *is* she?" Templar said, looking around him

"I didn't see her in the canteen," Caswell said.

Nor had Templar; he had ordered and paid for her beef stroganoff, but she had failed to appear.

"Maybe she's making a call or something," Caswell said further.

Templar said: "Or maybe she's sick." Then, abruptly: "I'll take a look in the bungalow." He struggled from his canvas chair, deep suspicion rising in him. Was she cheating on him again? Something told him she was

"Let me send a boy," Caswell offered.

"No, no, I'll go myself," Templar said quickly, remembering the *last* time a call-boy had been sent to fetch her. (The call-boy had failed to return, so Templar had gone looking for her himself, and found her in his lot bungalow. Her dress was bunched around her neck, and the call-boy was entering her from behind. Incensed, Templar had leapt on to the call-boy's back, called him a dirty sonofabitch and tried to break his neck. Afterwards he told Honey he wanted her out of his life, he never wanted to see her again. But Honey, lowering her head, had wept – or so it had seemed to Templar – and he had forgiven her. He had forgiven her a second time, a third time and a fourth time. Recently he'd begun to wonder if he was capable of forgiving her a fifth time.)

Outside, he climbed into a Paragon electric buggy, turned it in the direction of his bungalow, and engaged it at its maximum speed of fifteen miles an hour. It was a hot day and the buggy's slip-stream was refreshing. As he passed the Administration building he saw Jake Blickerman getting into his pearl-grey Cadillac. Their eyes met briefly and Templar experienced a pang of anxiety. He knew that Blickerman, having seen him, would return to his office and dictate a message to *Tom Thumb Meets Count Dracula*'s Head of Production, Ellis Duxborough, complaining that the picture's star was seen riding in a Paragon buggy during shooting hours. He, Templar, would be asked to give an explanation in writing.

"Well, you can go take a running jump at yourself, Blickerman, you bastard," he said to himself. He felt tears of self-pity burn in his eyes. It wasn't fair. After all he'd done for Paragon – the money he'd made for them. And Honey…He'd given her most of the things she'd asked for, insisted she get bigger parts and more lines to speak; he'd even lied to get her crowned a Paragon Princess. He heard Blickerman's words again – "That fat slut a Paragon Princess? Not over my mother's dead body will she be a Paragon Princess. You hear that, Alice? He wants we should make his fat slut a Paragon Princess." But Templar hadn't given Alice (Mrs Blickerman) opportunity to respond: he had gotten in first, saying that he and Honey were to be married; that it would be "great publicity" for his next picture if he were to marry a Paragon Princess. The Blickermans had looked at each other for a long time, Blickerman with his mouth open. Eventually Mrs Blickerman, touching her throat, had said: "Well, maybe if Miss Bunn was to go on my fish diet for a month…"

Templar parked the buggy and noticed that the bungalow's curtains were drawn. He clenched his fists. There would be no let-off this time. This time he would kick her out. He wouldn't be made a fool of again. But even as he reached to place the key in the door he felt his determination falter. He loved her. She was, as Blickerman had said, a slut, but she was the only woman in his life, including his mother, who hadn't been ashamed to be seen with him, who had *wanted* to be seen with him. At premiers, before photographers, she crouched to kiss him or to brush his cheek with her fingers. He was aware that she did this to get her picture in magazines, but no matter, she kissed him. Her predecessors had simply stood with him and smiled; had sometimes moved away from him as if they had suddenly discovered they were standing next to a steaming pile of horse manure.

His determination returned when he opened the door and saw Honey in fellatio with his stand-in, Tony 'Titch' Pio.

Had she been with a man of normal size, the pain he felt would not have been quite so great. A normal-sized male would have been competition he could more easily have coped with. He could have forgiven her. But Pio was half an inch smaller than himself and less prepossessing – a thin-faced, squint-eyed fifty-year-old who smelled of stale wine and unwashed feet. Templar felt insulted.

They hadn't heard him enter. He stared down at them for a few moments, then said flatly: "You're finished, both of you."

Honey, her face flushed, looked up quickly. "Baby – " she began.

"Finished," Templar repeated. "Dead. Don't bother to come back on set." He turned and walked briskly out the door. There was a bright red light behind his eyes and the muscles in his neck were in spasm.

"Baby!" He heard Honey call after him. "It's not what you think. It's wasn't the way it… Baby, don't – "

Templar hurled himself into the buggy and started it up.

"Baby!" Honey called again, and then, as he drove away: "Aw, go join a circus!"

On the set Templar told Caswell he was unwell and couldn't work that day; that Honey and Pio would have to be replaced; that he never wanted to see either of them again. They were to be paid up and got rid of. Then he had a call-boy fetch Max from the studio Games' Room to drive him home. Before leaving, he told Caswell to get Honey to hand over the duplicate keys to his house and bungalow and to leave them with Sam the gateman for his, Templar's, collection. If necessary, Caswell was to use force to get them. "Have a couple of security men stand by ready to jump her if she starts acting up," he told him.

When he got home he chained the door, poured himself a large gin, and sat with it in his study. He gave himself a mental pat on the back for feeling as calm as he did.

He had two more drinks, swallowed a sleeping pill and went to bed. Sometime in the night he was awoken by a hammering at the door. He listened for a while, and then went back to sleep.

He rose late, bathed and returned to the studio. At the gate he asked Sam if any keys had been left for him, and was handed an envelope. Inside were the duplicate keys to his house and bungalow and a note from Caswell which said: *You have no idea what it took in terms of muscle to get these.*

Templar thanked Sam and told him that if Honey or Pio showed up, they were not to be allowed into the studio and that he should ask them to give up their passes. If necessary he should use force to get them. He repeated what he had told Caswell: "Have a couple of security men stand by in case they give you trouble."

"Whatever you say, Mr Templar," Sam said and saluted.

Templar felt a great rush of affection for Sam. He was the only person to have shown him any kind of loyalty.

Caswell was on the set when Templar got there. He looked handsome in a pepper and salt suit, and his handsomeness irritated Templar. If *I* looked like him, he thought, things would be different.

Caswell greeted him excitedly. "Jesus, Tiny, the trouble we had with Honey yesterday. She went crazy. Couldn't *see*, she was so mad. Harry the security man had a finger bitten through and the forest props are a write-off. If she turns up today, I don't intend waiting around to see what happens."

"She won't," Templar said with finality.

They re-arranged the shooting schedule and then went to the studio bar to discuss finding a replacement for Honey.

Over their drinks, Templar said: "Why don't we have the old dame we used in *Knee Hi!*? She's the right size and nobody can scream the way she can." He took a sip of the martini he was holding. "Maybe an older dame would be better for the part. We could have her bite the vampire." The coolness of the bar relaxed him. He felt a slow returning of confidence. "That's not a bad idea," he went on. "Instead of having the vampire bite the professor, we'll have the dame bite the vampire."

"She's drying out," Caswell said.

"Well, *get* her," Templar said, suddenly aggressive. "Find out where she is, settle her bill and have her brought here."

Caswell sipped his drink. "What about finding a replacement for Pio?" he asked, and immediately regretted the question: it might lead to his having to use the word *midget*, a word he would have difficulty in using in front of Templar; he would feel as he had felt at a studio party when, during a conversation with Jake Blickerman, he had inadvertently used the word 'kike'.

Templar sensed Caswell's unease and the reason for it. He deliberately remained silent. He would make him squirm.

"It's going to be difficult," Caswell continued.

"Why?" Templar asked.

Caswell cleared his throat. "People like Pio – " He broke off. Then, finding the right words: "People of Pio's size are not easy to find."

Templar recalled Honey's insult to him. He gave a tight smile and said: "Why don't you try a circus? That's where the midgets hang out, isn't it?"

"Well, I – " Caswell moved his head from side to side, as if his collar had suddenly become tight.

"Forget it," Templar said. "I'll do my own stunts for the time being."

They had a second drink and left the bar.

Outside, Caswell said: "By the way, I forgot to tell you: Duxborough's secretary called. She'd like a word with you."

"I thought she might," Templar said.

Max drew up in the car, and Templar got in.

At the gate he asked Sam if Honey had put in an appearance.

"Not yet," Sam said. "I guess she must have overslept."

"Well, don't forget what I told you," Templar said. "She doesn't get in."

CHAPTER 10

Sam had been right: Honey *had* overslept. She had beaten on Templar's door until three in the morning, and then, swollen with rage, gone to an hotel and taken a room. It wasn't until five o'clock that she had got to sleep. Now, at 11.30, she dressed hurriedly, ran a comb through her hair, left the hotel, and arrived at the studio at midday.

As she waited for the gate to open she saw Sam look at her from his box, then lift the receiver of his telephone. After a while he left the box and came up to her. Through the gate's bars, he said: "I'm sorry, Miss Bunn, but I've got instructions not to let you in."

Honey said: "Cut the comic games, Sam, I'm late on set."

Sam said: "I've been told by Mr Templar not to let you in – and you're to hand over your pass."

"Open the goddamn gate, Sam."

"I can't do that, Miss Bunn."

"Open the gate, Sam." Her tone was threatening.

"I'm sorry, Miss Bunn."

"Open the gate, you dumbcluck, or I'll hang it on your ear."

As she spoke, a Paragon security car turned a corner and drew to a halt a few feet from where Sam was standing. Two heavily-built men in uniform got out.

"Okay, Sam, *we'll* take it from here," the taller of the men said. And to Honey: "I'm afraid we have to ask you to relinquish your pass, Miss Bunn."

"Go shit in your hat," Honey said.

"That's no way for a Paragon Princess to talk, Miss Bunn," the smaller guard said peevishly. "Hand over your pass and don't give us trouble."

"Like hell I will," Honey said.

"I'm asking you to hand over your pass, Miss Bunn. You don't, we'll have to take it from you by force."

"You and the *rest* of the boy scouts," Honey said.

"Open the gate, Sam," the taller guard ordered.

Sam returned to his box and a second or two later the gate swung open.

"Okay, George, grab her!"

The smaller guard darted forward, and, as Honey swung her purse at him, his partner grabbed her from behind and pinned her arms to her sides. The smaller guard, avoiding Honeys kicks, took hold of her purse and pulled it from her grasp. After a few moments he called: "Okay, George, I got it." He held up Honey's pass. "Let her loose." He threw the purse on the ground and took up a position at the gate.

"You lousy sonsofbitches!" Honey fought to free herself from the taller guard, but he had a tight hold on her. He half dragged, half carried her to a distance along the road, set her down and sprinted back.

"Okay, Sam!"

Sam from his box pressed a button and the gate swung shut.

Honey stayed at the gate screaming insults for a few minutes, then left and got a taxi to Templar's house.

On the porch were two piles of her clothes. Again she beat on the door and again got no answer. She threw the clothes into the taxi and was driven to her hotel.

Next morning, in a dimly lit bar that she and Templar had made their meeting place, she telephoned the studio and in Templar's voice asked to be put through to the gatehouse.

"Hi, Sam," she said when she was connected, "this is Mr Templar."

She heard Sam say brightly: "Morning, Mr Templar – what can I do for you?"

"Look, Sam, about that business with Miss Bunn: well, it's all okay now. If she shows up today, let her through, will you? And give her back her pass. The whole thing was a misunderstanding."

"Well, sure, Mr Templar," Sam said, "only I don't *have* Miss Bunn's pass, it's gone to administration – and you know the rules: no pass, no admittance."

"Don't worry about that, Sam, I'll fix it with administration. Just let her through."

"Well, I don't know, Mr Templar. The last time I let someone in without a pass I got two days' pay stopped."

"Sam, don't worry – everything will be okay."

"Well, if you say so, Mr Templar." There was still a note of doubt in his voice, so Honey said: "Say, Sam, how would you and the wife like a couple of tickets for the Cagney premiere? I can't use them. It'll be a swell evening."

"The Cagney premiere! Jeez, Carrie'll be over the moon. Not counting you, Mr Templar, Jimmy Cagney's just about our favourite movie star."

"All right, Sam, I'll drop them off. In the meantime, let Miss Bunn through – okay?"

"Sure, Mr Templar. Don't worry about a thing."

Honey left the bar and decided to walk the half-mile to the studio. It was a rule of Blickerman's that Paragon Princesses, when unaccompanied, should travel by limousine or taxi: they were Paragon 'royalty' and as such should distance themselves from the public. But Honey wanted time to get her thoughts in order: she did not quite know what she would say to Templar when she confronted him. Perhaps she should again feign tears, but would he be moved by them this time? She doubted he would. Perhaps she should try a different approach this time. She remembered a Rosemary Winthrope picture in which Winthrope had played an adulterous wife who had helped win back her husband's affection with the words: "My dear, it is not my betrayal of you that makes you so bitter. No – you are bitter because your pride, your colossal pride has been hurt." But Rosemary Winthrope, Honey reminded herself, had not been found on the floor with a midget's member in her mouth.

At the gate, Sam came out to greet her. He smiled nervously. "Good morning, Miss Bunn. Welcome back."

Without slackening her pace and without looking at him, Honey said: "You know something, Sam? You're not worth a squeeze of dog shit."

When Sam had digested her words, he wondered why she hadn't asked for her pass.

As Honey neared Stage Eight she saw Templar's car parked outside and experienced a twinge of uncertainty. What if she were unable to win him over, if he refused to take her back? She would be on her own. She wouldn't even have Finn to return to. A picture of Finn came into her mind and she recalled her dream of the night before: Finn had been laughing at her and telling her she looked a mess. She had aimed blows at him with her fists, but an invisible barrier had prevented them from landing. She had screamed insults at him, swore at him, but Finn had only laughed louder.

She tidied her hair and opened the stage door.

Templar was on set. He was dressed in a doublet and hose, and wore a hat with a point – the type of hat pixies wear. He held a wooden stake that outmeasured him by a good six inches and was standing against a backcloth of a medieval castle at dusk. To his left was an artificial tree, around which peeped a chalky-faced extra wearing fangs.

Honey heard Caswell call: "All right! Ready to go! Quiet!" There was a silence. "We'll take it now! Lights!"

"Hold it." Templar walked to the edge of the set and looked disbelievingly at Honey. He looked at the crew. "How did *she* get in here? Get her out!" His voice rose. "Get her out!"

Honey came from behind Caswell's chair. "Now listen, Tiny," she said.

"GET HER OUT!" Templar threw aside his stake. "I want her off the set. Now!"

Caswell stood up and placed a hand on Honey's shoulder. "Come on, Honey," he said softly, "this won't do you any good."

As if she hadn't heard, Honey said: "Tiny, I got to – "

"GET HER OFF THE SET!"

Caswell turned to two lighting men and nodded in Honey's direction.

Honey moved forward. "It didn't mean a thing, baby," she said. "Jesus! A freak like Pio!"

One of the lighting men got hold of Honey by the arm, but she quickly freed herself, spun round and hit him across the mouth with the flat of her hand.

Templar shouted: "Call security!" He removed his pixie's hat and tossed it to one side.

"Look, Tiny," Honey continued, "you got to understand…Me and Pio…It was just – "

Before she could finish, the man she had hit came up to her again and this time she caught him with a punch beneath the eye.

He staggered backwards and fell into a tangle of lighting equipment.

Honey went up close to Templar and said: "Baby, why you making a big thing out of this?"

Templar said: "I want you off this set. I've told you: you're finished here." He called to Caswell: "Is somebody getting security?"

Honey tried to recall Rosemary Winthrope's words, but her encounter with the lighting man had submerged them. Instead she murmured: "Come on, baby, let's go home and get out the glass. Boy, have I got a pile stored up for *you*!"

Templar tried to pass her, but she caught hold of him by the sleeve of his doublet.

"Let go, you crazy bitch." He pulled back to break free, and there was a tearing sound as the sleeve came away.

Seeing this, the chalky-faced extra with the fangs tittered.

Templar looked witheringly at him for an instant, then said to Honey: "I'll make you wish you hadn't done that."

"You're not ditching me, Tiny," Honey said. "You're not throwing me over."

"Just watch me," Templar said.

Some of Rosemary Winthrope's words surfaced. "It's your pride's been hurt, baby – your colossal fucking pride." Then suddenly security men had hold of her and she was being run from the building.

Two days later she again impersonated Templar's voice and was asked by Sam: "How many fish in the barrel?"

"Huh?"

"Sorry, Miss Bunn," Sam said, and replaced the receiver.

After two weeks of trying to guess how many fish there were in the barrel Honey gave up and applied for work with Allied International. She was told they had finished testing and that the Extras' Book was closed.

There was a similar response from Galaxy Pictures, Sapphire Inc., and World Wide.

She approached Global Studios and was taken on as a dress extra in *California Or Bust!*, but at the end of the first day's shooting she was paid off without explanation.

Over lunch in a restaurant in West Hollywood she said to Lever:

"If ever I meet up with that sonofabitch, I'll beat piss out of him."

Lever said: "Why don't you forget Templar and get back into the theatre?"

"Doing what?" Honey said, "handing Mister Marvel his magic wand? Finn's dead, remember?"

"Who says you need a partner?" Lever said. "You can make it on your own. You've a big talent."

"Yeah." Honey surveyed her breasts. "Only nobody appreciates 'em anymore."

"I'm not talking about your handles," Lever said. "You're a great impressionist."

Honey furrowed her brow. "You mean Cagney, and all that stuff?"

"Cagney, Bogart, Cantor...I've never heard anyone do them better. And the icing is, you're female. In all the halls you've played, you ever seen a female impersonate a male? And I don't mean a dike in a bow tie. You get an act together, I'll get you top billing."

Honey took a mouthful of food and shook her head. She tapped the table with her fork as she swallowed. "Uh-uh," she said, "I want to make it here. Screw the theatre and all that look-how-good-I-can-juggle crap. I want to make it here."

"But here don't want *you*," Lever said firmly. "Don't you know? Templar's slammed the door on you. Why d'you think you can't get work? You couldn't get a part as a shit stain on Rusty The Wonder Dog's ass."

Honey narrowed her eyes and said: "You know for sure it's Templar?"

"It's from a twenty-four carat source," Lever said. "Templar's put the word round you're unstable – a crazy."

"I figured something like that," Honey said.

They sat in silence for a long time, Honey looking at her plate. Eventually she stood up. "I'll think over what you said," she said, "but first I got a midget to fix."

CHAPTER 11

The party was to celebrate Stewart Fields' thirtieth birthday and the renewal of his contract with Galaxy Pictures. Fields was a Galaxy leading man whose screen image was that of a witty socialite and *bon vivant*. He was known as Tuxedo Fields because he was rarely seen out of one. Galaxy's publicity department proclaimed him *Every Woman's Ideal Man*, while *Flickthroo!* columnist, Eddie Pinkerton, once described him as: "The man with more smooth than a baby's butt." Off screen, Fields beat his Basset hound and whispered crudities to old ladies. It was rumoured that Fields and Galaxy's *femme fatale*, Carmita Jurez (real name Gladys Weintraub), were the parents of a hunchbacked son whom they cruelly referred to as Quasi. It was further rumoured that Fields and Jurez had placed 'Quasi' in a filthy orphanage somewhere in southern Italy, where he now languished miserably.

"Bring a few friends along," Fields had said to Sylvia Cannon, a researcher in Galaxy's script department, handing her an invitation to the party and smiling his famous screen smile. "And I don't mean those of the hung variety."

Sylvia had invited Honey.

They knew each other from their days at Paragon together: Sylvia had worked there as a stenographer in the administration department and they had often shared a table in the studio canteen; a friendship of sorts had developed between them. Sylvia had left Paragon to join Galaxy, and although the two women hadn't kept in touch, they would meet by accident occasionally at Sammy's, a bar in Little Italy that played loud music. On the last occasion, Sylvia, as she was leaving, had shouted: "Hey, I got this juicy party on Friday; real big names. How about coming along? Call me and we'll fix a time." Honey had telephoned Sylvia the next day and arranged to collect her in the car she would hire for the occasion (if she was going to a 'juicy' party, she would go in style, she had decided). She hired a powder blue Chevrolet with white-walled tires.

"Aren't you being a little extravagant?" Sylvia said as they started out.

"It's not me who's paying for it," Honey said. She told Sylvia of her break with Templar and how just that morning she had sold a five-hundred-dollar necklace given to her by him on her last birthday. "I never *did* like it much," she said. "Kind of cheap-looking."

They arrived at Fields' house just as a thirty-foot-high hoarding on the front lawn broke out in red, white and blue lights that spelled *Happy Birthday, Mr Wonderful*.

"He's not exactly a shrinking violet," Honey said.

"He's his own number one fan," Sylvia said.

They watched the spectacle for a while, then went into the house and into a room where music and voices were coming from and where there was a bar.

When Honey had a glass of whiskey in her hand and Sylvia a glass of gin, Honey looked around the room and saw groups of men and women talking and laughing together. Most of the women were young and beautiful, their bodies sheathed in gold or silver, their hair beautifully coiffed. Looking at them, Honey thought they looked *special* – felt special, too, she bet.

Honey did not feel special. She felt secondary, marginalised. She was here, she told herself, because Fields had taken a shine to a girl in Galaxy's Script Department. She recalled her days at Paragon and the parties she'd attended with Templar. How different it had been then. Then the invitations had come not second-hand from scriipt girls but on cards with her name printed on them. "So where's Mr Wonderful?" she asked Sylvia.

Sylvia shook her head. "Probably getting laid somewhere," she said.

They moved to another room, then, armed with fresh drinks, made their way to the terrace at the back of the house.

"Jeez!" Sylvia said as they stepped out.

The terrace was illuminated by blue and white spotlights and paved with black marble slabs, many bearing in gold letters the titles of the pictures in which Fields had played a leading role. In front of the terrace was a long kidney-shaped swimming pool strung with Chinese lanterns and filled with turquoise-coloured water. Spaced around it at regular intervals were ornate tables and chairs and large crystal urns that held ferns and other plants and reflected in tiny points of light the colours that came from the house and its grounds. Beyond the pool, centred on a great sweep of lawn, was a raised circular platform which slowly revolved and upon which sat musicians in gaucho costume playing *La Cucharacha*. High above the musicians' heads hung a glass crescent that glowed milk green and revolved in keeping with the platform.

"Jeez!" Sylvia said again.

A waiter in a wine-red jacket came up to them and held out a tray of drinks. Honey and Sylvia drained their glasses and exchanged them for full ones.

"Let's go find Fields," Sylvia said eagerly.

"You go," Honey said, "I'll stay here for a while." Suddenly she found Sylvia's high spirits tiresome. Suddenly she despised her for them.

"Sure?"

"Sure," Honey said. "I wanna see the elephants come on."

Sylvia gave a high-pitched laugh. "Okay, but if you get to Fields first, save a piece for me."

Honey watched her until she was out of sight, then carried her drink to a table close to the swimming pool but away from the lights.

She sat down and took a cigarette from a box that was on the table. She noticed that printed on the box and cigarette were Fields' initials.

Another waiter came up and this time Honey took *four* drinks. "I got some people joining me," she told him.

She took four drinks the *next* time a waiter came up, and when she had drunk all eight and listened to three playings of *La Cucharacha* she decided to leave.

She changed her mind when she saw Templar.

He was coming towards her with Fields and a girl with light red hair who had hold of Fields' arm. They stopped by the side of the pool and after a brief conversation and handshakes Fields and the girl walked away, the girl with her head thrown back, laughing.

From her table, Honey watched Templar move to the edge of the pool and look down at the water. He remained looking at the water for a minute, then took a pipe from his jacket pocket, tamped the tobacco and lighted it. When it was burning and after he had exhaled two clouds of smoke, Honey called: "Hello, Tiny."

Templar turned and narrowed his eyes.

"It's me – Honey." She stood up and went across to him.

Templar removed the pipe from his mouth and glanced over his shoulder, as if seeking an escape route. "Now, look – " he began.

"Okay, don't get jerky," Honey said. "I'm not here to make trouble. I just thought we maybe could have a drink together."

Templar stared at her for a long time. Eventually he said: "Don't you understand, can't you get it into your head, it's over between us." He spoke the works emphatically, as though he were trying to communicate with a particularly stupid child. "I don't want to see you any more. I don't want anything more to do with you. Can't you understand that?"

"For old time's sake," Honey said, smiling.

"Christ!" Templar looked away in exasperation.

"Aw, come on, Tiny, loosen up. One drink's not gonna hurt. Nothing's gonna happen, you got my word on it."

Templar regarded her steadily. Her voice had a ring of sincerity about it, which made him uncertain. He returned his pipe to his mouth and after drawing on it a few times said: "All right, but just so long as – "

"Sure," Honey interrupted breezily. "Jesus, I'm not gonna eatcha!"

They went to Honey's table and Templar beckoned to a waiter. As the waiter served them drinks, Templar said: "You won't have heard, but I'm to be married."

Honey took a sip of her drink and, because of the anger she felt, had difficulty in swallowing it.

When her anger had subsided, she smiled and said: "That's swell. Who's the plucky girl?"

"She's new at the studio. Rita Schilling – a big talent. Blickerman plans to Princess her."

"You didn't waste much time," Honey said, still smiling.

"That's the way things happen," Templar said.

Honey looked around. "So where *is* the future Mrs Templar? Why isn't she with you?"

"She couldn't be here," Templar said. He took a drink and continued: "Her kid brother was hurt in a work accident and she's flown out to be with him. They're very close."

"That's tough – about the accident, I mean."

Templar nodded solemnly.

"Where she from, Rita?" Honey asked.

"Philadelphia," Templar said.

"I played there with Finn a couple times," Honey said.

There was a short silence, then Honey said: "I didn't see anything in the trades about the engagement."

"Paragon are putting out a release when she gets back." Templar looked briefly at Honey's breasts.

Noticing this, Honey said: "We had some good times together, didn't we?"

"Some good, a lot bad," Templar said. He looked into Honey's face, and, although he tried not to, looked again at her breasts. He was missing Rita Schilling.

As if reading his mind, Honey said: "How is she?"

"How is she?"

"Rita. How is she in bed?"

"I don't know that that's any of your concern," Templar said coldly.

"Come on, Tiny, we're not kids in a bible class."

Templar looked into his glass. After a moment he said: "She's okay."

"You don't sound like you're waving a flag," Honey said.

"She's okay." Templar spoke the words more forcibly.

"As good as me?"

Templar was silent.

"She do the stuff I used t'do?"

Templar knocked his pipe on the side of his chair and laid it on the table. "I think we should end this conversation," he said.

"She do the glass bit and the other stuff?" Honey persisted.

"That's in the past."

"My ass it's in the past. You're stuck with it, Tiny. That's the way you're made."

"If we're going to have this drink together, let's talk about something else."

After a short silence, Honey said: "You don't like me any more, Tiny."

"I wouldn't piss against you," Templar said.

Honey laughed. "You did *one* time, remember?" Without waiting for a reply, she caught hold of a passing waiter's jacket and took two drinks from his tray. She pushed one across the table to Templar. "You're making things tough for me," she said.

"You made things difficult for *me*."

"Because of you, I can't get work here."

Templar shrugged and looked away.

Honey felt the anger return, then a plan formed in her mind and she said brightly: "What the hell! Who *cares* I won't be another Garbo! I'll be glad to get the hell *out* of this dream-shit place. Who *needs* it? I got an act lined up Lever says'll hit the top."

"I'm happy for you," Templar said without conviction.

"One thing I'll miss, though" – Honey raised her glass to him – "is all that stuff we had going together. Boy, you've sure got a wild imagination, Tiny, I'll say that for you." She took a drink and went on: "One time I didn't think I could handle it, but it worked out I got as big a kick from it as you." She lowered her voice. "I never had it so good as I had it with you, Tiny," she lied. "You're the best I ever had." She paused for a moment, and then said: "I miss it, Tiny." She paused again. "You do too."

Templar looked into her eyes for a long time. He wanted to say: "Yes, I miss it", but thought it wiser not to. Soon Rita Schilling would return; he would be patient. It wasn't as interesting with Rita as it had been with Honey – Rita was a little squeamish – but neither was it dull.

"What d'you say we have one last fling together?" Honey said.

Templar shook his head.

"I need it with you, Tiny." Honey made her voice sound pleading. "Just one last piece of fun. No strings. We'll do whatever you want. We'll get out the glass." She let out a sigh. "Jesus, do I *want* it with you." She slowly rotated her right palm over the point of her left breast.

Templar, as he watched her, pictured the breast uncovered and felt a change in the rhythm of his breathing. After a minute he heard himself say: "If we do, you have to remember that it won't mean anything. Like you said, no strings. When it's over I don't ever want to see you again."

Honey said: "You won't – I'm catching a plane for New York first thing tomorrow."

Templar finished his drink and pocketed his pipe. "You leave first," he said. "I'll follow behind. I can't have anyone see us together."

Honey thought: You're gonna wish you never said that, you bag of midget shit.

"Do you have a car?" Templar asked.

"I hired one," Honey said.

"We'll use *your* car," Templar said. "I'll meet you out front."

At Templar's house, Honey swallowed the double-strength, rapid-action purgative he had handed her, and after they each had had two tall drinks and undressed, Honey said soothingly: "Let mommy and daddy have fun now." She eased his hands from her thighs, went upstairs to his bedroom and returned with an eighteen-inch-square pane of glass.

She laid the glass on a couch and went to him. "Come on, baby." She placed her hands on his shoulders and gently forced him to the floor.

He lay on his back, and Honey knelt beside him. "I'm feeling good, lover," she said. "I've not felt this good in a long time." She ran a hand over his body and murmured: "It'd be swell if we could get back together."

Templar said coldly, "No way."

"Not ever?"

"Not ever."

Honey leaned over him and brushed her lips against his cheek. "Okay, it don't matter." She paused. "We'll have our fun now, baby."

She got to her feet, went to the couch and took up the pane of glass and a cushion. She carried the cushion behind her back. "Here." She handed the glass to Templar, who held it with both hands a few inches above his face.

"This is gonna be just like old times, baby," she said cosily. She swung a leg over him, protected her buttocks with the cushion, and let herself drop.

She heard his cries as she gathered up her clothes and left the house, heard a terrible guttural cry (perhaps he had caught sight of himself in a mirror and seen that one of his eyes was gushing blood and that he no longer had a nose) as she quickly dressed and got into the car.

She drove at seventy miles an hour: she could feel the purgative beginning to take effect.

* * *

On her arrival in New York, Honey made two telephone calls – the first to Calvino to let him know she was back, and the second to Lever to tell him she would take his advice: she would "go solo".

Next day she went into Honnegan's Music Store on East Forty Second Street and bought a phonograph and recordings of songs by Al Jolsen, Eddie Cantor, Bing Crosby, Jimmy Durante, Frank Sinatra, Tony Martin, and Louis Armstrong.

She played the records repeatedly for six weeks and when she was able to impersonate the singers to a point approaching perfection, she began work on what she had decided would be the first part of her act – impersonations of James Cagney, W.C. Fields, Sydney Greenstreet, Peter Lorre, Humphrey Bogart, Charles Laughton, and George Raft.

After three months of visiting the City's picture houses, she again telephoned Lever and this time told him she was ready to begin rehearsing.

CHAPTER 12

"This is mutiny, Mister Christian! Mutiny, sir!"

The numbing voice of Charles Laughton as Captain Bligh reverberated around Jersey City's Tivoli Theatre.

"I will see you hanged for this. I will have you flogged until your backbone shows, then have you hanged from the highest yard-arm in the British fleet – you and the *rest* of your mutinous dogs. You will pay for this treachery with your life, sir. By God you will!"

Honey let the words fade and die, then stepped from behind a screen and half ran to the edge of the stage. "I will live to see you *hanged*, Mister Christian!" she bellowed. "Hanged!"

There was a short, stunned silence from the audience followed by a burst of applause. Someone at the back of the theatre whistled appreciatively.

Smiling, Honey gave a low, supplicatory bow (the bow she had seen Rosemary Winthrope give in *Always The Actress*) and with the applause still in the air, turned and walked briskly to a table that was placed in the centre of the stage, a few feet forward of the screen. On the table were a telephone and three hats – a bowler, a trilby, and a cap.

She picked up the trilby, set it at an angle on her head and lifted the telephone receiver. She dialled, then turned and faced the audience. After a moment, she said in Humphrey Bogart's voice: "Hello, Jimmy, this is Bogey." A pause. "Yeah, sure. You, too, kid." A moment's silence again, and then a dry laugh. "Say, listen, pal, I need a favour. I got this job set up that's a real pushover – a payroll heist on East Forty Fifth – only I don't have a wheel man. The guy I had in mind just got himself a ten to twenty stretch for knocking over a bank in Detroit." Pause. "Yeah, that's the one. Those saps couldn't open a can of peaches. Anyway, like I said, I don't have a wheel man, and Sidney and me – " A small pause. "Yeah, the *big* man – and Sidney and me, well, we figured you might be interested in helping out. Come along for the ride, so to speak."

Honey removed the trilby and replaced it with the cap. She spread her legs, narrowed her eyes and gave a slight shrug of the shoulders. Now she was James Cagney. "You kidding? I'm still owed my cut from the last job we pulled. Brother, have you got a nerve."

Honey donned the trilby again. "Like I told you before, kid, nobody got their cut. Someone tipped off the cops."

Again a change of hats. "If ever I get my hands on the dirty rat – "

"Sure, sure, kid; we can take care of that later. Right now I need a wheel man. What d'you say, pal? You're the best there is."

"Okay, but this time I don't work for chumpchange. You want me, you've gotta come up with the right kind of dough." Pause. "What's the deal?"

"I'm not fronting this one, kid – Sidney is. *He* decides how the split's made. He's here now. Why don't you talk with him. I'll put him on."

Honey exchanged the trilby for a bowler. She gave a rich belly laugh followed by a sharp intake of breath. "Mr Cagney, Sir. Delighted to make your acquaintance. Yes, Sir, I can give you a categorical assurance that you will receive not less than two thousand American dollars. Now, Sir, how does that strike you? With all the force of a particularly fine Tintoretto, I would suggest." A longish pause, then Greenstreet's belly laugh. "Very well, Sir, I shall allow generosity to get the better of me. Ten thousand it shall be. Yes, Sir. Ha, ha. Good day to you, Sir. I shall look forward to working with you."

And so it went on:

George Raft: "Hiya, pal. How about cutting me in on this payroll number you're cooking up?"

Peter Lorre, apoplectic, to Sydney Greenstreet: "You stupid fat idiot. You crazy oversized slug…"

W.C. Fields: "W-e-l-l n-o-o-o-w, this sounds like a plot positively pulsing with pecuniary possibilities."

Then came the songs: Frank Sinatra: *I Get A Kick Out Of You*. Louis Armstrong: *Gone Fishin'*. Bing Crosby: *Moonlight Becomes You*. Eddie Cantor: *Making Whoopee*. Tony Martin: *Begin The Beguine*. And finally Al Jolsen: *California Here I Come*.

Next day in his showpage column for the *Jersey City Post*, Rupert Girling wrote: *The Tivoli Theatre can boast the first appearance of a bright new star in the rising. I refer to Miss Honey Bunn, a voice impressionist of quite breathtaking ability and originality. Yes, readers, originality. The word is used unhesitatingly, for Miss Bunn's impersonations are of men! Yes, dear reader, men! – C. Laughton, H. Bogart, J. Cagney, S. Greenstreet, P. Lorre, G. Raft, B. Crosby...All pour splendidly forth from the ivory throat of this most accomplished entertainer. There is no doubt in this recorder's mind that Miss Bunn is destined to reach the very pinnacle of her profession. DO NOT MISS HER!*

As a postscript Girling wrote: *Unfortunately, not every artiste appearing at The Tivoli is blessed with Miss Bunn's talent. Miss Alice Davies, billed as Atlantic City's Own Songthrush, sang as if she had earlier undergone a tonsilectomy."*

By the end of the week Honey had received offers from three New York nightclubs – *The Top Hat, The Blue Strawberry,* and *The Flamingo.* On Lever's advice, she accepted the offer from *The Flamingo*: of the three it was the most prestigious. It also offered the most money.

To celebrate, Honey went to Silvers, a back-street Irish bar within walking distance of the Tivoli that attracted the district's heavy drinkers – mostly coarsely-spoken men with calloused hands and unkempt hair. Silvers was owned by Patrick Sylvester, a former dancer who, it was rumoured, had once partnered Ginger Rogers in a carioca. Sylvester had been the bar's proprietor for twenty years and in that time had neither redecorated it nor replaced any of its furniture. Horsehair poked through holes in the red-leather bench seats and the wallpaper was stained and peeling. It was the type of bar in which Honey felt most at home.

She ordered a glass of beer and carried it to one of a row of tables that were placed ends-on to the counter. Standing in line at the counter were half a dozen men, two in conversation.

Honey studied their faces for a few minutes, then let her mind drift easily into thoughts of the future. She saw it as a long sunlit road strewn with prizes, each with her name written on it in tall, ineffaceable letters. The Flamingo was the first of the prizes, but farther along the road where the light pulsed and radiated were others that were bigger and more exciting. The Starlight Roof...The Coconut Grove...The Copacabana. She pictured herself at the Copacabana taking a bow to frenzied applause and afterwards sweeping into a dressing room – a large, sumptuously-furnished dressing room with a gold star on its door – filled with flowers and admirers.

She drank quickly. After three glasses of beer she changed her drink to whiskey.

When she was halfway through her fourth measure, a man came in and joined the two men who were in conversation at the bar. He was tall and slim and aged about fifty. He had a full head of wiry hair and a broad, short nose. He wore a reefer jacket, the right sleeve of which swung loose below the elbow. From time to time he turned to look at Honey. Honey met his looks and at the fifth look smiled.

The man came over to her and said: "Care for a drink?"

Honey held up her glass. "Scotch. Thanks."

The man went to the bar and after a few moments returned with two glasses – one containing whiskey – and a bottle of beer, the bottle carried in his jacket pocket. "Mind if I sit down?"

"Be my guest."

The man set the glasses and bottle on the table, pulled up a battered chair and sat down. "I got to say this – " He poured beer into his glass and took a swallow. "You've got the best pair of handles I've ever seen."

Honey said: "You think so?"

"I ain't never seen anything like 'em." He put down his glass, reached across the table and cupped Honey's right breast.

Honey did not pull back.

"That's some piece of cargo you're carrying," the man said.

Honey smiled. "How'd you come to lose your arm."

The man withdrew his hand and glanced at his right sleeve. "I got it caught in a tug wire." He took another swallow of beer. "Wanna see something?"

Honey nodded.

The man shrugged off his jacket and let it fall to the back of his chair.

Beneath the jacket he wore a blue short-sleeved shirt that was stained with sweat.

The arm had been amputated just below the elbow so that enough of the forearm remained to take an artificial limb.

"Watch this," the man said. He extended the stump towards

Honey, and, working the elbow joint, made the end piece jump convulsively. "How d'you like it?"

"I like it," Honey said.

The man repeated the movement.

Honey reached across the table and ran her hand over the stump.

"That feels good," the man said.

"Feels good to me, too," Honey said. She grasped the end piece. "Make it move again," she said.

The mutilated arm jerked into life.

"Some women go crazy for it," the man said softly.

"I bet," Honey said.

"How'd you like to try it for size?"

"Where can we go?" Honey said.

"There's a parking lot out back that ain't used much."

They finished their drinks.

As they were leaving, Honey, taking hold of the man's good arm, said: "Why don't you bring your pals along."

CHAPTER 13

Wracked by a feeling of betrayal, Henry lifted the receiver of the telephone in his study and dialled the number of his lawyer and friend of many years, Milburn Pool.

"Milburn," he said when he was put through, "I have to see you immediately. It's Jessica. She...She's ..." but he couldn't continue, he burst into tears.

A half hour later, seated in Pool's walnut-panelled office, Henry broke into tears again, and it was only when Pool said in a harsh voice: "For God's sake, Henry, get a grip on yourself" that he was able to blurt out the reason for them:

He had awoken in the middle of the night, and hearing noises coming from beneath the bedclothes – "dis*gusting* noises, Milburn" – he had thrown them back – and found Jessica with her face buried in Sonny's groin. "In his *groin*, Milburn. Jessica was...She was ..." He had dragged her from the bed, slapped her face – "It was covered with perspiration, Milburn" – and ordered her from the room. "She threw herself on me and begged my forgiveness, but I couldn't even *look* at her, let alone forgive her." Henry wiped tears from his cheeks with the tips of his fingers. "I hate her, Milburn."

Pool, tall, silver haired with a small beaked nose, did not reply immediately: it took him a minute or two to digest his good fortune. He had been practicing law for thirty years and in that time had never received the publicity his ego so badly craved. He placed the blame for this on the cases he handled; they were not what newspapers call 'good copy' (reports of minor accidents and insurance claims do not make for increased readership). Now his name would be in every newspaper in the country. He looked into Henry's red-rimmed eyes and saw the headline: *Husband Names Boy, 12, As Wife's Lover.* He wanted to shout *Hooray!*

"You have got to be strong about this, Henry." he said when the headline had faded. "You have to *divorce* Jessica. If you stay married to that" – he paused and grimaced – "to that woman, and it got out that she had had sexual congress – in *your* bed and in *your* presence – with a minor – a minor in *your* care – " He broke off. "How long has this been going on? Do you know?" Henry shook his head. "No matter. If it got out that she had had sexual congress in *your* bed and in *your* presence with a minor in *your* care, you would be seen to have con*doned* the act. You would be seen to be some kind of pervert. It would ruin you, Henry."

Henry bowed his head and thought of his position at Staley's. At last, looking up, he said: "I guess you're right, Milburn." He got to his feet and moved to the door. "I guess you're right."

As soon as Henry was gone, Pool drew up the divorce paper, sealed it in an envelope addressed to Jessica, and instructed his clerk to deliver it that afternoon. "Make sure that whoever receives it, signs for it," he ordered. He wanted everything watertight.

* * *

The envelope was received by Millie.

She took it into the kitchen, and after giving Sonny his lunch (Sonny having complained to Henry of a head cold that morning had been allowed to miss school), carried it upstairs to Jessica.

Jessica lay on a four-poster bed in the main guest room.

"This has just come from Milburn Pool's office," Millie said, extending the envelope.

Jessica turned on her side, away from Millie. The shame she felt made her want to hide her face.

"Ain't you gonna see what it is?"

Jessica was silent.

Millie placed the envelope on the bedside table and said, "Ain't you feelin' well?" She had asked the question earlier when she had brought Jessica her breakfast and had had it waved away.

"I'm all right, Millie. I just want to be left alone."

"Can I get you anything?"

"No thank you."

"You know Sonny's got a cold – least, that's what he says – and ain't gone to school?" Millie said.

"Please, Millie!" Jessica beat the bed with her fist.

"Okay, I'm going, I'm going," Millie said. "I'm not *that* dumb I don't know when I'm not wanted."

She returned to the kitchen and found Sonny tapping at a slice of chicken breast with his fork. "Don't play with it, eat it," she said brusquely.

"I've no appetite," Sonny said fretfully.

"I've no appetite," Millie mimicked. "You don't sound like you got a cold to *me*."

"Perhaps I have, perhaps I haven't."

Millie chopped chives. "Your aunt Jessica ain't well today, so I don't want you making a noise round the house."

"Henry is angry with her," Sonny said.

"I don't want to hear about that," Millie lied.

"About what she was doing to me last night," Sonny went on.

Millie continued to chop. After a while she said in a casual tone: "What d'you mean, what she was doing to you last night?"

"Henry found her kissing me."

Millie snorted and said: "So what's new about that? Your aunt does nothing *else* but kiss you. I've never known a child kissed so much. One of these days you'll be kissed clean away."

"She was kissing my delight."

Millie stopped chopping, and in a faintly bemused, faintly troubled voice said: "Kissing your what?"

"My delight. That's what Henry calls it. *He* kisses it, too."

Millie felt a stirring in her stomach. "And what might your de*light* be?"

Sonny stroked the chicken breast with his fork. "My dangle," he said carelessly.

It was a word Millie had taught him as a three-year-old. She had used it when bathing him (a duty Jessica had relieved her of (without explanation) a few days after her second visit to Dr Schneider).

"Kissing your dangle? You know what you're saying, Sonny? You know what happens to boys who tell lies?"

"It's true," Sonny said. "It happens all the time." He paused. "I don't mind."

Millie thought: Yes, it *is* true. Sonny doesn't lie. He's a little no-good, but he doesn't lie. She recalled an incident she had witnessed last summer: Jessica, picnicking with Sonny in the garden, had asked him: "Do you love me, Sonny?" and Sonny, absently and looking off into the distance, had replied: "Not really."

She worked again at the chives and pictured Jessica in bed with Sonny. She saw Jessica's mouth on the boy, on his sex, and abruptly and without warning her opinion of Jessica changed. She had always been reasonably fond of Jessica (Jessica, unlike Henry, never raised her voice and was always civil when issuing instructions), but at the same time she had despised her for her timidity, for allowing herself to be subordinated by Henry. No longer. Now she saw Jessica as an heroic figure, a woman of reckless passion; a debaucher who, in the presence of her husband, had hurled caution to the wind (with both hands, it seemed to Millie) and taken as a lover a twelve-year-old boy – a boy who was as close to her as any son could be. Perhaps it was the appeal that incest held for Millie (from an early age she had desired her eldest brother Clarence – Clarence who could touch the tip of his nose with his tongue) that gave her this new depth of feeling; though the idea of an over-intimate relationship with her *own* son made her hair rise. He was much too ugly.

"What else she…What else they do?" she asked.

* * *

On her third day in the guest room Jessica opened the envelope, read its contents, leaned over the side of the bed, and vomited copiously.

She had been married to Henry for twenty-two years, and although during the last five of them they had grown increasingly apart, they still displayed a protectiveness towards each other which made life tolerable. A winter chill in Henry would always be met with a fuss of hot water bottles, and Jessica's frequent headaches never failed to draw from Henry a *Can-I-get-you-anything?* Jessica had once asked herself what answer she would give if God or the Pope or her best friend Verna Lugmann were to ask her: "Tell me, dear, are you happy with Henry?" and she had decided that it would be: "No, but neither am I *un*happy with him." She felt secure with Henry, protected by him. Now that security and protection were about to be taken away.

She wiped a dribble of bile from her mouth with her night handkerchief. She deserved this punishment, she told herself. Henry was *right* to divorce her. What she had done was horrible. She had corrupted a child, taken advantage of a child's innocence to satisfy her lust, and she had betrayed her husband, betrayed him in his own bed – Henry who had provided for her for twenty-two years. She was depraved; a seducer of children; a deceitful, wicked wife. She beat herself with the words Henry had beaten her with: Disgusting. Filthy. Slut. (It did not matter to her that Henry had ignored her sexual needs, that Sonny had taken her hand in bed and guided it to that part of his body which she had come to find so irresistible; she would allow herself no excuses.) "I must leave here," she said aloud.

She rose, dressed and packed a case. She had no idea where she would go. Away from Henry and Sonny and her friends, especially away from her friends: they would soon learn of the divorce and the incident that had led to it; it would be impossible to face them. Jessica broke out in a cold sweat as her mind's eye saw Connie van Lodz and the others at the weekly bridge party. First there would be a hushed discussion of the matter, then the dirty talk would start. Jessica heard Connie van Lodz say: "The next time Sonny comes round, it'll be *me* who plays with him, not Carly!" She pressed home the clips of the case and went downstairs.

In the study, she sat at the heavy redwood desk that was Henry's reward for fifteen years of sickness-free service with Staley's and wrote on a leaf of her lilac notepaper: *Dear Henry, I am going away. I understand your feelings. Of course we cannot remain married. I will let you know my address (for legal purposes) once I am settled. Forgive me. Jessica.*

She searched for an envelope, but could not find one, so she placed the note unfolded in the housekeeping ledger where Henry would see it when he made that day's entry. She noticed that recorded among the previous day's entries was the purchase of a bottle of hair tonic. Poor Henry, she thought, still concerned about his hair, still feeding it with lotions.

From the study she went to the kitchen. Through the half open door she saw Millie seated at the table, drinking from a mug. She listened at the door for a minute and when she was certain that Millie was alone, that Sonny wasn't with her, she put down her case and went in.

Millie looked up and smiled warmly.

"Like some coffee?" she said. "It's fresh made."

Jessica smiled weakly and shook her head. "No thank you. No, I…" She faltered. She hadn't rehearsed her words to Millie and she puzzled that Millie was looking at her with such interest – looking *into* her rather than at her. It piled up the fog in her brain. "Millie, I have to go away for a while. I don't know exactly for how long; or where I shall be staying. I'll write to you once I have an address – in case I need anything."

"You don't look in much of a condition for travelling," Millie said.

"I'm perfectly well, Millie," Jessica lied. Her legs and arms were dead weights and her eyes seemed not to be focussing as they should.

There was a silence between them.

After a while, Millie said: "Mister Lansbury know you're going?"

"Well, of course he knows," replied Jessica, quickly. "Do you think I would leave without telling him? Heavens, Millie, of course he knows."

"Ain't you takin' anything with you?"

Jessica gestured limply towards the door. "I have a case outside," she said.

Millie took a sip of coffee and said: "What about Sonny?"

Jessica felt a lump grow in her throat. She looked abstractedly around the kitchen. When she was able to speak, she said: "Sonny?" She paused. "He'll be in safe hands with you and Mister Lansbury."

Millie thought: In *my* hands he will, in Henry Lansbury's I ain't so sure.

Jessica gave a weak smile. "Well, Millie, I must be going. Do take good care of things while I'm away. Do make sure" – her eyes misted over – "that Sonny isn't cruel to his rats."

Millie stood up. "You got a cab?"

"Oh, dear – " Jessica put a hand to her brow as the oversight registered.

"You want me to call one?"

"Oh, if you would, Millie; I quite forgot." She had also, she realised, forgotten to provide herself with money.

While Millie telephoned for a taxi she went back into the study and from a drawer in the redwood desk took out Henry's cash box. From a second drawer she took a key that had been hidden beneath brown lining paper. She opened the box and saw that it contained five one-hundred-dollar bills. She took two hundred dollars and returned the box and the key to their places. Next she opened the housekeeping ledger and added to the note she had written: *I have taken two hundred dollars for living expenses, which I shall repay as soon as I am able to find work.*

She read what she had just written, and felt despair. What work would she find? She had no skills, no training. She closed the ledger and went back into the kitchen.

"You've got five minutes, if you want a coffee," Millie said.

"No thank you, Millie," Jessica said.

They were silent.

After a while Jessica went to the window and gazed out. Among a scattering of leaves on the lawn she saw one of her silk squares. Sonny, she remembered, had asked her for it to use as a shroud for a dead rat (although Sonny treated his rats cruelly, he always gave them a decent burial), and at her refusal he had snatched it from her neck and run with it from the house. A breeze caught and rippled it, and Jessica saw it as she saw herself – a wretched, soiled thing, vulnerable and exposed.

She turned from the window and said: "When you have a moment, Millie, perhaps you'll fetch my silk square from the garden. I must have dropped it when I was pruning the dogwood last week."

Millie said: "I'll do that."

There was the sound of a car horn and Jessica said: "The cab's here."

* * *

When Jessica had been gone a week, Henry, as he was leaving for work, summoned Millie to his study and told her that his wife would not be returning.

He went on: "Before you hear it second-hand, I might as well tell you: Mrs Lansbury and I have decided to separate. Something has come between us which makes it impossible for us to continue living together. We are to be divorced."

The words came as a surprise to Millie. From the talk she had had with Sonny, it hadn't been too difficult to guess the reason for Jessica's departure; but she hadn't considered the possibility of divorce; she had assumed that after a period of contrition Jessica would return, and their lives – Jessica's and Henry's – would, with a change in sleeping arrangements, carry on where they had left off. She said: "I'm sorry to hear that, Mr Lansbury."

Sonny suddenly appeared in the doorway, and Henry, seeing a concerned look come into Millie's eyes, said: "It's all right, Sonny knows." He went on: "I've had a letter from Mrs Lansbury asking that you take a few of her things to her. I have a list here." He drew from his pocket a piece of paper and handed it to Millie. "I've written the address on the back. It's just a few clothes she requires. I'll be sending on the rest of her things later."

Millie studied the list, then turned the paper over and studied the address – and felt a rush of pity for Jessica. She knew the district as a place of run-down houses and second-hand furniture shops and guessed how someone of Jessica's sensitivity would hate living there. She looked at Henry and had an impulse to say: 'You're as guilty as she is, you slippery little hypocrite. You've been messin' with the boy, too.' In a cold voice, she said: "I'll see that she gets them."

Henry took out his wallet, opened it, and withdrew a ten-dollar bill. "You'll need your cab fare," he said. "It's quite a distance, but this should take care of it." He handed Millie the bill and turned to Sonny. In a Western drawl, he said: "Shouldn't you be saddlin' up for school, old timer?"

"Do I have to?" Sonny asked irritably.

"Do you have to what, pardner?"

"Go to school, of course!"

In a serious voice, Henry said: "You've been absent for a week now, Sonny, and that's not good. If you fall too far behind, you'll never catch up."

Sonny made a face and looked abruptly away. Henry turned back to Millie and said: "I'll call in on the van Lodzs on my way to the office and have Mrs van Lodz pick the boy up."

Millie looked at him uncertainly and said: "What if Mrs van Lodz asks after Mrs Lansbury? What do I tell her?"

"Don't worry about that," Henry said. "The van Lodzs know the situation. I felt it best to tell them. They are our friends and it would have been wrong not to." He added after a small pause: "They would have found out, anyway." He moved to the door and said to Sonny: "Adios, amigo."

Sonny fluttered his lashes, gave a coy smile, and in a voice that sounded exactly like that of Shirley Temple aged six said: "Please, Sweets. Please let Sonny stay home today."

Henry laughed appreciatively and said: "I'm sorry, Sonny, but Millie has to go out, and we caint have a young critter like you left alone in the house all day. I hear tell there's a Sioux raidin' party in the vicinity."

Sonny slammed out of the room, and Henry, smiling after him, murmured to Millie: "*I'll* bathe the boy tonight."

CHAPTER 14

Jessica said: "Here, let *me* take that." She was wearing a black twin-set and black skirt, and it occurred to her that with her pink-tinged eyes she must look as if she was in mourning.

Millie glanced around the room and handed her the Gladstone bag she was carrying.

"Sit down and rest," Jessica said. "You must be tired after the climb up those stairs."

She tried to make her voice sound bright saying this: she did not want Millie to feel sorry for her, to think that she minded living in an apartment that had stained wallpaper and a thin carpet and windows that hadn't been washed in heaven knows how long. She placed the bag on an ancient couch and said: "Would you like some tea? I was just about to make some. Or coffee? I've coffee if you'd prefer it." She felt a little disorientated: she had gotten used to silence, to being on her own.

"Tea'll do fine," Millie said. She unbuttoned her coat and sat on one of two high-backed chairs that stood at a scarred oval dining table.

Jessica left the room and a few minutes later returned with two ugly white cups on thick blue saucers. She handed one to Millie and said: "It's a little strong, I'm afraid. I forgot to get more milk in."

Millie said: "It looks good."

Jessica sat at the table, smiled and said: "It's so nice to see you again, Millie. I've missed you." She raised her cup to her lips. "It hasn't been very…" She tried to stop her smile from faltering. "It's been rather…I haven't been…" She felt her eyes brim with sudden tears, and she put down her cup.

After a moment, Millie said angrily: "What you doin' livin' in a place like this? Go back to your home. Come back with me."

In a dull voice, Jessica said: "I can't Millie. It's not possible. Something has… You don't understand. I can't explain."

A few seconds went by, then Millie said gently: "I know all about it, Mrs Lansbury. Sonny told me."

Jessica felt panic sweep through her. She half rose from her chair, but Millie got to her feet and placed a hand on her arm and she sat heavily down again.

"I know about the divorce, too," Millie went on. "Mister Lansbury told me about it this mornin'." She added: "Maybe it ain't right what went on between you and Sonny, but the way I see it, Mister Lansbury ain't in no position to be divorcin' anyone. He's been with the boy too."

Jessica furrowed her brow, doubting she had heard correctly. "Mister Lansbury and Sonny?"

"It's true," Millie said. "Sonny told me. And Sonny don't tell lies. You know he don't."

Jessica said dazedly: "No, Sonny doesn't tell lies. He never lies. But..." She looked at Millie with an expression of baffled anguish. "Are you quite sure?"

"Sonny told me hisself," Millie said.

Jessica shook her head and turned away. "Henry and Sonny? I just can't – " She shook her head again, as if by doing so the words would register, or at least make some progress towards registering. "It's too – " Suddenly there were voices clamouring in her brain and they all seemed to be railing at Henry and telling her what a fool she had been. "Bastard, bastard, bastard", one of the more disturbing voices kept repeating. Another said: "He reviled you, left you flailing in a mess of shame and embarrassment and all the while – " She looked at the thin carpet and the mildewed wallpaper and simultaneously felt hate, contempt and pity – hate and contempt for Henry, pity for herself. "Why are you telling me this, Millie?" she asked emptily.

"I don't know," Millie said. "I guess I just don't like seein' you takin' all the blame. It don't seem fair."

Jessica thought: It *isn't* fair. Henry is as guilty as I am, but he's not living in this mean apartment with its worn-out furniture and execrable pictures (two yellowing prints; both in the bedroom and both of stampeding bison); he's not alone; he's not without money and friends. A blurred vision of Connie van Lodz's face appeared, and a quick, uneasy question occurred to her. She asked: "Does anyone else know? About..."

In a quiet voice, Millie said: "The van Lodzs. I think Mr Lansbury may've told the van Lodzs."

"Oh God!" Jessica jumped to her feet and began beating her thighs with her fists. "Oh, no!" In the time she had spent in the apartment she had conditioned herself into accepting that her friends would learn of the divorce and that after discovering the reason for it would ostracise her, become her enemies, but she had supposed they would get their information second hand, not first hand from Henry. Even though her marriage was over, she still expected a degree of loyalty from Henry: their years together *had* to count for *some*thing. But no; he had denounced her.

"Oh no!" She wanted to tear at her hair and scream imprecations from an open window, as she had seen bereaved Arab women do in newsreel pictures. To her astonishment she heard herself cry: "Bastard! You fucking bastard, Henry!" She covered her face with her hands and sobbed.

Millie went to her and guided her back to her chair. "That's good," she murmured. "That's good. Cry it out."

Jessica continued to weep for a minute, then stopped abruptly and said: "He's not going to get away with it, Millie. I won't let him. I'll make that – I'll make him suffer as I've suffered."

Her voice, although faint, was extraordinarily steady.

CHAPTER 15

As he waited to be put through, Henry read again the part of the letter that had made him feel that something small and icy and alien was moving among his intestines: *My client cites as the third party one Sonny Bunn, a male minor in your charge.*

The letter had arrived with two circulars and he had opened it when he was half way through his breakfast of scrambled eggs.

He hadn't finished his breakfast; he had stared at the letter for a time, then gone to the telephone and dialled Milburn Pool's office.

Now Pool's voice said: "Hello, Pool speaking."

"Milburn, this is Henry."

"Oh, hello, Henry. How are you? Isn't this grand weather we're having. I was just remarking to old man – "

"Look, Milburn," Henry interrupted, "I want you to halt the divorce proceeding. I've decided not to go through with it. I want you to write to Jessica informing her of this."

"What? But – " Pool's voice had dropped a few notches. "But, Henry, you can't do that. I mean – I mean, it would be unwise. As I told you, if ever it got out that – "

"I don't care about that, Milburn. *I don't want to go through with the divorce.*"

There was a small pocket of silence, then Pool in a voice that sounded thick with disappointment said: "I'm sorry to hear this Henry, *extremely* sorry – and surprised – " His voice picked up slightly, as if he were clutching at straws " – yes, surprised – that you are prepared to allow the child to be put at risk from Jessica again. Have you thought about Sonny, Henry, and the moral danger he'll be exposed to? It could damage his whole life. You really should think most carefully before – "

"That will be taken care of," Henry said quickly.

After a further silence, Pool said: "What made you change your mind?"

Henry said: "It was a difficult decision, but Jessica and I have been married a long time. It would be wrong to throw all those years away. The marriage should be given a second chance." Before Pool could reply, he went on: "I'd appreciate it if you would get the letter out today."

He read over Jessica's address, replaced the receiver and went back to his breakfast. He tried a mouthful of scrambled egg, but it was cold, so he pushed the plate away.

A week later Pool contacted Henry at his office to say that he had received a letter from Jessica's lawyer – "from Jessica's *lawyer*, Henry" – informing him that Jessica intended to proceed with her action. "With her *action*, Henry! Jessica is *cross-petitioning*!"

Henry did not answer. He closed his eyes and wished he was somewhere else.

"Are you there, Henry?"

"Yes, Milburn, yes. Now listen, this is what I want you to do. You must write to Jessica's lawyer and tell him that I am desirous of a reconcilliation. Tell them – him – that I acted hastily." He hesitated. "Point out that I am still very much in love with my wife."

"Henry, did you hear what I said? I said Jessica is cross-petitioning. Henry, *what is going on?*"

"Milburn, please do as I ask."

Next day Henry did something he had never done before: at lunchtime he went into a bar and had a glass of whiskey. He did the same the following day, and when on Friday Pool again contacted him and in a cheerful voice told him that Jessica had rejected his request for a reconcilliation, he went into the bar and had *two* glasses of whiskey.

From the bar he telephoned his office to say he would be late in returning from lunch. Then he drove to the apartment hotel where Jessica was staying.

He did not leave his car immediately, but sat for four or five minutes absorbing the building's decrepitude. He noticed the broken limestone steps leading to the door, and the neglected window frames, and, moving lower in his seat, he saw that high up and to the left of a set of windows hung with torn, dun-colored curtains some kind of plant had rooted itself in a gap in the brickwork.

He stepped from the car and walked briskly up the steps of the building and into its vestibule.

The vestibule had green stone floor-tiles ingrained with dirt, and heavy fuscous wallpaper that was broken in places and marked in others by large patches of damp. An overpowering, unhealthy smell came from somewhere. As he climbed the stairs he wondered how anyone could possibly live in such a place.

He found Jessica's apartment without difficulty and pressed the buzzer.

The door opened, and he said: "Hello, Jessica."

Jessica stared at him without answering.

As casually as he could, he said: "May I come in?"

"No," Jessica said curtly.

"It's important."

Jessica was silent, and Henry thought: She looks strong and straight and purposeful. He said: "Please, Jessica."

"No."

His tone became authoritative. "Jessica, this is silly. Let me in."

Again she was silent.

Henry looked anxiously around the hallway, then, in a much softer voice and leaning forward slightly, said: "I want you back, Jessica. I behaved badly. Please come back. We can forget what has happened." Solemnly, almost accusingly, he added: "I love you, Jessica."

Jessica closed the door in his face.

* * *

He returned the following day and told Jessica what Pool had told him – that if she went ahead with the divorce, there was a strong possibility of child corruption charges being brought against them. But Jessica was unmoved.

He made one further visit – on the eve of the divorce proceeding, and when Jessica told him to go away, he dropped to his knees in the hallway.

"Look, I'm on my knees," he cried, patting them with his palms. "See, Jessica, I'm begging you on my knees! Don't go through with the divorce Jessica!"

Jessica walked past him, down the stairs and into the street.

CHAPTER 16

The temperature according to the radio station's weather announcer was the lowest of the year, but even so, Henry could feel sweat breaking out on his face: the man approaching him held a camera and he knew with terrible certainty that he was a newspaper photographer.

He had got to the courthouse early to waylay Jessica before she entered the building. He would, he had decided, make one final appeal to her; if necessary go down on his knees again. He had been waiting half an hour.

"Mr Lansbury? Henry Lansbury?"

"Why, yes, but – " Before Henry had time to shield his face the man focussed his camera on him and pressed the shutter button.

"Hey, wait a minute!" Henry ran forward. "Please!" He took out his wallet. "Here…Here's twenty dollars. Take it – only please don't publish the picture."

"I'm sorry, Mr Lansbury, I can't do that," the photographer said. He was tall, balding and wore a tartan windcheater. Henry thought he looked a little seedy.

"Look, I'll make it fifty. A hundred!"

"I'm sorry, Mr Lansbury."

"I beg you – " Henry looked wildly around, and to his relief saw Milburn Pool step from a taxi. "Milburn!" He hurried towards him. "Milburn…This man" – he pointed frantically in the direction of the photographer – "is a newspaperman. He has taken my picture. For God's sake do something!"

Pool, his nose red with cold, said comfortingly: "Now calm down, Henry."

"But, Milburn, don't you understand – this man has – "

"All right, Henry," Pool said. "Wait here. I'll see what I can do."

Henry watched Pool converse (conspiratorially, it seemed to him) with the photographer for a few minutes, then saw him nod in the direction of the road and the photographer move off and converge, camera poised, on a car which had pulled up and out of which was stepping Jessica. A small round-faced man carrying a brief-case was holding open the door for her.

"Jessica!" Henry sprinted past the photographer and took hold of her arm. "Jessica, I have to talk with you." He tried to pull her to one side, but she stood her ground. "Jessica, don't do this to me. Don't go through with it. Jessica, please…" But Jessica, her mouth set in a rigid, barely discernible smile, removed his hand from her arm and walked quickly away and into the courthouse, the man with the brief-case (her lawyer, Henry dully guessed) following a pace behind. A moment later Henry heard Pool say: "Come, Henry, let's go in." Aware of Pool linking his arm into his, of the photographer aiming his camera at them, of a man in a trenchcoat holding a spiral-bound reporter's notebook appearing from somewhere, Henry, as if in a dream, moved slowly towards the heavy doors of the courthouse. "Oh God," he said silently.

Inside the courtroom a sonorous voice called: "All rise!" and a second later the Judge hurried in, his robes swirling about him and disturbing a bar of pale sunlight that came from a transom in the ceiling and fell on Milburn Pool's head.

The judge was tall and gaunt and had small hard eyes overhung with black spiky eyebrows. He nodded perfunctorily and seated himself at his bench.

Pool and Jessica's lawyer went forward to confer with him, and after a while, after documents had been produced and the Judge's eyebrows had merged into what seemed to Henry to be a furious scowl, the lawyers stepped back.

Suddenly Jessica's lawyer was speaking: "Sonny…same bed… carnal knowledge … several years…their help's signed testament…"

There was a short silence, then the Judge beckoned Henry to step forward.

After a moment's hesitation, Henry approached the bench.

"Mr Pool informs me that you instituted, but later withdrew, divorce proceedings against your wife, naming as the third party in your petition the child that is named in your wife's petition?"

"Yes, your Honour," Henry said. "I wanted to – "

The judge waved the words away and beckoned to Jessica.

Jessica, her chin raised and her eyes steady, took a position alongside Henry.

To both of them, the judge said: "This is without doubt a most disgusting story. In the twenty years that I have been on the divorce circuit I have never before had to preside over anything quite so" – he faltered – "*unspeakable*." Without pausing, he said to Jessica: "Is this your signature?" and held an affidavit towards her.

Jessica studied it for a moment and in a ringing voice said: "Yes, it is."

"And do you, as this paper states, agree that your marriage has irretrievably broken down?"

"Yes," Jessica said.

"I have to tell you," the judge said, his eyes switching from one to the other, "that I intend personally to acquaint the District Attorney's office with the facts of this proceeding and urge that you both be investigated under the terms contained in the Prevention of Child Corruption Act. I also intend to see that the child, Sonny Bunn, is immediately placed in the care of the State's Welfare Department." He paused, then added: "If I had *my* way, you both would be standing here in chains." Rising, he said: "The divorce application is granted."

Henry thought: I am ruined.

Jessica thought: I will gladly accept whatever punishment is given to me.

Milburn Pool thought of the trial to come and of the extra newspaper publicity it would bring him. He saw a new headline: *Husband And Wife Shared Boy Lover, 12,* and had difficulty in suppressing a titter.

CHAPTER 17

For her marriage to Calvino, Honey had her hair lightened to near platinum blonde and fashioned into corkscrew curls. She wore a cerise suit, a wide-brimmed hat of pink straw, and cerise shoes.

Calvino wore a light blue suit, a pale-yellow shirt, and a silver-blue tie.

The marriage took place at the Two Hearts Wedding Parlour on Biloxi Heights and was attended by Calvino's mother, Frank Lever, Mastrioni, and a plump brown-haired boy, who throughout the ceremony held Mastrioni's hand.

Afterwards the party drove in two cars to La Busola, a small restaurant in Little Italy which, together with its one musician – a violinist – Calvino had commandeered for the day.

They were greeted by the proprietor, a small, round man with an imperfectly-trimmed black moustache, who, with low sweeping gestures, ushered them to a table covered with a white cloth.

Honey and Calvino sat with Calvino's mother on one side of the table, and Lever, Mastrioni and the boy on the other.

"I bring in the food in a couple of minutes," the proprietor said and went off.

They settled themselves, and Calvino poured wine from a caráfe. As he filled Honey's glass he glanced at her and smiled. He smiled at his mother. "It went well, didn't it, Momma?" he said.

Mrs Calvino shrugged. "It wen' okay, you don' min' a preacher keep scratchin' his nuts," she said

Honey laughed.

"Momma!" Calvino closed his eyes in exasperation. "Cut the language." He looked at Mastrioni and shook his head apologetically.

Mastrioni gave Calvino a smile which said: *It ain't important. I unnerstand. It ain't your fault your mother she's a slob.*

The boy said to Mastrioni: "Can I have ice-cream?"

Mastrioni looked at him and murmured: "Sure, sure."

Calvino's mother said to Mastrioni: "Tha's a nice boy you got there, Mr Mastrioni. Real priddy."

Mastrioni nodded appreciatively.

"Tommy here" – Mrs Calvino smiled briefly at her son – "looked a liddle like him as a kid. Same mowt." She said to the boy: "Wha's youse name, sweedheart?"

The boy said: "Harold, but Sylvano calls me Harry."

In a surprised voice Calvino's mother said: "Sylvano? Ain't Mr Mastrioni youse farder?" She looked at Mastrioni for confirmation.

"Momma!" Calvino said angrily.

"Tha's all right, Tommy," Mastrioni said. To Calvino's mother he said: "He's a little friend of mine." He touched the boy's cheek. "Ain't you, Harry?"

The boy smiled at him without replying.

There was a small, awkward silence, then Honey said to the boy: "I got a kid about your age, Harry. A little younger may – " She broke off abruptly and turning to Calvino, said excitedly: "Hey, you realise something? You realise you're a daddy now?" She laughed stridently and tugged at Calvino's arm. "Remember I told you about Sonny, my kid? You're his daddy now!" Before Calvino could reply, she leaned across the table to Mastrioni and in a stage whisper said: "I got this kid, Sylvano, who's got a tube that ain't real. Sylvano, you've never seen a kid with a tube like my kid's got. It's a hosepipe!" She laughed explosively.

Mastrioni smiled minutely and sipped his wine. He placed the glass on the table. "You got a little boy, Honey?" he said sweetly. He picked up a linen napkin, unfolded it and punctiliously wiped his mouth. "How old you say your boy is?"

"I dunno, twelve, thirteen maybe," Honey said. "The last time I saw him was when he was six and that was back in – " She turned to Calvino. "When was it, baby?"

Calvino shook his head.

Honey thought for a moment, then said: "I guess it has to be six years since I last seen him." She turned to Lever, who was studying a menu, and said: "Six years, Frank? Remember I told you I bought him a baseball bat for his birthday?"

"About six years, I'd say," Lever said.

"He's got to be some good-lookin' kid if he takes after his momma," Mastrioni said. He folded the napkin and tossed it on to the table.

"He's a knockout," Honey said.

Mastrioni looked at Calvino. "You ain't never told me Honey's got a kid, Tommy," he said evenly.

Calvino shifted uneasily in his chair. "I guess I forgot," he said.

"Where's the boy now, Honey?" Mastrioni asked, his voice sweet again.

"I got him with an aunt and uncle in Boston."

"And you don't never see him?"

"Last time was six years ago, on his sixth birthday."

The boy said: "Can I have ice-cream, Sylvano?"

Mastrioni, without looking at the boy, said: "Shuddup." He sipped his wine contemplatively. After a few moments he looked at Honey and the others and addressing them, said: "You know, Tommy here's like a son to me." He smiled at Calvino's mother. "You don't mind me sayin' that do you, Mrs Calvino? You ain't offended by what I say?"

Calvino's mother shrugged.

"Good." Mastrioni nodded a few times as if judiciously cogitating, then went on: "Like I said, Tommy here's like a son to me and when a son marries, then the wife she becomes like a daughter." He reached across and touched Honey's hand. "And if the daughter happens to have a kid, then the kid he becomes like a gran'child. That makes sense, don' it?" He looked at each of them in turn. "Sure it does. The little kid becomes like a gran'child. Tha's the way things are. Tha's the way they always bin." He looked at Calvino. "I ain't never had a gran'child, Tommy." He paused. "Now I got one." He fractionally narrowed his eyes. "I'd sure as hell like to see my little gran'son, Tommy."

The message registered and Calvino turned to Honey and said eagerly: "Hey, that'd be nice, baby. Why don't we have the kid come live with us?"

Honey looked at him incredulously and said: "Are you loco? What do I want with a kid? I got my work. Who's gonna look after him?"

Calvino said: "We can get a woman in." He glanced at Mastrioni who was smoothing the tablecloth with a fork, seemingly disinterested in what was going on.

Calvino touched Honey's cheek. "For *me*, baby," he crooned. He kissed her.

Honey said: "Are you serious?"

"Cross my heart, baby. I'd like to have the kid come live with us."

Honey studied his face for a sign of insincerity and not finding one jerked upright in her chair and said happily: "Okay, if that's what you want." She looked at Mastrioni and laughed. "Today, *any*thing goes." She kissed Calvino roughly and murmured: "Anything you want, lover."

Listening to the conversation, Lever felt a small weight lifted from his shoulders. The previous day, while having his hair trimmed, his barber, out of the blue, had handed him a newspaper with the words: "How d'you figure out something like this? A guy and his wife screwing with a twelve-year-old kid and all they get is six years. I'd have given 'em life."

Lever had read the report without interest, but a line in the third paragraph had stayed in his mind: *Lansbury, a chief executive with the giant Staley group…*Then he'd remembered Finn's words – "The kid'll be okay…the old man's a big shot with Staley's." The 'child' in the report had to be Sonny. From Sonny and the newspaper report, Lever's thoughts had gone to Honey and his ten per cent agent's fee. Honey's career was blossoming and if ever it became known that her son was living in a State welfare home she would be branded a callous, uncaring mother – and audiences did not take kindly to callous, uncaring mothers. But how could he persuade Honey to take the boy back? Honey liked her freedom; she would see him as an obstacle, a hindrance. Now, thanks to Mastrioni and Calvino, the problem was solved. "I've something to tell you concerning Sonny," he said to Honey.

"Sonny?"

"It'll keep," Lever said.

Before Honey could question him, Mastrioni said: "What you say your boy's name is, Honey?"

"Sonny," Honey said.

"Tha's a nice name," Mastrioni said. "When you gonna collect

Son – " he smiled and corrected himself – "my little gran'son?"

Honey took a swallow of wine. "I got a week to go at The Garden Room, then I got three weeks free before starting at the Pink Pencil." She turned to Calvino. "Maybe we can pick the kid up then?"

Calvino kissed her again and said: "Whatever you say, sugar." He smiled briefly at Mastrioni.

The proprietor came in carrying a tureen of spaghetti and placed it on the table.

The boy whispered to Mastrioni: "Can I have ice-cream?"

Mastrioni said to the proprietor: "Bring the kid a plate of ice-cream." He looked down at the boy and noticed for the first time a fine covering of hair on the boy's upper lip. He thought: If this kid's thirteen, then that ain't a dish of spaghetti I got in front of me, it's a bunch of fuckin' bananas. You'll do for the time bein', kid, but soon you gotta be replaced.

He said to the boy: "What you want, strawberry or vanilla-flavoured?"

"Both," the boy said firmly.

CHAPTER 18

They arrived in Boston just before midday and went by taxi to the Carlton Hotel, which Lever had recommended for its breakfasts and the comfort of its beds (he had once stayed there while negotiating a contract with a young illusionist who was appearing at the Boston Empire).

They registered, and after freshening themselves, took a second taxi to *The Boston Evening Herald* building, where Lever asked a uniformed receptionist for the Back Copies' office and was directed to a room at the end of a long, dimly lit corridor.

They went in and saw a tall, round-shouldered man of about sixty standing at a linoleum-covered table entering something in a ledger. After a minute the man looked up and in a piping voice said: "Yes, folks, what can I do for you?"

Lever said: "I'm interested in the Lansbury case. I'd be grateful for anything you have on it."

The man said tiredly: "The Lansbury case…Everybody wants to read about the Lansbury case." He coughed phlegmatically. "How many copies?"

"Just one," Lever said.

"Trial lasted three days. You want all three issues?"

"Yes; thanks," Lever said.

The man went away and returned five minutes later with a fold of newspapers. "Sixty cents," he said. "There's an extra charge for back numbers."

Lever gave him a dollar and told him to keep the change.

Outside, they opened the newspapers and stood reading them.

The report of the trial, together with pictures of Jessica and Henry, appeared on all three front pages.

Honey, as she studied the pictures, said: "They haven't changed much. Uncle Henry's lost a little weight, but apart from that …"

Lever said suddenly: "This is the guy we want – Pool." He folded his paper. "Let's get something to eat, I'm hungry."

They found a hamburger bar and went in. When they were seated, Honey said: "Jesus, who'd've believed it of Aunt Jessica? To look at her you wouldn't think she would know what it was for."

Calvino said: "When I was a kid, I always wanted to get laid by a married dame."

"Not by a guy, though, I bet," Honey said.

Calvino left this unanswered.

They ordered, and Lever said to the waitress: "Where can I find a lawyer by the name of Pool?"

"Pool as in the Lansbury case?"

"That's the one."

"You're practically sitting in his lap. Make a left leaving here, and his office is four doors along."

The waitress went away, and Honey said absently: "I feel kind of sorry for them."

"Jesus, they've been screwin' with your kid for Chrissake!" Calvino said.

Honey gave a throaty laugh and said: "I know, it's crazy!" Tapping a newspaper, she said to Lever: "The judge said Uncle Henry could've damaged Sonny's personality. What'd he mean by that?"

"He meant that Sonny could turn out to be a fruit."

Honey said: "The kid *is* kind of girlie." After a pause she said: "I ever tell you about this guy I worked with on a Templar picture? Jesus! what a faggot. Big black guy. Used to wear fur and paint his nails. The crew called him Queen Kong."

They ate their food and after they had drunk coffee and Calvino had paid the bill, they left.

A few minutes later they were in an outer office and Lever was saying to a silver-haired man in shirtsleeves standing over a woman at a desk: "Mr Pool?"

Pool looked Lever up and down. "Yes," he said, "but I'm afraid I can't see you right now. You'll have to make an appointment with my secretary here."

Lever, touching Honey's arm, said: "Mr Pool, this is the mother of the Lansbury boy."

Without a change of expression, Pool said: "Step into my office, won't you." To his secretary, he said: "I don't want to be interrupted."

In Pool's office, Lever gave their names, and when they were seated said to Pool: "Mrs Calvino is in Boston to collect her son."

Pool took some time to reply. Eventually he said: "The authorities will want proof of identity." He looked at Honey. "You have the boy's birth certificate?"

Honey said: "I never got around to getting one."

"Due to illness, Mrs Calvino was unable to register the birth," Lever invented.

Pool looked at Calvino. "Why didn't *you* register the birth? It's a legal requirement. You're the boy's father."

"Not me," Calvino said.

Pool furrowed his brow.

"He's the boy's stepfather," Lever explained. "Mr and Mrs Calvino were married just a few weeks ago."

"Where's the boy's father?" Pool asked Honey.

Honey raised her eyebrows and shrugged. "It happened when I was a kid," she said.

"Jessica Lansbury will identify Mrs Calvino as the boy's mother," Lever said.

Pool nodded. "I see. And *Henry* Lansbury?"

"No problem," Honey said.

Pool studied their faces and after he had pictured another newspaper headline – one that read: *Lawyer Reunites Lansbury Boy With His Mother* – he sat up suddenly and said: "This is what I propose we do."

CHAPTER 19

Henry's appearance had shocked them all. They had expected him to look as he had looked in the newspaper pictures taken of him at his trial. But no – his mouth had hung loose, and his eyes had had a hunted, vacant look. His hair – what was left of it – was bone white, and he had lost an alarming amount of weight. Also, signing the paper that Pool had drawn up, his hand had shaken. A prison guard had had to wipe his nose for him. Clearly he was a broken man.

Jessica, on the other hand, standing before them now in the office of Martha Rogerson, Superintendent of the Boston Penitentiary for Women, plainly was flourishing. Her eyes were bright and clear, and her skin (from spells of sunbathing in the prison's excercise yard) golden brown. Her posture spoke of self-confidence and her figure of many hours spent in a gymnasium lifting weights. Her hair had a high shine to it; it bounced a little when she moved.

"You look swell, Aunt Jessica," Honey said.

Thank you," Jessica said. "You look good, too, Honey."

"We just come from seeing Uncle Henry," Honey said.

Jessica lowered her eyes slightly and said: "I'm sorry, Honey. Forgive me."

Honey linked her arm with Calvino's and in a carefree tone said: "Forget it." She scratched beneath her left breast, causing Pool to frown. "How you making out?" she asked.

"It isn't so bad," Jessica said.

"Jessica is one of our model prisoners," Miss Rogerson said. She had iron-grey hair and wore a white cotton shirt, and a navy skirt that hugged her hips. "If every prisoner were like Jessica …" She sighed lavishly.

"I'm married now," Honey said to Jessica, and took a tighter hold on Calvino's arm.

"I'm happy for you, Honey," Jessica said. She smiled at Calvino. "For *both* of you," she amended.

"This is Frank Lever, my agent," Honey said, glancing at Lever.

Jessica and Lever exchanged nods.

Honey turned to Pool. "And this is – "

"I know Mr Pool," Jessica said in a slightly narrower tone.

"Jessica," Pool said, "Mrs Calvino has come from New York to collect Sonny from the welfare home. She would like to have Sonny live with her."

"I understand," Jessica said.

"But unfortunately Mrs Calvino failed to" – Pool paused – "was unable, because of health reasons, to register the boy's birth. We would like your signature recognising Mrs Calvino as the child's mother."

"Of course," Jessica said with precision.

"We have *Henry's* signature."

"Yes."

Pool unfastened the briefcase he was carrying and drew out a foolscap sheet of paper.

"Use my desk," Miss Rogerson said. She cleared a space and handed Jessica a pen.

"Miss Rogerson will witness the signature," Pool said.

Jessica wrote her name, and as she did so, felt a large knot of hurt begin to untie itself in her stomach. The knowledge that Sonny was in a welfare home hurt her deeply, hurt her to the point where she found it difficult to sleep at night, to concentrate on anything for longer than a minute or two. Her cellmate, Betty 'Butch' Gluttman, had repeatedly assured her that life in a welfare home was not too terrible (Betty had spent five years in one before escaping to take up bank robbery), but she had remained unconvinced.

She drew a line under her name and returned the pen to Miss Rogerson, a warm glow inside her. Soon, she told herself, Sonny would have a *proper* home, parents to take care of him (she hoped that Honey and her husband would be kind to him and was sure that they would; how could they *not* be kind to such a beautiful child?), a room to himself, a pet rat or two to keep him company on dark evenings. She sighed contentedly. Now she could rest easier at night. Now she could lie in Betty 'Butch' Gluttman's arms and pay full attention to Betty's whispered endearments.

CHAPTER 20

"And when momma's working, daddy and Gran'ma Calvino'll look after you – mostly Gran'ma Calvino. You'll like Gran'ma – she's a yell. And tomorrow daddy'll – " Honey broke off and squeezed Calvino's thigh. "Daddy here" – she laughed briefly – "'ll take you out and buy you something nice. Some clothes, maybe." She tugged at Sonny's velvet knickerbockers. "We can't have you looking like Little Molly Make-Believe, can we?" She laughed again and said: "How'd you like some blue jeans and sneakers?"

Sonny, seated opposite her in the Pullman compartment, was silent. He hadn't spoken, hadn't made a sound since the moment in the welfare home when Honey had put her face close to his and said: "Hi, baby, it's mommie come to c'llectya." He hated her; hated her size and sound and the vivid colors she wore; hated her coarseness (when straightening up after greeting him, something – a button or stitch – in her skirt had given and she had said violently: "Shit!"). He fixed his eyes on the yellow corkscrew curls that swung in rhythm with the train, and thought: "How is it possible that this hideous woman is my mother? Why haven't I a mother who wears lavender chiffon and speaks like a Henry James heroine?" In imagination he saw Jessica reading to him from *Washington Square,* heard her speak one of Catherine Sloper's lines – *It is useless for us to attempt to be friends.* He looked out of the window at the flat, unchanging landscape and pictured Jessica reading Henry James in a prison cell. He saw her through iron bars turning pages with unhappy hands, saw a tear fall and blur the words. He coughed to stifle a giggle.

Honey in mock surprise said: "Oh, so at least he can cough. At least I don't have a *total* dumb-dumb for a kid." She leaned forward. "Well, if you can cough, let's hear you *say* something. Let's, for instance, hear you say, 'Hello, Mommie', or 'Hello, Daddy', or 'Hi, Mr Lever.'"

Sonny continued to look out the window.

Honey glared at him. "Well, come on," she demanded.

Sonny remained silent.

To ease the tension, Lever said: "You know, Sonny, your mother's getting to be a real big name in the theatre. Your mother's a terrific entertainer. You didn't know that, I bet. She's what theatre people call an impressionist. She impersonates all the big movie stars, all the big *male* movie stars. Your mother's a very special impressionist."

Sonny turned slowly from the window and faced Lever. He looked at him coldly for a few moments, then opened his eyes wide and gave a pinched smile. In Bette Davis' clipped voice he said: "But dahling, what's so clever about that?"

Lever felt a movement in his stomach and in the hairs on the back of his neck. He glanced at Honey and saw that she was looking at Sonny with stunned disbelief.

Calvino said: "Bette Davis! Hey, that was great, Sonny."

Lever said to Sonny: "Where'd you learn to do that, Sonny?"

Sonny fluttered his eyelids and, again in Bette Davis's voice, said: "Why, at the movies of course, where else?"

Lever smiled and said: "Who else d'you do?"

Sonny glanced at Honey and smiled inwardly. The impersonation had hurt her, had hurt her deeply, he could tell. Well, he would hurt her again. He struck a superior pose – head raised, eyes narrowed – and said: "Why, I can do prac-ti-cally anyone I cay-er to."

Calvino said quickly: "Katharine Hepburn! Hey, waddayaknow!"

Honey, her neck beginning to redden, her lips compressed, said to Sonny: "Okay, Mister Smartass, now suppose you let us hear you say something in your *own* voice."

As if he hadn't heard, Sonny turned and gazed out the window.

"Hey, I'm talking to you."

Sonny stayed silent.

"Hey!" Honey reached across and poked Sonny's shoulder with her forefinger.

Still Sonny stayed silent.

Honey took hold of the front of his jacket and pulled him roughly towards her. Between her teeth she said: "Answer me, you little runt, or I'll kick your ass from here to next week."

Sonny looked at her, and without emotion said: "Take your hands off me, you fat, ugly cow." His voice had a depth and mellifluence to it that made Lever think: "I bet he does a great Joan Crawford."

Honey said: "Why you – " and swung her arm.

Sonny had only once before been hit – by a boy at the welfare home who had taken a dislike to him. Sonny guessed the reason for the boy's dislike to be jealousy – the boy was ugly. The bad feeling between them had started with taunts about Sonny's curls. It flared one night in the dormitory. Just before lights out the boy gave Sonny a push. Sonny pushed him back. Enraged, the boy struck out with his fist, knocking Sonny to the ground. Sonny unhurriedly got to his feet, picked up a baseball bat that was lying on a bed, and smashed in half the boy's face and five of his ribs. The next morning an appointment had been made for Sonny to see the home's visiting psychiatrist.

Honey's palm landed on Sonny's temple and sent his head thudding against the window. A bright red light filled a space behind his eyes and he heard someone say: "Hey, tighten up!" He heard Honey say: "Nobody talks to *me* that way."

She added: "You ever to talk to me that way again, you little asshole, and I'll wipe the fucking – "

The red light faded, and Sonny launched himself from his seat. He heard Honey gasp as he grasped her hair, and as his face closed on hers he heard her grunt with pain.

"Hey!" Calvino was on his feet.

Sonny felt arms encircle his chest and begin to pull him away. He took a tighter hold on Honey's hair, gripping it as a jockey grips reins, and hauled himself back. "For Chris*sake*!" he heard Honey say.

Other arms (Lever's) went round his legs and ankles and suddenly he was in a horizontal position.

He pulled for all his worth. His nose brushed Honey's nose, then her cheek. He bared his teeth to strike, and, as he did so, was conscious of a hand searching for his testicles. All at once the red light returned and a split second later a great burst of white light filled his head. He screamed and released his grip.

When the pain had subsided and he felt sure he could control his voice, he said to Honey: "I hate everything about you. I always will."

Calvino, at Sonny's side on the seat, restraining him with an arm across his chest, said: "Hey, that's your momma you're talkin' to."

Sonny looked up at him and said: "And *you're* not my father."

Honey lowered a small oblong purse mirror in which she was

repairing her hair, stared at him with malevolent eyes and said: "He isn't, huh? How d'you know he isn't?"

"I just do," Sonny said shortly.

"Well, you're right," Honey said. "He's *not* your old man." She half smiled. "You wanna know who your old man was? I'll tell you who he was, Mr Hoity goddamn Toity. His name was Joe Backhouse and he drove a truck for Maxi's Miracle Meatloaf Company." She gave a short, contemptuous laugh. "Now, how does that grabya, you little creep?"

Sonny gave an involuntary shudder. For as far back as he could remember he had carried in his mind a picture of his father as The Artist – a poet or a concert pianist; a man of ineffable elegance and charm who strolled through life with a silver-topped malacca cane amusing and delighting those who were lucky enough to make his acquaintance. Jessica had done nothing to dispel that image – rather she had embellished it. Whenever they had spoken of him, a dreamy look had come into her eyes. "I'm sure he must have been utterly handsome," she would say. She would look at Sonny and sigh. "Oh, yes, utterly handsome, and frightfully well bred (for some reason, talk of Sonny's father caused Jessica to use English upper-class speech); a nobleman, perhaps; someone with exquisite taste. A divine, Byronic creature."

They invented names for him. Sonny would have had him called Julian Lushcurl, but Jessica preferred Sir Harry Maltravers. ("Lushcurl! Heavens, Sonny, what kind of name is that? Oh, all right, if you're going to sulk, Lushcurl it is; but let there be a compromise. Let his name be Sir *Harry* Lushcurl.") Sonny wished he were with Jessica now so that he could say to her: "Do you know who my father *really* was? He wasn't a *nobleman*, you stupid bitch. His name was Joe Backhouse and he drove a truck for Maxie's Miracle Meatloaf Company."

He pondered the name: Joe Backhouse…Sonny Backhouse… Sonny Backhouse requests the pleasure of…Starring Sonny Backhouse…It was too disgusting, There was something of the sewers about it. He had an urge to say Ugh!

Honey threw the mirror into her purse, clipped the purse shut and said to Calvino: "You don't want a dead kid on your hands, you better keep the little creep away from me. Next time it won't be his nuts I break, it'll be his goddamn head."

"Can we please cool this?" Calvino said angrily.

"You know he tried to take a bite out of me?" Honey said in an accusing tone.

Sonny said: "Don't ever hit me again."

Honey sneered and said: "Hitya, I'll beat the daylights outofya."

Lever said: "Come on, Sonny, let's take a walk along the train."

"Take him for a walk along the track," Honey said.

Lever and Sonny went to the restaurant car and found an unoccupied table. An attendant came up to them, and Lever said to Sonny: "What will you have?"

"Hibiscus tea," Sonny said peremptorily.

"We don't, ah, serve hibiscus tea, sir," the attendant said.

"Hibiscus tea's out," Lever said.

Sonny ordered chilled milk, and Lever coffee.

No further words were exchanged until the drinks were before them; then Lever, stirring sugar into his coffee, said: "That milk looks good, Sonny."

Sonny said: "Appearances can sometimes deceive."

Lever took a sip of coffee, swallowed and said: "Those are big words for a small boy – but you're right," – he replaced the coffee cup in its saucer – "things are *not* always as they seem." Feigning nervousness, he glanced over his shoulder, then leaning forward and nodding at Sonny's milk, he whispered: "You think that might be spiked?"

Sonny gave a blank look, which made Lever feel he'd made a fool of himself. He resolved not to treat Sonny as a child in future.

"Quite often, though," Sonny said, "appearances *don't* deceive. Take the Calvino woman, for instance. She looks disgusting and she is."

Lever said: "That 'Calvino woman' you're talking about happens to be your mother."

"So far as I'm concerned, she's *not*," Sonny said.

"She has many good qualities," Lever lied.

"She's monstrous," Sonny said.

"Where'd you get all these words from?" Lever asked.

"Jessica, my aunt, was always reading to me," Sonny said.

Lever made a guess. "You like Jessica, don't you, Sonny?"

"No," Sonny said. "She's stupid and weak."

"That's not the way she came across to me."

"Well, she is," said Sonny.

"Is there anyone you *don't* dislike?"

"Not really," Sonny said.

"Don't you have any friends?"

"No."

"Why do you think that is?"

"I don't know."

"Could it be that you're not a very friendly person."

Sonny shrugged in a disinterested way.

"Doesn't it worry you that you have no friends?"

"No."

Lever decided he wasn't getting anywhere, so he said: "Those impersonations you did were very good."

"I know," Sonny said. "I'm a very good mimic. I'm probably a great deal better than I think I am."

Lever smiled at this and said: "Do you impersonate male movie stars?"

"No," said Sonny, "only women. I prefer impersonating actresses."

"Why's that?"

"I don't know, I just do. I suppose it's because my voice is better suited to them. I have a quite delicate voice."

"It may change as you get older," Lever said.

"It won't," Sonny said, and Lever believed him.

"You need to do a little work on your Bette Davis. You haven't quite got the expression. The eyes need to be opened wider to get that mock innocent look. And you need to straighten your back. Haven't you noticed how Bette Davis has a kind of rigid look about her? It's the way she holds her shoulders. You need to do a little more work in that department."

"Perhaps," Sonny said.

"Who else do you do?"

Sonny with calculated indifference said: "Claudette Colbert, Barbara Stanwyck – quite a few."

"Will you do Barbara Stanwyck for me?"

"No."

"Why not?"

"Because I don't care to."

Lever sipped his coffee. "It's weird – you doing impressions of women, and your mother doing – "

"She's not my mother," Sonny interrupted.

"She is whether you like it or not," Lever said.

They fell silent.

After a while Lever said: "How would you like to go on stage one day and be an entertainer?"

Sonny shrugged again.

Lever said laconically: "Appearances can sometimes deceive. I take that shrug to mean that you'd give *any*thing to go on stage."

"I rather think I was *made* for the theatre," Sonny said.

"I think you were, too," Lever said. Without pausing, he said: "Do Barbara Stanwyck for me."

Sonny considered for a moment, and then, deciding that Lever wasn't being patronising, suddenly sat upright, a tormented look in his eyes. "Why didn't you take me in your arms that first day?" Barbara Stanwyck was saying. "Why didn't you know I'd never want anybody else? Why did you let me go? Didn't you know I was crazy for you, that I'd have gone anywhere with you? Why didn't you want me as I wanted you? We could have been so good for each other."

An elderly woman in a heavy tweed coat who was passing at that moment stopped and stared at Sonny in amazement. "Why, that's the most extraordinary thing I've ever heard," she said. "Barbara Stanwyck is my favourite actress and you sounded so very much – " She shook her head as though bewildered.

Sonny looked up at her, narrowed his eyes, and hardening the Stanwyck voice, said: "Go fly a kite."

Reddening, the woman said: "Why, er – " She hesitated for a moment, giggled nervously and moved on.

They returned to their compartment.

Honey and Calvino were asleep, Honey with her mouth open and making tiny gurgling sounds.

Lever loosened his tie and took off his jacket.

Sonny returned to his seat opposite Honey.

Lever placed his jacket on the luggage rack, sat down and closed his eyes.

Sonny waited until Lever was audibly asleep, then gathered saliva in his mouth and began working it into a ball. When he was satisfied with its consistency, he got to his feet, lined up his mouth with Honey's, and spat.

CHAPTER 21

After four days of ministering to Sonny's needs – and they were many – Calvino's mother said to Honey: "I can't take it no more. Tha' kid of yours...Everything I cook, he don' eat. And he looks at me like I was some kinda bug. You know what he called me over breakfas' this morning? A slut. Tha's wha' he called me – me, his gran'ma. Wha' tha' kid needs is a slap in the mowt, and if I stay around here much longer tha's eggzaggly wha' he's gonna get." She wiped her hands on the stained apron she was wearing. "A slut." She shook her head disbelievingly. "Nobody don' ever call me a slut before." She looked at Calvino. "Not even your farder when he was alive don' call me a slut." Her voice broke slightly. "Tha' kid: he ain't *like* other kids. Other kids, they out playin' stick ball. All tha' kid does is look at his hands." She said to Honey, "You got a fruit for a kid, tha's what you got." She paused. "And tha' hairahis – tha's another thing... Jesus, the time he takes fixin' it! You'd think he was some kinda movie queen." She sat down. "It ain't natcheral."

They were in the Calvinos' apartment, bathed in a pink glow. All was pink. Rose-pink wallpaper, pink and silver upholstery, dusty-pink rugs, pink curtains, pink bric-a-brac, pink and white squares of candy in a pink dish.

Calvino's mother went on: "It ain't right him callin' me a slut. Who the hell he think he is? He was *my* kid, I'd beat a hole in his goddamn head."

In exact imitation of Mrs Calvino's voice and not taking his eyes off the pink lampshade he was staring at, Sonny said: "He was *my* kid, I'd beat a hole in his goddamn head."

Mrs Calvino sprang from her chair and took a step towards Sonny, her hand raised.

"Hold it!" Calvino put himself between his mother and Sonny and held out his arms to form a barrier. "Just hold it." After a moment he looked down at Sonny and in a menacing tone said: "You ever act that way towards my old lady – your gran'ma – again and I'll take your fuckin' head off."

Watching this, Honey wondered how she would feel if Sonny were to imitate *her* voice – she felt sure he could – and had an overwhelming urge to compete with him, to imitate Calvino's voice. Sonny was good, but she was better.

Calvino's mother said: "Tha's it! I ain't stayin' here no longer. You want someone to look after tha' asshole kid of yours, you find someone else."

"Momma, please…" Honey pleaded, but Mrs Calvino collected her things and put on her coat. At the door she said to Sonny: "You don' deserve a gran'ma cookin' and cleanin' for you. You don' deserve no lookin' after." She opened the door. Turning her head, she said: "You lucky I don' break your ass."

The door slammed.

Honey glared at Sonny and said: "Well, you're really something, aren'tya? You really fixed things. I ought to knock your teeth loose."

Sonny, with a tired sigh, got to his feet and walked slowly, undulatingly towards his room. It was a walk that reminded Honey of Mae West.

When he was out of sight, she said: "*Now* whadda we do? I got a show coming up next week and no way am I cancelling to play nursemaid to that little creep. Jesus!" She closed her eyes in exasperation.

"It's okay, I'll take care of things," Calvino said.

"Christ, why'd we have to have him come live with us in the first place?" Honey said. "What a dumb idea."

"I said I'd take care of things," Calvino said.

"You do that," Honey said. She added after a small pause: "How you gonna take care of things, throw him off a bridge?" She paused again. "Maybe that's not such a bad idea."

"I'll come up with somethin'," Calvino said confidently. He patted her arm reassuringly. The situation had developed in the way he had suspected it might. If by some miracle Honey and his mother had taken to Sonny and he to them, the carrying out of Mastrioni's instructions (Mastrioni had visited them on their second day back in New York and on seeing Sonny had taken Calvino to one side and said: "I want that boy, Tommy. You get him for me. You get him for me quick, you hear?') might have proved difficult. But Honey and his mother disliked Sonny almost as much as Sonny disliked them. The matter could be settled without fuss. He went to Sonny's room.

Sonny, his eyes closed, was stretched out on his bed, toying with his hair.

Calvino stood over him and said: "How'd you like to go visiting tomorrow, Sonny? See Mr Mastrioni. Remember Mr Mastrioni who called on us the other day?"

Sonny said nothing.

"He likes you, Sonny. He told me. Likes you a *lot*. You should see where he lives. You'd like it. Plenty of space – not like the shoebox we got here. Lots of other kids there, too. You do what you want there, nobody gettin' in your hair all the time. Swell food…anythin' you want…people waitin' on you all the time. How'd you like to go see Mr Mastrioni?"

Still with his eyes closed, Sonny gave a small shrug.

"Okay, we go tomorrow first thing. You be nice to Mr Mastrioni and he'll give you anythin' you want. Maybe even let you stay for a while."

"Rats?" Sonny said in a dreamy voice.

"Huh?"

"Would he allow me to keep rats?"

"Rats? Sure. Sure he'd allow you t'keep rats. Why not?"

INTERLUDE

Sylvano Mastrioni started life in America at the age of sixteen in a three-storey tenement on East 108th Street in the East Harlem district of Manhattan. He had arrived there from Palermo, Sicily, with his father, Alberto, and his mother, Constanta.

Alberto found work as a road digger, and Constanta took in washing. Sylvano organised back-street dice games and robbed vending machines and small stores.

A year after his arrival the young Mastrioni was arrested for assault and robbery: he and a friend, Benjamino 'Benjie' Cantaro, had followed a coal dealer into an alleyway and after beating him over the head with a hammer had stolen his wallet containing fifteen dollars. Both were sentenced to a year's imprisonment, but because of good behaviour served only eight months.

A week after their release the two friends were introduced to a member of the East Harlem Mafiosa who, liking their 'style', employed them to collect rents from a tenement block he owned.

With the money he earned from rent collecting, Mastrioni bought himself a Colt .45, and within a year of owning it had shot dead two policemen.

Impressed by the cold bloodedness of the killings, Mastrioni's Mafiosa acquaintances elevated him to the position of executioner.

Five years and twenty-six executions later Mastrioni broke away from the East Harlem brotherhood and, with Benjie as his chief lieutenant, went into business for himself.

By the time he was forty he owned twenty nightclubs, ran fifty brothels, ruled (with an iron fist) a thousand call girls, controlled New York's waterfront and garment industry unions, extorted five million dollars a year from shopkeepers and restaurateurs, governed the city's drug trafficking and pornography trades, and operated distilleries in ten states. He was also the nation's leading distributor of olive oil, mayonnaise and sacramental wafers. Such was his power that he could place judges on the bench, elect mayors, and have high-ranking police officers promoted to higher ranks.

On his forty-fifth birthday, as a token of appreciation for all that he had done to further the Organisation's cause, his confederates honoured him with the title of capo di tutti capi – boss of all bosses.

CHAPTER 22

Mastrioni occupied two floors of a twenty-floor hotel he owned on Park Avenue. One floor was for his personal use, and the other for the use of his former lovers – their reward for services rendered. Featured on Mastrioni's floor, away from his private quarters, in a space the size of a football pitch, were a circular glass bar in which two hundred rainbow-coloured fish swam; three snooker tables imported from England; a nickelodeon; six pinball machines; a pale green grand piano that stood on a granite platform in the middle of a rockpool, a miniature stone bridge leading to it; a vine-covered ceiling in which lived a score or more tiny birds and a perfectly harmless snake; and a stainless steel cage containing the embalmed, dinner-suited body of Angelo Ludovici – the first and, to date, most formidable of Mastrioni's gangland rivals.

There were other, more mundane objects to be seen: a roller skate, a puzzle book, a popgun with the cork fired, and, on the seat of the electrically-powered cart in which Mastrioni traversed the area, a pair of boy's underpants.

"You'll like it here," Calvino said to Sonny as they ascended in Mastrioni's smoked glass, bullet-proof lift.

Sonny was silent.

The lift stopped and Calvino spoke his name into a metal grill above the button panel. Almost immediately there was the sound of a lock being disengaged. A moment later the lift's door swung open. "Neat, huh?" Calvino said.

They stepped into a small ante-room lined with ice-blue mirrors.

Sonny had just time enough to admire his reflection before two of the mirrors parted and Mastrioni, his arms outstretched in welcome, came towards them.

"Tommy…" Mastrioni placed his hands on Calvino's shoulders. "You lookin' good, Tommy," he said. He looked down at Sonny and felt his heartbeat quicken. "And Sonny, beautiful Sonny." He shook his head as if unable to believe his eyes. "Come," he said eventually.

He guided Sonny past the cage where Ludovici sat, a bird clinging to his nose and tugging at a hair that protruded from it (it was nesting time), and on to the bar.

"You want a drink, Tommy?" Mastrioni asked. "Or is it too early?"

"Not right now, Sylvano," Calvino said.

"Sure...Sure..." Mastrioni spoke the words tenderly, compassionately, as if Calvino were a hospital patient suffering from some excruciatingly painful disease of the jaw and he a visitor who had just offered a slab of peanut brittle and had had it refused. He squeezed Calvino's arm. "Why don't you go sit up the end there, read a magazine, let me and Sonny have a little talk. We got to get properly acquainted."

Calvino left them, and Mastrioni went behind the bar. "You like a drink of somethin', Sonny?" he asked.

"No thank you," Sonny replied. He looked at the fish that swam vacantly before him. He noticed a water pistol lying among a tangle of lilac sea fern, but had no wish to possess it; he looked at it with contempt.

"I got lemonade, or I could get a cherry soda sent up. They make great cherry sodas here."

"Please don't trouble yourself," Sonny said disdainfully.

"You got good manners," Mastrioni said. "Real good manners. Not many kids today got good manners." He poured himself a drink and joined Sonny on the other side of the bar. "You like fish?" he asked. He placed a hand on Sonny's shoulder.

"I prefer rats," Sonny said.

"Rats?"

Sonny, not taking his eyes off the fish, nodded.

"Rats are good," Mastrioni said vaguely. He moved his index finger so that it rested on Sonny's neck. "I used to keep mice when I was a kid but it ain't the same as keepin' rats. With rats you got somethin' to get hold of. With a rat you got a real friend. Gimme a rat any time." He was aware that he was talking nonsense, but it didn't seem to matter.

They stood in silence for a minute, then Mastrioni said: "Why don't we sit down?" He didn't feel in control of himself.

Sonny said coldly: "No thank you, I'd rather stand."

"You got young legs, you can stand. Me, I got old legs, I gotta sit." Mastrioni went to a leather couch close to the bar and sat down.

Sonny looked at the vines.

"We got a snake up there, Sonny," Mastrioni said. "You scared of snakes?"

"I'm not scared of *any*thing," Sonny said. He paused. "What sort of snake is it?"

"I ain't sure, but it's real priddy."

"Who's the man in the cage?" Sonny asked.

"Tha's *another* kind of snake," Mastrioni said. "*Was* a snake. Ain't no more." He chuckled and took a drink. "Come and stand near me, Sonny." He wanted the boy close to him, to be within touching distance.

Sonny did not move. He looked at Mastrioni and smiled a slow, seductive smile. Still smiling, he lowered his lids. "No," he said bewitchingly.

Mastrioni sighed. He was dazzled by Sonny's beauty and manner, by his self-assuredness and authoritativeness. He heard Sonny's words again: *I'm not afraid of anything... No thank you, I'd rather stand.* He felt a fulfilment he had never experienced before. He thought he could spend the rest of his life with someone as beautiful and as authoritative as Sonny. He saw himself in old age, his eyeglasses needing polishing, and Sonny, still beautiful, briskly, authoritatively polishing them and returning them to his nose, perhaps with the merest reprimand. He got to his feet. "Sonny, I bin thinkin'." His voice sounded strange to him. "We both got the same taste in things – *you* like rats, *I* like rats – so why don't you come live here with me? We get ourselves plenty of rats." He ran his hand over his mouth. "When I last seen you I could tell you ain't happy livin' with your momma. It'd make sense for you to come and live *here*." A small, vivid bird flew from the vines, settled on his shoulder, defecated, and flew off. "It'd make sense, Sonny," Mastrioni repeated. "You know it would."

Sonny, standing beside the green piano now, one hand resting on its top, conscious of his beauty, stared at Mastrioni and thought him an ill-educated thug. Henry James, he guessed, would have termed him a vulgarian; but his eyes were quite exciting and he *did* appear to be rich, much richer than Uncle Henry. More importantly he offered an escape from the hideous pink apartment and the abomination who called herself his mother. He said: "If I were to live here, I should want to redecorate this room. The colours are horrid, utterly horrid."

"Utterly – " Bewildered, Mastrioni looked around. "Redec – " The words penetrated. "Sure! Sure! Redecorate!" he said brightly. "The room's a mess. You redecorate it whatever way you want." He had risen from the couch and taken a position close to Sonny.

"*And*," Sonny went on, "I should like some spending money. Five hundred dollars should suffice."

Unhesitatingly Mastrioni took out his wallet and withdrew from it a five-hundred-dollar bill. He turned and called to Calvino: "Tommy! Tommy, come here quick. I got good news." Handing the bill to Sonny, he said: "Tomorrow we go out and buy you anythin' you want. You want rats, we get you a set in mink coats and gold hats."

"If I'm to stay, I should like to make a tour of inspection," Sonny said.

"A tour of… Sure, sure. You look around," Mastrioni said. "We got other kids here. Maybe you find yourself a playmate."

"I doubt there's any likelihood of *that* happening," Sonny said crisply.

Calvino arrived.

"Sonny here's gonna stay, Tommy. He wants to see over the place. Take him see the kids."

"He do his movie star take-offs for you?" Calvino asked.

"Movie star take-offs? You do movie star take-offs like your momma, Sonny?"

Sonny shrugged.

"You should catch his Bette Davis," Calvino said.

"You do Bette Davis, Sonny?"

"You got to hear it to believe it," Calvino said.

"Lemme hear you do Bette Davis, Sonny."

Sonny was silent.

Mastrioni took another five-hundred-dollar bill from his wallet. "Do Bette Davis for me, Sonny," he said. He held out the bill.

Sonny accepted it, gave an acid smile, and in the actress's voice and looking straight at Mastrioni said: "Dahling, do please try to stay sober tonight. You know how impossible you are when you've had too much to drink. And *do* try to wear a suit that doesn't look as if it had been in a traffic accident."

Mastrioni stared at Sonny for a few moments, then turned to Calvino. In a voice thick with emotion he said: "Sonny's special to me, Tommy. Real special. I want you to know that."

Calvino nodded uneasily.

To Sonny, Mastrioni said: "I ain't ever heard anythin' like that before. What you just done was" – he shook his head, searching for the right words – "was somethin' special. You just a kid talkin' Bette Davis. It don' seem possible." He smiled beatifically. "Who else you do, Sonny? You do Junie Allyson?"

"Yes, but not now," Sonny said dismissively.

"Okay, okay; later maybe. You go with Tommy now. Have a look over the place. Meet some of the other kids. We have Junie later." To Calvino he said deliberately: "You give him anythin' he wants, Tommy. He asks for anythin', you get it for him, unnerstand?"

"Sure, Sylvano," Calvino said in a peeved tone. He felt a little disturbed by the amount of attention Sonny was getting. Normally a new boy would be given a cherry soda or, if he were fretful, a bat with a ball attached to it by a rubber band and left to amuse himself until Mastrioni was ready for him.

Mastrioni said: "Okay, Sonny, I got to see to a coupla things now." He was reluctant to leave the boy, but there was an Inland Revenue problem to be discussed with his lawyers. He touched Sonny's cheek. "You got beaudiful brown eyes, Sonny," he said.

"They're more raven than brown," Sonny said.

"Raven..." Mastrioni repeated the word as if it were the key to eternal life or a billion dollar cocaine haul. "Raven..." Shaking his head, he walked away.

"Come on," Calvino said brusquely.

They returned to the lift and went to the floor above.

"You're doin' okay for yourself," Calvino said as they waited for the door to open. "Five hundred dollars. That ain't bad for first time around."

"A thousand," Sonny said.

"A thousand? You havin' me on?"

Sonny took the two notes from his pocket and held them up for Calvino's inspection.

In a dry voice, Calvino said: "Some shine the man's taken to you."

The door opened and they stepped into a corridor thronged with scantily-clad youths and filled with noise. Music blared from radios and phonographs and somewhere in the background a violin was being tuned. In a room close to where Calvino and Sonny stood, two people argued in loud voices. The air was hot and there was the acrid smell of half-washed clothes being dried over radiators.

"Hi, Tommy." A youth wearing only a G-string waved to Calvino.

"Hiya, Jimmy," Calvino said. "Howya doin'?"

"Fine," the youth replied. "You?"

"Swell."

"Who's your little friend?"

"Not mine, Sylvano's," Calvino said.

"Cute," the youth said as they passed.

There were similar greetings – one from a black youth with bleached-blond hair and rouged knees.

"Who *are* these people?" Sonny asked crossly.

"Friends of Sylvano's," Calvino replied. "Some go back a long time."

"Why have you brought me here?"

"You said you wanted to look the place over."

A door opened and a man of Calvino's age appeared. He wore a towel round his head in turban fashion and a rose-pink bathrobe that came six inches above his knees. His face was heavily made up. "Tommy, baby!" he cried.

"Hi, Maxine."

"You look divine, Sweets."

"Right back at ya," Calvino said.

The man looked down at Sonny. "Hello, pretty boy," he said. As he spoke a rivulet of hair-dye escaped from his turban and ran down his forehead. "You come to visit fairyland?"

Sonny stared at him without speaking.

The man swept the dye away with a practiced finger.

"What colour're you *this* week?" Calvino asked.

The man threw back his head and in a strident, theatrical voice said: "Blonde, darling. Blissfully, blindingly blonde!" He fluttered his lids. "It's *me*!" He stepped forward and quickly kissed Calvino on the cheek. "Must dash, darling," he said. "I've a heavy date coming up and I want to grab a bath before the kids move in with their Donald Ducks." Glancing at Sonny, he said: "Sylvano'll soon have to learn how to change a diaper."

They moved on.

"That was Maxine," Calvino said.

"He's ugly," Sonny said.

"He was a peach once."

They hadn't gone more than a dozen paces when another door opened and a boy no older than fourteen emerged. He was naked except for horn-rimmed spectacles and a pair of blue-spangled high-heeled shoes that were two or three sizes too big for him. He was reading a comic book.

"Hiya, Lindsay." Calvino ruffled the boy's hair.

The boy glanced at Calvino, gave him a brief, nervous smile and clunked off.

"What you think of the place so far?" Calvino asked.

"It smells," Sonny said.

"It stinks," Calvino said.

"Do all these people live here?"

"Yeah," Calvino said. "Some they've been here five, six years. Maxine's been here ten."

"What do they do?"

"Have a good time mostly. Run a few errands. Do a little film work."

"Film work?"

"Not the kind Bette Davis'd be interested in."

They continued along the corridor, passing rooms in which youths could be seen engaged on some task or other – exercising their bodies (many seemed to be doing this), repairing a radio, painting a toe-nail, peeling an apple, or simply relaxing with a newspaper or magazine.

"I want you should meet someone," Calvino said.

"I want to go back," Sonny said. The ambient noise and smell were making him nauseous.

"Okay, but first meet Derek." There was a note of pride in Calvino's voice.

"Who's Derek?"

"He's what you might call the star of the show. It was me who discovered him. Maybe discovered ain't the right word. I fixed it so he came to live here."

They stopped outside a room where a violin was being tuned. The door of the room was slightly ajar. Without knocking, Calvino pushed it open.

They saw a tall youth with lank blond hair that fell to his shoulders. He wore faded blue shorts, a sweatshirt torn at the breast and a thin band of copper around his wrist. He held a violin ready for playing. At the sight of Calvino, the youth gave a look of undiluted contempt.

Calvino said to him: "I brought someone to see you." He said to Sonny: "This is Derek. Derek plays violin sweeter than Ray Robinson throws a punch – when he ain't too high, that is."

Sonny experienced a dart of hatred for the youth. Here was someone who could play the violin – one of the most difficult of instruments to master, so Jessica had told him – and who was almost as beautiful as himself. He felt a little inferior, a little murderous. "Can we go?" he said to Calvino.

"Wait'll we hear Derek play somethin'."

Sonny recalled Jessica's favourite violin music, and, hoping to catch the youth out, said suavely: "Do you play the Brahms Concerto in D?"

"Who are you?" the youth replied good-naturedly. Sonny noticed that his eyes had a dazed look.

"He's Sylvano's little buddy," Calvino said.

The youth smiled at Sonny. "Yes, it's a fine piece. Would you like to hear it?" His words were faintly blurred, dragged out.

Sonny forced himself to return the smile and said: "Yes, but not now." He looked at Calvino and said: "I'm going." He left the room and hurried back along the corridor, his face hot with frustration: he wasn't used to having young people behave kindly towards him.

As he reached the lift Calvino caught up with him and said: "Don't you want to find yourself a little pal?"

"No," Sonny said sharply.

They got into the lift.

"Derek's a good kid," Calvino said when they were back in Mastrioni's apartment.

"He seemed to be drunk," Sonny said.

"That ain't drink that makes him look that way," Calvino said.

"What is it, then?"

"Derek's got what you might call a habit."

"You mean he takes drugs."

"For a kid, you're a pretty smart number," Calvino said.

In the distance Mastrioni came towards them. He was followed by two men each carrying a document case.

"Sonny…" Mastrioni opened his arms and quickened his step. Calvino thought he had never seen him show so much enthusiasm for a boy.

When Mastrioni was close to them he reached out to touch Sonny's face.

Sonny pulled back, widened his nostrils and said firmly: "I want all those awful people on the floor above to leave."

"Wha'?" Mastrioni's expression changed from adoration to incredulity. One of the men with him said: "I really think we should get to grips with this matter as soon as possible, Sylvano. If it's left unattended we could find ourselves in very serious trouble."

Mastrioni turned on him and said angrily: "I told you, I ain't got time now. You get out now." He looked at Calvino. "I want you should leave, too, Tommy. You done good, but I wanna be alone with Sonny."

Calvino and the two men got into the lift, Calvino hesitantly. Before the door closed, Mastrioni touched Calvino's sleeve and said: "You did good, Tommy. I see you soon. We have a drink together." He smiled.

Calvino did not return the smile. He had a sudden sense of being shut out, abolished. "Sure," he said sullenly.

Mastrioni waited until the lift had disappeared, then said to Sonny: "What you ask for ain't possible, Sonny. Those kids, they do work for me. Im*portant* work. Besides, this is their home. I kick those kids out, they ain't got no place to go; they'd have to go live on the street."

Sonny glared at Mastrioni and in a raised voice said: "Well, pro*vide* them with a place! Find them another hotel – *any*thing. I don't want them here. If they stay, I go."

"Sonny – " Mastrioni put out his hand again, tentatively this time, and Sonny, precisely, scrupulously certain of his hold over him, slapped it. "No!" he said.

For a moment Mastrioni could not speak. He was fourteen again and back in Sicily, walking on a hillside with a boy of ten. He was teasing the boy about his girlish looks, and the boy, with angry tears in his eyes, was attacking him with his fists. At first he danced out of range of the blows, but after a while he stood still and allowed the boy to beat him on the chest. He feigned hurt and fell to the ground. The boy leapt astride him and pounded his face. He let the boy beat his face until blood ran from his nose and mouth and until the boy, exhausted and sobbing, lay prostrate upon him. He put his arms around the boy, stroked his hair, and had his first orgasm.

Mastrioni knew now why he was so smitten with Sonny: Sonny was almost identical to the boy on the hillside.

"I get rid of them, Sonny," he said.

"When?"

"Tomorrow. I get Tommy to find them another place."

"Good." Sonny gave a beautiful smile. "We could misbehave now, if you wish," he said.

PART THREE

CHAPTER 1

The President, sensing the presence of the First Lady, stopped scratching his neck and turned around. The First Lady raised her head and sniffed the air. When she was satisfied that all was well, she approached the President and gently touched his nose with hers. The President positioned himself behind her and prepared to mount.

The President had ginger hair and a tail eight inches long. The First Lady had black hair and a slightly shorter tail. They occupied a large papiér-maché maze that rested on two straight-backed chairs in Mastrioni's apartment.

Before the President could mount, Sonny extended a half-eaten grape to the First Lady, who snatched it from him and carried it in her mouth to a corner of the maze.

"The President…all he wants to do is screw," Mastrioni said. "No wonder the First Lady don' look so good, she's gettin' too much."

Sonny picked up the President, held him close to his chest and stroked his head.

"Sometimes I think you like those rats better than you do me," Mastrioni said without rancour.

"So you keep telling me," Sonny said. He paused. "I neither *like* them nor *dis*like them. I enjoy watching them, that's all."

After a while Sonny tossed the President to its mate and inspected himself for stray hairs. He was wearing a lemon polo-necked cashmere sweater, Bedford cord trousers from Savile Row, England, and a pair of suede ankle boots the colour of wet sand. At twenty-two he was astonishingly handsome: dark eyed and dark lashed, with a sweeping jawline and a straight-cut, chisel-tipped nose set above a full but not fleshy mouth – features that aroused carnal feelings in both sexes.

"I'm bored, Sylv," Sonny said. He forced a grape into Mastrioni's mouth.

"We take a vacation soon," Mastrioni said over the grape.

"Yes, I know. But at this moment – *now* – I'm bored." Sonny went to the bar (no longer filled with fish (one day in a fit of pique Sonny had emptied ten bottles of bourbon into it) and made himself a gimlet.

"What you wanna do?" Mastrioni asked. "Whatever you wanna do, we do it." He spat pips.

"I don't know – *anything*," Sonny said. He looked around. "Perhaps have the room redecorated."

"We only just had it done last year," Mastrioni said. He joined Sonny at the bar.

"Let's go out tonight," Sonny said.

"We been out every night this week."

Sonny widened perfect, opaque nostrils, raised perfectly-shaped eyebrows, and said: "Well, let's go out again. LET'S, GO, OUT, AGAIN!"

Mastrioni made himself a drink.

"Okay, we go out. Where you wanna go? The movies?"

"No, *not* the movies," Sonny said quietly. "I don't want to go to the fucking movies. I'm tired of going to the fucking movies." He spoke the expletive resonantly, made it ring the way an English Shakespearean actor or a Church of England bishop might. "Let's go somewhere different for a change."

"You *like* the movies."

"Yes, but not tonight."

"Okay, we go somewhere else. You name a place where you wanna go."

"I don't know," Sonny said irritably. "Somewhere different."

Mastrioni finished his drink and in a cautious voice said: "Honey opened at the Starlight Room last night."

Sonny looked at Mastrioni and blinked. "Do you want to upset me today?" he asked.

"Okay," Mastrioni said quickly, "the Starlight's out. We go someplace else."

There was a long silence between them. Suddenly Sonny set down his glass and strode across the room to a tall silver-framed mirror. Standing before it, he studied his face and hair. He looked for the smallest imperfection, the merest irregularity, and could not find one. He had never looked better, he thought. He would never look as good as he did now. A line of Wilde's came into his head – *A youth made for olive groves starred with white narcissi.* He smiled. "All right," he said brightly

"Huh?" Mastrioni said.

"We'll go to the Starlight Room."

Sonny had not seen Honey since the day of his departure from the pink apartment; had *avoided* seeing her. His loathing of her had not diminished. Whenever her name was mentioned he felt a cramping sensation in his stomach, and whenever Calvino brought tickets for a new show in which she was appearing he tore them up and scattered the pieces on the floor. Now, suddenly, he wanted to see her, wanted her to see *him*, wanted her to be dazzled by his looks and youthfulness, to be made to feel gross and ugly. In his mind he saw her face as he had last seen it and tried to imagine it as it would look now. It would have aged a good deal in ten years. It would be going to fat. The jaw-line would be heavier and there would be a slackening of the skin around the eyes and mouth. He turned sideways and studied his figure. "I shall wear my uniform, and you the dinner suit I chose for you. And I want six of your thugs – the ugliest – to accompany us." He returned to the bar and patted Mastrioni's cheek. In Ida Lupino's voice he said: "We'll make the old has-been wish she'd stayed at home, won't we, Ma?"

"I'll get Tommy fix us a table," Mastrioni said.

"The best," Sonny said.

"Sure the best," Mastrioni said with an expansive gesture. "I ever get you anythin' else?"

Sonny made himself another drink and carried it to the lift. "I'm going to rest for a while," he said. "If I'm not down by seven, have someone call me."

"Why don' you come rest in *my* room," Mastrioni invited.

"No, not today," Sonny said simply.

Mastrioni gave a resigned smile. The rejection hurt but he accepted it. He would accept *any* hurt from Sonny. He was mesmerised by him. Sonny was all that mattered. Everyone and everything else took second place; not even the Organisation came before Sonny. To be at his side he cancelled meetings, postponed expansion plans, let telephone calls and messages go unanswered – behaviour that worried and irritated his associates. More worrying to them was that they were no longer taken into his confidence, no longer consulted. Where once he had sought their advice, or at least their views, before making important decisions he now sought only Sonny's. More often than not it was Sonny who made the decisions – impatiently and with a sigh, for Sonny found decision-making tiresome. Those foolish enough to criticise Mastrioni were immediately banished. Those who criticised Sonny were maimed. Not even Benjie, who had been with Mastrioni from the beginning, was allowed to speak his mind (he once, in the presence of Mastrioni, had taken Sonny to task for torturing to death an elderly arthritic rat and had had his own Luger held to his head).

"Okay," Mastrioni said, "I get Benjie give you a call, you ain't down."

Sonny went to the floor above.

He left the lift and, as always when he stepped into the corridor, was a little unsettled by the silence; as always, he half expected a great noise to start up and to hear somewhere in the background a violin being tuned.

He opened a door facing the lift and entered a large room contrived to look ancestral. The floor was laid with solid lengths of untreated oak, and against the walls stood heavy chests and settles and tall, wide chairs covered in old tapestries. To one side of the room was a wooden staircase stained nut brown that led to a narrow gallery, on the walls of which were, with one exception, sombre portraits of elderly men in wigs and richly coloured robes. The one exception was a portrait of Sonny painted in the style of the impressionists and showing him at age fourteen seated naked at a beach table, a turquoise sea behind him, sucking (suggestively, some thought) on a triangular stick of lime-green ice.

Other attractions were a handsome Victorian grandfather clock, a suit of armour, a Florentine cabinet, and an eighteenth century tumbril preserved in thick coatings of shellac.

Sonny went to a second door and opened that. Now he was in a room of pale greens and pinks; a pleasant, airy room furnished with bamboo chairs and couches and dappled with artificial sunlight that came through striped canvas blinds. On a white slatted table that stood beneath a life-size photograph of him taken on the steps of the Casino Rothschild in Monte Carlo were a phonograph and a stack of records. He selected a record, placed it on the phonograph and set it in motion. Very soon Noel Coward was singing *Mad Dogs and Englishmen.*

> *In tropical climes*
> *There are certain times of the day*
> *When all the citizens retire*
> *To take their clothes off and perspire*

Sonny finished his drink and went to a swing bed that hung between two pairs of white poles garlanded with small, bright flowers made of silk. He threw himself expertly on to the bed and lay back.

> *In the Mangrove swamps where the python romps*
> *There is peace from twelve to two*
> *Even cariboos lie around and snooze*
> *For there's nothing else to do*

He closed his eyes and listened to Coward's clever lyrics. He wished vaguely that *Mastrioni* possessed Coward's sophistication; rolled his r's the way Coward did. He decided that Mastrioni would have to take lessons in elocution.

He slept for an hour, rose and went into his bathroom.

Of the half dozen rooms he occupied, the bathroom, because of its luxuriousness, was the one that gave him the most pleasure; the one in which he felt most at home. Prior to its construction he had consulted an interior decorator known for his criminally high fees and eccentricity of dress (purple woollen hood and mittens in all weathers). "I can see you in a setting of sybaritic decadence," he had said to Sonny at their first meeting, and Sonny had agreed with him. Together they had ordered black marble from Italy, tall gold-framed mirrors from Venice, two hundred boxes of hand painted tiles, a chandelier once owned by the Singer family, a rug made from the pelts of seventy or more white mink, and an alabaster replica of Michelangelo's David. The bath itself was square-shaped and big enough to accommodate three average-sized males (which it sometimes did) or four smallish females (which it never did). Water flowed from solid gold faucets, and tablets of sweet-smelling soap rested on solid gold wings. Gold-plated handrails were fixed to steps leading into the bath, and two black marble urns filled with perfumed crystals stood like sentinels on either side of a gold-plated basin. The floor was made of inch-thick frosted glass which, when a button was pressed, showed a pale green light, giving Sonny, so he thought, an ethereal look.

He soaked himself until he became bored, then put on a white bathrobe and went into his dressing room. This room had primrose-silk wall covering and contained a chaise-longue (also done in primrose-silk), a small bar, a standing swing mirror, and a closet which took up the whole of one wall.

He made himself a long drink of rum and iced lime juice and after tasting it went to the closet and slid back a door. From a line of eighty or more suits he took out a navy blue uniform that buttoned to the throat and had gold braid encircling the cuffs and running down the outside seams of the trousers.

He placed the uniform on the chaise-longue, returned to the closet and selected a pristine set of underclothes and a pair of highly polished black ankle boots with a pointed toe.

He sat for a while sipping his drink and looking forward to the moments when he would slip into the uniform and pull on the boots. He picked up a boot and admired its shape and the excellence of the craftsmanship that had gone into its making. It was almost too beautiful to wear, he thought. He was half inclined to put it to his cheek, but he was perspiring slightly (he had taken a very hot bath) and he worried that the perspiration might mark it.

He dressed carefully, swallowed what remained of his drink and returned to Mastrioni's apartment.

Mastrioni was at the bar with Benjie. He was wearing a dinner suit with silk reveres, patent leather shoes and a stiff-fronted shirt with a flyaway collar. Benjie was similarly dressed. Catching sight of Sonny, Mastrioni put the fingers and thumb of his right hand together and kissed their tips. "Bellissima!" he cried flinging the kiss into the air. He smiled adoringly. "You look a hundred million dollars, Sonny." He turned to Benjie. "Do he or don' he look a hundred million dollars, Benjie?" he asked.

Benjie nodded. "You look real sharp, Sonny," he said.

Sonny glanced at himself in the wall mirror and said cheerfully: "Yes, I rather think I do." To Mastrioni and Benjie he said: "If I didn't know you, I'd take you for a couple of gangsters." He laughed briefly and added: "Make me a drink, Sylv, will you? Something a little military."

"Military?"

"A pink gin," Sonny said, a slight edge creeping into his voice. He went to his rats and stood looking down at them. The President was scratching an ear, his leg a blur of motion. Sonny lifted him from the maze and carried him by the tail to the bar.

"I ain't never seen you in that outfit before," Benjie said.

"We got it in England," Mastrioni said. "It's what the military they wear out there. Tha's twenty four carat he's got on those cuffs and pants." He handed Sonny a pink gin.

Sonny, still holding the President by his tail, swung him round his head three or four times, then released him. The President flew across the room and landed unhurt on a leather armchair.

"He always go flying without a parachute?" Benjie asked.

Sonny ignored the remark and said to Mastrioni: "I want you to take elocution classes, Mum." He sipped his drink.

"Elocution classes?"

"I want you to improve your speech. I want you to speak like Noel Coward."

"Coward's a faggot," Benjie said, and, realising his faux pas, added quickly: "I mean his voice…It's kinda lavender-soundin'."

Again ignoring Benjie, Sonny said to Mastrioni: "Repeat this: 'I am too terribly tired, Teresa.'" He rolled the r's and clipped the words the way Coward would.

Mastrioni was silent.

"Say it," Sonny ordered.

"Sonny, c'*mon*," Mastrioni said pleadingly.

"Say it."

Mastrioni shrugged and said: "Okay, say it over for me."

"I am too terribly tired, Teresa."

Mastrioni gathered himself and said: "I am too terribly tired, Teresa."

"No," Sonny said. "Roll the r's, like this: 'I am too terribly tired, Teresa.'"

204

"I am too terribly tired, Teresa."

"Terrrrrrribly," Sonny said, annoyed.

"Terribly," Mastrioni said.

"God!" Sonny took a swallow of his drink and turned away. There was a stiff silence until Benjie said to Sonny: "I was havin' a bite to eat with our White House feed a coupla days ago and when I told him you got a rat you call the President he nearly choked on his salami."

"Really," Sonny said. He spoke the word as if he had just been given the most colossal piece of useless information – a rise in the price of sheep-dip. To Mastrioni he said: "Which of your gorillas have you detailed for escort duty?"

"Who you got, Benjie?"

Benjie said: "Hammernose Hymie, Jimmy the Eye, Big Pacco, Jake the Chin – " He stopped to think.

"Did you get the one with the huge feet and the hernia?" Sonny asked.

"Oh, yeah, Willie the Shoe," Benjie said. "We got him." In a chagrined tone he added: "That ain't a hernia he's got. He walks that way 'cos he took it in the knees one time."

"The knees?" Sonny said in a dreamy voice. "You're sure it wasn't the face?"

Ignoring this, Benjie said: "We also got Max the Lip."

Sonny finished his drink and said: "Well, let's inspect the troops, shall we?"

They took the lift to the ground floor and found the escort party standing in a group in the lobby. Seeing them, Sonny said to Mastrioni: "You didn't tell me the Martians had landed."

Mastrioni grinned and in a loud voice said: "Ugly bunch of bananas, ain't they?"

Sonny let his eyes wander from disfigurement to disfigurement. They were exactly right; a perfect foil to his radiance. Seated with them in the Starlight Room he would be as salient as a diamond ring on a charred finger, a fallow deer amongst a sounder of warthogs. "Excellent," he said.

Mastrioni, pleased that Sonny was pleased, said to Benjie: "You did good, Benjie."

"Yes, you did well, Benjie," Sonny said grudgingly. He said to

Mastrioni: "Have the cars been taken care of?"

"They're waitin' outside," Mastrioni said.

In Lauren Bacall's voice, Sonny called to the escorts: "Okay, girls, let's go." To the one he took to be Hammernose Hymie, he said: "And no stopping on the way for soda pops, Alice."

They travelled in three cars – Sonny and Mastrioni in Sonny's cream Studebaker – a gift from Mastrioni – and Benjie and the others in two black limousines, the Studebaker protected front and rear by the limousines.

On the way, Mastrioni placed a hand on Sonny's knee and in an apologetic voice said: "I ain't no good at talkin' Noel Coward, Sonny."

"It doesn't matter," Sonny said coldly, removing Mastrioni's hand.

"You ain't sore?"

"Not in the least." His tone was unconvincing.

"You want I should take classes, I take 'em."

"It's not important."

"You sure you ain't sore?"

"Please stop it," Sonny said.

Mastrioni smiled. "Okay." He gave a contented sigh. "Now we have a good time."

Outside the Starlight Room, they left their cars and when they were assembled Sonny said to Mastrioni: "You lead the way with Benjie, and I'll follow behind with" – he studied faces – "The Lip" – he paused – "and The Nose."

"Why don' you wanna go in with me?" Mastrioni asked peevishly.

"I want to make an entrance," Sonny said. "You're not ugly enough."

Mastrioni, not entirely satisfied, said: "Okay, if tha's what you want."

"Get them for me, will you?" Sonny said.

Mastrioni called to Max the Lip and Hammernose Hymie and they came over.

Sonny, without the least hesitation, took up a position between them and linked his arms into theirs. Looking miserable, Max the Lip said to Mastrioni: "Do we have to do this, boss?" He shuffled his feet.

In a threatening voice, Mastrioni said: "You do what he wants." He said to Sonny: "Okay? We ready?"

"Not yet," Sonny said. He called to the rest of the group: "Will you fall in behind in twos, gentlemen." Imperatively he added: "Quickly now!" To himself he said: 'I think I might be quite good for the army.' For an instant he saw himself in a trench, calmly smoking a cigarette in a holder while shells exploded all around him.

They fell in behind in twos.

"All right, Mum, lead on," Sonny said to Mastrioni.

As they moved off, Sonny looked up at Max the Lip, smiled, and in his Barbara Stanwyck voice said: "This is fun, isn't it, Max?"

Their entrance had the effect Sonny knew it would have. Heads turned and remained turned for a long time. There was a perceptible lessening of the sound of cutlery on china. And as they were shown to their table a woman was heard to say urgently: "Who *are* they?"

They seated themselves, and almost immediately Calvino came up to them and, after greeting Mastrioni, said to Sonny: "You look real neat, Sonny."

Sonny gave a sardonic smile and said: "How long do we have to wait before we have the pleasure of seeing your lady wife perform?" He made the question sound pornographic.

"She's due on at ten," Calvino said, his voice hardening.

"Get a chair and sit down," Mastrioni said.

"I'm with someone," Calvino said.

"Who you with?"

"Frank Lever," Calvino said.

"Go get him; bring him over."

"Yes, do," said Sonny.

As Calvino went off, Mastrioni said to Sonny: "You wanna order now?"

Sonny said: "I don't want anything to eat, just something to drink."

"You ain't had nothin' to eat all day."

"I'm not hungry," Sonny said. "I'll have something to eat later perhaps."

"You ought to eat, if you're drinkin'"

"I've just told you, I'm not hungry."

"You sure?"

"Don't be a boring cow," Sonny said tiredly.

"If *you* ain't eatin', *I* ain't," Mastrioni said. "What you wanna drink, champagne?"

"Why not?" Sonny said.

Mastrioni beckoned to a waiter, who hurried over.

"What champagne you got?" Mastrioni asked.

"We have most champagnes, sir. Dom Perignon, Bollinger, Mumm – "

"Dom Perignon," Sonny interrupted.

"A dozen bottles," Mastrioni said.

"That won't be enough," Sonny said, knowing that it would.

"Make it two dozen," Mastrioni said. To Benjie and the others he said: "You want food, order what you want."

Calvino returned with Lever, who, after paying his respects to Mastrioni, turned to Sonny and said: "Hello, Sonny. It's been a long time."

Sonny gave a small smile and nodded. He was quite pleased to see Lever. Lever, if his childhood memory of him could be relied upon, had an easiness of manner, a certain cynicism, which he found appealing. Nothing seemed overly to impress or surprise him. He detected something of himself in Lever.

Indicating Sonny's uniform, Lever said: "Should I salute?"

"That won't be necessary," Sonny replied. He noticed that Lever's appearance had hardly changed from when he last saw him. His hair was a little greyer, but everything else about him was the same. "We're very informal this evening," he added. For effect and hoping to shock Lever, he said to Mastrioni: "Aren't we, Mum?"

Calvino and Benjie exchanged a glance and Lever smiled.

"Tha's right, no salutin'," Mastrioni said. He chuckled. "We're on furlough tonight." He made a sweeping gesture with his arm. "Get chairs and siddown."

Calvino had a waiter bring two chairs, and he and Lever sat down opposite Mastrioni and Sonny.

The champagne was brought and opened. As they drank, Lever said to Sonny: "You still do your impersonations?"

"Occasionally," Sonny said agreeably.

"I haven't forgotten the time on the train when you nearly had the old girl in the tweed coat swallowing her false teeth with your Barbara Stanwyck impersonation."

Sonny gave a slight smile and said: "Stanwyck's *easy* to do." He turned to Max the Lip, who was seated on his right, and crinkling his eyes, said huskily, Barbara Stanwyckly: "Isn't she, killer?"

Max the Lip moved uneasily in his chair and took a swallow of champagne. He wasn't enjoying himself. He would have preferred to be on a street somewhere breaking someone's neck or leg.

Lever gave an appreciative laugh. "If ever you want an agent, I'd be –"

"Sonny ain't looking for no agent,"Mastrioni broke in, scowling, annoyed with Lever for putting ideas into Sonny's head. Sonny on stage would mean Sonny being away from him and that would be unthinkable. He would rather be parted from his eyes than be parted from Sonny.

Ignoring Mastrioni, Lever said: "I expected your name to be spelt out in lights by this time." After a small pause he said: "What do you do with yourself?"

"Travel," Sonny said.

"Is that *it* – travel?"

"It's enough."

"What happens when you run out of places to visit?"

"I start again with the A's," Sonny said.

"You're letting a fine talent go to waste."

Sonny shrugged. "There are those who say that we should *conceal* our talent; that by concealing our talent we spare the *un*talented the feeling of inferiority."

"Crackpots," Lever said.

"Perhaps."

"If Leonardo de Vinci had thought that – "

"We wouldn't have had to put up with his dreary little pictures."

"We wouldn't have had Beethoven."

"Beethoven's tedious."

"Shakespeare."

"Who enjoys reading Shakespeare?"

"Quite a few people watch his plays."

"And fall asleep."

"Baloney. You're talking baloney."

Sonny, his baiting of Lever over, laughed.

Mastrioni leaned forward and said to Lever: "You don' watch

your mouth, you'll find something' in it – "

"And it won't be angel cake, will it, Sylv?" Sonny said, finishing the sentence he had heard many times before, his voice intimate but drenched with sarcasm. He added viciously: "For heaven's sake shut up." After a short silence, he said in a calm voice: "Mr Lever is right – we *shouldn't* let talent go to waste." He glanced sideways at Mastrioni. "Just imagine what would happen if we were to allow *your* talent to go to waste: half the mortuaries in New York would have to close." Without pausing, he said to Lever: "You enjoy da Vinci's pictures?"

"Never seen one."

"Beethoven?"

"Wouldn't know him from Beiderbecke."

"Shakespeare?"

"I once saw a play of his and fell asleep."

Sonny smiled. He let a moment pass, then said: "Perhaps you're right, perhaps I *should* go on stage."

"You once told me you were made for it," Lever said.

"I think I could be good."

"I'm darn sure you could."

Sonny looked from Lever to Calvino, who was turning his glass on the table. Addressing Lever but with his eyes on Calvino, he said: "Better than the Calvino slut?"

Calvino stopped turning the glass and jerked up his head. "Why, you little – " He pushed back his chair as if to get to his feet, but remained seated when Mastrioni said quickly, threateningly: "You little *what*, Tommy?"

"Nothin'," Calvino said. His voice was full of bitterness.

"You got somethin' to say, you better say it," Mastrioni said.

"Forget it," Calvino said.

Mastrioni's face whitened. He leaned forward. "Forget it? FORGET IT!"

Heads turned.

"I'm sorry, Sylvano," Calvino said. His shoulders sagged.

Mastrioni wiped a speck of saliva from his mouth with a table napkin. "Tha's bedder. Tha's bedder you're sorry," he said.

Sonny turned back to Lever. "Better than the Calvino slut?" he persisted.

Lever studied Sonny's face. He had once read an article in *Variety* in which the writer described Greta Garbo's features as impeccable. Sonny's features, he thought, were impeccable. He wondered how his libido would cope with them if ever he were to find himself alone with Sonny on a desert island. He said: "With hard work you could be as good as – " He hesitated: what he had to say might upset Sonny, and he knew from a conversation he had had with Calvino that to upset Sonny would be to incur the wrath of Mastrioni. He glanced at the appalling face of Hammernose Hymie, pictured him grinning down at him as he lay broken and bleeding in some dark alley. The hell with it, he thought, and said: "With hard work, you could be as good as your mother." He saw Mastrioni dart an anxious look at Sonny, and thought he detected two points of red appear in Sonny's cheeks. Recklessly he continued: "Your mother's the best there is."

Sonny calmly sipped champagne. He would not allow the anger he felt to surface. If it was Lever's intention to goad him – and he wasn't sure that it was – he would disappoint him; he would display exquisite self-control; he would surprise them all. He smiled dazzlingly. "Dear mother," he said sweetly. "All tits and talent." He went on: "Does she still have those ghastly ringlets? The last time I saw her she looked like a terribly ancient Shirley Temple." He snickered. "Someone really should tell her about them – it would be a kindness." He paused. "Perhaps *I* should be the one to do that." He took another sip of champagne. "Later, perhaps, after she's performed." He said to Calvino: "Mother *will* be joining us, won't she?"

Calvino was silent.

"Sure she will," Mastrioni said. "One big happy family tonight."

They drank and talked, or rather Mastrioni, Lever and Sonny talked; the others for the most part were silent. They found Sonny's presence inhibiting. His sneering remarks and closeness with Mastrioni prevented them from being their natural selves. But they listened, and whenever Sonny said something belittling to Mastrioni ("Do you *have* to make that filthy smacking noise every time you take a drink?") or whenever Mastrioni's manner towards Sonny became too servile, they exchanged covert, tense glances which said: "Can you believe what you're hearing?"

Suddenly the lights dimmed and a disembodied voice announced gravely: "And now ladies and gentlemen, for your entertainment, New York's Starlight Room is privileged to present that amazing impersonator of stage and screen personalities...the voice of Hollywood...Miss Honey Bunn." A band struck up *This Could Be The Start Of Something Big* and a moment later a spotlight came on and picked out a shimmering silver-blue curtain which faced the diners beyond an area reserved for dancing. There was a murmur of approval as the curtain parted and revealed a three dimensional representation of New York's skyline at dusk, the windows of the buildings flickering points of yellow and white. Standing before the skyline on a glass stage were the silhouetted figures of seventeen musicians. "Ladies and gentlemen, Miss Honey Bunn!" The musicians took a step sideways and Honey, who had hidden herself behind them, strode forward smiling and swinging her shoulders. She wore a charcoal double-breasted suit with a wide pin-stripe, a black shirt, a yellow silk tie, and black-patent shoes.

Looking at her, Sonny smiled to himself. She *had* changed. Her face had seemingly doubled in size. The flesh around the mouth had spilled over into her neck and engulfed it. *There was no neck*, just a sac that hung from her chin and disappeared into her shirt collar. She looked bloated, goitrous. She looked disgusting, Sonny thought.

One of the musicians handed Honey a microphone, and raising it to her mouth, she took up the tune:

> *You're lunching at Twenty-One and watching your diet*
> *Declining a charlotte russe, accepting a fig*
> *When out of a clear blue sky, it's suddenly gal and guy*
> *And this could be the start of something big*

It was Howard Keel's voice. The singer's rich, virile tones reverberated around the heads of the audience, drowning all sounds, and, because of the excellence of the impersonation, making all conversation cease.

As he listened, Sonny was conscious of a twinge of annoyance. He hadn't expected her to be quite so good: he'd expected an *above average* performance but not a *masterly* one. He looked at Lever and saw that Lever was looking at him. He raised his eyebrows and inclined his head, as if to say: "She's very good."

Lever smiled. He didn't know why, but Sonny's acknowledgement of Honey's talent, albeit tacit and condescending, gave him immense satisfaction.

This could be the start of something BIG!

Ending the song, Honey punched the air with her fist. Immediately a great crackle of applause broke out and with it more murmurings of approval. Calvino sprang to his feet and began whistling through his teeth. Once or twice he glanced down at Sonny with eyes that said: "How'd you like *that* for openers, smartass?"

When the applause had subsided, Honey thanked the audience, and after bowing her head for a moment, said quietly: "You know, ladies and gentlemen, there's no place in the world like Hollywood, and there are no movie stars in the world like the ones Hollywood produces; there's no other country that makes them the way *we* make them. England may have Laurence Olivier (here she called out in Olivier's voice: "It's Heathcliffe, Cathy! Cathy, come back! Don't leave me, Cathy!"), and France, Maurice Chevalier (she gave the Chevalier chuckle and in the Frenchman's distinctive broken English sang: "Every leetle breeze seems to whisper Louise.").

There was laughter from the audience and some uncertain applause.

"But they haven't got what we've got," Honey went on. "They haven't got the names that make Hollywood the movie capital of the world. Names like...Cary Grant." She stiffened her body, leaned backwards a little and gave a bemused half smile. For a moment, despite her platinum hair and her ballooned face, she resembled the suave dark-haired star of romantic comedies. "Well, bless my soul, if it isn't Judith Davenport. Well, well, well, I scarcely recognised you with that soufflé on your head. It is a soufflé, isn't it? Or is it a hat? No, silly me. Of course it isn't a hat, it's cousin Betsy's pekinese."

More laughter and this time solid applause.

"And Broderick Crawford..." Honey swayed her head and made fidgety body movements. "Okay, the whole thing went wrong, the whole thing blew up in my face. What do you want me to *do*, cut my throat? I cut my throat, where will that leave you?... without a patsy."

Louder applause.

"And Henry Fonda..." She spoke the name reverentially, smiled wistfully. "Now there's one beautiful actor." She paused. "You ever

213

see him in that great movie, *The Grapes Of Wrath*? Remember the scene with his mother when he's about to leave the family to become a union man? It went something like this ..."

And so it went on: John Wayne...William Holden (the boardroom speech from *Executive Suite*)...Spencer Tracey...Frederick March...Gary Cooper...Burt Lancaster...Fred McMurray...Claude Raines...Cagney...Bogart...Groucho Marx, and finally Al Jolsen. The band struck up, and Honey spread her legs and held clenched hands to her chest.

Cal-i-for-nia here I come
Right back where I started from

Sonny, sipping champagne, lowered his glass. A picture of himself at age six standing on a chair singing *Sonny Boy* had sprung into his mind. He put down his glass and stood up.

A sun-kissed miss said don't be late
That's why I can hardly wait

The rasping voice of Ethel Merman joined Al Jolsen's.

Honey, taken aback, faltered momentarily and looked in the direction of Sonny's table, her eyes narrowed to penetrate the dark and identify the singer. Perhaps it *was* Ethel Merman. Perhaps the great Broadway star had called in unexpectedly. These things happened. Hadn't she once seen Tony Martin in the audience? (His lack of height had disappointed her.) She sang louder. Nobody was going to get the better of *her* – not even Ethel fucking Merman.

Sonny, still singing, moved from behind the table and on to the dance area. In the style of the Broadway actress, he strode quickly back and forth before the audience, his head held high and his chest thrown out.

The audience laughed and applauded.

Aware now that it wasn't Merman, Honey increased her volume. Inside she swore at the floor manager for not having had the interloper thrown out.

Open up those golden gates

The voices of Jolsen and Merman soared in unison.

Cali-for-nia here I come!

The lights came on and there were cries of "More!"

Sonny faced Honey and saw her brow furrow, then her mouth

drop open. Identified, he smiled cynically and gave a slight bow.

Honey, her face reddening, turned to leave the stage

"MORE!"

Honey hesitated, considered her position. To walk off at that moment would make her appear a bad loser; she would be jeered. She looked at the bandleader and snapped: "Broadway." She would make Sonny wish he'd never taken her on.

> Come on along and listen to
> The lullaby of Broadway

Frank Sinatra's voice filled the room.

So, too, did Doris Day's. Sonny, his eyes crinkled and his mouth stretched to its limit in a Colgate smile, *was* Doris Day:

> A Hip-hooray and a bally-hoo
> The lullaby of Broadway

The audience cheered.

After Frank Sinatra and Doris Day came Dean Martin and Dinah Shore (*Green Eyes*); Louis Armstrong and Ella Fitzgerald (*Can't Get Started*); Fred Astaire and Judy Garland (*Heaven*); Bing Crosby and Rosemary Clooney (*Begin The Beguine*); Bob Hope and Peggy Lee (*The Folk Who Live On The Hill*).

The applause was the loudest that had ever been heard at the Starlight Room, and when it died, Sonny took a deep, contented breath. Honey, had she been standing on a chair, would have kicked in its back.

Sonny returned to his table and when he was seated, Lever said to him: "What you did wasn't good. You know that, don't you?"

"Do I?"

"You ruined her act."

"She once ruined mine. Anyway, the audience loved it."

"Sure, they loved it," Mastrioni said. His face glowed with pride. He poured Sonny champagne and wished it could be liquid gold.

"They may have loved it," Lever said, "but you ruined Honey's – your mother's act."

"Yes, I did, didn't I?" Sonny said.

Calvino got to his feet.

"Where you going?" Mastrioni asked him.

Calvino looked at Sonny with stone cold eyes. "To talk to Honey," he said.

"Bring her back here," Mastrioni ordered.

Calvino, his teeth clenched, nodded and left.

The disembodied voice said: "There will now be dancing for the remainder of the evening, ladies and gentlemen. Please enjoy the music of Roy Whiting and his orchestra."

Couples moved on to the floor to dance a quickstep. As they danced, they looked across at Sonny.

"Did you enjoy it?" Sonny asked Lever.

"I don't enjoy seeing a person's act ruined."

"Give me an honest answer. Did you enjoy it?"

"'I've been in the entertainment business for thirty years and it was the second best thing I've ever seen."

"What was the best?"

"A sword swallower who welshed on me for a hundred bucks choking to death on the Piermont stage in Cincinnati."

Sonny gave a short laugh. "How did you score us?"

"Nothing in it."

Sonny turned to Mastrioni. "What do *you* say, Mum?"

"No contest. You won from here to Belmont Park," Mastrioni said.

"I *thought* you might say that," Sonny said dryly.

After twenty minutes Calvino returned with Honey. A waiter brought her a chair and she sat down. She had changed into an ankle length gold lamé evening gown, but still wore her stage make-up, which away from the glare of the spotlight was a bright orange. Mastrioni filled a glass with champagne and handed it to her. "A swell act, Honey," he said. "Jolsen: I love him. Sinatra…" He smiled sublimely for a moment, then, leaning forward: "You know he has connections with friends of ours?"

Honey had not heard Mastrioni. Her thoughts were concentrated on Sonny. She wanted to throw her champagne in his face, but was held back by what Calvino had said to her in her dressing room a few minutes before ("You say or do anything to hurt Sonny and we'll both of us be sleepin' in oxygen tents tonight").

Sonny said to her: "Hello, mother dear. How are you? You've put on a little weight since last I saw you."

"You enjoy yourself tonight?" Honey asked contemptuously.

"Fun, wasn't it?" Sonny said.

"Depends on how you take your fun," Honey replied. Seeing him at close quarters she felt herself age and become ugly. She hated him for looking as beautiful as he did. She felt no pride in knowing that this beautiful young man was her son.

"I thought your Crosby a little high," Sonny said.

Ignoring Calvino's warning, Honey said: "You should know all about stinkers."

Calvino audibly drew in his breath, and Sonny laid a calming hand on the fist Mastrioni had made. "I meant that you made him sound a little falsetto," he said charmingly.

Lever, tit-for-tat, said: "Your Dinah Shore needs working on."

"Your Dinah Shore was perfect," Mastrioni said.

"Thank you, Sylv," Sonny said, and heard Honey gasp.

It was a reaction he had become accustomed to. Strangers found his emasculation of someone as powerful as Mastrioni an alarming experience. It was as if they had been in a room with Attila The Hun and heard him addressed as Tilly. Sonny decided he would give Honey something *else* to think about. He turned to Max The Lip and said: "Let's dance, shall we, Max?"

Max The Lip recoiled.

Sonny turned to Mastrioni. "Tell him to dance," he said coldly.

Mastrioni leaned forward and looked around Sonny at Max The Lip.

"I can't dance, boss," Max said before Mastrioni could speak.

"You *dance*," Mastrioni ordered.

Sonny moved back his chair and stood up. In Ingrid Bergman's voice, he said to Max The Lip: "They're playing our song, Rick."

Max The Lip slowly got to his feet, a miserable death-sentence look in his eyes.

On the dance area Sonny placed an arm round Max The Lip's waist and held out his right hand. "You lead," he said.

Max The Lip *could* dance. He danced extremely well. He was light on his feet, as many big men are. His feather-step was excellent.

As they danced, there were sniggers from the other dancers and from the people sitting at the tables. At Mastrioni's table, Honey looked at Calvino and saw him give a tiny shake of his head, as if to say: "Take it easy. Don't say anything." (She wanted to say: "Jesus, what a cream puff *he* turned out to be.")

Sonny danced twice with Max The Lip and once with Willie The Shoe (a foxtrot – *Tea For Two* – which Willie, despite his size fifteen feet and ruined knees, performed with consummate skill).

As Sonny was leaving the floor after the foxtrot, a tall grey-haired man with watery eyes came up to him and in a loud upper-crust English accent said: "You, sir, are a disgrace to the uniform you wear." The man swayed a little and his words were not quite formed.

Sonny brushed him aside and returned to his table.

The man followed, and, as Sonny was about to sit down, reached out as if to take hold of his tunic.

Sonny gave him the merest, contemptuous glance, knocked his arm away and sat down.

Mastrioni stood up. He took hold of the man by the neckband of his shirt, pulled him towards him so that their faces almost touched and said: "You ever try layin' a hand on him again and I'll have it taken off at the wrist and sewn to your mouth."

"Wha – " The man started to say something but Mastrioni gave him a violent push and he staggered backwards, his mouth open and his arms flailing.

"Get outta here. Beat it," Mastrioni growled.

The man recovered his balance, looked balefully at Mastrioni for a few seconds, then turned on his heel and went to his table.

"You okay?" Mastrioni asked Sonny.

"Yes, of course," Sonny said unperturbedly.

"You don't seem so popular all of a sudden," Honey said.

Sonny sighed. "The English …" he said. "They *do* tend to get emotional over the wrong things." He enveloped Honey in a look of disgust and added: "Do you *always* look as you do now?" Quickly, before Honey could reply, he said to Lever: "I don't suppose *you* would care to dance?"

"Sorry, I'm all booked up," Lever said.

They talked and drank, Honey and Calvino speaking only when spoken to and then in monosyllables.

Towards the end of the evening, Honey, her brow wrinkled as if she were in pain, suddenly got to her feet. To nobody in particular, she said in a dull voice: "I have to go to the powder room", and taking up her purse, went off.

When she returned fifteen minutes later, her eyes were bright and urgent and she was smiling. She kissed Calvino on the cheek. "So," she said cosily, sitting down and addressing Sonny, "what's little sugar plum fairy been up to while Momma's been away?"

"For chrissake!" Calvino gripped her wrist, but she wrenched it free.

Sonny stared at her for a few moments, then turned to Mastrioni and said: "The lady's a little drunk, wouldn't you say, Mum?"

"Mum!" Honey laughed explosively. "That what you call him: *Mum*? Jesus!" She looked at Max The Lip and said sneeringly: "What'ds he call *you*, Frankenstein: *Gran'ma*?"

"Or is she on dope?" Sonny asked, as if he hadn't heard. "She has that look in her eyes, wouldn't you say?" He snatched up her purse and, avoiding her attempt to retrieve it, unfastened its clip and emptied the contents on to the table. Among a collection of garishly-packaged cosmetics was a small silver box. Sonny picked it up and opened it. "Now…what have we here?"

"Lemme have that," Honey said angrily.

"What would you say that is, Sylv?" Sonny extended the box to Mastrioni, who took a small pinch of white powder from it and tasted it. "Snow," he said without hesitation. He tasted it a second time. "It's good. Grade One."

"Well, well…so mother's a dope fiend," Sonny said. "How very squalid." He closed the box and tossed it on to the table.

"How long you been on junk?" Mastrioni asked.

Honey, refilling her purse, didn't answer.

"How long she been on junk, Tommy?"

"I dunno; a few years now, I guess," Calvino said.

"That our merchandise she's usin'?"

Calvino nodded.

"Paid for?"

"Sure it's paid for," Calvino said hotly.

"It'd better be," Mastrioni said. "I ever find out – "

"It's paid for," Benjie confirmed.

Honey snapped her purse shut and glared at Sonny.

"Yes?" Sonny asked. He smiled ravishingly. "Do you have something to say?"

Honey drew a deep breath. Her hatred of him had shifted to

unmitigated loathing. He had ruined her act, criticised her appearance and exposed her weakness in a way that had made her feel and look cheap. She had come to the Starlight Room in a happy mood. She and Calvino had made love before leaving the apartment and they had both enjoyed it. Afterwards, flushed and naked and looking at herself in a mirror, she had remarked on her size, and Calvino, laughingly and with a tiny slap, had said: "There can't be too much of you for *me*, baby." His words had pleased her and put her in good spirits. In the car on their way to the Starlight Room, she had sung a romantic song to him in her Fats Waller voice. Then, thanks to Sonny, it had all gone wrong. Yes, she *did* have something to say. "Plenty," she said and stood up.

"Ladies and gentlemen – " She caught the attention of the bandleader and signalled to him to stop the music.

Calvino got to his feet and took hold of her by the arm, but she shrugged him off.

"Ladies and gentlemen, you may not know it but we have with us tonight a very special guest – one of New York's most prominent citizens – in fact, one of the United States' most prominent citizens. I know you will want to say a big hello to" – she indicated Mastrioni – "Mr Sylvano Mastrioni."

There was a little half-hearted applause and Mastrioni, smiling grimly, raised a hand in acknowledgement.

"Mr Mastrioni," Honey went on, "is here with his faggot boyfriend, Sonny – " She paused and looked down at Sonny. "Sonny *Backhouse*." She reached across the table and ruffled Sonny's hair. "Stand up, Sonny, and give the folks a curtsy."

There was laughter.

Sonny remained seated. He was smiling, but his throat and brain burned with anger.

"No-o-o-o?" Honey asked soothingly, as if she were addressing a petulant child. She smiled and winked at the audience. "She's a little tired tonight, folks; must be all that dancing she's been doing. Tires a girl out, doesn't it?"

Calvino linked his arm into Honey's and gripped it tightly. "Move," he said, barely moving his lips. He exerted body pressure.

Honey pointed to Sonny. "Sonny Craphouse, folks," she shouted as Calvino's strength prevailed and she was led away.

For several minutes there was an awkward silence; then Lever got to his feet and bid Sonny and Mastrioni goodnight.

Mastrioni and Sonny left soon afterwards.

During their drive to the hotel – a journey punctuated with threats from Mastrioni (*She's dead…The next place she plays in'll be a garbage sack…She's gonna wish she never opened that fat mouth of hers…*) – Sonny was silent. He spoke only when he was in Mastrioni's apartment with the President in his hand, and then he said: "I've made up my mind: I'm going on stage. It's – "

"Sonny, please… " Mastrioni shook his head. "Don't do this." His voice sounded hollow and unreal.

"I've made up my mind," Sonny repeated. "I'm going on stage. And I'm going on stage with *her*, so I don't want anything to happen to her." He faced Mastrioni. "Do you understand? I don't want anything to happen to her. Get hold of Lever tomorrow and tell him I should like to see him as soon as possible." He threw the President to one side, waved away Mastrioni's pleadings, and took the lift to the next floor.

He undressed slowly and got into bed. As he relaxed, he considered the step he was about to take. He would hate the constant travelling and the hotel accommodation and the disgusting dressing rooms (he had seen enough 'backstage' movies to know that an entertainer's life was not an easy one) but there would be compensations; there would be the pleasure of appearing before audiences, of hearing their applause, of seeing his name on posters outside theatres. But most of all there would be the exquisite pleasure of making Honey suffer. For the first time in his life he went to sleep looking forward to the next day.

* * *

On the floor below, Mastrioni paced back and forth. The tiredness that had suddenly come over him on the drive home from the Starlight Room had been chilled away by the shock of Sonny's announcement. He was tormented by thoughts of a Sonny distanced from him, of Sonny the entertainer mixing with other entertainers. He had had experience of these people: he owned, or extorted money from many of the clubs and theatres in which they appeared, owned many of the entertainers themselves. He knew how dissolute they were, how dissolute Sonny was.

He had first learned of Sonny's dissoluteness during a holiday they had taken in Venice to mark Sonny's seventeenth birthday. Returning unexpectedly to their hotel suite, he had found him on a bed with two of the locals – one a short wiry man with dark blacksmith's arms, and the other a gap-toothed youth of about twenty. Sonny was wearing only a gold half-mask (a relic from a costume ball they (Sonny and Mastrioni) had attended the previous evening (Sonny masquerading as Narcissus, and Mastrioni, at Sonny's insistence, as Charles Dickens) and was standing looking down at the man and the youth as they copulated. A few weeks later, when they were back in New York, a search party led by Benjie had discovered Sonny, who had been missing for two days, in a derelict building, drunk and naked and surrounded by a dozen salivating down-and-outs.

Mastrioni did not hold Sonny's dissoluteness against him: Sonny was Sonny. What he feared was that it might lead to his meeting someone with whom he would want a permanent relationship. Away from his watchful eye (Mastrioni had constantly to detail Calvino or Benjie to 'take care' of a partner who'd become too intrusive), the greater, he felt, would be the likelihood of that happening, especially if he were in the company of entertainers; many of the entertainers Mastriioni had encountered had been witty and amusing – traits that a bored twenty-two-year-old would find compellingly attractive.

He continued to pace back and forth.

* * *

"You look ghastly," Sonny said as he took his place at the breakfast table the next morning. (Sonny and Mastrioni always breakfasted together. It was a routine they had gotten into since their first days together.)

"I didn't sleep too good," Mastrioni said.

"You look haggard," Sonny said.

There was a long silence before Mastrioni said: "You mean what you said last night?"

"Yes," Sonny said. He reached for a slice of toast. "Have you contacted Lever yet?"

"Not yet."

"Have him meet me in Chad's at seven."

"It ain't good, this, Sonny."

"Don't be bloody, Sylv, I'm not in the mood." He bit into the toast.

"Why you want this theatre shit? You want more money, I give you more."

"It has nothing to do with money."

"What's it to do with then? You tell me."

"I'm bored."

"*You're* bored, we're *both* bored. Okay, we'll take a trip – we'll catch a ship somewhere. We'll take over the whole ship and do the fuckin' world," Mastrioni said wildly.

"Please don't swear," Sonny said. He sipped coffee. "I need to do something different."

"We will. We'll go somewhere different and have a good time, have some fun. You don' need this theatre shit, Sonny."

"I do," Sonny said resolutely.

"Honey: she won' have you in the act."

"She will. You'll make sure of that."

"Why you wanna work with her, you hate her so much?"

"She needs to be taught a lesson."

And it was left at that.

CHAPTER 2

Chad's Tap Room on 26th Street smelled of old frying and bad drains, and some of the men who stood at the bar had the vacuous, half-demented look that comes from drinking raw alcohol. Their clothes were torn and stained and their faces rough with five-day beards. When they opened their mouths to order a drink or to shout suddenly and briefly at a wall or the reflection of themselves in the flyblown mirror at the back of the bar, they showed broken, carious teeth. One man coughed, and, clearing his throat, made the sound a soda siphon makes when run down.

"What time does Dorothy Parker and her gang get here?" Lever asked, looking around and seating himself opposite Sonny in a dimly lit booth.

"Pleasant, isn't it?" Sonny said. "Unpretentious."

In the background an adenoidal singer crooned through the zinc-meshed front of a boxwood radio.

Sonny was dressed in a Prince of Wales check suit, a dazzlingly white shirt, and a silver and red cravat. The cuffs of his shirt showed three-quarters of an inch below the sleeves of his jacket and were held together with wafer-thin tablets of unembellished gold. On the table in front of him were a bottle of gin, two glasses – one empty – and a pitcher of water. "Will you have gin, or would you prefer something else?"

"Gin's fine," Lever said.

Sonny poured a large measure of gin, which Lever topped up with water. "Chin-chin," Sonny said, raising his glass.

"Cheers," Lever responded.

When they each had taken a swallow, Sonny said: "Did Mastrioni tell you why I wanted to see you?"

"I got the message from Calvino. I was told to meet you here, that's all."

"I intend becoming an entertainer," Sonny said.

"That's good," Lever said.

"With Honey as my partner."

Lever smiled and said: "She wouldn't work with you for a million a week, platinum toothpicks thrown in."

Sonny took another drink. He glanced round the bar and, coming back to Lever, said: "If she refuses, I'll have Mastrioni close doors on her; there'd be no club or theatre she could work in. He can do that, you know – Mastrioni. He's an extremely powerful man. All he has to do is pick up a telephone. You're aware, of course, that Mastrioni is the boss of bosses – the capo di tutti fruity, or whatever it is they call him

"Capo di tutti capi. Yes, I *had* heard."

"The other families do what he tells them to do. If he tells them to shut her out, she's shut out. She'd never work again."

"You'd have him do that?"

"Of course."

"You don't need Honey. You have enough talent to make it on your own."

"I know, but it wouldn't be any fun."

"Why not?"

"There'd be no competition."

Lever looked puzzled.

"Last night at the Starlight Room was enjoyable – *most* of the time it was. I enjoyed being in front of an audience. But what gave me the greatest pleasure was competing against the Calvino slut and beating her. I did, you know – beat her. My impersonations were much the better."

"You were better, but not much," Lever said.

Sonny gave a pleasant, negligent smile and went on: "I would have no fun appearing on my own; after a while it would become tedious – a not very pleasant job. I would get no satisfaction from it. I would – will – get tremendous satisfaction from dimming the Calvino slut's lights; humiliating her."

"That sounds a little like sadism to me."

"Perhaps."

"You must hate her like that bunch over there" – Lever nodded towards the drinkers at the bar – "hate water."

"I do."

"Because she ditched you when you were a kid, and then dumped you on Mastrioni?"

"Oh, good heavens, no. No, not at all. I would have *hated* to be brought up by her." He laughed, showing flawless teeth. "God, what a thought!" He paused and went on: "No; Henry and Jessica treated me very well; Mastrioni gives me everything I ask for. If I were to ask him for a million dollars he would give it to me unhesitatingly. He rather dotes on me, you know."

"Yes, I had noticed."

"No, I haven't quite worked out why it is that I hate her."

"Maybe it's because she hates *you*."

"Possibly, but I think there's more to it than that. I rather fancy it's because she turned out differently from what I'd expected. As a child I always had it in my mind – perhaps Jessica put it there – that she was a great actress, a beautiful, fragile creature who wore wonderfully elegant gowns and smelled faintly of curacao. She was something of a disappointment."

"That doesn't sound like a good reason for hating someone."

"Ever hear of Marcel Proust?"

"He the guy with the elephant act?"

"He was a writer. He got to hate his mother because she once failed to kiss him goodnight."

"My old lady used to *hit* me goodnight but I never hated her. I didn't like her a lot, but I never hated her."

"Some people are more sensitive than others. A shock to the nervous system of a sensitive person can have the most dire psychological repercussions."

Lever looked away briefly. "So you want to go into show-business?"

"I've bored you."

"I'm short on time."

"You accept that I will be working with Honey?"

"Like you said, Mastrioni is a powerful man."

"A routine will have to be worked out. I will want your advice."

"What do you have in mind?"

"Something similar to the little show we put on at the Starlight Room last night – musical numbers plus dialogue between big screen names – Bogart and Bergman, Tracey and Hepburn, Garfield and

Crawford – that sort of thing. The musical numbers would come at the end of the act, of course."

"It sounds good to me."

"It will be *very* good. When can we get started?"

"Honey's got a twelve-week Vegas spot when she finishes at the Starlight and after that she's at the Crystal Club for – "

"You'll have to cancel all engagements."

Lever lowered his glass. "Now wait a minute," he said slowly. "Those are firm bookings, contracts have been signed. If we pull out, we're going to be hit for everything we've got."

"Mastrioni will fix it. When can we start? I'd like to work out something as soon as possible. I would suggest that you and the Calvino slut meet with me at my apartment ten a.m., Monday."

Lever was silent. He clenched his teeth and looked at his drink.

"We'll need copies of movies. Can you get them? If you have any trouble, let me know and I'll have Mastrioni pull strings. Get as many as you can. Those with big names." Sonny swallowed more drink. "I think the act should have one rather special scene – something glamorous and glowing. *Gone With The Wind* – a scene featuring Gable and Vivien Leigh. The Calvino woman will have to lose weight; she's hideously fat; ideal for Sydney Greenstreet but not Gable." He paused and set down his glass. "By the way," he said, "I won't expect any payment for my appearances. I'll arrange to have all monies due to me turned over to you. You'll do very well out of this."

"I'll drink to that," Lever said.

* * *

When Lever had gone, Sonny had two more drinks, then, looking round the bar, chose his partner for the night – a tall, broad-shouldered man with a five-day beard and long club-like arms.

CHAPTER 3

When Honey had calmed down, they lapsed into a difficult, confined silence, like mourners in a funeral parlour who had known the deceased but were not known to each other. Eventually Calvino said: "The whole set-up's crazy; the little creep's practically running the outfit. He blinks, Mastrioni jumps through hoops."

They were seated in Honey's and Calvino's apartment on the day following Lever's conversation with Sonny. Lever had come there and told them of it. At first Honey had refused to believe him. "You're kidding; you're putting me on," she'd said. But Lever had said no, he wasn't putting her on; and Honey, her whole body trembling with rage, had launched into an attack on Sonny that had lasted a solid forty minutes. The volume of her voice had given Lever a headache; he sat now with his eyes closed.

There was silence again until Honey, out of the blue, said to Calvino: "And you *don't*, I suppose. You and all the *other* tough guys."

Calvino, taken aback, sat up suddenly. "Huh?" he said.

"Jump through hoops," Honey said. Like a bad general beaten in battle, she had turned on her second in command.

"How many times I have to tellya?" Calvino said tiredly. "Anyone steps out of line with Sonny, it's 'Goodbye world'. You're lucky you're not in a drum of cement someplace."

Honey lighted a cigarette, pursed her lips and blew out a thin stream of smoke. "What'ds Mastrioni see in the little crud, *any*way?" she asked, determined to keep the topic alive. "Why'ds he let him walk all over him? He getting shaky in the head?"

"Some of the boys in the organisation, they're askin' the same thing," Calvino said. "They're sayin' that maybe he's losin' his grip, that maybe it's time for a change." He turned to Lever. "It's not *me* who's sayin' it, you understand, Frank."

Lever opened his eyes and smiled sardonically. "Of course not, Tommy," he said.

"Jesus!" Honey burst out. "If you can't trust Frank, who *can* you trust? What's wrong with you, for chrissake? If anyone's losing his grip, it's you. Any other guy whose wife had to take what I took from that rat-assed bastard prick the other night would've hit the roof."

"We've been over that," Calvino said.

"Yeah, haven't we though," Honey sneered. She turned to Lever. "You know what Mister Tough Guy here told me before you called, Frank?" She gave Calvino a withering look that lasted a good three seconds. "Sonny throws shit at us, we eat it." She laughed contemptuously. "That's what he told me." She flicked ash into a pink ashtray. "Some fucking tough guy."

"If *you'd* of eaten the shit he threw at you instead of squirting your mouth off, you wouldn't be in the mess you're in now," Calvino said.

Honey took a long moment to digest his words. "You think that's why he's doing what he's doing – to even the score with me for having made him squirm a little, not because he wants a quick way in?" She looked at Lever. "You think that, Frank?"

"I don't know," Lever lied. He hadn't divulged the whole of his conversation with Sonny: he had seen no point in telling Honey that Sonny was out to humiliate her. "Like you, I figured he wanted a quick way in," he added.

Calvino snorted. "A quick way in? If Sonny wanted a quick way in he'da had Sylvano buy him MGM. People like Sonny: you hurt them, they hurt back."

Honey narrowed her eyes. "Hurt me? How's he gonna hurt me?"

"Christ, how do *I* know!" Calvino said. "He's *already* got you climbin' walls, hasn't he?"

"Jesus," Honey said, "every time I think of that little snot I wanna throw up. I'd sooner work with a barrel of rattlesnakes than work with him."

"You know, Honey," Lever said, "however much the idea of working with Sonny makes you want to reach for a monkey wrench, one thing's for sure: you're going to have one hell of an act. Your Gable to his Colbert…His Bergman to your Bogart…It'll knock their socks off."

"I'd like to play Henry Eight to his Ann Boleyn," Honey said. "Take his fucking head off."

"I think we have to get used to the idea that Sonny's calling the shots," Lever said, and they lapsed into silence again.

CHAPTER 4

Honey's morning dosage of heroin was one generous pinch. On the morning of her meeting with Sonny and Lever she allowed herself two. Her railing against Sonny had left her mind worn; she needed a second pinch to refurbish it. Her introduction to the drug had come via a chorus girl in Cincinnati, whose boyfriend was an agent in the narcotics branch of the FBI. She had tried it at the girl's apartment late one evening and enjoyed the sense of euphoria it had given her. By the time of her marriage to Calvino she was addicted to it. She would sooner be without her lipstick than without heroin.

After the second pinch she left the apartment feeling relaxed and quite young.

Lever was waiting for her in the lobby of Mastrioni's hotel. "Would you like something to drink or shall we go straight up?" he asked.

"Let's get it over with," Honey said. She wore a grey suit, a white shirt with a frilled lace front, and red high-heeled shoes. Looking at her, Lever thought: 'If it wasn't for her shape and her hair and her over-made-up face she wouldn't look half bad.' He heard Sonny's words again: *She was something of a disappointment.*

They crossed the lobby to Mastrioni's private lift, and, as they drew near, two men who were seated on either side of the lift's door got to their feet and perceptibly stiffened their bodies.

"It's okay, we're expected," Lever said. "I'm Frank Lever, and this is Mrs Calvino – Tommy Calvino's wife. We're here to see Sonny."

"I seen you someplace before?" the taller of the two men asked Lever.

"I don't think so," Lever replied.

"I gotta check you out," the man said. He nodded to Honey. "Mrs Calvino," he said respectfully.

"We got our tickets, y'know," Honey said sarcastically.

"We gotta check everybody out," the man said.

Honey made an impatient face and looked away.

The man pressed a button beneath a grill at the side of the lift and a few seconds later a small red light came on and the man said into the grill: "I got a Frank Lever and Mrs Calvino down here to see Sonny." A green light came on. "Okay," the man said to Lever, and opened the lift's door. As Honey and Lever got in, the man said to Honey: "How's Tommy? I ain't seen him in a while."

"Still jumping through hoops," Honey replied.

"Huh?" the man said.

"Forget it," Honey said.

Sonny met them in the corridor. He was wearing a lightweight double-breasted grey suit, a white silk shirt open at the neck, and lightweight dark brown leather shoes. He had one hand in his jacket pocket and with the other held an unlighted cigarette. "We're both in grey, I see," he said to Honey. "How exciting."

"Ain't it though," Honey said.

Sonny smiled, and after nodding a greeting to Lever, said: "This way."

He walked ahead of them until he came to a door halfway along the corridor. "In here." He opened the door and stood aside to allow them to enter.

They found themselves in a room that had been styled to look like the foyer of a cinema – a warmly lit, richly carpeted foyer with a bar and a popcorn machine and two other machines that dispensed candy and chocolates and chilled soft drinks in paper cups. On the walls beneath brass-shaded wall lights were large portraits of past and present Hollywood stars and luridly illustrated posters of old movies – *Ben Hur, Blue Angel, The Hunchback of Nottre Dame*. Next to the *Ben Hur* poster was a black peg-board, which playfully announced in small white letters that 'Coming Soon' was *The Gold Rush*. Part of the foyer had been cordoned off with a thick gold rope to make a VIP lounge, and here were featured deep leather armchairs, low smoked-glass tables, and standing chromium-plated ashtrays. From a speaker above a portrait of Yvonne de Carlo in décolleté gypsy costume came intermission music played on a whirlitzer.

"Would you care for a drink?" Sonny asked, his eyes going from Honey to Lever.

"Scotch," Honey said coldly.

"Nothing for me," Lever said.

Sonny went behind the bar, and noticing that Lever was interested in his surroundings, said: "It's a little cinema that Sylv installed for me. Awfully vulgar, isn't it? The cinema itself is through that door over there." Sonny nodded at a quilted leather door that had an Entrance sign above it. He poured a drink. "Would anyone care for popcorn?" he asked.

"Not right now," Lever said. "Let's save it for the Mickey Mouse feature."

Sonny left the bar and handed Honey her drink. "We have *most* of the Mickey Mouse cartoons," Sonny said to Lever. "Sylv loves them. He loves the Popeye cartoons too. He identifies with Bluto."

He said to Honey: "Popeye's fun, don't you think? Perhaps we should include a Popeye-Olive Oyl sketch in the act." He smiled. "You do do Popeye, don't you? I do a very good Olive Oyl."

"I can do Popeye," Honey said flatly, and seeing mirth rise in Sonny's eyes realised he was trying to make a fool of her. She became hot with embarrassment – something that had never happened to her before.

"I was sure that you could," Sonny said. "It's such an *ugly* voice."

"Now listen, you," Honey said angrily. "I've just about had all – "

"Please don't," Sonny said. "Please don't." His eyes had changed to stone cold and his voice, although controlled, was charged with menace. For the first time in her life Honey experienced fear. She looked away.

Sonny turned to Lever and said: "Let's get started, shall we?" He went to the VIP section. "We'll be more comfortable here." He unhooked the gold rope.

When they were seated, he said: "There are things that need to be discussed before we can begin rehearsing. We need to decide what shape the act will take; what dialogue and what songs will be featured; what sort of opening the act should have." Not taking a breath, he went on: "Will we open with a song? If so, what song? What costumes will be worn?"

"I go for a musical opening and closing," Lever said.

"I've given some thought to the matter and I agree with you," Sonny said.

"What about you, Honey?" Lever asked kindly.

Honey shrugged, said nothing.

"So," Sonny said to Lever, "let's try to visualise it. We're standing together on stage; the curtain rises; the orchestra begins to play; we sing." He paused. "Hardly original." He paused again. "*I* have an idea for an opening, but first I'd like to hear yours, if you have one."

Lever rubbed ruminatively at the side of his nose. "How about if you're both on stage, back of stage, with your backs to the audience. The band starts up with – " He thought for a moment. "I don't know, *Lullaby of Broadway*, say – and Honey turns and starts singing Gordon McCrae. She sings the first verse; and then *you*, Sonny, turn and give the second verse in Doris Day."

"And the remainder of the song is sung as a duet?" Sonny said. "That sounds good." After a pause he said: "Or what if the curtain were to rise on an empty stage, with the orchestra playing – let's keep to the song you suggested, *Lullaby of Broadway* – and suddenly from the wings *right* of stage – " Sonny broke off and looked at Honey. "I have to call you something," he said, "so I shall call you something suitably ironic." He raised his eyebrows. "I shall call you 'Mother-dear.'" His voice was loaded with sarcasm.

"Then you won't mind if I call you 'Sonny-dear,'" Honey said with equal sarcasm.

Sonny ignored her and continued: " – and suddenly from the wings *right* of stage Mother-dear here starts to sing *a la* Gordon McCrae. She sings the first verse, and halfway through the second verse comes on stage. I, who will be standing in the wings *left* of stage, take up the third verse *a la* Doris Day or Ethel Merman, complete it, and when I'm halfway through the fourth verse, make *my* entrance. I complete the fourth verse and am joined in the fifth by Mother-dear. As we sing, we move towards each other until we are positioned side by side *centre* stage, where we end the song."

There was silence. Then Lever said suddenly: "I like it." He nodded. "Yeah, it's good."

"I think my opening has a certain drama which yours lacks," Sonny said. "But there's no reason why we shouldn't try both." He paused before saying breezily: "Costumes. What should we wear? For the opening, I mean; something that immediately identifies us as male and female. I shall wear light slacks, a navy shirt and a white silk square knotted cowboy fashion at my throat; something entirely masculine."

Honey smiled to herself, but was silent.

"There must be no doubt in the audience's mind as to our gender," Sonny went on. "Mother-dear must look very feminine. I see her in a gingham frock and" – he looked at Honey for a long moment with an expression of distaste – "and, God help us, bows in her hair."

Honey banged down her glass on the table in front of her and looked at Sonny with hate-filled eyes. She opened her mouth to say something, but Lever got in first and said: "We have a problem here. When you've finished your opening number you'll go straight into dialogue, which means we'll have Honey here dressed in gingham talking Bogart and Cagney, and *you*, Sonny, dressed like Roy Rogers, talking Hepburn and Crawford. It won't work. It'll turn the whole thing into a farce. Somehow you have to make a costume change immediately following the opening number."

"Perhaps if we had a screen on stage that we could change behind?" Sonny suggested.

Lever shook his head. "No," he said. "You've hardly begun the act and already you're disappearing. That's school concert stuff." He lighted a cigarette. "Let's take things one step at a time; we're moving too fast." Blowing out smoke, he said: "So far, we have an *opening* – and the more I think about *your* idea, Sonny, the more I like it – and we have costumes for it. What comes next? The lead-in, the spiel comes next. That's Honey's department – she's *known*, you're not, Sonny." He thought for a while. Eventually he said: "This is a brand new act and that's what has to be put over; that's what the lead-in has to be about. Honey has to explain why it is she's taken on a partner." He focussed on Honey. "How does this sound: Until a few weeks ago you were working solo, then something happened to change that. What happened is, you were reunited with the son you hadn't seen in twenty-two years, since the day you placed him with a family who you knew could give him all the things you couldn't. And what do you discover about your son? You discover that he has a terrific talent for voice impersonation. So terrific is his talent for voice impersonation that you just had to have him in your act."

Honey gave a short, dry laugh. "Excuse me while I throw up," she said.

"It'll work," Lever said. "It'll go big with the trades, too. The trades'll love it. I'll get something down on paper tonight." He drew on his cigarette. Through smoke he said: "Okay, we have our lead-in: next the costume change. From gingham and pants into what? Honey should stick to the outfit she wears – *wore* – at the Starlight Room – the pin-stripe. It's exactly right." He said to Sonny: "How about *you*? You have any ideas about what *you* want to wear? There should be only one change, two at the most. Too many changes and you lose continuity."

"I should wear something that would be suited to the personality of each of the stars I impersonate – a simply-tailored beige jacket and skirt, perhaps…with high-heeled shoes."

Lever said: "I can't see Mae West or Dietrich in a simple beige jacket and skirt."

Sonny inclined his head briefly, acknowledging the logic of the remark. "Good point," he said.

Lever said: "How about a pair of silk lounging pyjamas? Crawford, Hepburn, Bergman, Mae West…It's the kind of outfit they all could wear and look good in."

"Ma Kettle?" Honey said.

"Let's be serious about this," Lever said, his voice hardening.

"I think silk lounging pyjamas would do very well," Sonny said.

"Okay, lounging pyjamas it is. Now, how do we make the change on stage in front of an audience?"

"In front of an audience?" Sonny said. "Wouldn't that be rather risqué?"

"If you mean will the customers see something they shouldn't, the answer is no."

"Explain," Sonny said.

Lever smiled cryptically. "As soon as Honey finishes her spiel, two dressers come on stage, stand in front of you and, to the sound of background music, fix you into new costumes. When I say *fix* you into them, that's exactly what I mean. The costumes you'll be wearing for the opening number will be what we call breakaways – costumes with no backs to them. They're held in place with steel bands – like cycle clips – that're sewn into the material. A couple of pulls and they're off. The replacement costumes will be breakaways also. The whole costume change won't take more than fifteen seconds; and the beauty of it is, it will add interest to the act. People get a *kick* out of seeing a person change from one set of clothes into a new set, especially if the clothes they're getting into are totally different from the ones they've just taken off – like a caterpillar changing into a butterfly."

"Metamorphosis," Sonny said.

"He was one hell of a ball player," Lever said, and without pausing: "Let's make it even more interesting. We'll have the dressers carry make-up. When they've completed the costume change, we'll have them get to work on your faces." He looked at Sonny. "You'll need your eyebrows reshaped and your lashes mascaraed." To Honey, he said: "And you'll need some chin shadow, Honey."

"And a few more facial lines, perhaps," Sonny said, and, by way of stifling a possible riposte, he added quickly: "It's an extremely clever idea, Lever."

"Call me Frank-dear," Lever said.

Sonny said scathingly to Honey: "You're not contributing very much to this discussion,"

"If I did, you maybe wouldn't like what I had to say," Honey said.

"Why wouldn't I?"

"I'm not sure I'm gonna go along with this thing."

"You will," Sonny said without emotion. "You will go along with it or you'll never work again. Didn't Lever make that clear to you?"

"Frank-dear," Lever corrected.

"*I* can get work," Honey said confidently. "I can go overseas and get work."

Sonny raised his eyebrows and in a bemused tone said: "Without vocal chords?" He stood up. "Let's have something to eat, shall we?" To Lever he said, "I shall need wigs, of course."

Sonny ordered food to be sent up and when they had eaten, Sonny and Lever began to a compile a list of the stars to be impersonated and the pictures from which dialogue would be taken. They had nearly completed the list when the door opened and Mastrioni entered.

Sonny glared at him and said: "I thought I told you we weren't to be disturbed."

"The First Lady ain't lookin' so good," Mastrioni said. "I figured you'd wanna know." His voice and eyes were flat. He felt desolate. He had paced his apartment considering what was taking place on the floor above. He had pictured matters being discussed that would take Sonny away from him. He had seen long days without Sonny, and seeing them had wanted to be very close to him. His pacings had taken him to the papiér-maché rat maze, and glancing at it, he had seen the President and the First Lady in mating mode. He had stopped to watch the act and on its completion had turned away. Something, a small noise, made him turn back, and he saw the First Lady stagger sideways and collapse, her legs moving convulsively as if she were trying to get to her feet. Her movements had become more rapid and there was a moment when he had felt an urge to help her. But he hadn't. Had he got her back on her feet she might have rallied and recovered; he would have lost an opportunity to be with Sonny.

"What's the matter with her?" Sonny asked.

"She's breathin' a little funny," Mastrioni said.

Sonny, looking from Honey to Lever, said: "Perhaps this would be a good time to break. We'll continue tomorrow." He stood up. "Would you like to see my little pets?"

"Sure, why not?" Lever said.

Honey was silent.

They took the lift.

"All that screwin' must have got to her," Mastrioni said as the door opened.

Sonny led them at an unhurried, almost carefree pace to the rat maze.

The First Lady was as Mastrioni had left her, only now her legs were still. The President, seemingly unconcerned, scratched an ear. Sonny, seeing Honey looking at the President, said to her: "Sweet, isn't he?" Honey gave a shrug of indifference, but when the President suddenly stopped scratching and looked directly into her eyes (perhaps attracted by the perfume she was wearing) she turned her head away.

Sonny gathered up the First Lady and studied her for a few

moments. He half rotated the hand in which he held her, and her head rolled to one side. "Oh dear," he murmured, "we *are* poorly, aren't we?"

He said to Mastrioni: "Call George, will you?"

Mastrioni went to a table that was placed by the side of a vine-covered pillar, picked up a small china hand-bell and sounded it.

"I think you might enjoy this," Sonny said, his eyes going from Lever to Honey. He smiled. "Come."

They joined Mastrioni at the table.

"Why 'The First Lady'?" Lever asked. "Any special reason?"

Sonny said: "Her mate is called the President; it makes sense that she should be called the First Lady." He placed the near-lifeless rat on the table.

"Why 'The President'?"

"It's as good a name as any. The last rat I had I called Balzac and the one before that Cardinal Wolsey. I name them as the mood takes me." He glanced up at the vine-covered ceiling. "When you think about it, 'The President' is an eminently suitable name for a rat. Presidents, being political animals, are great survivors. They'd do anything to survive. So, too, would a rat. Did you know that if I were to imprison the President beneath a tin helmet on your bare stomach he would chew into your stomach in order to escape?"

"Peachy," Lever said.

As he spoke there was a rustling above their heads.

Looking up, they saw a snake emerge from a cluster of vine leaves and begin a mid-air slow-motion descent towards them. It was coloured gun-metal blue and had a body as thick as a child's thigh.

"And this, I suppose, is George," Lever said. "Sanders or Gershwin?"

"Neither," Sonny said. "He was named after a boy I knew at school."

"I take it you didn't much like George?"

"He had scaly skin and hideously small eyes."

As the snake drew near, Lever took a step back.

"It's all right, he won't harm you," Sonny said. "His fangs have been removed."

"Maybe he's taken up wrestling," Lever said.

When the snake was almost within touching distance, it stretched effortlessly across to the pillar, coiled itself around it and continued its journey.

Sonny reached out a hand. "George is two years my senior, would you believe?" He stroked the snake's head with the backs of his fingers. "We're rather fond of him, aren't we, Sylv?"

"He's family," Mastrioni said solemnly.

The snake uncoiled the first yard or so of its body from the pillar, lowered it to the table, and moved towards the First Lady, who was perfectly still. The only sound was Mastrioni's heavy breathing.

The snake settled its head a few inches from where the First Lady lay and ceased all movement. It stayed this way for perhaps fifteen seconds, then, as if triggered by some inner timing mechanism, oozed forward and very slowly, very gently, took the First Lady, tail first, into its mouth.

Lever glanced at Honey and saw that her brow was furrowed in concentration. He looked back at the snake, and for an instant, a split second before the First Lady disappeared into its mouth, he had the notion that her eyes had opened wide and an expression of panic come into them.

"So long, Mrs President," Mastrioni said carelessly.

"Wonderfully efficient creatures, snakes," Sonny said. "Never any mess when they feed."

"I saw her eyes move," Lever said flatly. "She was still alive,"

"George wouldn't have had her any other way," said Sonny, smiling.

The snake made its way back up the pillar and when it had vanished into the vine leaves, Sonny turned to Lever and said: "Well, I'll see you" – he glanced at Honey – "and Mother-dear same time tomorrow. It's been very interesting, very constructive." He ushered them towards the lift. "Do you think we should have some dialogue between Herbert Marshall and Ethel Barrymore?" He opened the lift's door. "I do a very good Ethel Barrymore." Without waiting for a reply, he said: "Until tomorrow, then." He closed the door on them and pressed a button.

CHAPTER 5

They met every day and watched films. On the fourth showing of *Double Indemnity* Lever noticed that Fred McMurray had flat feet; and on the third showing of *Adam's Rib* Honey decided that Katherine Hepburn was a "pain in the ass". "I can't stand the sight of her," she told Calvino. "That voice! And those teary eyes! Why'n't somebody put her out of her misery, why don't they?"

* * *

Late one Friday, just as Lever and Honey were about to leave Sonny's apartment (after having sat through four showings of *Gone With The Wind*), Sonny suggested that they take a week's break and then begin rehearsing. "I think we've earned one, don't you?" he said. "Anyway, I've building work to be done and the noise would distract us."

They went their separate ways; and now, on their return, Sonny led them into a large room, the beauty of which made Lever catch his breath. For a moment he was back in a theatre on the outskirts of Paris, a tiny theatre painted in blue and gold and hung with nests of amber lights that burned in fragile shades of frosted glass, the very same theatre where, after months of searching, he had found his wife with her French baritone lover.

"Do you like it?" Sonny asked. "I had thirty people working on it night and day for four days. I think they did splendidly, don't you?"

Lever smiled ruefully and said: "The last place I was in that looked like this I made a soprano out of a baritone. I'll tell you about it one day."

"I thought you'd appreciate it," Sonny said with brio, as if Lever's words were lost on him.

Lever nodded in the direction of a pale young man with thinning hair and large protruding ears who sat at a piano at the back of a brilliantly lit stage. "What's Duke Ellington doing here?" he asked.

"Our accompanist," Sonny said. "He's very good. Later, when

we're proficient, I'll arrange for orchestral accompaniment." He drew a gold cigarette case from his inside pocket. "We'll smoke a cigarette, then get started." In Marlene Dietrich's voice, he called to the pianist: "Play something tropical, will you, snooks?"

Honey chose *not* to smoke a cigarette. She sat in one of a bank of blue-velvet seats away from where Lever and Sonny sat and closed her eyes. Her head ached. The heroin she had taken that morning hadn't yet countered the effects of the previous night's gin. She and Calvino had drunk gin. Later they had argued, and when towards the end of the evening she had called him a "Mastrioni brown-noser", he had responded with hot, dangerous words; words that had excited her and made her proud of him. She heard the words again now, and again was excited by them. After a while she swivelled open the top of a pill-box opal ring she had taken to wearing and took from it a pinch of heroin. She heard Sonny call: "Are you fit, Mother-dear?" and saw him, laughing, get to his feet. As she inhaled the heroin, she said to herself: "Have a good time while you can, asshole."

CHAPTER 6

It was the evening preceding the last day of four weeks' of rehearsals and Sonny and Mastrioni were standing at the bar in Mastrioni's apartment, Sonny sipping a martini, and Mastrioni a Scotch and soda, Mastrioni having just suggested to Sonny that he and Honey appear before a specially invited audience.

"It'd be like a try-out for you, Sonny," Mastrioni went on.

"You mean a trial run," Sonny said absently. His thoughts were on Honey and an incident that had taken place between them earlier that day. He had cut one of Honey's Edward G. Robinson lines ("You're good kid, but not *that* good, see. You're still a punk, a two-bit punk"); and Honey, having already seen him cut her lines by half, had refused to rehearse, had walked off stage. Calmly, matter-of-factly, as if commenting on the weather, Sonny had told her that if she didn't return immediately, she would be taken to the roof of the hotel and thrown from it. Ashen faced, Honey had returned immediately.

Sonny let the incident repeat itself in his mind and gave a satisfied smile. He must, he thought, have scared her half to death. Still smiling, he said to Mastrioni: "You know, Sylv, you might *have* something there." He added: "Fix a day – make it a Saturday. And draw up a list of guests. No thugs." He finished his drink, bid Mastrioni goodnight, coolly, and took the lift to his apartment.

* * *

Next morning Mastrioni sat at his desk and drew up a list of guests. Later, handing the list to Benjie, he instructed: "Tell them they don't turn up, they're in trouble."

* * *

There were no absentees. On Mastrioni's left sat a senator, and on his right a police chief. On the police chief's left sat a judge, and next to the judge a Presidential aide. Also in the audience were nightclub and casino owners; a former Broadway leading lady; two film stars; an Anglican bishop; a male opera singer; a diplomat; the world organiser of the Save The Children Fund; a leading heart surgeon; an English photographer of royalty; two film producers; and the owner of twenty million dollars worth of silver bullion and four race tracks.

Following the entertainment there was a cocktail party, and Sonny surprised and delighted guests by appearing in his stage costume (blue-satin lounging pyjamas) and Mae West wig. There was laughter when, in his Mae West voice, he was heard to say to the opera singer: "Hey, fat stuff, is that a bun in your pocket, or is it hernia time?"

Towards the end of the evening an incident occurred: Sonny, disengaging himself from an embrace with the more muscular of the two film stars – a former ventilation engineer adored by countless women and not a few men for his animal good looks – strode up to Mastrioni and to gasps of astonishment slapped him hard across the face. "*Now*, you appalling old cow," he said angrily, "perhaps you'll stop watching me."

But Sonny's anger soon passed and later when everyone was gone and Mastrioni said to him: "You sure look good in those pyjamas, Sonny", Sonny, because he was leaving with Honey and Lever for a theatre engagement in Baltimore the following day and, sadistically, wanted Mastrioni to miss him badly, removed them and went with him to his bedroom. He did not remove his Mae West wig, nor was he asked to.

Next morning Sonny awoke tired and irritable. He was silent at breakfast and ignored Mastrioni's attempts at conversation. He was angry with himself for having stayed too long in Mastrioni's bed. He had given too much of himself.

Later, as he was dressing for the airport, Mastrioni took hold of his hand and with tears in his eyes said: "I'm gonna miss you, Sonny." But Sonny, still irritable, said: "Oh, for heavens sake!" and pulled away. Mastrioni's words, though, remained with him, and on the plane, as he tried to collect a few minutes sleep, they returned, and to his annoyance he was moved by them.

In the days following Sonny's departure, Mastrioni sat alone in his apartment and refused to see or to speak to anyone. Sometimes he sat with the President on his knee and fed him Parmesan cheese. Having the President close to him made him feel close to Sonny. Sometimes he spoke to the President: "What you suppose Sonny's doin' now?" and looking at his watch and seeing that it was late, he would picture Sonny with a handsome entertainer – a black tap-dancer, say – one with a gold-capped tooth and a hard flat stomach – and he would be swept with jealousy and despair.

After five days of pining, he said to Benjie: "I'm going to Baltimore. Have someone take care of the President."

Accompanied by six bodyguards, he boarded his private aircraft and two hours later booked into the hotel where Sonny was staying.

He did not contact Sonny immediately: he kept to his rooms and pondered the reason he should give for his being there. He knew that whatever reason he gave it would not be accepted. Sonny would insult him and scream at him, but in the end, after he had been sufficiently humiliated, he would be allowed to stay.

CHAPTER 7

Baby,

I don't know I can take much more of this. Things are getting so I can't think straight. Everything I do Pretty Boy don't like. Last night he cut me out of the Sinatra/Doris Day number and had himself singing solo. He cut my lines, now he's cutting my numbers. It's getting to be all him and nothing of me. I keep telling him you're not doing this to me but he says you walk out and you're dead. He means what he says, baby. Baby, he scares me, and you know me, I don't scare easy. You were right, he's out to pull the plug on me. Jesus, he hates my guts and I hate his. Frank does what he can but don't get nowhere.

Baby, remember what you told me the night we fought? Did you mean what you said? Jesus, I hope so. With Mastrioni out of the way I'd maybe get my life back.

You know, we get great notices every place we play – we could play in Vegas if we wanted to – but all we do is play in dumps nobody's heard of. Pretty Boy wants it that way. We open at some dump in Pittsburgh next week.

Sylvano hangs around Pretty Boy like he's a million dollar movie queen. It makes me want to throw up. Pretty Boy treats him like dog-dirt, brings his pick-ups back to the hotel three and four at a time and, excuse my language, sugar, fucks with them in front of him. You should see some of the bums he brings back. Some of them they stink.

Baby, I want you so I can't think straight.

I can't give you an address because I don't know where we'll be staying next.

Baby, if I don't get out of this soon I'll finish up in a crazy house.

Jesus, I miss you, baby. Baby, I just want to get my hand round it. You know what I mean.

A million hugs and kisses.

Honey

Had Honey been writing to a close woman friend instead of Calvino she might have mentioned that her weight had risen, that her skin was becoming dry from the amount of drink and drugs she was taking, that dark roots showed in her hair, that she often fell asleep over her meals, that her nail polish was chipped, and that she was beginning to slur her lines.

CHAPTER 8

Calvino's words to Honey had not been spoken out of bravado; he had meant what he said when he told her that she had a surprise coming to her, that he would show her if he was a Mastrioni brown-noser or not, that she shouldn't be surprised if Mastrioni wasn't around for much longer. Suddenly he'd become tired of Mastrioni's treatment of him. He'd served Mastrioni well, yet Mastrioni allowed Sonny to insult and belittle him, belittle Honey. He lived in fear of upsetting Sonny. Suddenly he'd decided he had had enough. Also, he wanted to improve his position within the Mafia; he'd fetched and carried for too long; he wanted something better. Mastrioni had many enemies; if he could find a way of eliminating him, he could go to any one of them and name his price. But how to eliminate someone who was never without an army of bodyguards? He needed a plan that would isolate Mastrioni long enough for a bullet to be put into his head. He had pondered the problem for many hours and not found a solution. Now, as he listened to the voice on the radio, a voice remarkably like Sonny's, one came to him. He shaved, dressed and made a telephone call.

CHAPTER 9

Angelo 'Rings' Torrelli, seated in his favourite booth in Augie's restaurant on East Forty Second Street, raised a pale manicured hand to his mouth and brushed away a crumb of blueberry pie, an extra large portion of which he had just consumed.

Aged 52, Torrelli had thinning black hair, a round over-fleshed face, small eyes that glittered beneath waxy, iridescent lids, and a large pitted nose. He weighed one hundred and fifty two pounds, and when wearing built up shoes, as he was today, reached a height of five feet six inches. He was dressed in a black birdseye suit, a white shirt, and a black and white crescent-patterned tie held together with an inch-wide platinum clip. On each finger of his left hand, set in heavy gold, was a diamond as big as a dried pea. Torrelli enjoyed displaying his wealth for the feeling of pride it gave him. He had worked hard and spilled a great deal of blood for it. He saw it as tangible evidence of his success as a racketeer.

Like Mastrioni, Torrelli started his criminal career as a raider of vending machines and small stores. Later, after serving a prison sentence for armed robbery, he successfully tried his hand at hi-jacking, and with the money he made from it invested in slot machines. Within six moths he controlled the market for them. He still did. He also controlled the gambling in Harlem and had investments in property development, trucking companies and ice cream factories.

Torrelli lived with his wife Lucille (a sufferer of chronic conjunctivitis, who, whenever Torrelli approached her, slipped on dark glasses to protect her eyes from the glare of his rings) and two children in a ten-roomed apartment in Central Park West and had a personal fortune of seventeen million dollars. It wasn't enough. He wanted more. He wanted what Mastrioni had.

"So – " He leaned back and smiled a creamy smile. "I understand you got a proposition you wanna put to me." His voice was thick with catarrh.

"That's right," Calvino said.

Torrelli pulled back the left sleeve of his jacket and glanced at a white-gold watch marked with tiny ice-blue diamonds. "You got ten minutes."

Calvino hesitated, then, his heart beating fiercely because of the enormity of what he was about to say, said: "You want Mastrioni taken out; I know a way to do it. I can do it for you. I'm the only one who can."

Torrelli opened his eyes wide. "I want Sylvano taken out? Why should I wanna thing like that? I ain't got nothin' against the man; me and Sylvano, we're pals. We go back a long way."

Calvino said wryly: "Come on, Rings, this ain't tell-junior-a-story time. You'd give your kids' shoes with their feet in 'em to get rid of Mastrioni."

Torrelli shrugged and smiled a guilty child's smile.

"There's no way you're gonna do it," Calvino went on. "Mastrioni's got a round-the-clock guard. You'll never get to him. You wouldn't get to first base. You wouldn't even get to swing the bat. You've got more chance of gettin' into Harlem in a Klan outfit than you have of gettin' to Mastrioni." He paused. "I got a way."

Torrelli, suddenly serious, leaned forward. "What's the deal?" he said.

CHAPTER 10

Two evenings later in fine, barely perceptible rain and carrying a small suitcase containing a change of clothes and a Luger pistol in a shoulder holster, Calvino made his way from Union Station, and after buying a copy of *The Pittsburgh Tribune* and studying its entertainments' pages hailed a taxi. He had left New York in a buoyant mood. His terms had been accepted and his plan of action greeted with enthusiasm (beautiful, Torrelli had called it). He had felt as if he were throwing open a new world for himself. But now, as the taxi carried him through a rapidly deepening gloom, he was gripped by a feeling of uncertainty. Now he had to make the plan work. He saw himself as a mountaineer who having in a moment of caprice committed himself to climbing the Eiger in frogman's flippers had taken his first step on the slope that led to its summit. Then, as suddenly as the uncertainty had appeared, it was gone, swept away by an almost messianic sense of purpose. Here he was about to set in motion a scheme that would dispose of one of the Underworld's most powerful figures; a ferocious manipulator of others; a man who in one breath could order the destruction of a dozen people and in the next give instructions to New York's Commissioner of Police. He felt liberatory, retributive. He felt wings of gold begin to sprout.

"This is it, bud – the Trocadero."

Without his realising it the taxi had come to a halt in a dimly lit street on the edge of the city. He paid the fare and got out.

As a small boy Calvino used often to visit the Rialto, a back-street picture house in New York's Little Italy where for ten cents he could watch the latest Disney cartoons. Looking at the Trocadero, seeing its flaking blue paint and torn posters, Calvino was reminded of the Rialto.

He checked the times of the last performance from a board inside the entrance, and after locating the stage door, walked for ten minutes until he found a bar. He went inside and had two glasses of beer. Then he returned to the Trocadero and waited in an unlit doorway across the street and a few yards down from the alley where the stage door was situated.

Almost immediately the theatre began to empty.

From where he stood, Calvino could see the faces of the people as they entered the foyer from the auditorium. He watched a young couple button their coats, the girl thin and tight-lipped and her companion overweight and showily masculine. He followed them with his eyes as they left the foyer and wondered if they were married. He fleetingly pictured them making love, the girl's features set in a rictus of distaste, the man's flesh jouncing heavily as he pumped away at her.

He let his eyes return to the theatre, and as he did so, a wind sprang up and caught a poster that hung across itself on the wall to the left of the theatre's entrance. The poster lifted and flattened and he had just enough time to read *SONNY AND HONEY – A NITE WITH THE STARS* before the wind dropped and the poster hung limp again.

So the entry in *The Pittsburgh Tribune hadn't* been wrongly put together. He had thought it odd that Sonny's name should take precedence over Honey's, but had dismissed it as a printer's error. Now, having seen the poster, he realised there was no question of a mistake having been made: Honey was having to play second fiddle to Sonny.

The last of the audience left and a few minutes later a uniformed commissionaire appeared and began locking the doors. He moved slowly, stiffly, as if his body was restricted in some way, and when he had locked the main door, remained before it, staring through the glass panel into the darkness. Eventually he turned and made his way to a point beyond the ticket booth and disappeared from sight. Shortly afterwards the foyer's lights went out.

Calvino now focussed his attention on the stage door, noting with satisfaction that a small light burned above it: he would have no trouble identifying Honey when she came out. He pictured her in her dressing-room applying fresh make-up, her fingers moving quickly, expertly across her face. He wondered if she would be as pleased to see him as he would her, and guessed that she would. He shifted his weight from one foot to the other, and as he did so a Cadillac turned the corner and stopped outside the theatre.

Calvino could just make out that the driver wore a chauffeur's cap and was smoking a cigarette.

After about six minutes and simultaneous with the driver winding down his side window and spinning out the end of his cigarette, the stage door opened and a figure appeared wearing a white coat.

The coat was vicuna and Sonny wore it un-belted, the belt hanging loose at his sides. Calvino had seen similar coats on sale at Saks Fifth Avenue for eight hundred dollars.

He watched Sonny cast the merest glance at the sky, then make his way to the Cadillac and get in. There was a moment's delay before the Cadillac started up and pulled away. Looking after it, Calvino saw it reach the end of the street and turn the corner. Almost at once a second Cadillac, its lights dimmed, came into view and after stopping momentarily at a spot a few yards past the theatre's entrance, took the same route the first Cadillac had taken.

Calvino guessed that Sonny was being followed and felt a twinge of sympathy for the person following him. (Mastrioni's obsession with Sonny could be a tiring business for those assigned to guard him or report on his movements, as Calvino well knew. He had once spent two days and nights waiting for Sonny to emerge from a run-down hotel in Greenwich Village.)

The stage-door opened again and two men carrying musicians' cases stepped into the alley. After exchanging a few words they walked briskly in opposite directions.

A half hour went by before Honey appeared.

She wore an off-white trenchcoat, the belt knotted tightly at the waist. She stood for a few moments, seemingly undecided, a step forward of the stage door's light, and because of the shadows that were cast on her face, Calvino could not see that her eyes were dull and that her mouth drooped. He called to her, and saw her turn in his direction. He called again and she ran to him.

"Baby." She pulled his head down and placed hurried kisses on his mouth. "Lover… " Her hand moved to his fly.

Aroused, Calvino took her quickly and methodically in the doorway.

Afterwards they headed for a bar, where, according to Honey, they could talk without being overheard.

As they walked, Calvino told her of the idea that had come to him while listening to the radio, and of his conversation with Torrelli.

"I get rid of Sylvano, I get to be top man in Harlem," he said. He glanced at her. "You know what the take is in Harlem? Twenty thousand a week." To please her, he added: "And with no Sylvano, there's no Sonny. He'll be out – finished."

"That's what I figured," Honey said. She linked her arm into his and pulled him close to her. In an urgent voice, she said: "So what is it I say to Sylvano when I make the call?"

"Let's get to the bar first," Calvino said, and, excited, they quickened their step.

The bar was to Calvino's liking: apart from themselves there were only four customers – three elderly men who stood in conversation at the far end of the counter and a man in a booth reading a newspaper.

Calvino ordered drinks and they carried them to a booth away from where the man with the newspaper was sitting.

When they were seated opposite each other and after they had taken a swallow of drink, Calvino said: "Would you have any trouble with Sonny's voice?" He had heard her impersonate Sonny many times, but now, seeing the dullness in her eyes and having heard the thickness of her tone, he wanted reassurance.

"You kidding?" Honey said. In Sonny's voice she said: "Mother dear, do you *have* to wear such garish colours?"

The impersonation was not up to her usual standard, and Calvino said: "We want this thing to work, you gotta lay off the shit."

"It's the only thing keeps me going," Honey said.

"You don't lay off it, it'll keep us permanently stationary," Calvino said. He lowered his voice. "When you make that call, you got to sound one hundred per cent Sonny."

"I can do it, baby." Honey reached across the table and lightly touched Calvino's sleeve. "You know I can. What is it I have to say?"

Calvino waved the question away. "We'll get to that later. First we got to work this thing out. What's Sonny's routine? How often does he go out?"

Honey took her hand from Calvino's sleeve and said: "Most nights – after the show."

"Where'ds he go?"

"Cruises the streets, looking for pick-ups."

"*Walks* the streets?"

"No, he's mobile; he's in a car."

"Who drives – who's at the wheel?"

"One of Mastrioni's men."

"Where does Sonny go with his pick-ups?"

"Back to his hotel, mostly. Maybe to a flop house, but mostly back to his hotel."

"Who was chauffeuring him to*night*? It wasn't one of the Mob."

"Saturday nights he has a hire-car pick him up. Saturday nights he takes in the bars, finds a party to go to. The hire-car drops him at the party house."

"Why a hire-car?"

"You tell me."

"What about afterwards, when the hire-car's dropped him at the party house – it wait around for him?"

"No."

"How'ds he get back to his hotel?"

"He calls Sylvano and has him send someone to collect him. Either that, or he'll take a cab. He might even walk. Depends where he is and what time of day it is."

"What time does he usually get back to the hotel?"

"Around mid-day next day, maybe later. Sometimes he don't get back until mid-day Monday."

"What about the tail car? I saw a tail car on him tonight. Don't he ever hitch a ride in that?"

"Sonny always loses it. That, or he tells the driver to get lost."

"How d'you know all this?"

"I hear things." She took a drink. "Hammernose Hymie's here with Sylvano; he lets me know what's going on."

Calvino smiled. He thought for a moment, then said: "So there's one day a week when it would be possible for Sonny to be snatched without Sylvano's men knowing about it. He shakes the tail car, and there's no chauffeured car, Mob or otherwise, standing by outside the party house waiting to take him back to his hotel. That's what you're telling me?"

"Right," Honey said.

"And every Saturday night he goes partying. You're sure about that?"

"Sure."

Calvino nodded. "Good." He took a sip of drink before saying: "Okay, here's what we do." Lowering his voice slightly and leaning forward, he said: "We tail Sonny to his party house and when we see the door close on back of him we go to a call box and you call Sylvano. You make like you're Sonny and you tell him two guys are holdin' you and he wants to see you again, he's gotta come up with two hundred thousand dollars. You tell him, the guys holdin' you don't get the money, they're gonna take you out. You make like you're nervous, that you're scared shitless. You – " He broke off, considered what he had said. Then: "On second thoughts you *don't* make like you're scared shitless. Sonny wouldn't play it that way; he wouldn't react that way; he'd play it zero cool." He looked at her hard. "You play it just the way Sonny would play it – like you've got a couple icicles up your ass."

He went on: "Real cool, you tell Sylvano that part of the deal is he comes alone. No protectors. The guys holdin' you see he's got someone with him, they're gonna blow your head off."

"You're forgetting something," Honey said. "Mastrioni doesn't carry that kind of money around with him. How's he gonna raise it? It's Saturday night Sunday morning remember – the banks are closed."

Calvino dismissed the words with an impatient movement of his head. "Mastrioni's got Mob connections here. He could raise that kind of dough in ten minutes flat. Two calls, that's all it'd take." He took another drink and said: "When you're through with the Sonny spiel, you make like you're one of the guys holdin' him. Use any kind of street voice. You tell Sylvano you want the money in one hour and you want it dropped – " He stopped short. "We'll have to find a spot. Somewhere quiet. A warehouse maybe – somewhere where a person can be blown away without the whole neighbourhood knowin' about it. I'll take a drive round town tomorrow, find a place." He went on: "You tell him, as soon as you've checked the money's good, as soon as you can see it ain't yesterday's newspapers, you'll let him know where he can find Sonny. When you've said all that, you make with the Sonny voice again and tell Sylvano to do exactly like the guy says. No *second* man. You make a point of that."

Calvino leaned his back against the booth. He exhaled, smiling a small, self-satisfied smile. "It's perfect," he said. "We take out Mastrioni, I get the Harlem racket, and we get two hundred gees on top." He looked intently at Honey. "You got it clear what you have to say? We'll keep goin' over it till you have. We'll keep goin' over it till you know it *backwards* what it is you have to say."

Honey said: "What if Sonny decides to leave the party early? I make the call, and the next thing we know he's on his way back to the hotel?"

Calvino was silent for a moment. "We couldn't allow him to do that – to get back into the hotel, I mean. We allow him to get back into the hotel and Mastrioni sees him walk in, the whole thing folds up on us. We'd be dead."

"What if he calls a cab from the party house? He leaves the party early, steps out of the house straight into a cab?"

"I'd have to take him out when he reaches the hotel; we'd follow him to the hotel. It shouldn't be too difficult…to take him out, I mean… it'd be dark…you'd be waitin' in a car with the engine running. Mastrioni'd think Sonny had somehow managed to get away from the guys holdin' him and that the guys had caught up with him and taken him out. They'd of had to do that 'cause he could put the finger on them." He thought for a moment. "The cab driver would have to be taken out too: the cops'd question him, get an address from him. Mastrioni'd find out Sonny was at a party. He'd figure it wasn't Sonnny made the call, it was somebody impersonatin' him. And there's only one person could do that – *you*. I'd have to waste the driver."

"There'd be a record of the call."

Calvino looked around the bar, his eyes narrowed in anger. Honey was making points he would rather not hear. Coming back to her, he said: "Jesus, you think I don't know that? You think I don't know there'd be a record of the fuckin' call?" He darted a look over his shoulder. Through clenched teeth, he went on: "If necessary I'll go to the cab office and take out the whole fuckin' staff. Burn the fuckin' place down." A tired expression came into his eyes. "Don't make this thing more difficult than it already is."

There was a brief silence before Honey said jauntily: "It won't be like that, anyhow. Sonny don't *leave* parties. He gets to a party, he don't leave till he's had everyone's pants off."

The words relaxed Calvino. He breathed more easily and said: "How d'you feel about havin' Sonny wasted? He's your kid. I know you hate his guts, but he's still your kid."

"I couldn't give a *shit* he's taken out," Honey said. "That asshole's making me eat dirt. He has to be taken out, I'd like to be the one who gets to pull the trigger."

Calvino smiled. He felt a tremendous admiration for her. He could not have admired her more had she been Jack Dempsey.

"When do we do it?" Honey asked.

"How long you in Pittsburgh for?"

"We got another four weeks, then we play Philadelphia."

"There's no hurry. We wait till we've got everythin' worked out. There're still some things we need to look at – like who says what to Sylvano. Is it Sonny tells him to come alone, or the guys holdin' him? And would Sylvano *come* alone?"

"He'd do anything you tell him, if it meant seeing Sonny again. And it'd be the guys who'd tell him, not Sonny. Sonny'd just tell him to do exactly what the guys told him to do. That's the way it works in the movies."

Calvino grinned and said: "I must be gettin' a little rusty."

Honey said: "Maybe we should get something down on paper." She paused. "I'll work something out when I get back to the hotel."

"Just so long as nobody sees it," Calvino said.

Ignoring his words, Honey said: "Another thing: while I'm making the call, shouldn't you be watching the party house? Just in case …"

Calvino frowned. It was something he hadn't considered. "We've got to think this thing out so it's solid all the way through," he said.

He went for more drinks and when he returned and after they had arranged to meet at the same time and place the next day and

258

spoken for a few more minutes on the subject of Mastrioni, Honey told Calvino of Sonny's treatment of her.

"He's trying to kill me off," she said. "He wants me in little pieces. All these dumps we play in…You'd seen the house we had tonight, you'da thought Professor Plum and his Magic Lantern was playing there. We could play the best places, full houses every time." She paused. "You get my letter?" Calvino nodded. "Sonny, though," Honey went on, "don't *wan't* the best places; he wants the dumps. He has people phone around finding places nobody who's anybody'd be seen dead in – joints for has-beens. You know who we got supporting us here? A ballroom dance act, a comic who's about as funny as having a leg off, and a sixty-year-old lush who whistles bird tunes through her teeth."

"How about money?" Calvino asked.

"Sonny pays me New York rates. I also get what the dumps we play in pay me. I wouldn't get more if I was playing the Stork Club. The pay's *good*. What's *not* good is that I'm not getting the exposure I need to keep my name up front. A couple more months of this and I'll be history."

"I see Sonny gets to have his name first on the bills."

"He's taken over," Honey said resignedly. She sipped her drink and was silent. She could not admit to Calvino that since her letter to him Sonny had undermined her confidence to the point where she could no longer go on stage without first taking a massive dose of heroin or drinking at least a half pint of whiskey; or that her performances, when Sonny allowed her to perform, were laughable and that he encouraged audiences to laugh at her, that he would say to an audience in his Barbara Stanwyck voice: "You ever seen anyone as pie-eyed as she is? The last person I saw as pie-eyed as she is was a Skid Row bum trying to shake hands with himself. She's so pie-eyed, if King Kong were to walk in here she'd call a dog-catcher."

They had two more drinks, then left – Calvino for a rooming house and Honey for the Gateway Hotel, two floors of which Mastrioni had taken over for the duration of Sonny's stay in Pittsburgh.

* * *

Next morning, after he'd shaved and dressed and breakfasted on ham and eggs in a snack and grill bar not far from the rooming house in which he'd installed himself, Calvino went to a car-hire office and rented a 1951 Ford convertible.

He drove slowly, first reconnoitring the city and its perimeter, then moving into the suburbs. After half an hour he came to a small park about three miles south of Penn Station, on Cheyne Avenue, a minor road restricted to cars and light-duty vehicles. He stopped the car and got out.

It was a children's park, not big enough for a child to get lost in, with swings and a steel climbing frame and overlooked on one side by a row of two-storey houses and on the other by a tin-roofed building with boarded up windows and doors and a high chain-link fence to keep out trespassers. At either end of the park and almost hidden by tall laurel bushes was a single row of bungalows.

There were, Calvino discovered, two entrances to the park – one close to the play area and the other close to adjoining brick-built men's and women's toilets. Neither entrance had a gate to it.

Calvino found a bench near the play area and sat down. By his watch he saw that it was twelve-thirty, the time of day when a park could be expected to have visitors: a few mothers walking with their children, old men admiring young limbs; but apart from two tawny dogs running together this one was empty.

He stayed on the bench for twenty minutes, then got to his feet and made his way to the men's toilet.

Inside were a marble urinal and a single cubicle. There were no odours coming from either. He went into the cubicle and saw that everything, including the lock on the door, was in good order and that there was no graffiti on the walls. He concluded that the toilet was rarely used. He returned to the bench and lighted a cigarette.

He sat on the bench for an hour, and during that time saw nobody enter the park.

Later, when he was with Honey, he told her he had "found a place".

He returned to the park the next day, arriving a little before ten in the evening. From the street's lights and the lights from the houses he was able to see anyone who entered or left.

He saw no one.

He stayed until midnight and before leaving made another inspection of the toilet. It was lighted by a single bulb shielded by a yellow glass box: he would not need a flashlight.

He paid further visits to the park – once accompanied by Honey – and made notes of the route he had taken and the landmarks he had passed – one a large illuminated billboard showing a silver Pan-Am airplane flying over an implausibly blue ocean. Mastrioni could not fail to see it.

Satisfied that the park provided adequate cover, he turned his attention to Sonny, and for the next three Saturday nights kept him under surveillance.

Sonny's routine never altered. A chauffeured limousine would collect him from the theatre and straight away take him to the Beau Geste, an all-night basement club on Tenth Street.

Sonny would enter the Beau Geste and after an interval of two or three hours reappear with a group of people, some holding a half finished drink and all speaking in loud voices and acting foolishly. Sonny would leap into his limousine and, with his companions following in taxis or their own vehicles, head at high speed for the poorest part of town – to Steggle Street and a piece of waste land to one side of it, where a dozen or more down-and-outs sat around a fire drinking from wine bottles.

By the light of the fire, Calvino would see Sonny leave his limousine and in a casual, easy manner, a hand raised in a gesture of greeting, approach the circle of drinkers and stand amongst them. A few words would be exchanged, and then Sonny would point to three or four of the faces that stared up at him and beckon them towards him. Those chosen would rise and receive from him a note (from where he was parked, Calvino could not see that the note was a twenty dollar bill) taken from his wallet.

A few more words would be exchanged before Sonny would herd the chosen ones into the back of the limousine, and after providing them with a bottle of something taken from the car's boot, seat himself alongside the chauffeur and be driven to a house in the smarter part of town.

On each of the three occasions that Calvino had kept watch Sonny had never left the house before mid-day the next day.

CHAPTER 11

"We go on Saturday," Calvino said. It was late Wednesday and they were seated in the bar they had gone to on Calvino's first night in Pittsburgh; it had become their regular meeting place. "How d'you feel about it?"

Honey smiled. "Good," she said. She beamed. "Like I've just hit a home run for the Giants."

"There's no point in puttin' it off. We could spend *months* looking for a better place."

"It's perfect," Honey said. She made the words sound as if they were discussing a honeymoon island.

"If we make the hit Saturday, I want you to cut down on the shit for a couple of days. Not just the shit, the booze too."

"You've heard me, I'm good," Honey said.

Calvino nodded. She was, he thought, better than good. After only a few hours of practise, her impersonation of Sonny was impossible to fault. He had put it to the test earlier that day. They had gone to adjoining telephone booths, and Honey, armed with a script she had prepared, had telephoned Calvino and spoken in Sonny's voice and in the voice of the 'kidnapper' – a hoarse voice that carried just the right level of menace – and Calvino had been delighted with what he had heard. Mastrioni wouldn't fail to be taken in.

"Just go easy," he said pleasantly. For some reason, now that he had fixed the date of Mastrioni's execution, he felt a great tenderness towards her, the tenderness a comrade feels for another before going into battle. At that moment he wanted to be very close to her and to place an arm around her shoulders. He looked into her eyes and noticed for perhaps the hundredth time since his arrival in Pittsburgh how dull they were and how puffed and dark the skin was beneath them. The tenderness he felt became suffused with pity. He had not told her that the previous night he had gone to the Trocadero and witnessed Sonny's humiliation of her. He had sat in the back row and seen Honey take unsteady steps on to the stage, her eyes fixed and sodden, and join Sonny in singing *There's No Business Like Show Business*, Sonny singing in Judy Garland's voice and Honey in Howard Keel's. They had sung together for a few minutes, then suddenly Sonny had increased the tempo, and Honey, obviously confused by what was happening, had stopped singing and stared blankly at the audience. Sonny had sung on alone, and, pointing at Honey, had swayed on his feet the way a drunk sways. The audience had laughed, and Calvino had heard a man in the seat in front of him say peevishly to the woman he was with: "She's oiled." At the end of the song Sonny had called to Honey in a superior English voice: "Excuse me, madam, do you work here, or are you just passing out – I mean through?" and again the audience had laughed. Then Sonnny had launched into a series of brilliant impersonations, and Honey, her brow furrowed, had remained staring out across the footlights. His throat dry with anger, Calvino had left the theatre. His intention had been to castigate Honey for having allowed Sonny to treat her in that way, but he had said nothing. He hadn't wanted to further unsettle her. He wanted her to be as settled as possible for what they had to do.

"Tomorrow we get you fixed up with a car," he said. "Somethin' simple – nothin' too bright."

"How about a hearse?" Honey said cheerfully, and seeing a sharp look come into Calvino's eyes, added: "For Sylvano, cornball."

They spent the night together in the house where Calvino had taken a room, and for the first time in their relationship both found their love-making unsatisfactory.

* * *

They rose late and went to the car-hire office that Calvino had gone to, and rented Honey a dark green Plymouth.

Calvino drove – first to a men's outfitters, where he bought a white Coronet shirt with a spearpoint collar (it was an idiosyncracy of his that he never killed without he wore some pristine item of clothing – usually a shirt or tie; once, brightly coloured suspenders), then to a restaurant on Fort Dequesne Boulevard.

Over a meal of cold lobster and tossed green salad, Calvino raised a glass of the wine the waiter had recommended and said: "To Easy Street."

In George Raft's voice, Honey, as they clinked glasses, said: "All the way, friend", and they both laughed.

They finished their meal and when they had drunk more wine and gone over what they had to do when next they met, they left the restaurant and parted.

CHAPTER 12

Calvino worried that the Coronet shirt would ride up or wrinkle when he strapped on the shoulder holster, but it did not, and he resolved to wear only Coronet shirts in future.

He went to the suitcase that lay open on the bed, took up the Luger that rested on a wad of handkerchiefs and slipped it into the holster. Then he went to the wall mirror that hung above a maplewood chest of drawers and studied the effect.

Satisfied with what he saw and glad to be reunited with an old friend, he drew on his jacket and left the house.

The night was still and clear and chill enough for a muffler to be worn. Perfect weather for an execution, Calvino thought. (Past experience had taught him that hot or humid weather made for discomfort and, as a result, loss of concentration.) He inhaled deeply and opened the door of his car. He felt wonderfully alive and confident. Soon, he told himself, it would be over and he would be on his way back to New York and a future as bright as the rings on Angelo Torelli's fingers. For an instant he saw himself in a year or two kneeling beside Torelli's lifeless body, a pair of pruning shears in his hand.

He engaged the car's engine and moved along Grant Street and into Bigelow Boulevard. As he drove, he moved his right hand from the wheel and slid it inside his jacket to the holster. He ran his hand over the holster and along the butt of the Luger. Out of habit he lifted the Luger from the holster to test its freedom of movement. He tried to remember when he had last used it and thought it might have been to pistol whip a restaurant owner who had fallen behind with his protection payments, but he couldn't be certain.

Halfway along Bigelow Boulevard he turned left into Chester Avenue and at the end of Chester Avenue turned left again into Dequesne Street, where he saw the miserable lights of the Trocadero. He drove slowly, glancing at the cars that were parked to the left and right of him.

Honey's Plymouth was parked almost opposite the Trocadero's entrance.

He reversed into a space two cars behind the Plymouth, stopped the engine and switched off the lights.

The theatre hadn't yet started to empty, but the commissionaire with the difficult walk was locking open the doors, so it wouldn't be long before it did.

After ten minutes he saw Honey. She had followed his instructions and stayed in her dressing room only long enough to change into her street clothes. He saw her look for his car, and finding it and seeing him wind down the side window and nod to her, cross the street and get into the Plymouth. Almost immediately the theatre began to empty.

From past vigils he knew what would happen next: Sonny's limousine would appear and come to a halt outside the foyer; the chauffeur would remove his cap, light a cigarette.

For an instant, as the match flared, he saw the chauffeur's face. He hadn't paid much attention to it before, but seeing it now he was reminded of his father's face – hollow- cheeked with an ugly receding chin. He thought himself fortunate to have inherited his mother's chin. He thought of his mother and of how the news of his becoming a top man would silence her. He recalled something she had said to him on the eve of his marriage to Honey – "All the Mob men I read abowd they got mansions. You, you're in the Mob an' you ain't got nothin'. All you got is a lousy apar'men'." Well, that would soon change. He'd show the greasy old ratbag.

A few minutes went by, then he saw Sonny in a black single-breasted topcoat, a poppy-red silk scarf tied loosely around his throat, approach the limousine and get in. After a moment the limousine pulled away.

He waited until the limousine was almost out of sight, then turned the key in the ignition and moved after it. In his rearview mirror he saw that Honey was following.

From Dequesne Street they sped through lethargic traffic to the hub of the city, to Tenth Street and the Beau Geste.

After the sulphurous lights of the Trocadero the flashing red and white neon of the Beau Geste looked immensely inviting, suggested laughter and the excitement of illicit meetings. For a moment, as he drew to a halt, Calvino worried that Honey might find it irresistible. He glanced through his rear window and saw her pull smoothly into the kerbside. He slipped his hand inside his jacket and once again moved the Luger in its holster. He was impatient to use it. He wanted to be in the park toilet pointing it at Mastrioni's head. He looked at his watch and saw that it was ten-thirty. It would be at least another four hours before he would withdraw the Luger with purpose.

He checked his watch at regular intervals and at twelve-thirty saw Sonny, his poppy-red scarf now dangling from a pocket of his topcoat, emerge from the club with a group of laughing people. He heard a glass smash and saw a man of about twenty-five with cropped blond hair stagger towards a yellow Armstrong Sidley coupé and climb in. He heard engines start up and suddenly he was following a stream of taxis and cars, and almost before he knew it he was watching Sonny move among the down-and-outs.

Fifteen minutes later he was parked opposite a large white house in a quiet square on Deighton Heights – the house of the blond-haired man, for it was he who, after fumbling with keys, threw open the door and with the urgent gestures of someone who knew that soon the *real* party would begin, that soon there would be the throwing off of clothes, usher the others inside.

Calvino waited ten minutes, then left his car and walked quickly to Honey's. He opened the door, and when he was seated next to her, said: "You okay?"

"Great." She leaned across and kissed his cheek.

"I ain't seen this place before," he said agitatedly. He twisted round and squinted through the car's windows. More to himself, he said: "You see a call box anywhere? Jesus, you'd think a place like this'd have a call box."

"We passed a hotel two blocks back," Honey said. "I'll make the call from there."

He looked at her and said: "You sure it'll have booths?"

"You ever hear of a hotel that didn't?"

Hearing the confidence in her voice and feeling foolish for having asked the question, he patted her leg. "We'll move in half an hour," he said.

Honey glanced at the white house across the square and murmured: "I'd sure like to be a fly on the wall in *there*."

They sat close together without speaking, Calvino every so often peering at his watch. Like Honey, he wondered what was going on inside the house, what Sonny was doing. He saw a window thrown open and heard music being played – Bunny Berrigan's *Can't Get Started*. He wound down his window better to hear it.

I've been consulted by Franklin D
And Greta Garbo had me to tea
Still I'm so downhearted
'Cause I can't get started with you

They listened to the music and when it was ended Calvino turned to Honey and said: "It's time." He gripped her arm tightly. "How d'you feel?"

Honey placed a hand on his, and, with a bright, eager smile, said: "Couldn't feel better."

They kissed briefly and Calvino left the Plymouth. As he watched it pull away, he hated Honey a little for her enthusiasm. This was no picnic they were on.

* * *

And Honey, turning and seeing him standing alone in the square, hated *him* a little. His grip on her arm had suggested nervousness, and nervousness, to her way of thinking, was contemptible, a sign of weakness.

As soon as she was out of the square she stopped the car, twisted open the top of her opal ring and took out a pinch of heroin. Inhaling it, she felt her head cloud and a few seconds later clear. Fortified, she drove on.

She reached the hotel just as a group of people in evening dress was pushing their way into it through glass revolving doors. Falling in with them, she entered the hotel and walked briskly past the reception desk to a line of telephone booths.

She entered the end booth, lifted the receiver and dialled. Almost at once she heard the switchboard operator's voice say: "Good evening, Gateway Hotel." In Sonny's voice, she asked to be put through to Mastrioni's suite and moments later she was saying to Benjie: "This is Sonny, put me on to Sylvano." As she waited, she looked at her reflection in the glass panel of the booth's door. Before she had time to decide whether she was fully satisfied with what she saw, she heard Mastrioni's voice: "Sonny?"

"Sylv, I'm in a spot of trouble. No, don't say anything; just listen. I'm being held by two people who want two-hundred-thousand-dollars for my release. If they don't get the money, they say they will kill me. A gun, would you believe, is being held at my head at this very moment. You have to do what they tell you to do. Do you understand? Do exactly – " Honey broke off, allowed herself a moment's pause, then in a hoarse whisper said: "Okay, you heard him, two hundred thousand. We don't get the money, you don't get to see pretty boy again. You get the money and you take it to a park in West Grafton. Take the Wind Gap Road until you come to Grafton Centre, then take the left fork into Sycamore Street. A mile along Sycamore Street you'll see a lit-up Pan-Am sign. The park's a coupla minutes' drive along from there – on your right. It's a kids' park. You can't miss it. You go into the park, go into the men's toilets near the end gate and leave the money in the cubicle. Then you go back to your hotel. Once we see the money's good we'll let you know where you can find pretty boy. You've got two hours to make the drop – two hours, no more. And no company. You come alone. You got that? *No company*. We see you got company we'll blow pretty boy's head off. Okay, you got where you got to go? Take the Wind Gap Road to Grafton Centre, then the left fork into Sycamore Street. *Sycamore* Street. Remember, you've got two hours."

Honey heard Mastrioni say: "Okay, I do everythin' you say, only don't hurt the boy. Don't hurt him."

Honey replaced the receiver and left the hotel. As she drove, she sang in the voice of Bunny Berrigan.

* * *

Mastrioni, when he was able to speak, when he had gulped back sobs, said to Benjie: "Sonny's bein' held. They want two hundred thousand. How much we carryin'?"

"Fifty grand, maybe sixty."

"We got two hours. Get hold of Charlie Bonzetti. Tell him we want a hundred and fifty grand. Don't take no shit from him. Tell him we want it in forty minutes, fifty the most.

Benjie, as he made the call, hoped the money wouldn't arrive in time.

* * *

Calvino was in the car with Honey as soon as she had switched off the engine. "How'd it go?" His voice sounded nervous, so she made him wait a few seconds before replying. "He swallowed it."

"The whole deal?"

"The whole deal."

"Money?"

"He'll get it."

"No back up?"

"No back up."

"Baby!" He pulled her to him and kissed her on the mouth. When they had parted, he said: "How'd he sound?"

"Like he was breaking up."

"He did!" Calvino gave a small, hysterical laugh. "Beautiful, just beautiful. Jesus, what a dumb-ass!" He became suddenly serious and said: "When this is over, the first thing we do is, we get you a mink."

"Fifth Avenue," Honey said bluntly.

"You bet Fifth Avenue. The best they got."

They stayed in the square for another half hour, then drove to the park.

On each of his previous nocturnal visits to the park Calvino had heard the persistent call of a barn owl, but tonight, as he left the car, he heard only the humming of a street lamp.

He went into the park and into the men's toilet. The light still burned, so the flashlight he had bought at the last minute – just in case – wouldn't be needed. He returned to his car and got in. He switched on the car's radio and tuned into a late music programme. Dinah Shore was singing *Two Silhouettes* and her soft, tremulous voice soothed him. He listened to four more songs, then went to Honey's car. He opened the door and thrust his head inside. "Okay, you know what you have to do. As soon as you see Mastrioni leave his car sound your horn."

"Good hunting," Honey said.

He went back into the toilet and waited in the cubicle.

Fifteen hours later (it may only have been forty minutes) he heard Honey's horn sound, and another fifteen hours later (it may only have been ten seconds) he heard footsteps approach.

He withdrew the Luger from its holster and stepped from the cubicle.

Mastrioni was dressed in a black Raglan coat buttoned to the throat and a black homburg hat. He was carrying a black leather Gladstone bag.

Calvino levelled the Luger at a point just below the brim of the hat. Before he fired he said: "This one's for you, Sylvano."

He saw Mastrioni raise an arm and, simultaneous with the shot sounding, saw him stagger backwards a pace, then collapse and spreadeagle face upwards on the floor. Calvino waited a second, then went over to him and fired a second bullet into his chest. He returned the Luger to its holster, picked up the Gladstone bag and walked unhurriedly from the toilet to his car. As he slid into the driver's seat, he heard the barn owl call and took this to be a good omen.

* * *

They travelled south through Brentwood and Baldwin and when they came to Pleasant Hills booked into a motel.

In their room, after they had counted the money and after Honey had brushed her cheek with a wad of thousand dollar bills and decided she wanted a mink coat like the one she had seen Rita Hayworth wearing at a Tiny Templar film premier, they half-undressed, lay on the bed and slept.

Calvino was the first to wake. He rose and by his watch saw that it was nine o'clock. He shaved with the electric razor provided by the motel and when he had combed his hair and buttoned his shirt, turned the knob on the radio that was fixed to the wall above the bed.

He heard the nasal sound of a blues singer, and reaching out to tune into another station, one where he might hear a news bulletin, heard the radio go silent and a moment later a grave voice say: "We interrupt this programme to bring you important news of the shooting of New York Underworld boss Sylvano Mastrioni. Mastrioni was found in the early hours of this morning slumped over the wheel of a car parked outside a public play area in Sycamore Street, West Grafton. He had bullet wounds to his head and chest.

"Believed to be the victim of a gangland vendetta, Mastrioni was taken to St Francis Central Hospital, where he underwent three-hour surgery. A spokesman later described his condition as critical. We will bring you further news of the incident as soon as we have it."

Calvino felt his head swim and his legs buckle. He sat down heavily on the bed. "Oh God." He placed his hands on his legs to stop the quivering spasms that ran through them. "Oh Jesus." He ran the back of his hand across his mouth. "Oh Jesus fuckin' Christ." He looked down at the still-sleeping figure of Honey and saw her cheeks slowly swell with air, then her lips part with a faint popping sound as the air was expelled. He took hold of her shoulder and shook it roughly. Her mouth popped again and he pounded her shoulder with the heel of his palm. "For chrissake wake up!"

Honey opened her eyes. "Wha – "

"Get dressed. Mastrioni ain't dead."

"Wha' – " Honey, her eyes sodden with sleep and heroin, sat up.

"Mastrioni's alive. It just came over the radio. He's in hospital. Jesus, we gotta get out of here." He got to his feet. "We gotta get outa here quick."

"What you talking about, *alive*? You told me you put two bullets in him."

"He's alive for chrissake! The guy just came over the radio with it."

Honey, fully awake now, said: "How bad is he?"

"Critical."

"Maybe he won't make it. Maybe we should wait till we know for sure if he'll make it or not."

Calvino sank to the bed again. In a barely audible voice, he said: "Jesus, I put a slug in his head and one through his chest. It ain't *possible* he's still alive." He paused. "They found him in his car. He must've made it back to his car." He paused again. "Maybe you're right. Maybe he won't make it. Maybe we should wait for the next bulletin."

The second bulletin gave details of Mastrioni's injuries and 'miraculous' escape:

The first bullet had been deflected by his arm and, striking him just behind his left ear, had furrowed under the scalp to the back of his head and emerged close to his right ear. Its impact had been enough to knock him unconscious. The second bullet had shattered his breastbone and entered his left lung. In order to save his life, it had been necessary to remove the lung. He was still in a critical condition, but the surgeon who performed the operation was confident of a recovery.

They didn't wait to hear a third bulletin. They divided the money, drove to Union Station and boarded separate trains: their chances of staying alive, they had decided, would be greater if they were to part company.

CHAPTER 13

Mastrioni, as soon as he was able to speak, summoned Sonny and Benjie to his bedside in his private room in St Francis Central Hospital.

In a faint voice, he said to Benjie: "Calvino…I want that bastard found. He was the one did this to me. You find the bastard and when you find him you deal with him. You deal with him good."

"Calvino?" Benjie said, surprised. "Calvino did this?"

"I *saw* the bastard. 'This one's for you, Sylvano,' he said. I saw him."

Benjie looked at Sonny who was leaning, legs crossed, against the wall to the right of Mastrioni's bed. Without taking his eyes off him, he said: "It was *Sonny's* voice you heard on the phone."

In a slow, drawn out voice, Sonny said: "What *are* you talking about?"

"Sylvano took a call from you sayin' you was bein' held by two guys who if they didn't get two hundred thousand were gonna blow your head off."

"Tha's right, Sonny," Mastrioni said half apologetically.

Sonny was silent. The words had taken him by surprise. Benjie had told him that Mastrioni had been shot, but that was all; he had said nothing about a demand for ransom money, and he hadn't questioned him; the party had left him too exhausted to ask questions.

After a while he grasped the situation, smiled, and said: "My, you *have* been had, haven't you?"

"What's *that* supposed to mean?" Benjie said.

"Call the hotel and ask to speak to Mother-dear," Sonny said. "I'll stake my life against yours she won't be there."

Benjie looked puzzled.

"Use your brain, blockhead. If I wanted two hundred thousand dollars, do you think I'd go to the trouble of staging my own kidnapping? If I wanted two hundred thousand dollars, I'd ask Sylv for it, and he'd give it to me." Sonny glanced at Mastrioni. "Wouldn't you?" he said threateningly.

Unhesitatingly, soothingly, Mastrioni said: "Sure, sure." He smiled feebly and raised a hand for Sonny to touch, but Sonny ignored it.

"I don't get it," Benjie said.

"It was Mother-dear *impersonating* me, moron," Sonny said.

"Sylvano spoke to one of the guys holdin' you," Benjie persisted.

"Mother-dear," Sonny said suavely.

Benjie was silent for a second or two, then he said: "Okay, so why put two slugs in Sylvano? You don't take out the guy who makes the drop. You maybe take out the person you're holdin' but not the guy who makes the drop. It ain't done that way. You let the guy make the drop, wait till he moves off, then you move in and collect."

Sonny sighed extravagantly. "To use your vernacular," he said, "he was set up."

A small revelationery light came into Mastrioni's eyes. "Tha's right," he whispered, "I was set up. The bastards set me up. They did'n wan' the money, they wanted *me*."

"Go and make the call," Sonny said to Benjie.

Benjie shuffled his feet, unhappy that what had been said made sense.

"Call the hotel," Mastrioni ordered. He said to Sonny: "I knew you had nothin' to do with it, Sonny."

"Don't fucking lie," Sonny said. "You suspected me." He went to the window and stared out.

Benjie left the room and after five minutes returned and announced sheepishly: "She ain't there."

"Of course she isn't there," said Sonny, "she's with Calvino."

"You find those bastards," Mastrioni said to Benjie. "You find them and deal with them."

"You deal with *Calvino*," Sonny said coldly. "I'll deal with Mother-dear." He went to the door and opened it. Before leaving, he said to Mastrioni: "Let's return to New York."

"I ain't well enough to travel, Sonny," Mastrioni said weakly.

"Then I'll go alone."

Mastrioni closed his eyes. "OK, Sonny," he said, "we go back to New York."

* * *

A month after leaving Pittsburgh Calvino was discovered living in a rented apartment in lower Manhattan. Two days later his body was found floating in New York harbour. His right hand (the hand that had held the Luger) and his genitals were missing and his skull split in two by a blow from an axe.

Three months went by before Honey was sighted. One of Mastrioni's lieutenants on holiday with his wife and children in Cape May, New Jersey, saw her leave a bar and followed her to a bungalow on Maple Avenue. She looked, he reported to Mastrioni, like she didn't know what day it was.

Sonny, when he was told the news, ordered that she be watched around the clock for two weeks and a record kept of her movements. He also ordered a floor plan of the bungalow.

When the report and the plan were delivered and he had studied and digested them, he announced to Mastrioni that he was leaving immediately for New Jersey with Max The Lip.

Included in his luggage was a small cardboard box containing the President.

CHAPTER 14

Like most fourteen-year olds, Joseph Flanagan had a favourite comic strip hero. Joseph Flanagan's was Dick Tracy. Sometimes he daydreamed that he *was* Dick Tracy, saw himself trenchcoated and fedora-hatted fighting a ceaseless war against crime and corruption. This fantasy took greater shape during school vacations, for it was then that he worked as a delivery boy for Jackson's grocery store, and quite a number of the people he made deliveries to were, it seemed to him, highly suspicious characters. Old man Harrison, for instance, whose bathrobe was always open at the waist, and the dark-haired man with the nervous tic, and the young couple who never seemed to be fully dressed; but *most* suspicious was the woman with the dyed yellow hair and the bloated face who had taken the lease on the third bungalow on Maple Avenue and who was rarely without a glass of whiskey in her hand. Didn't the gangsters' molls in the Dick Tracy strip drink whiskey and have dyed yellow hair? Definitely someone to keep an eye on, young Joseph Flanagan thought.

CHAPTER 15

Shortly after ten p.m. on the day of their arrival in New Jersey, Sonny and Max The Lip walked the two blocks from their hotel on Kentucky Avenue to Honey's bungalow on Maple Avenue, Sonny carrying the cardboard box with the President inside.

There was a chill in the air, and Max The Lip blew on his hands before slipping the lock on the bungalow's back door.

Inside the bungalow they made their way to the living-room, where a ceiling light burned in a yellow shade.

Honey was asleep in a cane-back easy chair, her head resting on one of the chair's wings. Her mouth was open and she was snoring. On a table at her side was an empty bottle of bourbon and a tumbler with a quarter of an inch of liquid in it.

Sonny carefully placed the box on the table; and after looking round the room and grimacing at its ugliness, removed the box's lid and lifted out the President.

Perhaps nervous of his surroundings or startled by his sudden exposure to light, the President let out a series of tiny squeals. To comfort him Sonny stroked his neck.

When the President was quiet, Sonny nodded to Max The Lip, who took up a position behind Honey.

Sonny nodded a second time, and Max The Lip crouched and encircled Honey with his arms.

Sonny quickly changed the President to his right hand, and, leaning over Honey, gripped her throat with his left. He saw her eyes roll and bulge, and as she opened her mouth wider to get more air, he thrust the President into it.

Joseph Flanagan, peering through the window, tried hard not to vomit.

CHAPTER 16

In a hot courtroom, so hot that many of the women who were present feared their mascara might run, and the judge – Judge Douglas Westbury – wished he'd applied more fixative to his hairpiece (in a hot atmosphere it tended to slip), District Attorney William Harrison got to his feet, and addressing the jury, apologised to them for the sickening nature of the case they were about to hear. The killing of the nightclub entertainer Honey Bunn was, he said, one of the most obscene, most monstrous acts of violence ever to be heard in an American courtroom. Forensic evidence, he went on, would show that the victim – the mother of the accused – was choked to death by the insertion into her mouth of a live rat – Exhibit A. Fortunately for the public at large, *un*fortunately for the accused (here District Attorney Harrison turned and looked contemptuously at Sonny, who, aristocratic in a navy blazer, was smoothing an eyebrow), this appalling act of matricide was witnessed by a young man who, in order to escape the attentions of the accused's mobster acquaintances, had had to suffer the indignity of being kept behind bars in Sing Sing penitentiary.

The jury, said District Attorney Harrison, would hear from this public-spirited young man that while returning to his home after visiting a friend, he saw two men enter the grounds of a bungalow on Maple Avenue – the residence of the deceased – and, taking it upon himself to investigate, had witnessed an act of homicide of such horrible dimensions that it was unlikely he would ever erase it from his mind.

District Attorney Harrison went on: "The jury has heard that the accused has refused to enter a plea as to his innocence or guilt and that a plea of not guilty has been entered on his behalf, but the witness will state on oath that Sonny Bunn was the person he saw choke Honey Bunn to death with a live rodent in the living-room of the bungalow on Maple Avenue on the night of March fourteen." After a small pause, he said: "I call as the State's first witness Doctor Martin Lehane."

Doctor Lehane, tall, stooped and bespectacled, moved to the witness box and was sworn in.

"You are Doctor Martin Lehane who carried out the autopsy on the deceased, are you not?"

"I am."

"And what in your opinion was the cause of death?"

"Asphyxiation."

"How did you arrive at that opinion?"

"There were external and internal injuries to the deceased's throat."

"What form did those injuries take?"

"The throat was contused and there was damage to the larynx and gullet."

"So the deceased met her death through strangulation?"

"No."

"How then did she meet her death?"

"She choked to death."

"And what in your opinion caused her to choke to death?"

"The insertion into her mouth of an animate object?"

"An animate object? You mean a live object?"

"Yes."

"I see. But the contusions – the bruises to the throat – how did *they* come about?"

"By the application of manual pressure."

"But not enough pressure to cause death?"

"That's correct."

"You are saying, then, that manual pressure was applied to the deceased's throat and that an animate object was inserted into her mouth?"

"Yes."

"What led you to believe that a live object had been inserted into the deceased's mouth?"

"From the appearance of the injuries to the tongue and gullet."

"What form did these injuries take?"

"There were lacerations to the tongue and damage to the larynx and the epiglottis."

"Epiglottis?"

"The Adam's Apple."

"What was the extent of this damage?"

"Most of the larynx was missing and part of the epiglottis."

"And in your opinion it was the live object that caused this damage?"

"Yes."

"How was that opinion formed?"

"From teeth marks to the larynx and epiglottis and claw marks to the tongue."

"Were your findings further borne out by further examination of the deceased?"

"Yes."

"Tell us about that."

"Among the contents of the deceased's stomach was a partly-digested rodent."

"A rat?"

"Yes."

District Attorney Harrison slowly cleared his throat and swallowed. "And did you make an examination of the rat's stomach?"

"Yes."

"And what did you find?"

"Remnants of the deceased's larynx and epiglottis."

District Attorney Harrison walked to a table in the centre of the courtroom and picked up a large glass jar with a screwed top. "And is this the rat that was found in the deceased's stomach and which in your opinion caused the deceased to choke to death?"

The President eddied in formaldehyde.

"Yes, it is."

"Thank you, Doctor Lehane, I have no further questions."

Judge Westbury looked across at Sonny's attorney. "Do you have any questions to put to this witness?"

Victor Galdez, olive-complexioned with a Ronald Colman moustache, scourge of countless prosecution witnesses, half rose from his chair. "No, your Honour."

Somewhat triumphantly, District Attorney Harrison called Joseph Flanagan to the stand.

Joseph, fresh-faced and clear-eyed after a restful night in Sing Sing penitentiary, took the oath in a light, airy voice that brought sighs of delight from jurors and spectators.

Yes, he *was* Joseph Flanagan and yes, he *did* have occasion to make his way along Maple Avenue on the night of March fourteen, and seeing two men enter the grounds of a bungalow on Maple Avenue, yes, he *did* become suspicious and investigate.

And what did he see when he looked through the window of the bungalow?

He saw a woman asleep in a chair and two men standing over her.

And what did he see the men do?

He saw one of the men hold the woman from behind while the other put a rat into her mouth, and when the rat had disappeared, place his hand over the woman's mouth and nose and keep it there until the woman stopped moving.

And did he later identify the accused from a publicity photograph – Exhibit B – taken of the deceased with the accused?

Yes, he did.

And was the man in the photograph and the man he saw deliver the rat into the mouth of the woman in the bungalow on Maple Avenue one and the same person, and was that person in this courtroom today?

Yes, he was.

Would he point him out?

Joseph directed a perfectly steady Dick Tracey finger at Sonny. And when he was asked by Victor Galdez if he made a habit of spying on people in their homes, Joseph shook his head so that his marmalade-coloured hair swung to and fro, and in his charming, airy voice lied and said, No sir, he did not.

Joseph was followed to the stand by Lieutenant Thomas Lloyd of the New Jersey Police Department, a heavily-set man with grey sideburns, who told the court that he had traced Sonny to an hotel in New York and after arresting him had returned him to New Jersey where he was charged with first degree murder.

"And what did the accused say at the time of his arrest?"

Lieutenant Lloyd glanced at his notebook. "He said: 'Oh dear.'"

A ripple of laughter ran through the court.

"And what did he say when he was formally charged with murder?"

Detective Lloyd made a pained expression. "He said: 'Is it fun being a policeman?'"

Judge Westbury called for silence as the laughter increased.

"That was all? He didn't protest his innocence?"

"No sir."

"Did he admit the charge?"

"No sir."

"Did he deny it?"

"No sir."

"Did he make a statement?"

"No sir."

"He refused to make one?"

"Yes sir."

"Did you put it to him that there was a witness to what took place in the bungalow on Maple Avenue on the night of March fourteen?"

"Yes sir."

"And what was his reaction?"

"He shrugged."

"What was the accused's attitude during your interrogation of him?"

"Objection!" Victor Galdez was on his feet. "The prosecution is – "

"Objection overruled," said Judge Westbury.

"He acted like he couldn't give a damn," said Lieutenant Lloyd.

"And finally, Lieutenant, when you arrested the accused in New York, in whose company was he?"

Victor Galdez was on his feet again. "Your Honour, I must object to this line of questioning. The company in which my client was found has no bearing whatso – "

"Objection overruled," Judge Westbury said.

"Sylvano Mastrioni," Lieutenant Lloyd went on.

"Sylvano Mastrioni, the mobster?"

"Your Honour, this is outrageous."

"Please sit down, Mr Galdez," said Judge Westbury.

"Sylvano Mastrioni the mobster?" persisted District Attorney Harrison.

"Yes sir."

"Thank you, Lieutenant. No further questions."

Galdez rose, and brushing the side of his nose with his forefinger, approached the witness. "Lieutenant Lloyd, how long have you been with the police department?"

"Twenty-two years."

"And during that time how many murder suspects have you interviewed?"

"I don't know, sir."

"Hazard a guess, Lieutenant."

"Forty, maybe fifty."

"Forty, maybe fifty…And of those forty or fifty, how many of them when they were accused of murder failed to protest their innocence?"

"Not many."

"Did you not find my client's attitude, his behaviour, a little – "

Before Galdez could continue, Sonny in an ice-cold voice called: "That's enough."

Startled, Galdez turned and faced him.

"That's enough," Sonny repeated.

After a moment's hesitation, Galdez said to the judge: "Your Honour, I would like to request a recess in order to confer with my client."

Judge Westbury, glad of the opportunity to adjust his hairpiece, brought his gavel down hard on the ebony block in front of him and said: "This court will adjourn until ten o'clock tomorrow morning."

* * *

Later in his cell in New Jersey's Detention House, after his attorney and Mastrioni had left, after he had again turned down their petitions to change his plea to one of guilty by reason of insanity, to allow to be called to the stand a psychiatrist who would testify as to his insanity, Sonny lay on his bed, closed his eyes and thought of the day in the not too distant future when he would be taken to the death chamber and have a hood placed over his head.

He had no fear of death; he was quite looking forward to it. For some time now, perhaps from the moment that Honey's face had turned a horrible shade of purple and she had stopped breathing, perhaps long before that, he had begun to find life remorselessly, inexpressibly boring. Nothing about it appealed to him. Life, he thought, should be amazing, and it wasn't. He had lived in the *hope* of one day being amazed, but never had been, knew instinctively that he never would be. He could see a star fall and explode and form itself into a three-masted schooner that sailed the sky and he would not be amazed. He might raise an eyebrow, but that would be all – he would not be amazed. So what was the point …?

Ho-hum! He picked up the volume of Walt Whitman's poems which the multiple rapist in the next cell had loaned him, and turning the pages and becoming bored with what he read, let it fall to the floor. Silly old Walt, he thought.

CHAPTER 17

"The accused will rise."

Sonny got to his feet.

"Have you anything to say before sentence is passed on you?"

"Your hairpiece appears to be slipping."

Judge Westbury resisted the temptation to raise a corrective hand, and in a grim, sonorous voice said: "You have been found guilty of the heinous crime of matricide. A worse case of matricide I have yet to come across. Your attitude throughout this trial has been one of colossal arrogance and indifference. You have shown not an ounce of remorse. Had you done so I might have been more leniently disposed towards you." He cleared his throat, paused, and went on: "The judgment of the court, therefore, is that you, Sonny Bunn, hereby are sentenced to the punishment of death, and it is ordered that you be delivered with the warrant of this court to the warden of New Jersey Prison, New Jersey, where you shall be kept in solitary confinement, and upon a date to be appointed, the said warden is commanded to do execution upon you in the mode and manner prescribed by the laws of the State of New Jersey."

Somewhere in the back of the courtroom Mastrioni sobbed.

CHAPTER 18

Apart from his attorney, in the three months Sonny would spend on Death Row he would have only two visitors – Mastrioni and Lever. Lever would visit him twice and Mastrioni every day.

* * *

Lever on his first visit attempted to persuade Sonny to appeal against sentence; but when Sonny tossed his head and in Susan Hayward's voice said: "You're treading on my toes, mister", he knew he was wasting his time and did not mention the subject again. Instead he spoke of showbusiness matters. He had taken on a group of young singers who called themselves The Bluetones, and predicted a bright future for them. Sonny said that any group who called themselves The Bluetones could not *possibly* be expected to have a bright future. The Heliotropetones or The Magentatones, yes, but not The Bluetones. At this Lever laughed and wished Finn were alive so that he might make Sonny's acquaintance. He speculated that the cynical Finn would have enjoyed his company.

On his second visit, a week before Sonny was due to die, there were awkward silences between them, and Lever was glad when it was time for him to leave. Before leaving, he put out his hand to Sonny, who, shaking it, said: "I quite like you, Lever"; and Lever, instead of saying: "That's big of you", simply smiled. Later he wished he'd said: "And I think you're one hell of an individual."

Mastrioni's visits were more emotional; most of the time he wept, which made Sonny angry ("Stop it at once!").

On his final visit, on the eve of Sonny's execution, Mastrioni had to be helped into the cell. He hadn't slept for a week and found it difficult to stand. Since the day of Sonny's sentencing, his weight had dropped from 200lbs to 160, a scaly rash had broken out on his scalp, and he spoke in tiny, barely audible gasps. Before he left, he placed his arms around Sonny and, eyes streaming, held him tightly. In normal circumstances, Sonny would have pushed him away with a "For heavens sake!" but on this occasion, although he found the show of affection tiresome, he did not; he owed him *some*thing, he supposed.

CHAPTER 19

They woke Sonny from a dream in which he had seen himself in his British guard's uniform high up on a ski slope, and when he had washed and the prison chaplain had asked him to kneel in prayer and he had said he would "rather not", they took him to the chamber at the end of the cell block, and there, to the sound of the chaplain intoning a psalm, strapped him into the heavy oak chair that was placed in the centre of the chamber.

It was not uncomfortable, the chair. The straps were a little tight, but it was a minor inconvenience. The chaplain's voice was not unpleasant.

After a while Sonny heard movements behind him, and as he waited for the hood to be drawn over his head, he recalled the dream he had had and realised that he had not been alone on the ski slope, that there had been someone with him, someone with ineffably sad eyes, looking at him from a distance. Mastrioni. To his amazement he felt tears begin to form. He looked up at the chaplain and spoke his last words.

EPILOGUE

Prison Warden Patrick Burridge, surrounded by ten or more Pressmen, said: "One at a time fellas, *please*." He rubbed his face with his hand. "Jesus, it's hot in here." Looking around, he said: "Okay, who's first?"

The reporter from *The New York Herald-Tribune* who, like Burridge, was overweight and balding, said: "What were Sonny's last words?"

Burridge smiled, then gave a deep, rich laugh. He laughed louder. "What were his last words? *Ha, ha, ha...*That Sonny...What a character...*Ha, ha, ha...*You wanna know what his last words were? I'll tell you what his last words were. He – *ha, ha, ha* – he looked up at the padre and in one of those crazy voices of his – *ha, ha, ha* – in one of those crazy voices of his – maybe it was Tallula Bankhead's... Yeah, that's whose it was, Tallulah Bankhead's. He looked up at the padre – *ha, ha, ha* – he looked up – *HA, HA, HA, HA...*" Convulsed now, Burridge wiped tears from his cheeks with a large handkerchief. He gathered himself, coughed, and went on: "He looked up at the padre, and in Tallulah Bankhead's voice said: 'I thought I told you – *HA, HA, HA, HA, HA* – I thought I told you...*to wait in the car.*'"

* * *

Reading the report of Sonny's execution in the *Tribune* the next day, Mastrioni was consumed by grief. He put aside the newspaper, went to Sonny's apartment, and stood before the photograph of Sonny taken on the steps of the Rothschild Casino in Monte Carlo. He looked at the photograph for a long time, then, raising a handsome pearl-handled Derringer to his temple, he pulled the trigger.

Lightning Source UK Ltd.
Milton Keynes UK
UKOW01f0534180817
307511UK00001B/30/P

9 781780 882659